JOHANNA LINDSEY

The Holiday Present

Originally published as *The Present*
and *Home for the Holidays*

AVON BOOKS
An Imprint of HarperCollinsPublishers

The Holiday Present was originally published in hardcover and mass market as two individual works entitled *The Present* and *Home for the Holidays* by William Morrow and Avon Books.

AVON BOOKS
An Imprint of HarperCollinsPublishers
10 East 53rd Street
New York, New York 10022-5299

Copyright © 2003 by Johanna Lindsey
The Present copyright © 1998 by Johanna Lindsey
Home for the Holidays copyright © 2000 by Johanna Lindsey
ISBN: 0-06-054284-5
www.avonromance.com

First Avon Books paperback printing: December 2003; November 1999; November 2001
First William Morrow hardcover printing: November 1998; November 2000

Avon Trademark Reg. U.S. Pat. Off. and in Other Countries, Marca Registrada, Hecho en U.S.A.
HarperCollins ® is a registered trademark of HarperCollins Publishers Inc.

Printed in the U.S.A.

10 9 8 7 6 5 4 3 2 1

Books by Johanna Lindsey

the Holiday Present

Malory Family Tree

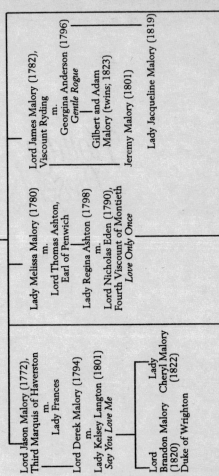

Gypsy grandmother
The Second Marquis of Haverston
m.
Marchioness of Haverston

Lord Jason Malory (1772),
Third Marquis of Haverston
m.
Lady Frances

Lord Derek Malory (1794)
m.
Lady Kelsey Langton (1801)
Say You Love Me

Lord Brandon Malory (1820)
Lady Cheryl Malory (1822)
Duke of Wrighton

Lady Melissa Malory (1780)
m.
Lord Thomas Ashton,
Earl of Penwich

Lady Regina Ashton (1798)
m.
Lord Nicholas Eden (1790),
Fourth Viscount of Montieth
Love Only Once

Lord James Malory (1782),
Viscount Ryding
m.
Georgina Anderson (1796)
Gentle Rogue

Gilbert and Adam
Malory (twins; 1823)

Jeremy Malory (1801)

Lady Jacqueline Malory (1819)

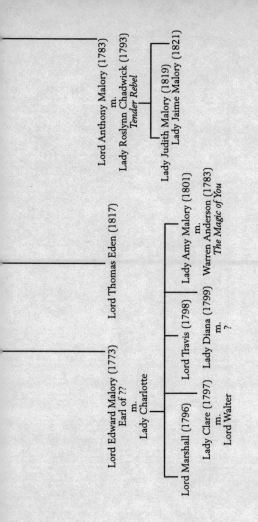

Lord Anthony Malory (1783)
m.
Lady Roslynn Chadwick (1793)
Tender Rebel

Lady Judith Malory (1819)
Lady Jaime Malory (1821)

Lord Thomas Eden (1817)

Lady Amy Malory (1801)
m.
Warren Anderson (1783)
The Magic of You

Lord Edward Malory (1773)
Earl of ??
m.
Lady Charlotte

Lord Travis (1798)
Lady Diana (1799)
m.
?

Lord Marshall (1796)
Lady Clare (1797)
m.
Lord Walter

Anderson Family Tree

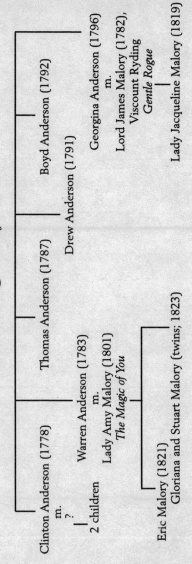

Clinton Anderson (1778)
m.
?
2 children

Thomas Anderson (1787)

Warren Anderson (1783)
m.
Lady Amy Malory (1801)
The Magic of You

Eric Malory (1821)
Gloriana and Stuart Malory (twins; 1823)

Boyd Anderson (1792)

Drew Anderson (1791)

Georgina Anderson (1796)
m.
Lord James Malory (1782),
Viscount Ryding
Gentle Rogue

Lady Jacqueline Malory (1819)

The Present

To the many fans
who love the Malorys as much as I do.
This present is for you.

Chapter 1

England, 1825

THE MALORY CLAN ALWAYS SPENT THE CHRISTMAS holidays at Haverston, the ancestral estate in the country where the oldest among them had been born and raised. Jason Malory, Third Marquis of Haverston and the oldest of four brothers, was the only family member who was still a permanent resident. The head of the family since he was only sixteen, Jason had raised his brothers—two of whom had been utterly scandalous in their pursuits—and a young sister.

At present the various Malorys and offspring were quite numerous and difficult to place, sometimes even for Jason himself. So it was a very large brood that gathered at Haverston these days for the Christmas season.

Jason's only son and heir, Derek, was the first to arrive, more than a week before Christmas. With him came his wife, Kelsey, and Jason's first two blond and green-eyed grandchildren.

Anthony, his youngest brother, was the next to arrive only a few days after Derek. Tony, as most of the family called him, admitted to Jason that he'd deserted London early after hearing that their brother James had a bone to pick with him. Annoying James was one thing, and something Anthony often strived to do, but when James was out for blood, well, Tony considered that a different matter entirely.

Anthony and James were his youngest brothers, yet only a year apart in age themselves. They were both skilled pugilists, and Anthony could hold his own with the best of them, yet James was heftier, and his fists were frequently likened to solid bricks.

With Anthony came his wife, Roslynn, and their two daughters. Judith, the oldest at six, had taken after both her parents, having her mother's glorious red-gold hair and her father's cobalt blue eyes, a seriously striking combination that Anthony feared was going to make her the reigning beauty of her day—which as her father and a reformed rake he was *not* looking forward to.

But his younger daughter, Jaime, was going to break some hearts as well.

But even with all his guests, Jason was the first one to notice the present that had appeared in the parlor while the family was breakfasting. It was hard to miss, actually, placed prominently up on a pedestal table next to the fireplace. Wrapped in gold cloth, banded with a red velvet ribbon and bow, it was oddly shaped, nearly like the size of a thick book, yet a round protrusion on top suggested it was nothing that simple.

Poking a finger at it showed that the protrusion could move, yet not very much, as he found out when he tilted the present sideways and it didn't change position. Strange, yet stranger still was that there was no indication of whom the present was from, nor whom it was for.

"A bit early to be passing out Christmas gifts, ain't it?" Anthony remarked as he sauntered into the room to find Jason holding the present. "The Christmas tree ain't even been brought in yet."

"That was my thought as well, since I didn't put it here," Jason replied.

"No? Then who?"

"I've no idea," Jason admitted.

"Who's it for, then?" Anthony asked.

"I'd like to know that myself."

Anthony raised a brow at that point. "No card?"

Jason shook his head. "None. I just found it here on this pedestal myself," he said, and put it back.

Anthony picked up the present as well to poke at it a bit. "Hmmm, someone sure dressed it up fancy. I'll wager it will fascinate the children—at least until we find out what it is."

As it happened, it fascinated the adults as well. In the following days, since none of the family owned up to having put it there, the present created a sensation. Just about all of the adults poked, shook, or otherwise examined it, yet no one could figure out what it might be, or whom it was for.

Those having arrived so far were gathered in the parlor the night when Amy walked in holding one of her twins. "Don't ask why we're late, you wouldn't believe it," she said, then in the next breath, "First the wheel on the coach fell off. Then not a mile down the road, one of the horses lost not one, but two of his shoes. After we finally get that all taken care of and we're almost here, the bloody axle broke. I thought surely Warren was going to kill that poor coach by then. He certainly kicked it enough. If I didn't think to wager with him that we *would* arrive here today, I really don't think we would have. But you know I never lose a wager, so . . . By the by, Uncle Jason, what's an unmarked grave doing in that lovely clearing east of here? The one close to the road that runs through your property? We ended up walking through it to get here, since it was the shorter route by that point, to just head across that clearing."

No one said a word at first, still in bemusement

after that long dissertation. But then Derek said, "Remember that grave m'self, now that you mention it, cousin. Reggie and I came across it when we were younguns gadding about the estate. Always meant to ask you about it, Father, just never got around to it, then forgot about it."

They were all looking toward Jason by then, but he merely shrugged his broad shoulders. "Devil if I know who was laid to rest there. That grave has been there since before I was born. Asked my father about it once, as I recall, but he put off answering, hemmed and hawed so much, actually, that I figured he just didn't know, so I didn't ask again."

"Think we've all come across that grave at one time or another, least those of us who were raised here," Anthony remarked to no one in particular. "Strange place for a grave, and a well-tended one at that, when there are two cemeteries nearby, not to mention the ancestral cemetery right here on the property."

Judith, who had been standing next to the pedestal staring at the mysterious present, came over to her cousin Amy and held up her arms to take the two-year-old twin from her. Judy was tall for her age, and very good with the toddlers. Amy was only surprised that she got no greeting, and said so.

"Where's my hug, puss?"

Those exquisite features just stared at her mulishly. Amy raised a brow toward the girl's father.

Anthony rolled his eyes, but explained, "She's pouting 'cause Jack ain't here yet."

Jack was James and Georgina's oldest daughter. Everyone knew that Jack and Judy, who were only months apart in age, were inseparable when they were together, and they were so fond of each other that their parents made sure they were often together—especially since neither was very happy when they were separated for very long.

"Am not," Judith denied in a pouting mumble as she marched back to the pedestal.

Jason was the only one to notice when Amy's attention centered on the present that had garnered everyone's curiosity. He would have thought nothing of it, except for her expression. Her brief frown made him wonder if she was getting one of her feelings about it. This niece of his had phenomenal luck, never having lost a wager in her life, which she attributed to these "feelings," as she called them, that she got. Jason considered such things as feelings exceeding strange, which was why he would as soon not hear if she was getting one now. So he was relieved when her frown eased and she gave her attention back to his brother.

"Uncle James hasn't arrived yet, then?" Amy surmised from Anthony's last response.

Anthony did some mumbling himself. "No, and hopefully he won't."

"Oh, dear. You two are fighting?" Amy surmised again.

"Me? Fight my dear brother? Wouldn't think of it," Anthony replied, then, "But someone bloody well ought to tell him this is the season for good cheer."

Derek chuckled at his uncle's sour expression. "Heard a rumor Uncle James was out for your hide. What's set him off this time?"

"If I knew, then I'd know how to defuse him, but I'm deuced if I know. Ain't seen James for a good week, not since I dropped off Jack after the outing I took the girls on."

"Well, James would have let me know if he wasn't coming," Jason pointed out. "So when he gets here, kindly take any altercations outside. Molly seriously objects to blood staining the carpets."

No one would think it strange that he called Haverston's housekeeper by her first name. After all, Molly Fletcher had held that position for more than twenty years. That she was also Jason's very longtime mistress—and Derek's mother—was not something that everyone in the family was aware of, however. In fact, only a couple of members had ever learned or guessed the truth. Jason had only told Derek, his son, about this time six years ago.

And around that Christmas, Jason, who deplored all scandals attached to the family, was willing to create one in giving his wife, Frances, the divorce she wanted, just to keep her from revealing what she knew about Molly.

But since then, Molly had remained the housekeeper. Jason had tried, ever since Derek found out the truth, to get her to marry him, but she was still refusing.

Molly didn't come from gentry. She had in fact been just a parlor maid when she and Jason fell in love more'n thirty years ago. And although he was willing to make one of the worst scandals possible, that of an esteemed lord marrying a commoner, she wasn't willing to let him.

Jason sighed, thinking of it. He had been forced to come to the conclusion that she would never give him the answer he so wanted to hear. Which didn't mean he was giving up, not by any means.

He was drawn back to the conversation when Amy said, "There is a little idiosyncrasy our twins have developed. Strangest behavior. When Stuart wants Warren's attention, I might as well be a stranger to him, he ignores me so thoroughly, and vise versa, when he wants my attention, Warren can't do a thing with him. And Glory does the same thing exactly."

"Least they do it at the same time," Warren,

who had finally arrived, added as he reached for Stuart and handed Gloriana to Amy.

"I've been meaning to ask Uncle James and Aunt George if they're having the same problem with theirs," Amy said with a sigh.

"Has he gotten used to them yet?" Jason asked Anthony, since Anthony, being closest to James, saw him the most often, and Jason didn't get to London often.

"Course he has," Anthony assured the family.

Yet they all still remembered his reaction when Amy had borne twins and he'd asked his wife Georgina, who was Warren's sister, where they came from. "Good God, George, you could have warned me that twins run in your family every other generation. We are *not* having any, d'you hear!"

Georgina had been pregnant again herself at the time, and had given birth to just that, twin boys.

Yes, the Malorys at Christmas were a wonderful sight, Jason thought. His life only lacked one thing to make it perfection.

Chapter 2

As the housekeeper, Molly usually wasn't present when the Malorys dined, but today she was supervising a new maid who was serving for the first time. By long practice, she managed to keep her eyes away from Jason's handsome face, sitting at the head of the table. It wasn't that she thought she might give herself away if she was caught staring at him, though she supposed that was a distinct possibility. Sometimes she simply couldn't keep her feelings from showing, and she had a lot of feelings where Jason Malory was concerned.

No, she wasn't so much worried that she might give herself away, it was that lately, *he* was revealing too much when he looked at her, and he didn't seem to care anymore who might notice. And with the house rapidly filling up with his entire family, there were a lot more people around who just might notice.

Molly was beginning to suspect that he was doing it on purpose, that he was hoping they would be found out. Not that it would change her mind about anything, but he might think it would.

It wouldn't, and she was going to have to assure him of that if he didn't return to his usual show of indifference when others were around. They had always been so careful, never giving away by look, word, or deed what they meant to each other, at least when they weren't alone. Until their son learned the truth, the only one who had ever come upon them in a moment of intimacy had been Jason's niece Amy, when she'd caught them kissing. And that wouldn't have happened if Jason hadn't been foxed at the time.

Keeping their relationship a secret had always been important to her. She wasn't gentry, after all, and she loved Jason too much to cause him embarrassment. Her lack of social status was also why she had convinced Jason that Derek should never know either, that she was his mother, though he hadn't wanted to keep that from his son. Not that Jason had considered marrying her back then. But he'd been young and, like anyone else of his class, adhered to the fact that a lord did not marry his lowborn mistress.

He had instead married an earl's daughter, just to give Derek and his niece Reggie a mother figure. Which had ended up a disastrous decision, since his wife, Frances, had been anything but maternal. A pale, thin woman, Frances hadn't wanted to marry Jason in the first place, had been forced to it by her father. She'd deplored his touch, and their marriage had never even been consummated. She had lived most of it separated from him, and had finally insisted on a divorce, which she had ultimately used blackmail to obtain.

Frances had been the only other member of the family to figure out that Molly was Jason's mistress and Derek's mother, and she had threatened to tell Derek this if Jason didn't end their marriage. The family had weathered that scandal fairly well, and six years later, it was rarely if ever mentioned anymore. Jason could have stopped it—Derek had actually learned the truth before the scandal of the divorce reached the gossip mills—yet he hadn't.

"This is something that should have been done years ago," he had told her at the time. "Actually, it's a marriage that never should have been. But then it's rarely easy, to correct the mistakes one makes in one's youth."

The reasons he had made the match had been good ones. The reasons he had ended it were good ones, too. But ever since it was ended, he'd been asking Molly to marry him, to her utter frustration, when he knew she'd never agree. And her reasons were no different than they'd ever been. She was *not* going to be the cause of yet another Malory scandal. She hadn't been raised that way. And besides she was already more a wife to him than Frances had ever been.

But she knew that her continued refusals to marry him, or even let him tell the rest of his family about their love, had been frustrating him as well for a very long time. Which was why she was afraid he was hoping the matter would come to light inadvertently. Not that he was being blatant in looks he was giving her, nothing the servants might take note of, at any rate. Yet his family was different. They knew him too well. And they would *all* be here soon . . .

More arrived even as Molly had the thought. Jason's niece Reggie and her husband, Nicholas, along with their young son, appeared in the dining room before lunch was finished. Anthony perked up immediately. Reggie might have been his favorite niece, but that didn't save her husband. Nicholas was his favorite verbal punching bag, so to speak, and without the presence of his brother James, whom he would just as soon trade barbs with, he'd been sorely missing a convenient target for his satirical wit.

Molly just managed to refrain from rolling her eyes. She knew Jason's family as well as he did, since he shared everything with her, including all the family secrets, foibles, and scandals.

So she wasn't the least bit surprised to hear Anthony say to Nicholas as he took the seat across from him, "Good of you to show up, dear boy. My teeth were getting a tad dull."

"Old age starting to set in, is it?" Nick shot back with a smirk.

Molly noticed the nudge Anthony's wife gave him before she said, "Remember it's Christmas and be nice for a change."

Up went Anthony's black brow. "For a change? I'm always nice. There's just nice, and then there's—nice. The latter gets reserved for bounders like Eden, is all."

Molly sighed. As fond as she was of all of Jason's family, she had a soft spot for Nicholas Eden, because he had befriended her son in their school days, when Derek had had to deal with his public illegitimacy. He and Derek had been close friends ever since. And typically, Derek jumped in now to take Anthony's attention off of Nick.

"Reggie, you remember that grave we found in the east clearing all those years ago?" Derek said to his cousin. "As I recall, you were going to ask one of the gardeners about it. Did you ever get around to doing that?"

Reggie gave him an owlish look. "Goodness, what made you think of that old grave? It's been so long since we found it, I'd forgotten all about it."

"Amy came across it last night and mentioned it. M'father don't even know who it belongs to."

Reggie peered at her cousin Amy. "What were you doing in that clearing last night?"

"Don't ask," Amy mumbled.

And Warren, obviously finding their catastrophes of the day before rather amusing now, after the fact, said, "A little coach trouble."

"A little!" Amy snorted indelicately. "That coach is cursed, I tell you. Who did you say you bought it from, Warren? Because you were definitely swindled."

He chuckled and patted her hand. "Don't worry about it, sweetheart. I'm sure the crew I sent over to dismantle it this morning will make good use of the kindling."

Amy nodded, then turned back to her cousin. "We ended up having to cross that clearing on foot last night. It just surprised me, to find a grave there, so far from the family plots, yet still on the property."

"Now that you mention it, it surprised Derek and me, too, when we found it all those years ago," Reggie replied thoughtfully. "But no, Derek, I don't believe I did ever get around to asking the gardeners. It's too far from the gardens, after all. Figured whoever was tending it probably didn't live at Haverston, so it wouldn't do much good to ask around."

"Unless one of the gardeners was specifically asked to tend it," Anthony pointed out. "Old John Markus was ancient when I still lived here, and he'd worked at Haverston for as long as anyone could remember. If anyone might know about that grave, it would be him. Don't suppose he'd still be around, would he, Jason?"

Like everyone else, Molly glanced toward Jason to hear his answer, and caught his tender expression on her. Her cheeks went up in flames. He'd done it! She couldn't believe he'd done it! And with half his family here to see it. But she was panicking for nothing. The look he'd given her had been brief, and no one was turning about to see who he'd been looking at, too interested in his answer, which he gave now.

"Here at Haverston, no," Jason replied. "He retired about fifteen years ago. But he's still alive, last I heard. Living with a daughter over in Havers Town."

"Think I'll ride over and pay my respects to Mr. Markus this afternoon," Derek said.

"I'll go with you," Reggie offered. "I've a few Christmas presents I still have to buy, so I was going to stop by Havers anyway."

Warren shook his head in bemusement. "I don't understand all this morbid curiosity about an old grave. It's obviously not someone in the family, or the grave would be in the family crypt."

"I suppose you'd think nothing of it if someone got buried in your backyard, and no one bothered to tell you who it was or why they picked your backyard?" Anthony asked. "Perfectly normal occurrence in America, is it, Yank, having unmarked graves show up on your properties?"

"I would imagine someone was asked and did know—at the time," Warren replied. "Or the grave would probably have been removed to a more proper location—at the time. And it seems pretty obvious that the grave is older than any of you, since none of you know when it got there or who's in it."

"Well, that's what I object to," Reggie put in. "It's just too sad, really, that whoever it was has been so completely forgotten. At the very least, her name should be added to that stone marker that merely says 'SHE RESTS.'"

"Think I'll join you as well for that jaunt to Havers," Amy said. "I was going to help Molly fetch the rest of the Christmas decorations from the attic this afternoon, but that can wait until tonight."

Molly was sure she'd learn later, whatever they found out in Havers Town, but right now she really couldn't care less. With her cheeks still heated, she slipped out of the room unnoticed.

And it was already going through her mind, what she was going to say to Jason when she got him alone tonight.

That had been too close by half. If his relatives hadn't all been so interested in the subject at hand, at least one of them would have noticed the way he had looked at her. And that would be the end of their secret.

But what good would it do? It still wouldn't change her mind about marrying him, though that was something she wished she could do, with all her heart. But one of them had to remain sensible about this. Even if he did marry her, she'd never be accepted by the ton. She'd be nothing but another Malory scandal.

Chapter 3

AS IT HAPPENED, THE TRIP TO HAVERS TOWN TURNED
out to be utterly unsatisfactory. John Markus was
indeed still living at the advanced age of ninety-
six. He was bed-ridden, yet his mind was quite
lively for his age, and he did indeed recall the
grave.

"I tended that grave for nigh on sixty-eight
years," John proudly told the group gathered
about his bed.

"Goodness!" Reggie exclaimed. "That's long
before even you were born, Uncle Jason."

"Aye." John nodded. "Since I was a lad of thir-
teen myself. Turned the task over to my nephew
when I retired fifteen years ago. Wouldn't trust
anyone else to do it proper. He ain't been slack-
ing, has he?"

"No, John, of course not," Jason assured him,
though he hadn't a clue, since he hadn't been out
to see that grave in over thirty years himself. But

he didn't want the old man worrying about it, so he added, "He's been doing an excellent job, indeed he has."

"We're delighted to have found someone who knows about that grave, Mr. Markus," Reggie told him, getting to the matter that had brought them there in mass. "It's been a point of curiosity for all of us, to know who is buried there."

The old man frowned. "Who is? Well now, I don't rightly know that."

The surprised silence that followed that answer was full of disappointment. It was Derek who finally asked, "Then why did you keep care of it all those years?"

"Because she asked me to."

"She?" Jason inquired.

"Why, your grandma, Lord Jason. Wasn't anything I wouldn't have done for that kind lady. Everyone at Haverston felt that way. She was well loved, your grandma was—not like your grandpa. Or at least not as he was regarded when he was young."

Up went a half dozen brows, but it was Jason who said indignantly, "I beg your pardon?"

The old man chuckled, too old to be intimidated by Jason Malory's ire. "No disrespect intended, m'lord, but the first marquis, he was a stiff one, though no different from other aristocrats of his day. He was given Haverston by the crown, but he had little care for it or its people. He preferred London, and came only once a year for an accounting by his estate agent, who was an arrogant coxcomb that ruled Haverston like a tyrant when the marquis wasn't there."

"A rather harsh testament against a man who can't defend himself," Jason said stiffly.

John shrugged thin shoulders before saying, "Merely the truth as I saw it, but that was before the marquis met and married Lady Anna. She changed him, she did, taught him to appreciate the little things in life, softened his edges. Haverston went from being a dismal, bleak place to work, to being a place her people took pride in calling home. A real shame about the rumors, though . . ."

"Rumors?" Reggie frowned. "Oh, you mean about her being a Gypsy?"

"Aye, that one. Just because she looked and sounded foreign, and there happened to have been Gypsies in the area just before her appearance, some folks got that silly notion. But the marquis, he put a stop to that rumor when he married her. After all, a lord like him would never marry so far beneath him, now would he?"

Jason intercepted his son's grin just before Derek remarked, "Depends on the lord."

Jason gave him a quelling look. The rest of the family didn't need to know—yet—that he, too, hoped to put his heart first.

John shook his head. "Back then it just wasn't done, Lord Derek. Today, maybe, but eighty-some years ago, a scandal like that would ruin a man."

"Well, rumor was all it ever was," Jason pointed out, "since it's never been proven, one way or the other. The rumor wasn't completely put to rest, though, or it wouldn't still be known. But as you say, it hardly matters in this day and age, whether Anna Malory was Gypsy or of Spanish descent, as most assumed. Only she could answer that, but my grandparents died before I was born. I'm sorry I never knew them."

"I've always wished to know the truth about her myself," Amy said. "I can remember being fascinated by the possibility when I was a child, and before you ask why again, recall that I take after her, or so I've been told. I wanted to think she really was a Gypsy—I still wish it was so. That would at least explain where I got such unusually perceptive instincts from, that are never wrong. And it must have been true love."

"Hell, if it's true love, I'm glad our ancestor realized it," Derek put in. "For some men, it takes years . . . and years . . . and—"

Jason didn't miss the subtle prodding directed his way, but before anyone else noticed, he said pointedly, "Didn't you say you had a bit of shopping to do while we were in town, Derek?" To which his son just grinned again, unrepentantly.

Jason sighed inwardly. He knew Derek was just teasing him. Actually, Derek was the only one in the family who ever dared tease him. And no one else, being aware of who Molly really was, would guess that he *was* teasing his father. But then Derek knew that Jason had been after Molly for a long time now to say yes to marrying him.

"Hmmm, wonder why I never thought to do that with Anna Malory," Amy remarked to herself, drawing everyone's attention again.

"Do what?" more than one Malory asked in unison.

"Make a bet that we'd learn the truth about her. Anyone care to take up the wager?"

But Jason interrupted with, "I'd prefer this speculation ended here."

Amy frowned. "You really don't want to know the truth, Uncle Jason?"

"I didn't say that, m'dear. I just don't want to see you break your perfect win record on something that can't possibly come to light. You would be devastated if that happened, now wouldn't you?"

Her sigh answered him, but didn't quite reassure him. After all, he was well aware that horrible odds had never stopped her from following her instincts in the past.

Chapter 4

THE FAMILY WAS SPREAD OUT IN THE LARGE COUNtry mansion that evening after dinner. Molly had carefully unpacked most of the Christmas paraphernalia from the attic earlier in the week, and it was Molly, just reaching the bottom of the stairs, who heard the horse come to a galloping halt out front and went to see who was visiting this late in the evening. Just as she reached to open the door, it was opened from without and Jason's brother James nearly knocked her over as he stomped in out of the cold.

Nonetheless, she was delighted to see he had arrived at last, even at that late hour, and offered a cheery, "Merry Christmas, Ja—"

To which he immediately cut her off with a very testy, "Bloody hell it is." Though he did halt his progress to offer her a brief smile, adding, "Good to see you, Molly," then in the same breath, "Where's that worthless brother of mine?"

She was surprised enough to ask, "Ah, which brother would that be?" when she knew very well he would never refer to Edward or Jason, whom the two younger brothers termed the elders, in that way. But then, Jason shared everything with her about his family, so she knew them as well as he did.

So his derogatory answer didn't really add to her surprise. "The infant."

She winced at his tone, though, as well as his expression, which had reverted to deadly menace at mention of the "infant." Big, blond, and handsome, James Malory was, just like his elder brothers, and rarely did anyone actually see him *looking* angry. When James was annoyed with someone, he usually very calmly ripped the person to shreds with his devilish wit, and by his inscrutable expression, the victim had absolutely no warning such pointed barbs would be headed his or her way.

The infant, or rather, Anthony, had heard James's voice and, unfortunately, stuck his head around the parlor door to determine James's mood, which wasn't hard to misinterpret with the baleful glare that came his way. Which was probably why the parlor door immediately slammed shut.

"Oh, dear," Molly said as James stormed off. Through the years she'd become accustomed to the Malorys' behavior, but at times it still alarmed her.

What ensued was a tug of war in the reverse, so to speak, with James shoving his considerable weight against the parlor door, and Anthony on the other side doing his best to keep it from opening. Anthony managed for a bit. He wasn't as hefty as his brother, but he was taller and well muscled. But he must have known he couldn't hold out indefinitely, especially when James started to slam his shoulder against the door, which got it nearly half open before Anthony could manage to slam it shut again.

But what Anthony did to solve his dilemma produced Molly's second "Oh, dear."

When James threw his weight against the door for the third time, it opened ahead of him and he unfortunately couldn't halt his progress into the room. A rather loud crash followed. A few moments later James was up again dusting pine needles off his shoulders.

Reggie and Molly, alarmed by the noise, soon followed the men into the room.

Anthony had picked up his daughter Jaime who had been looking at the tree with her nursemaid and was now holding her like a shield in front of him while the tree lay ingloriously on its side. Anthony knew his brother wouldn't risk harming one of the children for any reason, and the ploy worked.

"Infants hiding behind infants, how apropos," James sneered.

"Is, ain't it?" Anthony grinned and kissed the top of his daughter's head. "Least it works."

James was not amused, and ordered, barked, actually, "Put my niece down."

"Wouldn't think of it, old man—least not until I find out why you want to murder me."

Anthony's wife, Roslynn, bent over one of the twins, didn't turn about to say, "Excuse me? There will be no murdering in front of the children."

The smirk that elicited from Anthony had James raising a golden brow at him. That, of course, gave Anthony ample warning that he wouldn't like what was coming, knowing his brother as he did.

And James didn't keep him in suspense, saying, "Ask yourself what would happen when Jack, out of the blue, mutters, 'bloody everlasting hell,' within her mother's hearing. Then ask yourself what would happen when George asks her daughter where she heard such a phrase. Then imagine what would happen when Jack, unaware that she had just shocked her mother, pipes up that Uncle Tony took Judy and her to Knighton's Hall. Finally, imagine George hunting me down to demand why I *let* you take our daughters to that strictly male establishment where blood flies freely in the ring, where gamblers swear most foully when they lose their wagers on the contenders who get too bloody, where every kind of topic unsuitable for six-year-olds gets discussed freely. And *then* picture George not believing me when I tell her that I didn't know you could be that bloody irresponsible. She blamed me for letting you take them there. And since I didn't even *know* you were taking them there, guess who I'm bloody well blaming?"

Even Reggie took a deep breath after that long diatribe. Anthony had looked rather shocked at first, but now he looked quite uncomfortable, especially when his wife turned to narrow her gold-flecked hazel eyes on him, her Scots temper obviously about to erupt.

"Och, mon, I canna believe what I just heard. You did that? You actually took Judy and Jack to Knighton's, of all places? You didna ken how damaging that could be to such impressionable young girls?"

Anthony winced and tried quickly to explain. "It wasn't like that, Ros, really it wasn't. I was taking the girls to the park. I stopped by Knighton's just to run in quickly to have a word with Amherst. You had asked me to invite him and Frances to dinner, and I knew he'd be at Knighton's Hall at that time of day. How was I to guess the girls would sneak out of the carriage and follow me in?"

"When those two darlings are known to be getting into things and places they shouldna?" she retorted stiffly, then turned to Reggie. "Fetch the other two bairns," she said as she scooped up the twins. "We're leaving James to get on with his murdering."

Reggie tried to hide her grin as she plucked Jaime from Anthony and grabbed the other toddler's hand, then followed Roslynn out of the room. It was accomplished within moments, as efficient as the women were with children.

James leaned back against the door after it closed, crossed his arms over his exceedingly wide chest, and said to his bemused brother, "How's it feel, old chap? Least she was still talking to you before she flounced out of here, whereas George ain't talked to me in a week."

"Bloody hell," Anthony growled. "*You* can stop blaming me. You heard what I said. Wasn't as if I deliberately took the girls to Knighton's. Same thing could have happened to you, you know."

"Beg to differ," James replied laconically. "I ain't that bloody stupid."

Anthony flushed angrily, but it was a bit of guilt that had him retorting, "I like that. You want a piece of me, then? Won't be satisfied without it? Have at me, then."

"Don't mind if I do."

Chapter 5

THE PROBLEMS THAT AROSE WITH THE STAFF WITH so many guests in the house were typically wearing on Molly, who prided herself on keeping everything running smoothly. So though she wanted to confront Jason about her suspicions, she'd been unable to stay awake long enough last night to wait for him to come to her room.

But he had joined her as usual, and he was still there in her bed when she awoke the next morning. In fact, it was his hand gently caressing her breast and his lips on the side of her neck that woke her. And although she did recall near immediately that she was annoyed with him, she selfishly kept that to herself for the moment and instead turned slightly so that he could better reach the areas of her body that he was showing an interest in.

She sighed and put her arms around him. She did so love this man. Even after more than thirty years, his touch still thrilled her beyond measure, his kisses able to fire her passions just as easily as he'd done in their youth. And she knew she had the same effect on him.

It wasn't long before they were kissing quite heatedly, and Molly knew where that would lead, which it did. But she was ready for him. She was always ready for him. She supposed that was one of the nicer benefits of loving someone and desiring him as well. And Jason never stinted in his endeavors. His lovemaking was done in no small measure and immensely satisfying—as always.

"Good morning," he said, leaning back to grin at her once they both regained their composure.

A morning could easily go sour, but he sure knew how to start one off "good." She returned his grin and then held him extra tight before she released him, perhaps because she knew she was going to scold before they parted, and she wanted to soften the blow.

The rest of his family, aside from their son, saw him as the sternest of the lot, even quite formidable. He was, after all, the head of his family and had had the responsibility of raising his younger siblings when he'd been young himself. But she knew his other side, his charm, his teasing, his tenderness. These were things that, from habit, he restrained in front of others due to his position, but not with her, never with her—except, of course, when they weren't alone.

That was the rub that was frustrating him, and yet she could see no way around it. He wanted to treat her at all times as he did when they were alone, yet he had to marry her to do so, and she wouldn't let him. And his insisting that they marry and her continued refusal was putting a strain on their relationship. One of them was going to have to give in, and as far as Molly was concerned, it wasn't going to be her.

She was nearly dressed before she put a damper on *his* morning with what she had to say, but it had to be said. "Do I need to hide from you in the day, Jason, while your family is here?"

He sat up more fully in the bed, where he had been lazily watching her as she went about her morning toilet. "Where did that question come from?"

"From the way you were looking at me yesterday in the dining room, which anyone there could have noticed. This isn't the first time. What has gotten into you, that you so forget that I'm merely your housekeeper?"

"The fact that you *aren't* merely my housekeeper?" he countered, but then sighed, admitting, "I think it's this time of year, Molly. I can't help but recall that it was at Christmas that Derek overcame Kelsey's objections to marrying him, and her reasons had been the same as yours."

She was surprised to hear that, that the very season was making him brood about it, and was quick to point out, "But there's a huge difference and you know it. Good God, Jason, she descends from a duke. Anyone can be forgiven with such an illustrious family as hers. Besides, the scandal she feared was avoided completely. *Yours* wouldn't be."

"How many times do I have to assure you that I don't care anymore? I want you for my wife, Molly. I obtained a special licence to marry you years ago. All you have to do is say yes and we could be married today."

"Oh, Jason, you're going to make me cry," she said sadly. "You know I'd like nothing better. But one of us has to consider the consequences, and since you won't, I must. And letting your family know, which you seem to be trying to do inadvertently, won't change anything, it will merely embarrass me horribly. I have a measure of respect in this household. I will have none if it becomes common knowledge that I'm your mistress."

He came to her then, completely naked as he still was and without a thought for it, to draw her into his arms. She heard his sigh before he said, "You don't think with your heart enough."

"And you don't think with your mind enough—lately," she rejoined.

He leaned back to give her a wry smile. "Well, we can agree on that at least."

Her hand rose to caress his cheek. "Jason, let it go, it can never happen. I'm sorry that my birth was common. I'm sorry that your peers would never accept me as one of their members, whether you marry me or not. I can't change any of that. I can only continue to love you and try to make you happy as best I can. You have to let it go."

"You know I'll never accept that," was his stubborn and not unexpected reply.

She sighed now. "I know."

"But I'll make the effort you want and *try* to ignore you during the day—at least when my family is around."

She almost laughed. It was damned hard, getting him to concede anything these days, at least on this subject. She supposed she was going to have to take what she could get—for now.

Chapter 6

WHEN JAMES ENTERED THE BREAKFAST ROOM THAT morning, it was to varied reactions. Those who hadn't known that he'd arrived started cheerful greetings that sputtered to an end as they got a good look at his face. Those who did know of his arrival and what subsequently followed it were either tactfully silent, grinning from ear to ear, or foolish enough to remark on it.

Jeremy fell into the middle and latter categories when he said with a chuckle, "Well, I know the poor Christmas tree didn't do that to you, though you did try valiantly to chop it down to size."

"And succeeded, as I recall," James grouched, though he did think to ask, "Was it salvageable, puppy?"

"Minus a few of its feathers is all, but those pretty little candles will dress it up so as not to notice—at least if someone other than me finishes the task. I'm much better at hanging the mistletoe."

"And making good use of it," Amy noted with a fond smile for her handsome cousin.

Jeremy winked at her. "That goes without saying."

Jeremy had turned twenty-five not too long ago and had turned out to be a charming scamp. Ironically, he so resembled his Uncle Anthony that he was nearly a mirror image of Anthony in his younger years. But then rather than taking after his own father, Jeremy had gained the cobalt blue eyes and black hair that only a few of the Malorys had possessed, those who took after the ancestor rumored to have been a Gypsy.

The mention of mistletoe and the use it was most noted for put James back into his sour mood, because he knew he wouldn't be doing any kissing under the festive greenery this year himself, not with his wife refusing to come to Haverston with him because of *her* sour mood. Bloody hell. He would get this settled between them, one way or another. Taking his frustration with the situation out on Anthony hadn't helped—well, perhaps it had a little.

Warren, still staring at the splendid black eye and several cuts on his face, remarked, "Hate to see what the other fellow looks like," which James supposed was a compliment of sorts, since Warren had personal experience of his fists from numerous occasions himself.

"Like to congratulate the other fellow myself," Nicholas said with a smirk, which got him a kick under the table from his wife.

James nodded to Reggie. "Appreciate it, m'dear. My feet wouldn't reach."

To which she blushed that her kick had been noticed. And Nicholas, still wincing, managed a scowl, which turned out rather comical looking, considering the two expressions didn't mix all that well.

"Is Uncle Tony still among the living?" Amy asked, probably because neither James nor his brother had returned back downstairs last night.

"Give me a few more days to figure that out, puss, 'cause I bloody well ain't sure just now," Anthony said as he came slowly into the room, an arm tucked to his side as if he were protecting some broken ribs.

A melodramatic groan escaped as he took the seat across from his brother. James rolled his eyes hearing it.

"Give over, you ass," he sneered. "Your wife ain't here to witness your theatrics."

"She's not?" Anthony glanced down the table, then made a moue and sat back in his chair—minus any groaning this time. However, he did complain to James, "You *did* break my ribs, you know."

"Devil I did, though I'll admit I considered it. And by the by, the option is still open."

Anthony glared at him. "We're too bloody old to be beating on each other."

"Speak for yourself, old man. One is never too old for a spot of exercise."

"Ah, so that's what we were doing?" Anthony shot back dryly, as he gently fingered his own black eye. "Exercising, was it?"

James raised a brow. "And that's not what you do weekly at Knighton's Hall? But I understand your confusion in the matter, since you're used to doling out the damage, rather than receiving any. Tends to give one a skewed perspective. Glad to have cleared that up for you."

It was at that point that Jason walked in, took one look at his two younger brothers' battered faces, and remarked, "Good God, and at this time of the year, no less? I'll see you both in my study."

That Jason said it in that not-to-be-disobeyed tone that he was renowned for, and promptly exited the room again, left little doubt, in James and Anthony's mind at least, that they were to follow immediately. James rose without expression and came around the table.

Anthony, however, huffed in annoyance, "Called on the carpet at our age? I bloody well don't believe it. And I won't forget who instigated—"

"Oh, put a lid on it, puppy," James said as he dragged Anthony out of the room with him. "It's been so long since we've had the pleasure of seeing Jason rant and rave, I'm looking forward to this myself."

"You would," Anthony replied in disgust. "You always did enjoy provoking his rages."

James grinned unrepentantly. "I did, didn't I? Well, what can I say? The elder is just so amusing when he flies through the roof."

"Well, then, let's make sure all his flying is directed at you first, shall we?" Anthony retorted, and opening the door to Jason's study, began to immediately place blame where it was due. "Jason, old man, I tried to calm this great hulking bull down last night, indeed I did, but he was having none of it. Blames me—"

"Great hulking bull?" James interrupted, one golden brow raised sharply.

"—because George ain't talking to him," Anthony continued without pause. "And now he's got me in the same bloody boat, because Roslynn ain't said a word to me since."

"Great *hulking* bull?" James repeated.

Anthony glanced at him and smirked, "The shoe fits, believe me."

Jason, standing stiffly behind his desk, snapped at them both, "Enough! I'll hear the whys and wherefores now, if you please."

James smiled. "Yes, you did leave out the best part, Tony."

Anthony sighed and told his elder brother, "It was the worst bloody luck, Jason, indeed it was, and could have happened to any one of us, if truth be told. Jack and Judy managed to sneak into Knighton's Hall while I wasn't looking, and just because I had the care of them that day, I am being blamed because the little darlings came away with a phrase or two that don't belong in their young vocabularies."

"That's dressing it up a bit too nicely," James interjected. "Let's not forget to mention that George didn't blame you a'tall, that she instead blames me, as if I could possibly have known you could be so witless as to take the girls anywhere near—"

"I'll fix things up with George soon as she gets here," Anthony mumbled. "You may depend upon it."

"Oh, I know you will, but you'll have to hie yourself back to London to do so, since she ain't coming here. Didn't want to inflict her dour mood on the festivities, so decided it would be best to absent herself."

Anthony looked appalled now and complained, "You didn't say she was *that* mad."

"Didn't I? Think you're wearing that black eye just because she's a mite annoyed?"

"That will do," Jason said sternly. "This entire situation is intolerable. And frankly, I find it beyond amazing that you have both utterly lost your finesse in dealing with women since you married."

That, of course, hit quite below the belt where these two ex-rakes were concerned. "Ouch," James muttered, then in his own defense, "American women are an exception to any known rule, and bloody stubborn besides."

"So are Scots, for that matter," Anthony added. "They just don't behave like normal English-women, Jason, indeed they don't."

"Regardless. You know my feelings on the *entire* family gathering here for Christmas. This is not the time for *any*one in the family to be harboring *any* ill will of *any* sort. You both should have patched this up before the holidays began. See that you do so immediately, if you both have to return to London to do so."

Having said his peace, Jason headed for the door to leave his brothers to mull over their conduct, or rather, misconduct, but added before he left, "You both look like bloody panda bears. D'you have any idea what kind of example that sets for the children?"

"Panda bears indeed," Anthony snorted as soon as the door closed.

James looked up to reply drolly, "Least the roof is still intact."

Chapter 7

THOUGH SHE HAD SAID SHE WASN'T COMING, James's wife showed up with their children late the next morning. Georgina also had the rest of her brothers in tow, much to James's chagrin, since he never did get along well with his many American brothers-in-law, and he hadn't been warned they were coming to England for Christmas this year.

Judy, delighted that her best friend was finally there, still said huffily, "It's about time," and grabbing Jack the moment she stepped in the front door, pulled her into the parlor to see "The Present," as it was already being termed by then. And the two young girls spent most of the rest of the day with their fingers pressed to the pedestal table, which was nearly as tall as they were, and doing a lot of whispering back and forth about the mysterious gift.

Their avid interest, though, managed to bring

The Present back fully to the attention of the adults in the house, who couldn't help noticing the girls more or less standing guard over it. A strange thing, curiosity. Occasionally, too much of it simply couldn't be contained . . .

But in the hall, without much more than a curt nod to Georgina's brothers, though the rest of his family converged on them with greetings, James followed his wife upstairs to the room they always shared at Haverston, while the children's nanny took the twins off to the nursery. She hadn't said a word to him yet, which didn't give him much hope that she was no longer annoyed with him, despite her showing up.

So he reminded her pointedly, "You said you weren't coming, George. What changed your mind?"

She didn't answer immediately, since a footman followed them into the room with one of her trunks, which she moved to start unpacking. James, hearing another one coming down the hall, promptly closed the door and leaned back against it, figuring the servant would get the message that his delivery could wait.

He watched her closely as he waited, no hard chore that. She was quite a beautiful woman, with rich brown hair and eyes of the same hue. She was petite yet nicely rounded; bearing one daughter and a set of twins had only enhanced her figure.

Theirs had been an unusual beginning, hardly what one would call a courtship. Georgina, wanting to return home to America, had signed onto James's ship as his cabin boy. He'd known, of course, that she wasn't the young lad she was pretending to be, and he'd had a splendid, if sometimes frustrated, time seducing her. He hadn't expected to fall in love, though, but that had happened easy enough, to his own jaded amazement. He had, however, sworn never to marry, so it had been a bit of a dilemma, figuring out how to make Georgina his permanently, without actually asking her to marry him.

Her brothers had solved that problem for him nicely. With a little subtle provoking on his part, they had forced him to the altar, which he'd always be grateful to them for, though he'd be twice damned if he'd ever admit that to *them*.

After wrapping up a few loose ends, like getting her to admit she loved him, too, they'd had a wonderful marriage ever since. She might blow up every once in a while—with her hot American temper, she'd never had any trouble expressing her displeasure. But then he'd never had any trouble charming her out of any snit she got into.

Which was why he didn't understand their current spat and why it was continuing as long as it was. When he'd left for Haverston, she still hadn't been speaking to him, hadn't been sleeping with him either, for that matter. And all because their daughter had uttered a few colorful phrases more suited to the adult male gender?

That had been her excuse, but he'd had time and enough to wonder if that was really what had made her temper blow up. It wasn't like Georgina to go overboard on trifles. And to blame him for Jacqueline's vocabulary when he wasn't even responsible for it . . .

"Well?" he prompted when she still hadn't answered.

If somewhat stiffly, she replied, "Thomas convinced me that I might have overreacted about Jack."

James sighed in relief. "Only levelheaded brother you've got. I'll remember to thank him later."

"Don't bother. I'm still upset, and you're the reason I'm upset, and I would *really* rather not discuss this just yet, James. I'm here for the children's sake, since Jack has been doing nothing but moping about, knowing that Judy is here while she isn't."

"Bloody hell, then I'm not forgiven yet?"

Her answer was to turn away and continue her unpacking. And he knew that mulish look of hers. She really wasn't going to discuss this with him, whatever it was that she was upset about. He was sure now that it had nothing to do with their daughter. But he was damned if he knew what it could be that she was obviously blaming him for, when he hadn't *done* anything to be blamed for.

And then he noticed her shoulders drooping, a clear indication, to his mind, that she didn't like this estrangement between them any more than he did. And of course, she wouldn't. He *knew* she loved him.

He took a step toward her, but made the mistake of whispering her name as well. "George."

She stiffened again, her moment of despair gone and her stubborn streak firmly back in place. James promptly swore a blue streak, which fortunately there were no children about to hear, but unfortunately had no effect whatsoever in getting Georgina to talk to him again.

Chapter 8

LATER IN THE AFTERNOON, EDWARD, THE SECOND oldest of the four Malory brothers, arrived with the rest of his family. It was when Edward was being "filled in" by Reggie about what they had discovered concerning the mysterious grave on the property that Amy got the feeling that The Present was not just a present. She felt that it was much more important than a mere gift, that it was actually somehow related to the mystery that was Anna Malory.

And the feeling wouldn't go away once it took root. It was so strong that she made the decision to open the gift that very night. She just was undecided about waiting until Warren fell asleep, or confiding in him. The fact that he didn't seem to be the least bit tired, even after some vigorous lovemaking, settled the matter.

Still held in his arms, with his hands idly caressing her, she whispered by his ear, "I'm going to go downstairs and open The Present tonight."

"Of course you aren't," he replied mildly. "You'll enjoy the suspense and wait until Christmas like the rest of us to find out what it is."

"I wish I could, Warren, really I do, but I know it will drive me crazy, especially after I made a bet with Jeremy, that we would find out about our great-grandmother before the end of the year."

"After Jason expressly forbade it?"

"He didn't exactly forbid it, and besides, it's too late to take it back."

He sat up to look down at her. "And what has that to do with that present?"

"That's just it. I have the strangest feeling that what's in that box is the answer. My feelings are rarely wrong, Warren. And knowing that, how can I wait until Christmas to find out what's in that box?"

He shook his head at her and said in such a disapproving tone that she was reminded of the old Warren who never laughed or smiled, "I would expect such behavior from the children, not from their mother."

She *tsk*ed at him, not even a little daunted. "Aren't you the least bit curious?"

"Certainly, but I can wait until—"

"But I *can't* wait," she cut in passionately. "Come with me, Warren. I'll be careful with it. And if it's nothing more'n a simple gift, albeit a mysterious one, then I'll have the box wrapped up again perfectly, so no one will know we tampered with it."

"You're serious about this?" he asked. "You're actually going to sneak downstairs in the middle of the night like an errant schoolgirl—"

"No, no, *we* are, like two perfectly sensible adults making a reasonable effort to solve a mystery that has been around far too long."

He chuckled at that point, used to his wife's strange logic, *and* used to her ignoring any of his attempts at sternness. But then that was the magic of Amy. She was unlike any other woman he'd ever known.

He gave in gracefully with a smile. "Very well, fetch our robes *and* some shoes. I would imagine the fire has been banked in the parlor, so it will be a mite chilly."

It wasn't long before they were standing next to The Present, Warren merely curious, Amy finding it hard to contain her excitement, considering what she expected to find beneath the pretty cloth wrapping. The parlor wasn't chilly at all, since whoever had left the room last had closed the doors to contain the earlier warmth, and Warren had closed them again before he lit several of the lamps.

But the doors opened once more, giving Amy quite a start since she was just reaching for The Present when it happened, and Jeremy said as he entered the room, "Caught in the act, eh? Amy, for shame."

Amy, noticeably embarrassed despite the fact that Jeremy wasn't just her cousin, but one of her closest friends, said stiffly, "And what, pray tell, are *you* doing down here at this hour?"

He winked at her and said dryly, "Same thing you are, I would imagine."

She chuckled then. "Scamp. Close the door while you're at it."

He started to, but stepped out of the way instead as Reggie sauntered in, barefoot and still in the process of tying her bed robe. When everyone else there just stared at her, she huffed indignantly, "I did *not* come down here to open The Present—well, maybe I did, but I *would* have chickened out before actually doing so."

"What a whopper, Reggie," Derek said as he came in right behind her. "Nice try, though. Mind if I borrow that lame excuse? Better than having none a'tall."

And Kelsey, close on his heels, said, "You amaze me, Derek. You said we'd be lucky if we were the first to open it, and goodness, you couldn't have been more right."

"Not a'tall, m'dear." He grinned at his wife. "Just know my cousins very well."

He did indeed, because next to arrive were Amy's brothers, Travis and Marshall, shoving their way through the doorway, or trying to, at the same time. So it took a moment for them to realize they weren't alone.

But one look at the crowd already present had Travis grumbling to his older brother, "Told you this wasn't a good idea."

"On the contrary, looks like we ain't the only ones who had it," Marshall replied cheerfully.

"Hell's bells, does the whole family think alike?" Jeremy asked with a chuckle.

"Hardly," Amy answered. "You don't see Uncle Jason and my father here, do you? Nor Uncle James and Tony. Not that those latter two don't think alike, they just don't think like the rest of us."

But there was a cough out in the hall that had Amy rolling her eyes, then grinning when she heard Anthony say, "Now, why do I get the feeling the younguns think we're too old to be up this time of night?"

"Harping about our ages *again*, dear boy?" James shot back. "You might be getting senile, but I'll have you know I'm in my prime."

"Deuced hard for me to get senile before you, old man, since you're the elder," Anthony pointed out with a good deal of pleasure.

"By one bloody year," James was heard to reply before they walked into the parlor.

Unlike their nieces and nephews, who were all

in their bedclothes, James and Anthony were both still fully clothed, since neither had gone to bed yet. They had in fact been commiserating over a bottle of brandy in Jason's study, since they'd both found their bedroom doors locked to them, and had heard one too many creaks on the stairs not to investigate.

They hadn't expected to find quite such a large gathering, however, and Anthony couldn't resist remarking, "My, my, now, what would draw so many children to this room in the middle of the night, I wonder? Jack and Judy aren't hiding behind you, are they? D'you get the feeling these younguns think it's Christmas already, James?"

James had already deduced what was causing so many red faces, and said, "Good God, take a gander at that, Tony. Even the Yank is blushing, damn me if he ain't."

Warren sighed and glanced down at his wife. "You see what your silliness has caused, love? Those two will never let me live this down."

"Course we will," Anthony replied with a wicked grin. "In ten or twenty years perhaps."

"If I'm right about what's in The Present, then no one will be calling this silliness," Amy said.

"*What's* in it?" Marshall piped up, staring at his sister. "You mean you've guessed what it is? You're not just here out of curiosity?"

"I made the bet with Jeremy," Amy explained, as if that was explanation enough.

It was actually, but Reggie reminded her, "Even after Uncle Jason pretty much forbade it?"

Jeremy blinked. "Hell's bells, cousin, you didn't tell me I wasn't *supposed* to accept your wager."

"Well, of course not, then you wouldn't have," Amy replied in perfect logic.

And Warren added, "Don't even try to figure that out, Jeremy. When she gets one of her 'feelings,' she gives new meaning to the word 'determination.' "

"Would have said 'mulish' myself, but I suppose you know her better than I these days."

"Oh, bosh," Amy mumbled, giving them a disgusted look. "You both will have my permission to eat your words, since I *am* going to be proven right."

Reggie said, "You actually think The Present has something to do with our great-grandmother?"

"I do," Amy replied excitedly. "When I first saw it, I had the feeling that it was important. But today I got the feeling that it was now related to my bet, so it *must* have something to do with Anna Malory."

"Let's not talk it into the ground, children, or we'll be here all night," James said. "Just open the bloody thing and be done with it."

Amy grinned at her uncle and did just that. But no one was expecting that under the wrapping, The Present would still be difficult to get at—under padlock to be exact.

Chapter 9

THE SILENCE THAT SETTLED ON THE ROOM AS EVERY-
one stared bemusedly at the padlock on top of
The Present was finally broken by one of James's
drier tones as he said, "I take it no one has the
key?"

Whatever the gift was, it was bound tightly in
thick leather that had been cut to fold over it in
triangular flaps, each flap having a metal ring on
the end of it that allowed the padlock to lock
them all together. It was very old-looking leather.
The padlock was also rusty, indicating it was very
old as well, so obviously, whatever was under it
would be just as old.

That, of course, lent credence to Amy's feeling
that The Present might be relevant to Anna Malory in some way. Yet no one could yet guess how,
or what it was, and especially who had put it
there. The shape of it could be a book, but why

would someone lock up a book? It was more likely a book-shaped box with something smaller in it, something of great value, something, as far as Amy was concerned, that would point clearly to Anna Malory's true ancestry. She tried to lift one of the flaps a bit to see if she could see under it, but the leather was just too stiff and tightly drawn to budge.

"An attached key would have been too simple, I suppose." Reggie sighed.

"The leather was cut to shape around it. It can be cut to unwrap it," Derek pointed out.

"So it can," James agreed, and reached down to lift a very sharp-looking dagger out of his boot. That, of course, had Anthony raising a brow at him, to which he replied with a shrug, "Old habits are hard to break."

"Quite so, and you did haunt some of the more disreputable waterfront establishments in your day, didn't you?" Anthony remarked.

"Are we doing the laundry now, or getting inside that box?" James shot back.

Anthony chuckled. "The box, of course, old man. Do slice away."

The leather was tougher to cut than they imagined it would be, particularly with so little room for a blade to slip under any of the flaps to do the job. In the end, it was more James's strength than the dagger that snapped the leather away from the rings, so the padlock could be set aside and the flaps peeled back.

He handed it back to Amy to do the honors. She wasted not a moment pulling the flaps out of the way and lifting the gift out. It was a book after all, leather-bound and untitled. There was also a folded parchment in it that fell out and floated to the floor.

Though a half dozen hands reached for it, Derek picked it up first, unfolded it, and after a quick glance, said, "Good God, Amy, you really do know how to call 'em, don't you? I hope you didn't wager too much, Jeremy."

Jeremy chuckled at that. "She wasn't interested in winning anything, just in making the bet so she *would* win it. Works for her every bloody time, if you ain't noticed. Ought to drag her to the races one of these days. She'd even put old Percy to shame in picking winners, and he's been amazingly lucky himself in that regard."

Percy was an old friend of the family, at least of the younger generation. He'd chummed about with Nicholas, Derek, and then Jeremy as well, when Derek took his newly found cousin under his wing years ago.

"If you don't say what's in that letter this instant, Derek Malory, I'm going to kick you, see if I don't," Reggie said impatiently.

She and Derek were more like brother and sister than cousins, having been raised together after Reggie's mother died, and she had been known to kick him quite frequently over the years, so he was quick to reply, "It's a journal they wrote together, a history so to speak. Gads, that was nice of them, considering there's no one left alive who knew them—*really* knew them, that is."

He handed the parchment to Reggie, who shared it aloud with the others.

To our children and their children and so forth,

This record we leave to you may be a surprise, or it may not. It's not something we talk of other than in private, nor have we ever told our son. And we are not assured of having more children that we may or may not speak of it to.

Know that it was not an easy task, getting my husband to agree to add his thoughts to this record, because he feels he does not express himself well with the written word. In the end, I had to promise him that I would not read his portion, so he would be free to include feelings and perspectives that I might not agree with, or might tease him about. He made me the same promise; thus, when we finished this record, we did securely lock it and throw away the key.

So we leave this written record to you, to be read at your leisure, and with your own imagina-

*tion lending it life. Though when you do read it,
it will most likely be when we are no longer with
you to be questioned about our motives and less
than honest dealings with the people who would
do us harm. And I give you fair warning: If you
have been led to believe that we are individuals
that could do no wrong, then read no further. We
are human, after all, with all the faults, passions,
and mistakes that humans are known for. Judge
us not, but perhaps learn from our mistakes.*

Anastasia Malory

Amy was beaming widely as she held the journal to her chest. She'd been right! And she
wanted to start reading this unexpected gift from
her great-grandparents immediately, but the others were still discussing the letter . . .

"Anastasia?" Anthony was saying. "Can't say I've
ever heard my grandmother called that before."

"It's not exactly an English name, is it, whereas
Anna is," James pointed out. "An obvious effort
to conceal the truth, if you ask me."

"But what truth?" Derek asked. "Anastasia
could be a Spanish name."

"Or not," Travis put in.

Marshall said, "No need to speculate at this
point, when we'll be reading the truth for ourselves. So who gets to read it first?"

"Amy does, of course," Derek suggested. "It might have shown up before she made that bet with Jeremy, but it's related as far as I'm concerned, though I'd still like to know who found it and wrapped it up for a Christmas gift, rather than just give it to m'father."

"It's likely been in this house all these years, with no one aware of it," Reggie speculated.

"I'll buy that," Derek said. "Hell, this house is so big, there's places in it even I haven't looked into, and I was raised here."

"Lot of us were born and raised here, dear boy," Anthony mentioned. "But you're right, not every little thing gets investigated when you're young. Depends what you find interesting, I suppose."

Amy couldn't stand the suspense anymore and offered at that point, "I'm willing to read it aloud, if some of you want to stay to hear it."

"I'm game for a chapter or two at least," Marshall said, and found himself a seat to get comfortable in.

"As thick as that journal is, it may take right up to Christmas day to get it all read," Warren noted as he sat on one of the couches and patted the spot next to him for Amy to settle into.

"Lucky then we opened it ahead of time, eh?" Jeremy grinned.

"Can't very well get to sleep now, not after that 'Judge us not, but perhaps learn from our mistakes,' " James said. "Too bloody intriguing, that."

"Think we should wake the elders first, though," Anthony replied.

James nodded. "I agree. You wake them while I find us another bottle of brandy. I get the feeling it's going to be a long bloody night."

Chapter 10

THERE WERE FOUR LARGE WAGONS IN THE CARAVAN. Three of them were nearly little houses on wheels, made entirely of wood, including the slightly curved roof, and replete with a door and windows covered in bright curtains. Some were ancient, a testimony to the superior quality of craftsmanship that made them. Even the fourth wagon showed this quality, though it was merely a typical supply wagon.

When the caravan would move off to the side of a road at night to make camp, tents would be removed from the fourth wagon, along with large kettles and the iron rods that formed triangles over campfires to hold them, and the food to throw into them. Within minutes of the caravan halting, the area would take on the atmosphere of a small, cheerful village. Pleasant aromas would drift off into the surrounding woods, as well as the gay sound of music and laughter.

The largest of the four wagons belonged to the *barossan*, the leader, Ivan Lautaru. Surrounding his wagon were the tents of his family, his wife's sisters, her mother, his sisters, and his unmarried daughters.

The second largest wagon belonged to Ivan's son, Nicolai, built in preparation for him to take a wife. It had been built six years ago. He had yet to take that wife. The omens were not right for it, according to Maria Stephanoff, the old woman who lived in the third wagon. First she claimed the wedding must take place on a certain day of the year to be fruitful, then she claimed each year that the omens weren't right for it on the appointed day, much to Nicolai's fury.

There were a total of six families in the small caravan, with forty-six people among them, including the children. They intermarried as they were able, yet sometimes there were not enough brides or grooms to choose from, from so few families, and in such times they would search for other caravans like theirs in hopes there would be marriageable young ones in the same need. They met and dealt with countless people in their travels, yet these were outsiders, *Gajos*, and those of pure blood would never consider these outsiders for marriage.

Ivan was losing patience with the delay of his son's wedding as well. He had already paid the bride price for this wife for Nicolai. His word was law, yet he would not gainsay Maria. She was their luck, their good fortune. To ignore Maria's predictions would be the death of them. They firmly believed this. Yet he could not choose another bride for his son either. Only Maria's granddaughter would do, her only living descendant, the only one who could continue to bring them their good fortune when Maria passed on.

Tonight, as usual, they made camp near the town they had passed through during the day. They never camped too close to a town, just close enough to give the townsfolk easy access to them, and vice versa. In the morning the women would walk to the town and knock on every door, offering their services, be it the selling of trinkets or finely made baskets, or the telling of fortunes, which their caravan was known for.

They would also advertise the skills of their men, for the Lautaru caravan possessed some of the finest wagonmakers in the world. Everything earned was shared by all, for ownership of property was alien to them. Which was why a few of those women might come home with a stolen chicken or two.

If a wagon was ordered, they might stay in the vicinity for a week; if not, they would be gone within a day or two. Occasionally, if it was taking too long, they would leave the wagonmakers behind to catch up with them once their job was finished. Signs would be left along the roads to guide them back to the caravan.

This was necessary when people such as they were the scapegoats for any crime, whether they committed it or not. If caravans like theirs were in the area, fingers would begin to point at them if they were there too long. They could make camp within minutes; they could pack up and leave even quicker. From long experience and the persecution of their kind for centuries, they had learned to be able to be back on the road again on a moment's notice.

They were wanderers; it was in their blood, the need to travel, to see what was over the next horizon. The young adults had seen most of Europe. The older ones had seen Russia, and the countries surrounding it. They tended to stay in a country long enough to learn its language fairly well, if circumstances didn't chase them out beforehand. A wealth of languages was a benefit to any traveler. Ivan prided himself on knowing sixteen different languages.

This was not their first visit to England, nor would it likely be their last, since the English laws dealing with them were not as harsh as they had been in centuries past. They found the English a strange people actually. Many young Englishmen of good family were so fascinated by their beliefs and love of freedom that they wanted to join them, to dress like them, to act like them.

Ivan would tolerate one or two of these *Gajos* for short periods of time, only because their presence had a calming effect on the English peasants, who would reason that if their own English lords found these people to be trustworthy, then they couldn't be the thieves they were reputed to be, now could they?

There was one such *Gajo* with them now, Sir William Thompson. He was not the usual sort to want to join them, far from it. He was an old man, older even than Maria, and she was the oldest among them. She had deigned to speak to him several months ago, not to tell his fortune, which she no longer did for *Gajos*, but because she had seen the pain in his eyes and had wanted to remove it.

This she did, relieving William of a guilt he had been burdened with for over forty years, so that he could go to his Maker in peace. He was so grateful, he swore to devote his remaining years to Maria. In truth, he had realized that she was dying, and wanted to make her last days as pleasant as he could, in repayment for what she had done for him. No one else knew. Those who had known Maria all their lives didn't know. Her own granddaughter didn't know. Yet William had guessed, and it was an unspoken knowledge between them.

Ivan, though, would not have permitted him to stay. His age was a detriment, it was decided. He was too old to contribute to the community coffers. But he demanded to prove himself and did, always returning to the camp with his pockets full of coins, so he was allowed to stay. It was a moot point, really, that he was a wealthy man and the coins were his own. He was merely paying for the privilege to remain near Maria. Besides, he ended up making a further contribution, in bettering their English, which was a good thing, since they had no plans to leave England this year.

Anastasia Stephanoff sat on the stoop of the wagon she shared with Maria, her grandmother next to her. They watched the camp as it settled down for the night. The campfires were banked. A few groups still sat around them talking quietly. Children were rolled up in their blankets wherever they had gotten drowsy. Sir William, whom they had more or less adopted, was snoring loudly under their own wagon.

Anastasia had become very fond of Sir William in the short time they had known him. She found him silly most of the time, in his courtly ways, his stiff hauteur that was so English, in his efforts to make Maria laugh. But there was nothing silly in his devotion to her grandmother, a devotion that was not in doubt.

She would often tease Maria that it was too bad she was too old for romance, to which she would usually get a chuckle, a wink, and the remark "There is never an age too old for romance. Love-making, now, that is a different matter. Some bones get too brittle for such nice exercise as that."

Romance, lovemaking, these were not subjects that might only be spoken of in embarrassed whispers. Their people would discuss anything openly and with passion that they found to be natural, and what could be more natural than romance and lovemaking?

Lovemaking was brought clearly to mind as Anastasia watched her future husband push his current lover toward his wagon. He was not gentle about it. The woman even stumbled and fell. He yanked her back to her feet by her hair and pushed her again. Anastasia shuddered. Nicolai was a vicious brute. She had felt the sting of his palm many times herself, when he did not like the way she talked back to him. And this was the man she was to marry.

Maria noticed the shudder, and the direction of her gaze. "It bothers you, that he makes love to others?"

"I wish it did, Gran, then I would not feel so hopeless about my future. Any woman is welcome to him as far as I am concerned, though I cannot understand how they can abide him, as mean as he is."

Maria shrugged. "The prestige, of being favored by Ivan's only son."

Anastasia snorted indelicately. "There is nothing but pain in such favor. I hear he is not even a good lover, that he takes his pleasure and gives none in return."

"There are many selfish men like that. His father was the same."

Anastasia grinned. "You know that from personal experience, Gran?"

"Pshaw, Ivan should have been so lucky. No, the *barossan* and I always had a perfect understanding of each other. He would not look at me with lust in his eyes, and I would not curse him to the end of his days."

Anastasia laughed. "Yes, that might tend to make a man a bit leery of you."

Maria smiled, but then her expression became serious, and she reached over to fold her gnarled fingers with Anastasia's. The young woman felt alarm rising. Maria did not hold her hand unless there was bad news to impart. She could not imagine what that bad news could be, but she held her breath with dread, for Maria's bad news tended to be really, really bad news of the devastating sort.

Chapter 11

Anastasia had turned eighteen a few months ago. That was considered far, far beyond the marriageable age, when twelve was considered just right among their people.

Some of the women teased her mercilessly, for not knowing the touch of a man yet. Foolish, to waste her best years. Foolish to not gain extra coins from the *Gajos* for a quick tumble. It was just another way to fleece them. It meant nothing. No husband, or future husband, would be jealous of it; they in fact *expected* it. Only if a husband caught his wife making eyes at another member of the band would there be serious consequences; divorce, severe beatings, sometimes death, or worse in their eyes, banishment.

Whenever Anastasia would talk to Maria about her feelings on this matter, that she felt such an aversion to the very thought of being touched by man after man after man, Maria would blame it on her father's blood. Many things over the years had been attributed to her father, some bad, some good. Maria had found him to be a wonderful scapegoat, when she could think of no other way to answer Anastasia's questions.

Many things flitted through Anastasia's mind as she waited for Maria's bad news, things other than speculation of what that news would be. She could guess if she put her mind to it, but she didn't want to know, not yet. The continued silence was a balm at first; it did not contain disaster. But it lasted too long. Suspense intruded, and became unbearable.

Finally Anastasia could stand it no longer and prompted, "What is it, Gran, that you do not want to tell me?"

A sigh, a brief, heartfelt one. "Something that I have delayed far too long, child. Two things, actually, both of which will cause you considerable distress. The distress, you are strong enough to deal with. The abrupt change that will occur to your life is what worries me, and why I want to see it done soonest, while I am here to aid you."

"You have foreseen something?"

Maria shook her head sadly. "I only wish I did know the future in this instance. But you must make that future yourself, and the decision you make will be for your good or ill, but it must be made. The alternative, you have said yourself, is unthinkable."

Anastasia knew then, what Maria was being so cryptic about. Her marriage, or rather, the husband she was to marry. "This is about Nicolai?"

"It is about marriage, yes. I must see you settled into it this week. It can wait no longer."

Anastasia panicked. "But the day you set, it is not for another two months!"

"This cannot wait until then."

"But you know I hate him, Gran!"

"Yes, and if only *you* had known it before I accepted the bride-price for you, then you could have married another long ago. But Ivan, that wily son of a goat, he came to me when you were only seven, five years before you would be old enough to marry, long before you realized that Nicolai would not suit you. Ivan, he was taking no chances, that someone else would beat him to you."

"I was so young," Anastasia said bitterly. "I cannot understand such haste. He could have waited until I was old enough to decide the matter for myself."

"Ah, but we were visiting with another band, you see. And the other *barossan* showed too much interest in our family, and asked too many questions about you. Ivan was no fool. He asked for you that night. The other *barossan* asked for you the next morning, a few hours too late. Ivan gloated over that for many years."

"Yes, I've heard him do so."

"Well, it is time for his gloating to end. He has always used underhanded means to keep me and mine bound to this band because of our gift of insight. I never told you, but when your mother announced that she was going to live with her *Gajo*, Ivan came to me and promised he would kill her before he let her waste her talent on those not of the blood—unless I agreed to bear another child to replace her. I was past childbearing years at the time, but did that fool take that into account?" Maria snorted.

"I take it you must have agreed?"

"Of course." Maria grinned. "I have never had any difficulty lying to Ivan Lautaru."

"Did he badger you about it?"

"No, there was no need. We learned soon enough that your mother was pregnant with you, and Ivan convinced himself that she would return to us with her child, which is why we did not leave that area. It is the longest ever that we have remained in one place."

"But why do you want me to marry Nicolai now? You have helped me to avoid it all these years. What has changed your mind?"

"My mind is not changed, Anna. I said nothing about marrying Nicolai, just that you must marry."

Anastasia's eyes widened, for this had never occurred to her. "Marry someone else? But how can I, when I have been bought and paid for?"

"Marry someone else among us? No, you cannot. It would be the gravest insult to Ivan. Nicolai would never accept such an insult either. He would kill whoever you would choose. But a *Gajo* would be another matter."

"A *Gajo*?" Anastasia said incredulously. "An outsider not of the blood? How can you even suggest it?"

"How can I not, child, when it is your only alternative—unless you wish to live under Nicolai's fist the rest of your life?"

As earlier, Anastasia shuddered. She had long known that she would leave the band first, before she would submit to Nicolai. And what difference, leaving or marrying an outsider? Either way, she would be leaving.

She sighed. "I suppose you have a plan, Gran? Please tell me that you do."

The old woman patted her hand with a smile. "Of course I do, and a very simple one at that. You must bewitch a *Gajo* into asking to marry you. Then you must convince the band that you love him. Love makes the difference on how this will be viewed. One can betray one's people and all that one believes in, for love. This is understandable, acceptable. You must be convincing, though. If it is thought that you do this just to avoid marrying Nicolai, then the Lautarus are insulted. You will do as your mother did. For her it was real. She really did love her *Gajo*. For you it will be a lie, but one used to escape the future you say you cannot accept. And perhaps, if you are lucky, it will not remain a lie."

Do as her mother had done? Maria's daughter, Anastasia's mother, had fallen in love with a Russian boyar, one of the princeling nobles in that land. She had died giving birth to his child, a child he would have kept if it had been a son. But he had no use for a daughter, and so Maria had been allowed to take her granddaughter and raise her.

Anastasia had never met her father, nor had she ever had the desire to. She didn't even know if he still lived. She didn't care. A man who had found no value in her was nothing to her. And if she carried a small bit of bitterness in her heart over his rejection of her, she kept it to herself.

Maria knew how she felt, of course. Maria knew everything. She could look into people's eyes and know exactly what was in their heart. Nothing could be hidden from Maria. But Maria did not always have the answers to the questions that went against the natural philosophies of their people, which was when she would conveniently use the Russian as an excuse.

She did this now, reminding Anastasia, "You are different from the rest of us. Your father's blood shows in this. But that is not a bad thing. You have never stolen, never told a *Gajo* a lie to fleece him of a few coins. These are natural things for us to do, and to brag of, making fools of *Gajos*, yet you scorn such behavior. In that you are your father's daughter, too noble of blood to belittle yourself in what you would deem dishonorable ways. I never tried to break this in you or teach you any differently. It is a good thing to have qualities from both parents, if both parents had good qualities for you to inherit."

"I never wanted to be different."

"I know," Maria said softly. "But one cannot help what one is born to be."

"But won't Ivan threaten to kill me if I leave, as he did my mother?"

"No, not this time. I will convince him that if he keeps you from your love, your broken heart will more likely bring him disaster, rather than good fortune. I will also remind him that you could divorce your *Gajo* at any time and return to the band. This is something you *can* do, Anna, so keep that in mind if you find yourself unhappy in your choice. And if you do return, you will not have to worry about Nicolai ever again. Your marriage to a *Gajo* will break your contract with the Lautarus. You can then do as you please, marry whom you please, marry no one if you please. The choice will once again be yours to be made at your leisure."

"But I know nothing of bewitching men. How can I do this? You expect too much of me."

"Do not doubt yourself, child. Look at you. This band has never seen a prettier woman. You have your mother's glorious black hair with just enough curl to look wanton. You have your father's purest blue eyes, his fair skin. You have your mother's insight, her compassion. Many was the fight she got into with the band, to protect some *Gajo* she felt sorry for. You have done the same. You bewitch every man who looks at you. You just do not notice, because until now, you have not cared."

"I just do not see how this can be done, in so short a time. Two months—"

"One week," Maria cut in adamantly.

"But—"

"One week, Anna, no longer. Go to that town near here tomorrow. Look carefully at every man you see. Speak to those who interest you. Use your talent to help you. But make a choice, then bring him to me. I will know if he is a good choice."

"But do I want a good choice?"

A question like that might have caused confusion in another, but not Maria. "You think to just use this man for a short time, then divorce him so you can return to the band? Only you can answer, child, if you can live with using a man this way. I would have no difficulty doing so, but I am not you. I think you would prefer to be happy in your choice, to make your first marriage be your only marriage."

Maria was right, of course. Going from marriage to marriage was not much different than going from man to man. Anastasia, at least, didn't see much difference in the two. She saw love as lasting forever. Anything less could not really be love.

Unfortunately, she didn't see how, under the time constraint Maria was giving her, she could possibly find a man, an Englishman at that, whom she would want to *stay* married to. She was about to question the time constraint again when Maria's expression, for the second time, turned very serious, and her hand was once again gripped by those gnarled fingers.

"There is something else that I must tell you, that I have also delayed too long in the telling. I will not be leaving this place."

Anastasia frowned, thinking Maria meant to stay here with her and the English husband she was to find. But as much as she would love that to be possible, she knew Ivan would never permit it.

Hating to do so, she had to point that out. "You have told me countless times that Ivan will not let you leave, that he would kill you first."

Maria smiled ironically. "There is nothing he can do to prevent my leaving this time, Anna. The privilege of age will not be denied a final resting place, and I have chosen this place. My time has come."

"No!"

"Shush, daughter of my heart. This is not something that can be debated or bargained aside. And I have no desire to prolong the inevitable. I welcome this gladly, to end the pains that have burdened my body these last few years. I just must see you settled first, or I will not go in peace . . . Now, stop that. There is no need for tears, for something that is so natural as the death of a very old woman."

Anastasia threw her arms around her grandmother, hiding her face against her shoulder so she would no longer see the tears that were absolutely impossible to stop. Maria had predicted distress. Distress was not exactly what Anastasia was feeling just now, with her world falling apart around her. This was much too much to withstand all at once.

But for Maria's sake, she said, "I will do whatever is necessary to give you your peace."

"I knew you would, child," Maria said, patting

her back soothingly. "And you see now why you must be married first? If you are all that Ivan has left, then he won't let you go no matter the reasoning. As long as he *thinks* he still has me, then he will let you go. Now take yourself to bed. You need a good night's sleep so you will have all your wits about you tomorrow, for tomorrow you search for your fate."

Chapter 12

"AND WHOSE BED WAS SHE FOUND IN THIS WEEK?"

"Lord Maldon's. Really thought he had more sense. He must realize she's got the pox by now, in her vain attempt to outdo the last great court Delilah."

"And what makes you think he don't already have it himself?"

"Hmmm, yes, I suppose it wouldn't matter then, would it? Ah, well, there's not much to be said for variety these days. Stick with a mistress that you keep to yourself, like I do. Might live longer that way."

"Why don't you just get married, then, if you want to stick with just one woman?"

"Gads, no. Nothing will put you in the grave quicker than a nagging wife. Do bite your tongue next time, before you make such an outlandish suggestion. 'Sides, what's marriage got to do with keeping to just one woman?"

Christopher Malory was only vaguely listening to his friends' gossip. He shouldn't have brought them with him. They would expect to be entertained, were already showing signs of boredom as they sprawled in their chairs in his estate office, gossiping about *old* gossip. But he didn't come to Haverston to entertain. He came twice a year to go over the account books, which he was trying to do this evening, then leave as quickly as possible.

It was not that he had any business or social engagements in London to draw him back in haste. It was that he never felt comfortable in Haverston, felt actually oppressed if he stayed too long.

It was a dark, gloomy place, with outdated furnishings, ugly grays and dull tans in the wall coverings throughout, even dour-looking servants who never said a word to him other than "Yes, m'lord," or "No, m'lord." He supposed he could redecorate it, but why bother, when he had no desire to remain in Haverston any longer than it took to go over the books and listen to his estate manager's complaints?

It was a fine enough estate in size and income, but he hadn't wanted or needed it. He'd already possessed a very nice estate in Ryding that he rarely visited either—he just didn't care for the quiet of country living—as well as the title of viscount. But Haverston had been given to him in gratitude, along with a lofty new title, for having unwittingly saved the king's life.

It hadn't been intentional, his helping the king. It had occurred purely by accident when he'd stepped out of his mired coach into the road at just the moment that a runaway horse was tearing past. He happened to startle the horse into stopping, whereupon the horse had dumped its rider more or less into Christopher's lap, as it were; at least Christopher had ended up flattened on the ground with a hefty weight on top of him.

As queer circumstances would have it, the rider turned out to be his king, who had been hunting in the nearby woods when his horse had been spooked by a small animal. King George, of course, had been exceedingly grateful for the interference which he swore had saved his life. And there'd been no talking him out of being quite generous in his gratitude.

His manager, Artemus Whipple, was sitting across the desk from him and avidly listening to the gossip, rather than the business at hand. Christopher had to say his name twice to draw his attention back to his last question, and repeat it once again.

Whipple was a portly, middle-aged man who had come with the estate, and Christopher had found no reason, really, to replace him. As long as the estate produced an income, which it did, he could hardly fault him, even if some of the expenses he incurred could boggle the mind. He *did* always have a ready excuse for them. But some were so outlandish, they demanded questioning.

"Fifty pounds for laborers to plow and plant the home farm? Did you ship them in from the Americas?"

Whipple noted the sarcasm and blushed uncomfortably. "They were outrageously overpriced, yes, but it's getting increasingly more difficult to find farmers to work here. There's a silly rumor that Haverston is haunted and that's why you won't stay in residence."

Christopher rolled his eyes. "What rubbish."

"Oh, I say," Walter Keats interjected. "First interesting thing I've heard since we got here. Who's the haunter supposed to be?"

Walter, the youngest of the three friends at twenty-eight, was the one who abhorred the thought of marriage. His powdered wig was askew at the moment, after an itch had been scratched absentmindedly. Though wigs, and powdered ones at that, were mostly worn only on formal occasions these days, Walter took his cue from the older aristocracy and didn't leave his dressing room without one. Fact was, it was vanity and nothing more, since his dull brown hair didn't give him quite the flair that a perfectly powdered wig did, coupled with his vivid green eyes.

"Who?" Whipple asked the young lord with a blank look, as if he hadn't expected his reason to be dissected, and in fact, Christopher rarely did question him further on any of his given excuses.

"Yes, who?" Walter persisted, putting the manager on the spot. "If a place is haunted, stands to reason some*one* is doing the haunting, now don't it?"

Whipple's blush increased as he said stiffly, "I really wouldn't know, Lord Keats. I don't give much credence to peasant superstition."

"Nor does it matter," Christopher added. "There are no ghosts here."

Walter sighed. "You're such a stick, Kit. If my home had history, as in the blood and gore type, I'd bloody well want to know it."

"I don't consider this my home, Walter."

"Whyever not?"

Christopher gave a careless shrug. "The town house in London has always been my home. This place is just a place—a chore."

David Rutherford, not as plump in the pockets as his two friends, shook his head. "Who but Kit would consider a place like this just a place. It does look a bit drab, I'll allow, but it's got such potential."

David, at thirty, wasn't quite as bored yet with life as Christopher was at thirty-two. He was handsome by any standards with his black hair and very light blue eyes, and most of his interests these days were centered around women, though he was game to try anything new, and especially anything that sounded the least bit adventurous or dangerous.

Christopher wished he felt the same, but he had developed a strange ennui this last year and couldn't seem to find any interest in *anything*. He had come to realize that he was bored with all aspects of his life. It was a boredom that was beginning to weigh heavily on his mind.

With his parents dying when he was quite young, and having no other relatives, he had been raised by the family solicitor and servants, who perhaps gave him a different outlook on things. He did not find amusing what his friends did. Actually, he found very little about his life amusing anymore, which was why his boredom had become so noticeable.

"Whatever potential Haverston has would depend on time and inclination," Christopher replied tiredly.

"You've got the time," Walter pointed out. "So it must be lack of inclination."

"Exactly," Christopher said with a pointed look that he hoped would end the discussion, but just to be sure, he added, "Now, if you two don't mind, I *do* have work to do here. I'd like to return to London before autumn."

Since that season was a good month away, his sarcasm was duly noted and the two younger gentlemen exchanged aggrieved looks and got back to their gossiping. But Christopher no sooner glanced down at the next entry in the estate books when the butler arrived to announce some unexpected visitors from Havers Town.

The mayor, the Reverend Biggs, and Mr. Stanley, oldest member of Havers's town council, had each shown up to welcome Christopher to the "neighborhood" on his first trip to Haverston several years ago. He had seen none of these men again, however, since there had been no occasion to visit the nearby town when he was in residence, and he couldn't imagine what would bring them to Haverston again, particularly so late of an evening. They didn't leave him guessing, though, got right to the point of their visit.

"We were invaded today, Lord Malory."

"By a bunch of ungodly thieves and sellers of sin," Reverend Biggs said most indignantly.

Walter latched on to the word "ungodly," asking, "These are different from Godly thieves, I take it?"

He was being sarcastic, but the good reverend took him seriously instead, answering stiffly, "Heathens usually are, m'lord."

David, however, had perked up considerably at

the mention of sin. "What kind of sin were they selling?"

But Christopher, annoyed at yet another interruption to his chore, wanted to know, "Why do you bring this matter to me? Why didn't you just have these criminals arrested?"

"Because they weren't *caught* stealing. They are very clever, these heathens."

Christopher impatiently waved that aside, since his question still hadn't been answered. "As mayor, you can just ask them to leave your good town, so I repeat, why do you bring this matter to me?"

"Because the Gypsies aren't staying in our town, Lord Malory, they are camping on your property, where we have no jurisdiction."

"Gypsies? Oh, *that* kind of sin," David said with a chuckle that earned him a disapproving frown from the reverend.

"So I take it you want *me* to ask them to leave?" Christopher said.

"Course he does, Kit. And Walter and I will come along to assist you. Couldn't let you go alone, now could we? Never think it."

Christopher rolled his eyes. His friends had found something to entertain them, after all, and by the look of them both, were quite looking forward to it.

Chapter 13

"I'VE NEVER SEEN SO MANY MARRIED MEN IN ONE place," Anastasia said in complete disgust as she joined her grandmother at their campfire that night. "For such a nice-sized town, it was sadly lacking for our purpose, Gran. I couldn't find a single man who wasn't either too old, too young, or too—unacceptable."

"Not *one*?" Maria said in surprise.

"None."

Maria frowned thoughtfully before asking, "What kind of 'unacceptable'?"

"The kind that it would never be believed that I would fall in love with."

Maria sighed with a nod. "No, that kind won't do. Very well, I will tell Ivan tonight that we must leave. He will not question why. You can try the next town."

"I thought you said you wanted to stay here, that you find this clearing a peaceful place to rest."

"So I will look for a peaceful place down the road. Do not worry about me, child. I have the will to last until you wed—as long as you wed within the week."

Anastasia's shoulders drooped upon hearing that. She had promised herself that she wouldn't cry again. If her grandmother really was suffering in her old age, then she would be truly selfish to wish her to remain with the living just because she knew she was going to be utterly lost without her love and guidance.

So little time left. So much she wanted to say to this woman who had raised her. So many things she wanted to thank her for. But she could think of nothing adequate enough to express it all, except . . .

"I love you, Gran."

Maria's face lit up with a smile and she reached over and squeezed Anastasia's hand. "You will do fine, daughter of my heart. Your instincts will guide you, your insight will aid you; these things I predict for you. But if you or yours ever need my help, you will have it."

It was a fanciful claim, to offer help from the beyond, yet it still gave Anastasia immense comfort. She returned the squeeze and, to take the edge off their seriousness, teased, "You will be too busy, fending off all those handsome angels that have been waiting for you."

"Pshaw! What do I want with more choices to make, when it's peace I'm looking for?"

"Excellent point," Sir William said as he joined them at the fire. "And besides, she will be waiting for me, so there won't be any choices to make between those handsome angels, who, alas, will be infinitely disappointed." He bowed to Maria, then dumped a handful of wildflowers into her lap. "Good evening, m'dear."

Anastasia smiled as she observed Maria's slight blush and the adoring look that the Englishman gave her. Another reason she liked William so much—he was good for her grandmother, was adding pleasure to her last days. She would always be grateful to him for that.

He didn't stay long, though, since the food Maria was cooking wasn't ready yet, and he took it upon himself to tend to her wagon horses several times each day. But no sooner did he move off toward the horses than some unexpected visitors arrived in the camp.

It was quite an entrance, three riders galloping in, stopping abruptly, one of the horses a large brown stallion that looked annoyed to have his brisk ride curtailed, if his tossing head, stomping feet, and, finally, rearing up on his back legs were any indication.

His rider controlled him admirably, though, and got him to settle down after a few moments.

Anastasia looked at this man who could so easily handle such a powerful horse, and looked no further; she for the first time actually mesmerized by the sight of someone.

He was big, very big and broad of shoulder, thick of chest. His hair was blond, unpowdered. Half the English people she came across wore wigs, men and women alike, and half of those wore them powdered. But if that thick, tied-back golden mane was a wig, it was superbly made and lacking the tightly rolled curls at the temples that the English found so fashionable.

He was amazingly handsome, at least Anastasia found him to be so, which was why she was so mesmerized, and why Maria, watching her stare at him, said, "So you have found one today after all."

"He could be married," Anastasia said in a small, awed voice.

"No," Maria said adamantly. "It is your time to be lucky, child. Now, go take control of your fate, before one of the other women gains his attention and you must wrest him from her. They would be all over him already, if not for that dangerous animal he sits. But do not fear his beast, he will not let it hurt you."

Anastasia didn't doubt what Maria said, she never did. She nodded absently and moved toward the middle of the camp, where the strangers had stopped—next to the largest camp-fire. Ivan sat there and had come to his feet at the intrusion, which was why the blond Englishman was addressing him in his demands, which she heard as she approached.

"You people are trespassing on my land. I will allow that you might not have been aware of this, but now that you are, you will have to leave—"

Ivan was quick to interrupt him before his in-sistence became irreversible, saying, "We have an old woman who is very ill. She cannot travel just yet."

It was an excuse used many times when they had been asked to move on. Little did Ivan know how true it was this time. But the landowner didn't look convinced. He looked about, ready to repeat his demand.

So Anastasia stepped forward to add her plea. "It is my grandmother who is ill, Lord English-man. She just needs a few days to rest. We will leave your property as we found it, without harm. Please, you must allow us a day or two, so she can recover her strength."

He almost didn't even turn to glance at her, he was frowning so sternly at Ivan, but when he did, his eyes widened slightly, for the barest moment, giving her an indication that he was as surprised by what he saw as she was. His eyes were very green, very intense. She could not look away from them, recognizing the heated emotion that slowly filled them, delighted by it, for it was what she could work with, this passion he did not think to hide.

When he continued to just stare at her, she added, "Come, meet her. Share a bottle of fine Russian vodka or French wine with us. You will see that we are a harmless people with a few unique services that we offer in our travels, some you might even be interested in."

She knew she was being blatantly provocative, knew what service he would think she was offering, knew that was why he nodded and dismounted to follow her, none of which mattered in the greater scheme of things. She had to get him to herself so they could talk, had to make it seem that they were both fascinated with each other so it would be believed that they had instantly fallen in love with each other, and this was the easiest way.

She led him back to her campfire. Maria had risen, was starting to walk away. Anastasia hadn't thought how she might not appear sick at all to the stranger, yet she needn't have worried. She was too used to seeing Maria daily, which was why she hadn't guessed herself how ill she was. But looking at her through a stranger's eyes, she appeared ancient, pale, feeble—tired of living. It wrenched her heart, to see her that way.

"Gran, I have someone for you to meet."

"Not tonight, child, I need to rest."

Anastasia hadn't expected that, especially since she knew Maria hadn't heard what had been said by Ivan's campfire. Yet she realized quick enough that Maria was attempting to give her some needed time alone with the Englishman. She would have stopped her, though, wanted her opinion of the man, which Maria couldn't formulate if she didn't speak to him herself. He changed her mind.

"Let her go," he said abruptly. "I can see she is not well."

Anastasia nodded and indicated one of the plump canvas pillows on the ground for him to sit on. "I will fetch you something to drink—"

"That won't be necessary," he cut in as he hobbled his horse a few feet away, then joined her. "Sit. I am intoxicated enough by the sight of you."

She couldn't have asked for a better response from him. She still blushed. She simply wasn't used to this game of enticement, wasn't sure how to play it. But she knew it was her only option, the only way that she could possibly get him to marry her.

She joined him by the fire. Close up, he was even more handsome than she had thought. Everything about him, in fact, was pleasing to the eye.

His clothes were elegant, rather than gaudy as some lords favored. The brown coat that came to his knees was embroidered only on the flaps of the pockets and the large cuffs; the wide skirt of it flared around him as he sat. His knee breeches fit snugly and, with one knee raised to rest his arm on, showed how thickly muscled his thighs were.

The gartered stockings were white silk, as was his shirt, though the only evidence of the shirt was in the ruffles that appeared below his wide, turned-back coat cuffs, and the frills of lace down the front of the shirt that formed his jabot. His body-conforming waistcoat was beige brocade, fastened with a long row of gold buttons, left open from hip to thigh to facilitate easy movement.

Many men wore corsets to improve the fit of these long, slim waistcoats—it was quite fashion-able to do so—yet she didn't think this one needed to. He was simply too tightly made, too physically fit—too big, but in a muscular way. She didn't think he would allow any excess flesh to get in the way of his superbly tailored look.

He was staring at her again. She was guilty of the same, actually, couldn't seem to help herself. Yet she knew they were being avidly watched. His two companions had been descended upon by the other women. Music had begun to play. One of the women was dancing one of their more provocative dances to entertain them.

But Anastasia was only barely aware of these things occurring in the camp, so thoroughly did the man next to her hold her attention. So she was a bit startled to finally hear his deep voice again.

"You mentioned services. I am interested in what service you, in particular, offer, pretty one."

She knew what he was expecting to hear, knew that he would be disappointed if she told him merely the truth instead, yet she wasn't going to lie to him any more than was absolutely necessary. Actually, she hoped she wouldn't have to lie to him at all, for that wasn't how she wanted their relationship to start. And she knew, suddenly, with the perfect insight that she was gifted with, that they *would* marry. She just wasn't at all sure yet how she was going to bring it about.

The aroma of Maria's stew was very pleasant. Anastasia stirred it for a moment as she considered what to say to the Englishman. The full truth? A partial truth?

She did not want him to think she was a sorceress with magical powers, as some Gypsies were thought to be. Magic frightened some people. Even things that seemed like magic but weren't frightened some people. She was not possessed of any kind of true magic, just a talent that seemed somewhat magical in nature because it was so accurate. The dilemma was, how to explain that to him.

Chapter 14

CHRISTOPHER HAD SEEN GYPSIES BEFORE, THOUGH never this close. Large bands of them came to camp on the outskirts of London occasionally, to ply their numerous trades and entertain those Londoners daring enough to venture into their camps, but he had never gone himself. He had heard many stories, though, about them. Most not so nice.

Generally they were thought to be thieves and exotic prostitutes, but were also possessed of the legitimate skills of tinkering, horse-trading, music, and dancing. They were considered a very happy, carefree people who abhorred the thought of settling down in any one place. To keep a Gypsy from wandering was to wither his soul, or so he had heard.

This band did indeed seem harmless enough. Their camp was orderly, clean. Their music and laughter were not overly loud. They were mostly dark-skinned and very exotic looking. They were all dressed colorfully in bright skirts and kerchiefs, with pale blouses, the men wearing bright sashes. There was much flashing of cheap jewelry, in long, dangling earrings and many rings, chains, and bracelets.

The wench who had caught his interest so thoroughly seemed different from the others, though. She had the long earrings, the many bracelets and rings. Her clothes were just as colorful, her full skirt a bright yellow and blue, her short-sleeved blouse a pale yellow. She had no kerchief tying back her hair, though, which flowed in free, curly abandon down her back and over her shoulders.

It was her eyes, however, that made her so different. They were tilted at a slight, exotic slant, but were of a brilliant cobalt blue. Her skin, too, was much lighter in color, very fair, smooth as ivory.

She was not very tall. Her head would probably not even reach the top of his shoulders. She was slim of build, petite, yet very nicely shaped. Ample breasts pushed against the thin cotton of her blouse. He had seen women more beautiful, but never one as alluring as this one. He had wanted her the moment he clapped eyes on her. That in itself he found utterly amazing, since it had never happened to him before.

She hadn't answered his question yet. Watching

her, enjoying doing so, he nearly forgot it, until she said, "I am a healer, a seer, a diviner of dreams." Then with a grin, "You do not look sickly, Lord Englishman."

He chuckled at her. "No, I'm hardly that. Nor do I dream often enough to remember any dream in particular for you to divine. As for seeing into my future, you'll have to excuse me, pretty one, but I'm not about to throw money away on something that cannot be proven until some future date when you are long gone from here."

"A smart man." She smiled, clearly not offended. "But I don't see into the future."

"No?" He raised a golden brow at her. "Then what *do* you see, to be a seer?"

"I see people for what they are, and perhaps help them to see themselves in a clearer light, so that they can correct their own faults and be happier with their lot."

He was amused by such fanciful claims. "I know myself well enough."

"Do you?"

She asked it with such meaning that it gave him pause. But he shook off the immediate curiosity that her insinuation aroused. He was not fooled. These people made their living by taking advantage of the ignorant and superstitious. He was neither. And besides, what he wanted from her, she had not mentioned yet.

"I have coins to spend," he told her matter-of-factly. "Surely you must have something else to sell—that I would find of interest?"

That his eyes moved down her body as he said it could leave little doubt of what he wanted from her. A look like that would have insulted a lady. The wench didn't take offense, though, not even a little. She actually smiled, as if she were delighted he was being so blatant in his desire. Which was why her answer confounded him.

"I am not for sale."

He felt poleaxed. That he couldn't have her had never occurred to him. His emotions rioted; he refused to accept a no where she was concerned.

He had been rendered speechless, which was perhaps why, after a few moments, she thought to add, "Which does not mean you cannot have me—"

"Excellent!" he jumped in, only to have her hold a hand up so she could finish.

"However, you would not like the condition, so it is not worth discussing."

For someone whose emotions had been pretty much dead for a very long time now, Christopher didn't know quite how to handle these extreme ups and downs the Gypsy was dealing him at the moment.

He ended up frowning and his tone was less than pleasant as he demanded, "What condition?"

She sighed. "Why mention it, when you would never agree to it?"

She turned away from him, started to rise, as if to leave. He grabbed her arm to detain her. He *would* have her. But he was suddenly very angry, that she obviously thought teasing him would up the price.

"How much will it cost me?" he bit out.

She blinked at his tone, yet she didn't try to placate his obvious anger, asked merely, "Why must everything have a price, Lord Englishman? You have made a mistake in thinking I am like these other women. Lying with a *Gajo* means nothing to them, is just another means to put food in the kettle."

"And what makes you different?"

"I am only half Gypsy. My father was as noble as yours, if not more so, a princeling in his own country. From him I have different ideals, one of which is that no man will touch me without benefit of marriage. Now do you understand why I say this is not worth discussing? You would not only have to agree to marry me, you would have to convince my grandmother that you are worthy of me, and I do not foresee either occurring. Now, if you will excuse me . . ."

He was not willing to let her go. Marriage to her was absurd, of course, just as she realized it was. A princeling father indeed. Such an outrageous lie. Yet he still wanted her. There had to be another way to have her. He just needed to figure out how, and needed to keep her here and talking to do that.

Which was why he said, "Tell me more about this 'seeing' thing you do."

She did not mince words with him. "Why, when you doubt me?"

He gave her an earnest smile that he hoped would put her at ease again. "So convince me."

She bit her lip for a moment in indecision. It was a luscious-looking lip. She stirred the kettle again. She stirred things in him as well, with each of her sensuous movements. She appeared deep in thought. Then she sat back and looked into his eyes, just stared, for the longest time, and so intently. He got the strangest, fanciful notion that she really was seeing into the darkest reaches of his soul. The suspense almost had him ready to shout.

At last she said in a mild tone, "Very well. You are not a happy man. It is not that anything has made you unhappy. Actually, there is much in your life that could make you happy, it just doesn't."

His ennui was apparently easy to discern. His friends had remarked on it as well, so he was not surprised that she would pretend to "see" this as his problem.

Annoyed that she called "seeing" what was so obvious that anyone could "see" it, he put her on the spot. "Perhaps you know why?"

"Perhaps I do," she replied, and for a moment, compassion filled her eyes, making him distinctly uncomfortable. "It is because you have lost interest in what you used to be interested in, and have found nothing new to take its place. Because of this you have become—disillusioned? Bored? I'm not quite sure, just that something is seriously lacking in your life. Only recently has it begun to bother you. Perhaps it is merely that you have been alone too long, without family. Everyone benefits from the caring involved in family, yet you have been deprived of this. Perhaps it is merely that you have not found a purpose to your life yet."

He knew it was no more than guessing on her part, and yet her guessing was so bloody accurate, it was frightening. He wanted to hear more, and yet he didn't. Actually, what he really wanted to hear was something that would leave no doubt in his mind that she was a charlatan.

"What else do you see?"

She shrugged carelessly. "Minor things that have nothing to do with your well-being and state of mind."

"Such as?"

"Such as, you could be rich, but you don't really care to pursue great wealth."

He raised a brow. "Excuse me? What makes you think I'm not rich?"

"By my standards, you are. By your standards, you are merely comfortably secure. Even your estate manager earns more than you do from what he manages for you."

Christopher went very still. "That is a slanderous remark, wench, that you had better explain this instant. How could you possibly know that?"

She didn't seem even a little alarmed that she had gained his full ire. "I couldn't," she replied simply. "But I could not help but hear a lot about you when I was in Havers today. Because you come here only rarely, when you do come, you are the subject on everyone's lips. Often was your manager mentioned, and how he has been gulling you ever since you first arrived. For some, the opinion is that it is no more than a lord deserves. For others, they have dealt personally with the man and despise him. Two different motives for saying the same thing usually discounts motive and just speaks the truth. And if it was not true, Lord Englishman, you would have laughed it off. Instead, your anger shows that I merely confirm your own suspicions about the man."

"Anything else?" he asked tightly.

She grinned at him. "Yes, but I think I have made you angry enough for one night. Would you care to share our meager dinner?"

"I've eaten, thank you. And I would prefer to get all of the anger out of the way now, to leave room for—other emotions. So do continue dissecting me."

She blushed at mention of those "other" emotions, understanding very well what he meant. This took the edge off his anger, reminding him that he was sitting there in a state of need because of her, and had yet to figure out a way to take care of that need.

"You do not like to draw attention to yourself," she said, "which is why you do not dress foppishly. It's not because you don't like foppish, it's because you know very well how handsome you are, and this already draws more attention than you are comfortable with."

He laughed. He couldn't help it. "How the devil do you come by that conclusion?"

"That you know very well how handsome you are? Any mirror would show you that. That you might like to dress more fashionably, but don't? I see your companions wearing their expensive jewels, their much brighter colors, their patches and wigs, all very stylish. Yet you dress more sedately, wear no jewelry, not even a velvet ribbon around your neck. You hope that eyes will be drawn to them rather than you. This is a futile hope, though. You are simply an extraordinary-looking man."

He blushed. He was thrilled. He was in pain, her words firing his desire even more.

His hand went to her cheek. He couldn't stop himself, he had to touch her. And she didn't try to prevent his doing so. She merely stared at him, yet with such a swirl of emotion in those startling blue eyes that he almost forgot that they were sitting in the open at her campfire, and pulled her into his arms.

"Come home with me tonight, Gypsy," he said huskily. "You won't regret it."

"You have a *Gajo* priest in residence, then, to give his blessing?"

His hand dropped from her. Frustration filled his eyes. "You are saying you *would* marry me?"

"I am saying I want you, too, Lord Englishman, but without the priest's words, I can't have you. It does not get more simple than that."

"Simple?" he all but snorted. "You must know that is impossible, that people from my social stature only marry within their class."

"Yes, I know very well how nobles are governed by the opinions of their peers, which does not leave them free to do as they please. A shame you aren't a common man, Lord Englishman. They have more freedom than you."

"And how free are you, to do as you want?" he shot back in a frustrated tone. "Or did you not just tell me that you want me?"

"I can't deny that. Yet I am restricted by my own morals, rather than the opinions of others. If you must know, my own people would be scandalized if I were to marry you. Ironically, you would not be an acceptable mate for me, for you are not one of us. Would I let that influence me? No. Only one's heart should matter in these things. Yet mine will not let me go to a man who will not be mine to keep. I do not hold myself that cheaply."

"Then we have nothing further to say." He stood up and tossed a few coins into her lap. "For your insight," he said with a measure of derision. "Too bad you couldn't 'see' a way for us to be together."

"But I did," she replied sadly. "Too bad you don't want me enough to keep me."

Chapter 15

TOO BAD YOU DON'T WANT ME ENOUGH TO KEEP ME.
Oddly enough, Christopher did want her that
much. He realized it about noon the next day,
when she simply would not get out of his mind.
He couldn't get any work done for thinking of
her. He rudely ignored his friends as well. They'd
had a very good time last evening, a good time
that included getting from the other Gypsy
wenches what he'd been denied himself. Not that
he begrudged them that. It was just driving him
crazy, that he hadn't been as lucky.

He started drinking in the early afternoon, in an
effort to dull his disappointment. It didn't really
help. What it did do was make it much easier for
him to decide to make the Gypsy his mistress.
Surely that would satisfy her "mine to keep"
morals, wouldn't it?

It was just barely dark when he rode to the
Gypsy camp again. He didn't bring David or Wal-

ter with him this time, didn't even tell them
where he was going, since he had every intention
of bringing the Gypsy home with him, yet he
didn't want his friends to know how completely
she had bewitched him, to the point of wanting to
set her up in London where she would always be
available to him.

She wasn't at the campfire where he had left her
last night. The old woman was there, though. He
tethered his horse near her. No one came to question what he was doing there, probably because
they didn't want to know if he was there to evict
them again.

"I'm looking for your granddaughter, madame,"
he said without preamble.

She looked up at him, her eyes crinkling as she
smiled. "Of course you are. Here, sit, and give me
your hand," she said, patting the pillow next to
her.

He sat, but he wasn't sure why he gave her his
hand. She held it loosely in her gnarled fingers;
there was no strength in her grip. Her eyes closed
briefly, then opened to stare into his. It was the
strangest sensation, feeling as if your soul were
being touched.

Fanciful. He shouldn't have drunk so much
today, shouldn't have brought a full bottle of rum
with him either, as if he needed extra courage to
ask the Gypsy to be his mistress. Actually, he

wasn't at all sure what her answer would be, and really just wanted his senses deadened somewhat, in case she turned him down.

"You are a very fortunate man," the old woman said to him at last. "What I give to you will bring you happiness for the rest of your life."

"And what is that?"

She was smiling at him again. "You will know when the time is right."

More nonsense. These people thrived on being mysterious. He supposed it was part of their allure. But he was impatient to see the girl again.

"Where is your granddaughter?"

"She has been asked to dance. She is preparing herself now. It won't be long."

Even another minute was too long as far as he was concerned. His impatience was incredible. After forcing himself to stay away all day, he refused to be put off, now that he was here.

"Yes, but *where* is she preparing? I merely wish to speak with her."

The old Gypsy chuckled. "And so you shall, but after she dances. She doesn't need the distraction you present, when the dance requires her full concentration. Patience, *Gajo*, you will get what you want."

"Will I? When what I want is her?"

He shouldn't have said that to her grandmother, of all people. It was beyond tactless. The one pitfall of too much drink was a loose tongue, and he'd just stumbled over it. But it was too late to take it back now. Fortunately, she didn't appear offended.

She merely nodded and asked in her heavily accented English, "You have one of your religious men ready to give his blessing, then?"

That nonsense again? "Preposterous. I'm an English lord, madame."

"So? She's a Romany princess, as noble in her birth-land as you are in yours. And if you want her, you will have to marry her."

"I have come up with an acceptable alternative," he told her stiffly.

"Have you indeed? One she will find more favorable than marrying that Gypsy there, whose father is our *barossan* and has already paid her bride-price?"

Christopher tensed, filling with a rage the likes of which he'd never felt before. "Which Gypsy?"

"The handsome one there leaning against that tree—who will be dancing the *tanana* with her tonight. It is very, very rare for a *Gajo* to ever witness the *tanana*. You are blessed, Englishman, to have come at the right time to see it."

That "dancing with her" seemed to have some significant meaning that he couldn't figure out in his drink-befuddled state. He did find the man she had waved toward, and saw him leaving the tree. Following the direction he headed in, he saw the girl who'd been haunting his mind and drew in his breath at her sensual beauty.

She wore a low-cut, off-the-shoulder white blouse, the deep scoop of it bordered with a lacy ruffle, dotted with tiny gold sequins. Her full skirt was a shiny gold, and glittered even more with large gold bangles sewn about the hem. Her only jewelry was the long earrings that flashed and tinkled with her slightest movement. A shawl-like white scarf, also dotted with gold sequins, draped over her gleaming black hair and down her sides.

She was shining from head to toe. She was beautiful. She didn't notice that Christopher was there. She was staring at the Gypsy as her arms lifted, beginning the dance . . .

The young man was indeed handsome, tall, slim, graceful in his leaps and movements. Christopher felt too big and utterly clumsy in comparison. The dance was mesmerizing. They never lost eye contact with each other, no matter how frenzied the tempo and movements became. It was a dance of passion, of temptation, of two lovers flirting, teasing, denying, offering, promising . . .

"He can't have her. I forbid it," Christopher said adamantly, proving just how intoxicated he was.

Not surprisingly, the old woman laughed at

him. "You can't forbid it, English. All you can do is prevent it by marrying her yourself."

"I *can't* marry her, madame."

A long, drawn-out sigh. "Then stop thinking you can have her, enjoy the dance, and go home. We will move on in the morning."

He hadn't taken his eyes off of the girl since she had appeared, nor did he now. But the old woman's words caused an unexpected panic he couldn't quite control. They'd leave—*she* would leave? He'd never see her again? Unacceptable. She *would* agree to be his mistress. He'd buy her anything she wanted, give her anything—short of a marriage license. How could she not agree?

Yet as much as he wanted to believe that money would solve this for him, that couldn't be depended on when dealing with a people so different from his own. He was out of his element. Who but foreigners would think that he could just *marry* her, just like that, ignoring the fact that he was a titled lord and she was a common vagrant? Well, not so common. Well, utterly beautiful, utterly desirable, but that was beside the point. It simply couldn't be done.

Why not?

The question startled him. He needed another drink. That, at least, was easily done, and he pulled the bottle of rum out of his wide coat pocket, opened it, and tipped it to his lips, still without taking his eyes from her.

She was desire. She was passion. She danced like an angel. She danced like a wanton. God, he wanted her. He had never wanted anything as much as he wanted her. She made him feel again. It had been so long since his emotions had been this alive. He had to have her. No matter the cost, he had to have her . . .

Chapter 16

THE GROAN WOKE HIM. CHRISTOPHER COULDN'T figure out where it had come from until he heard it again and realized he was the one groaning. His head was splitting apart. A bloody hangover, and no more than he deserved, he supposed, for drinking rum, of all things. It certainly wasn't his normal libation, but he'd wanted something strong yesterday, and there had been nothing else left in the house—which he would see about rectifying first thing today.

"I can fix that for you."

The voice was lightly accented, soft as a whisper. He turned to see who it belonged to. He wasn't surprised to see that it was *her*, lying on the pillow next to him, smiling at him. Ann, Anna, no, Anastasia, yes, that was the name he had finally got from her at some point last night, though he couldn't remember just when.

"Fix what?"

"The pain you're experiencing from your overindulgence last night."

"Oh, that?" He winced as another pain shot through his temples. "Think nothing of it. If you'll just come a little closer and let me hold you, the pleasure of that will make me forget all about my aching head."

She touched his brow gently. "No it won't, but it's sweet of you to say so."

She moved closer anyway, pressing to his side and resting her head on his chest. He sighed blissfully as he realized she was quite naked under the sheet. Whatever had happened last night between them—why the deuce couldn't he remember?—he had little doubt that he had enjoyed it.

"So you agreed?" he said with a good deal of male satisfaction as he ran a hand through her soft hair. "Knew you would, though I'm damned if I can remember it."

"You insisted, if you must know."

"I did? Well, good for me."

She chuckled. It was a husky sound that provoked a quick response in his lower regions. Amazing, how easily she could make him want her.

"Not recalling the best part of the evening leaves me feeling distinctly—unsatisfied," he told her with some chagrin. "But I'm ready to have a go at it again, so I can remember it this time."

Her head lifted so she could look at him. Her lovely eyes held humor, but tenderness as well. "Again? I hate to disappoint you, Christoph, but the moment your head touched that pillow last night, you were fast asleep. You didn't even stir once when I undressed you, and that was no easy task, as big and heavy as you are. A cannon could have gone off in this room, and you wouldn't have—"

"I get the idea," he grouched. "Bloody hell, I drank *that* much?"

She nodded with a grin. "You really are quite funny deep in your cups. You don't slur your speech. You don't stagger or sway in your movements. You don't appear intoxicated at all. But the things you say—I really doubt you would say them if you had a clear mind."

"Such as?"

"Oh, such as when you told me I would *never* dance again. So silly, of course I will—whenever you ask me to. And when you tossed me up onto your horse and told me to stay there while you killed Nicolai."

His eyes widened. "I didn't, did I?"

"No, you got distracted, trying to find a weapon in one of your pockets, then finally couldn't remember what you were looking for."

He grimaced. "Never again. If I ever see another bottle of rum, I'll—"

"Yes, I know, you'll break it over your head before you drink it."

"I wouldn't go *that* far."

She chuckled. "I didn't think so, but that *is* what you said last night."

The sound of her humor again stirred him. He pulled her farther up his chest, so that her mouth was within reach of his. His eyes locked with hers. He had no doubt she would recognize the desire she could see in his.

"So we haven't made love yet?" he said huskily.

"No, nor will we," she said matter-of-factly, "not until I rid you of that awful headache I know you are suffering. When I make love to you, Christoph, I want you to feel only pleasure. I did not exaggerate when I told you I was skilled at healing. The knowledge of herb lore has been in my family for many generations. This will not take long."

He was beset by several different emotions at once, hotter desire when she spoke of making love *to* him, acute disappointment when she left the bed, abrupt awe as he was treated to a full view of her nakedness.

She behaved as if it were a perfectly normal thing to do, to walk about unclothed. Not a bit of self-consciousness or embarrassment did she show. Nor was she proudly flaunting that luscious body before him, though she certainly had reason to. She simply went to a cloth satchel that was hers, rummaged through it until she found what she was looking for, then looked about the room until she spotted what else she needed—glasses and several decanters, one that was replenished with fresh water each day.

She opened each decanter to sniff it, then, surprising, chose the brandy to sprinkle some crushed herbs into. Stirring it briskly with her finger, which she then sucked clean, much to Christopher's horror—what that did to his already stiff condition was quite painful—she came back to the bed and handed him the glass.

There was barely a half inch of the golden spirits in the glass, made murky, though, by the powdered herb, which had him staring at it with a frown. "Why the brandy rather than the water?"

"Because the cure isn't very pleasant tasting, and the brandy will mask the taste. Drink it. You will feel much better in only, oh, fifteen minutes or so. Just enough time for me to take a quick bath."

The thought of her in his large tub had him gulping down her concoction to set it aside. "I'll join you—if you don't mind."

"I don't mind." She smiled down at him. "If you will promise to keep your hands to yourself until you are feeling no more pain."

He sighed. "Never mind, I'll suffer here—er, wait here for you."

She nodded, leaned over to kiss his brow, then paused to whisper by his ear, "Good things come to those who wait, Christoph."

It was on the tip of his tongue to point out to her that his name wasn't that foreign-sounding Christoph, but he chose instead to savor the sight of those magnificent breasts that had come so close to his mouth when she leaned over him. He heard the door to the bathroom close and sighed again. But it wasn't long before he was fantasizing about her in that decadent bathroom.

It was the only room in the entire house that didn't fit the current decor and had been a complete surprise to him, on his first inspection of the estate. It was as if some puritan of the last century had decorated the house, but that single room had been hidden from them and so left intact. It was ancient Roman in design, huge, with a sunken tub that could easily fit six adults, entered by marble steps, surrounded by Grecian columns. Naked gold cherubs formed the waterspouts on the tub and the ornate sink.

He *would* bathe with her in there, and before they left for London. London . . . which reminded him, where the deuce was he going to keep her until he could find a suitable place for her? The servants in his town house couldn't be trusted not to gossip about her. Here in the country it hardly mattered; servant gossip didn't travel that far. But in London it certainly did, and he didn't care to have it run through the mills that he'd been bewitched by a Gypsy, despite the fact that it was absolutely true.

The door opened. She came back into the room as naked as when she'd left it. She came straight to the bed. She kneeled on it, threw back the sheet, then kneeled over him. He sucked in his breath at her boldness as she settled herself to sit on his loins. Her hip-length hair, which had graced her sides, curled on his belly in front of her.

"How is your headache?" she asked matter-of-factly, as if he weren't mesmerized by her actions.

"What headache?"

She smiled at that answer. "Any regrets, Christoph?"

He chuckled and moved his hips against her. "You must be joking."

She rolled her eyes. "I mean beyond what we are about to do. I know I can make you happy. I just wonder if you regret what fate has dealt you. I certainly do not."

He reached up to caress her cheek. "I don't think you realize how much you have already done for me. You were more accurate than I care to admit, in what you saw in me. I had become a dead shell. You've brought me back to life."

Her smile became brilliant. "We will be good

for each other." She braced her hands on the bed at his shoulders to lean over him and whisper against his lips, "Very good."

He groaned, his arms going around her, pulling her down to feel all of her against him. And her lips, he captured those, too, his mouth closing with a voracious demand on hers. He felt her tense. It was too much passion all at once, yet he couldn't seem to slow down. It was as if he'd waited years and years for this one moment, this one woman, and there was no stopping him now that both were his.

But she stopped him. She forced herself out of his hold, and in his momentary surprise, she cupped his cheeks and ordered sharply, "Listen to me, Christoph. I will not let you hurt me because you are so intoxicated with passion that you are not thinking about what you are doing. Do you forget this is my first time with a man? Some other time we can do this swiftly, if that is your wish, but not this time. This time you will have a care for what you must break. I am prepared for the pain, but only you can lessen its impact. Or does it not matter to you if I suffer more?"

"Of course it matters," he said automatically.

Yet he was still reeling over her words. Good God, how could she be a virgin and be as bold as she'd been? Yet the truth would be discovered within moments, so this couldn't be a pretense on her part.

"You are awful brazen for a virgin," he pointed out, rather tactlessly, he realized too late.

But she laughed, rather than taking offense. "We are going to spend the rest of our lives together. For what reason would I conceal anything from you? I am yours, Christoph. It would be silly for me to hide myself from you, would it not?"

I am yours. Strangely enough, hearing her say that filled him with tenderness. He rolled them over, so that he was the one leaning over her. He kissed her, gently this time. There was much to be said for savoring the moment.

She tasted heavenly. Her lips parted easily for him, pulled on his tongue as he sent it exploring. His hand moved over her firm breast. She arched upward, filling his hand completely. He nearly laughed in delight. A wanton virgin, what more could a man ask for?

"You will tell me, then, when you are ready?" he asked huskily.

"I think . . . you will know," she gasped out.

So he would. He smiled, continuing his exploration. Her skin was silken smooth, warm. He found himself caressing her reverently, marveling at her perfect shape, her softness, her reactions to his touch. He was hard, aching to be inside her, yet he was so fascinated by her that it was the sweetest bliss, watching her experience lovemaking for the first time. She shivered, she groaned, she thrust against his touch. She made him feel as if he were experiencing lovemaking for the first time as well.

And he did indeed know when she was ready. He was careful of his weight when he moved over her to settle between her thighs, and even more careful in entering her. The barrier was there as she'd claimed, and he did more teeth-gritting than she as he sundered it open. Her gasp was loud, but no more than a gasp. His kiss soothed her further.

He gave her a few moments to recover from the discomfort, didn't continue until she began returning his kiss. Her passion reignited, he slid the rest of the way into her depths, slowly, exquisitely, until at last she fit all of him. It was nearly more than he could bear without losing control, such tight heat gripping him, so much pleasure, yet he managed to hold off the final bliss, to withdraw and begin a gentle thrusting that she could tolerate. Yet it was soon apparent that she was beyond the need for moderation, and one deep thrust sent them both on that glorious ride to fruition.

Chapter 17

CHRISTOPHER HAD NEVER REALIZED JUST HOW pleasant it could be, to simply hold a woman close to him and savor the feel of her warm body. He supposed he'd never really taken the time before to find out, always impatient to either sleep or be off about his business, once he finished satisfying his needs. Then, too, he'd never "kept" a mistress before, or brought one into his own bed.

Not that he hadn't had many mistresses over the years, but they'd had their own abodes, their own agendas separate from his, and the typical arrangement with these types of mistresses was that they'd merely agree to accommodate each other exclusively for a time. They'd cost him no more than the occasional expensive trinket.

Anastasia, now, would be completely "kept." He'd be supplying her with a home where he could visit her, servants to see to her comfort, clothes, food, as well as the expensive trinkets. She was going to be costly. She was most definitely worth it.

"You sound famished," she said when they'd both heard his belly rumble for the third time.

"Perhaps because I am," he replied lazily, still in no hurry to get up. "Come to think of it, don't recall having dinner last night—bloody hell, it's no wonder that rum went right to my head. Any idea what time it is?"

"Quite late, midmorning at least."

He chuckled. "You call that late?"

"When you're used to rising with the dawn, yes, that's very late."

He smiled. "There'll be no reason for you to rise that early anymore."

"I happen to like the dawn, to watch the sunrise. Don't you?"

"Hmmm, never thought about it—actually, don't recall seeing too many sunrises. Sunsets are more in line with my habits."

"I think you'll enjoy the dawn with me, Christoph," she predicted.

"I *know* you'll enjoy sunsets with me," he countered.

"And why can't we enjoy both?"

He sat up to look down at her. "You aren't thinking of changing my habits, are you? And why do you persist in calling me Christoph?

Didn't I tell you last night that my name was Christopher?"

"You did. Kit, too, you said your friends call you. But I happen to like Christoph much better. It sounds more lyrical to my ears. Consider it an endearment."

"Must I?"

She chuckled and rolled to the side of the bed, then headed for her clothes. "I think we must feed you immediately. Empty bellies lead to grouchiness."

He blinked, then grinned to himself. She was right, of course. There was nothing wrong with her having a pet name for him. And besides, when she sashayed about the room naked like that, he simply couldn't find anything really worth complaining about.

He got up to dress as well. When he finished and glanced at her again, it was to find that she was wearing that flashy dancing costume from last night, which would draw more attention to her than he would like.

"Have you nothing else to wear?" he asked.

"You didn't exactly give me the opportunity to pack last night, Christoph. All I have is my satchel, which my grandmother tossed up to me just before you sent that mad stallion of yours galloping out of the camp."

He grimaced with the reminder that he'd been

less than gentlemanly last night. "I'll take you back today to collect your things—and perhaps to town to buy something more . . . normal looking."

She raised a brow at his choice of words. "You think my clothes are not normal?"

"Well, certainly they are." His tone turned conciliatory. "It is just, they are . . . well . . ."

He couldn't come up with an appropriate word that wouldn't insult her. She supplied some for him, and it wasn't difficult to see that she *was* insulted.

"Common perhaps? Peasantlike? Suitable only for Gypsy vagabonds?"

"There is no need for you to take offense, Anastasia. Your clothes were perfectly fine for the life you were living on the road. But you'll be living differently from now on. It's as simple as that."

She was frowning now, not at all placated. "Are you going to have trouble, Christoph, dealing with what I am?"

"What you are?"

"That I'm a Gypsy?"

"Half Gypsy, or so you've claimed."

She waved that aside. "I was raised as a Gypsy, not as a Russian. I may not think or do exactly as most Gypsies, but I am still one of them."

He came over to her and put his arms around her. "We are not having our first fight."

"We aren't?"

"No, we aren't. I forbid it."

She leaned back to stare into his eyes. "I will make some allowances to accommodate you. You must do the same for me. In such a way we can come to agree on everything in the end. Fair enough?"

"You have a unique way of looking at things that I think I can get quite used to. For right now, shall we agree to raid the kitchen?"

"If that is what it takes to obtain some breakfast, certainly." She waved her arm toward the door with a flourish and a bow. "After you—Lord Englishman."

He rolled his eyes and pushed her in front of him so he could swat her backside playfully. "No more of that. Christoph will most definitely do."

She giggled. "If you insist."

Chapter 18

IT WAS TOO MUCH TO HOPE, REALLY, THAT THEY would continue to get along perfectly, yet a few days or weeks wouldn't have been too much to expect—rather than the time it took them to walk downstairs that morning.

Thinking back on it, Christopher allowed that he could have been more tactful. But guarding his words was simply not his habit, especially among his friends. Who else, after all, would he feel like bragging to about his splendid acquisition than his closest friends?

Walter and David were that, but he could have wished they hadn't appeared in the hallway below just as he was coming down the stairs, Anastasia's hand in his, though she was a few steps behind him. And both men couldn't help but notice them, of course, when that flashy gold skirt of hers was like a beacon in the dark.

"What's this?" David asked, eyeing Anastasia,

though his question was for Christopher. "So *that's* where you went off to last night?"

"Taking her back to her camp?" Walter surmised, then with a grin, "We'll come along."

"Not exactly," Christopher corrected. "I'll take her later to collect her belongings, but she'll be staying with me from now on. She's agreed to let me keep her."

"Oh, I say, d'you think that's wise, Kit?" David asked. "She's not exactly typical mistress material."

Anastasia yanked her hand out of Christopher's at that point, but with David's remark in his mind, he barely noticed. "What has typical got to do with it?" he asked. "I've had 'typical,' David, and lose interest in it in a matter of days, same as you do. Which certainly won't be the case with my Anna here. Besides, I didn't ask her to be my mistress to introduce her to society, so it hardly matters whether she's typical or unique, now does it?"

"Er, not to be the bearer of dire tidings, old chum," Walter remarked. "But I'd say your Anna is about to take your head off—metaphorically speaking."

Christopher spun around just in time to receive a resounding slap across his cheek and watch Anastasia hike her skirt and run back up the stairs. "What the devil was that for?" he called after her.

But she didn't stop, and a moment later he heard the door slam shut to his room. The entire house likely heard it, actually.

"Bloody hell," he muttered.

Behind him, David was tactfully coughing into his hand, but Walter was outright chuckling. "No, indeed, nothing typical about that a'tall. Though it might help you to know, Kit, that she began frowning as soon as David introduced the subject of mistresses."

"Sure, blame it on me," David grumbled.

Christopher ignored his friends and marched back to his room. The door wasn't locked against him. He found Anastasia stuffing a few things that had been left out of her satchel back into it.

He closed the door behind him and leaned back against it. He wasn't angry, but he was certainly annoyed, and not just a little confused. A mistress had no conceivable reason to get upset at being called a mistress.

"Just what do you think you're doing?" he demanded. "And why the devil did you hit me?"

She paused long enough to glare at him. "I did not take you for a fool, Christopher Malory. Do not pretend to be one now."

"I beg your pardon?" he replied stiffly.

"As well you should," she snapped. "But you are *not* forgiven!"

"I wasn't asking to be. If I said anything wrong,

I'm bloody well damned if I know what it was. So why don't you tell me what you objected to, then perhaps—*perhaps*, mind you—I will apologize."

Her face flushed furiously. "I take it back, *Gajo*, you are a fool." She marched toward him. "Get out of my way. I am going home."

He didn't move away from the door. He did grab her shoulders to keep her in front of him, though he refrained, just barely, from shaking her.

"You aren't going anywhere until you at least explain yourself. You owe me that much."

Her lovely cobalt eyes flared. "I owe you nothing after what you just did!"

"*What* did I do?"

"You not only let those men insult me, but you stood there and did exactly the same thing. How could you speak of me like that? How could you?!"

He sighed at that point. "Those are my closest friends, Anastasia. Do you think I wouldn't be proud to show you off to them?"

"Show me off? I am not a toy. You didn't purchase me. And I am *not* your mistress!"

"The devil you aren't," he snapped, but then he paused and frowned. "Don't tell me I forgot to ask you last night. That's why I went back to your camp. Why else would you be here, unless I asked you and you accepted?"

"Oh, you asked me," she said in a soft, furious whisper. "And this was my answer."

For the second time, she slapped him. His face turned quite red this time, and not just from the slap. *Now* he was angry.

"Do *not* hit me again, Anna. It was a natural assumption for me to make, that you had agreed to be my mistress, particularly since I woke up to find you lying naked in my bed. Blister it, you even *said* you agreed. I distinctly remember you saying so this morning. What the devil did you agree to, if not that?"

"You have only to recall what I told you was the only way you could have me, and you'd have your answer. I'm not your mistress, I'm your wife!"

"The devil you are!"

It was probably because he looked so horrified that she shoved her way past him and out the door. That he was utterly horrified was why he stood there in complete bemusement, rather than try to stop her. He just couldn't believe that, drunk or not, he would so totally ignore the strictures of his class. A marquis did *not* marry a common Gypsy, well, not so common, but still a Gypsy, well, half Gypsy, but still . . . it just wasn't done.

She was obviously lying, a ruse to trick him into thinking that he'd married her, and she'd been able to do it because he got so sotted with drink last night that he couldn't remember what he'd done. Of all the bloody nerve, and especially when he only had to demand some proof and she'd have to fess up that she'd lied, since there wouldn't be any proof. He would have thought she was more intelligent than that, to think she could get away with it. Some of his fast-rising rage stemmed from disappointment in her.

He went after her. She'd already left the house. He just barely spotted that bright skirt disappearing into the woods quite some distance away. It was too far for him to catch up to her on foot, though, so he ran to his stable.

She was no more than halfway to her camp when his stallion came galloping up behind her and was yanked to a rearing stop a bit in front of her. She ignored him and the beast and continued her march, merely veering around him. It was an easy matter to move the horse in front of her again, and again, until she got the idea and stopped.

He extended a hand to her, to lift her up. When she just stared at it, he explained, "I took you away from your camp last night, I'll return you to it today. It's the gentlemanly thing to do."

She snorted. "How convenient, to play the gentleman only when it suits you."

That was a serious insult that had him retaliating in kind. "I wouldn't expect a Gypsy to grasp the intricacies of the nobility."

She raised a brow at him. "Is that a roundabout way of saying that the intricacies of common courtesy are beyond the grasp of the nobility?"

He blinked. "I beg your pardon?"

"Don't bother. I already mentioned that you won't be forgiven, didn't I?"

He gritted his teeth. "That's a blasted phrase that requests an explanation when delivered in that tone, *not* a request for forgiveness!"

"Is it indeed? When a simple 'what' would have gotten the point across without causing confusion? Another one of those subtle 'intricacies' understood only by you lordly types, I suppose?"

He rolled his eyes and said in a weary tone, "You are being obtuse, Anastasia."

She matched his tone and added a sigh. "And you are being dense, Lord Englishman, or have you not grasped yet that I have nothing further to say to you?"

He stiffened. "Very well, but before we part, I would like to know how you thought you could possibly convince me that I had married you."

"Convince you?" She laughed unpleasantly. "There is probably a paper in your coat pocket with our signatures on it, unless you managed to lose it last night. But then you could always ask the Reverend Biggs—I believe that was the name he supplied. You threatened to beat him to within an inch of his life if he didn't marry us, and poor man, he quite believed you. So do whatever needs doing to unmarry us. There will be no need to inform me when it is done, since I have no doubt whatsoever that you will see to it posthaste."

She was able to walk away from him again, because again, she'd rendered him quite beyond speech.

Chapter 19

SHE WASN'T GOING TO CRY. HE WAS AN INSENSITIVE beast, an arrogant wretch, and as he might put it, a "bloody" snob. But she wasn't going to cry. She had seen his confusion and wanted to help him. She had seen his pain and wanted to heal it. She had seen his emptiness and wanted to fill him with happiness instead. But she hadn't seen that he could be so foolish as to put the opinions of others before his own needs. She hadn't seen that he would sacrifice his own happiness because "it just wasn't done."

It was appalling, to have been so wrong about him, and worse, to let her own emotions take over. Her heart wasn't supposed to get so involved—yet. She shouldn't be devastated that he couldn't stand the thought of being married to her, when she'd known from the start that he felt that way—when he wasn't drunk. Drunk, he let his heart guide him. Drunk, nothing was going to stand in the way of what he wanted, certainly not his silly "it just wasn't done."

Anastasia entered the camp blindly, her mind too filled with misery to notice Nicolai until he caught her arm and painfully jerked her around to face him. His fingers would leave bruises. She was always left with bruises whenever he touched her.

"Where did you spend the night?" he demanded.

She should have been wise enough to lie, especially since he looked quite furious, but with her emotions in such turmoil already, it was defiance that reared its ugly head. Chin raised, she answered, "With my husband."

The slap was not unexpected. Even the brutality of it that sent her to the ground was no more than typical of Nicolai. Anastasia tossed her hair out of the way and glared up at him balefully.

"Perhaps you did not hear me correctly, Nico. I was with my husband, the *Gajo* I married last night, the *Gajo* who will see you end up in an English prison if you ever lay a hand on me again."

He looked suitably uncertain, as she had hoped he would. He even paled slightly at the mention of prison, since most Gypsies would rather die than be locked up for any length of time. Yet he still doubted her, and with good reason.

"You are promised to me!" he reminded her. "You would not dare marry another."

"Promised to you, but not by me, never by me. You were never my choice, Nico, nor would I have ever agreed to marry you. I would have chosen anyone other than you, whom we both know I hate. Yet I chose for love instead, yes, love, a concept you know nothing about!"

He would have hit her again if she weren't lying on the ground, out of his immediate reach. And they had gathered an audience, not close, but just about everyone in the camp was listening and watching, including his father—including Maria, who was approaching them as fast as her old bones allowed. She did not usually witness Anastasia's confrontations with Nicolai. This one had her enraged.

Nicolai saw her coming and stiffened. There wasn't a one among them, even his father, who wasn't just a little afraid of Maria. Her insights were *too* accurate, as were her curses. And she *was* their luck. You did not take chances with guaranteed luck.

Yet he was too furious to consider any of that for more than a moment, and raised a hand to ward her off. "This does not concern you, old woman."

Her answer was to throw gold coins at him. Each one hit him squarely, each hit a different spot, each stung worse than it should have, coming from such a weak-armed throw.

"There is your bride-price," Maria spat contemptuously. "My granddaughter is now nothing to you, a stranger, and you will treat her as such, keeping your eyes off her, keeping your hands off her."

"You can't do this!" he growled.

"It is done. Even if she wanted you, I would not let you have her. You are not worthy of a dog, much less a woman. Your father is to be pitied, having such a son as you."

"Your words are worse than harsh, Maria," Ivan blustered, coming to stand next to them. "I understand anger prompts them, but—"

"Not anger, Ivan, but the unfortunate truth," Maria interrupted. "No one else dares to speak it to you, but I do. The dying know no fear."

He had heard enough before he joined them to pale at the significance of those last words. "No! We cannot lose you both."

"You have no choice this time. You cannot keep Anna when her heart leads her elsewhere. To try would bring no benefit, would instead bring disaster. But you have no one to blame but yourself, Ivan. Had you taught Nicolai better, had you curbed his cruel tendencies, she might have come to love him, instead of hating him."

Ivan was blushing furiously after that, yet he couldn't dispute such brutal truths, when Nicolai was indeed a disappointment to him. Yet their good fortune was at stake here, their incredibly long reign of luck, which he could not bear to see ended.

"Does it mean nothing, that we have always taken care of you Stephanoffs, that you have always had your home with us?" he said, trying to use guilt to reach her. "Where has your loyalty gone?"

"Loyalty?" Maria scoffed. "You lost mine years ago when you threatened me, Ivan, over my daughter's leaving. Or did you think this old woman would ever forget that? What you have had since then is mere apathy on my part, since there is no other band that I cared to join. But we come again to the crossroads, of one of mine needing to go her own way, and she will *not* be hindered in this."

"Maria—"

"No!" she cut in sharply. "There is no more to say, except this. I have given my life in service to you and yours, but it is over. If you don't want me dying with a curse on my lips that will follow you until the end of your days, you will bid your farewells to my granddaughter and wish her happiness in the path she has chosen. Good fortune will still be yours as long as you are wise enough not to interfere with love."

It was a sop for him to salvage his pride and walk away with dignity. This he did with a curt nod to first her, then Anastasia. His son had no dignity to begin with, however, so it was not surprising that he spat on the ground at Maria's feet before he stalked off.

Anastasia had gotten to her feet when Maria arrived. She put her arm around her shoulders now to help her back to their wagon. She could feel her weakness, hear her labored breath, now that the confrontation was over.

"You strained yourself," she scolded. "I thought we agreed that I would handle that."

"You would deny me my last great fury?"

Anastasia sighed. "No, of course not. Did you at least enjoy it?"

"Immensely, child, immensely. Now, where is this husband of yours? Why isn't he with you?"

At which point, considering what she must answer, Anastasia promptly burst into tears.

Chapter 20

IT WAS STILL MORNING, BUT ANASTASIA HAD PUT her grandmother to bed. There was very little life's essence left in Maria now. Anastasia could feel none as she sat there and held her cold hand.

A death vigil. She knew that was what this was. Sir William shared it with her, standing silently behind her, his hand on her shoulder. It was all she could do to assure Maria that she would be fine, when she had no idea if that would be so, when she was trying to deal with her grief as well. Yet it all needed saying.

"He holds himself unaccountable for what he did while he was drunk last night," Anastasia said in answer to why the marquis wasn't there with her. "He thought I agreed to be his mistress, and he was delighted with that assumption. He refused to believe he'd married me instead. He actually thought I would lie about such a thing."

"So you think he didn't really want you?"

Maria asked. "After meeting him, I know this isn't so."

"He wants me, just not for his wife. Which is fine. I aspired too high, apparently, to the likes of him. I will be wiser next time."

"Next time?" Maria chuckled softly. "There will be no next time."

Anastasia misunderstood. "Then I will remain without a husband. It makes no difference to me," she tried to assure Maria. "The English lord, he served the purpose we needed. I am no longer promised to Nicolai because of him. For that, I am grateful."

The old woman smiled. "You have a husband. You will keep that husband."

"I don't want him now," Anastasia tried to insist, though she was never very good at lying, and particularly to Maria, who could unravel a lie so easily.

"You do."

"Really, Gran, I don't. And besides, as soon as he finds proof that we married, other than my word, which he would *not* believe, he'll have the marriage dissolved quicker than it takes to blink."

"He won't."

Anastasia sighed, but then chuckled wryly. "Very well, I am sure you have good reason to be so stubborn about this. Why won't he divorce me?"

"Because you showed him light, daughter of my heart. He won't go back to the darkness that was his before he met you. He is not a complete fool, though it may seem otherwise to you just now. It may take him a while to figure this out. You need only wait, and be prepared to forgive him when he comes to his senses."

"Or nudge him a bit, to hurry him along," Sir William suggested.

Anastasia swung around in surprise at the Englishman's unexpected remark. "I would not ask you to speak with him, William."

"Nor would I be so presumptuous," he said in his stiff English way. "He *is* a marquis, after all, while I'm merely a lowly knight."

"Then how would you go about nudging a marquis?" Maria questioned.

William grinned, somewhat conspiratorially. "I could take her to London, dress her in fine gowns, introduce her as my niece. It would show that young pup that appearances and origins mean very little in the end, that happiness is all that really matters."

"You would do that for us?"

"I would do anything for you, Maria," William replied softly.

She reached for his hand, brought it to her leathery cheek. "Perhaps I will ignore those handsome young angels after all, *Gajo*."

He beamed at her. "I will fend them off when I get there, if you forget."

She made a semblance of a smile. Her eyes closed slowly, the light gone out of them.

Her voice was but a whisper now. "I leave her in your care, then. Guard well this treasure of mine. And thank you . . . for letting me go in peace."

Her breathing stopped, as did her heartbeat. Anastasia stared at her in shocked silence, yet inside she wailed, she keened, she futilely beat her breast, and it changed nothing. Her grandmother was dead.

"Maria wouldn't want you to cry, lass, but sometimes that is the only way to get the pain out."

This was said kindly and with a catch; William was crying silently himself. Yet he was right, on both counts. Maria wouldn't want her to grieve, wouldn't want either of them to grieve. She'd said as much.

Anastasia began to cry, not for her grandmother, who had found peace from her pain, who really wouldn't want tears shed for her after she'd lived such a full life, but for her own loneliness . . .

Sir William helped her dig the grave. She had had many offers from the stronger of the men to do this, but had refused all but the Englishman's help. The others had respected Maria, were in awe of her, but they hadn't loved her.

By custom, everything that Maria had owned was buried with her or destroyed. Even the old wagon was put to the torch. But Anastasia defied Gypsy tradition in two things. She let Maria's horses go free, rather than slaughter them as was usually done whenever it was assured the legal authorities wouldn't interfere. And she kept the ring that had been given to Maria by her first husband.

"The first was the one I most loved," Maria had said often, when they sat before the campfire at night and she spoke of the many men she had known and married over the years. "He also gave me your mother."

The ring had little value, was a cheap trinket really, yet it had been valued by both of her grandparents, and for that alone, she would keep it.

William had wanted to go to Havers to order a stone marker for the grave. Anastasia had to explain her grandmother's last wishes on the matter.

"My body will rest here, my memory will rest with you, child," Maria had told her that same night she confessed she was dying. "But my name, I wish to keep to myself. If I must rest here, rather than in my own homeland, let there be no evidence of it."

"I will put a marker here someday," Anastasia told Sir William. "But it will not bear her name."

Everyone in the camp placed food on the grave that night. It was the duty of the family of the deceased to do so. Dead ones had been known to come and berate their family if this hadn't been done, or so the tales at campfires would relate. This was not the responsibility of friends or mere acquaintances, only family members. Yet everyone in the band honored Maria in this way.

Chapter 21

"THIS IS GOING TO BE SO MUCH FUN! WE CAN'T thank you enough, Will, for thinking of us and letting us share in this endeavor of yours."

Sir William blushed and did a little mumbling that had the three old women giggling to themselves. Anastasia, watching them, hid a smile.

She had heard much about these ladies on the way to London. They were dear friends of William's whom he had known since childhood. Near his age and still quite socially active. His sisters by choice, he fondly called them, and they apparently felt the same way about him.

Victoria Siddons was a widow—for the fourth time, her last husband having left her exceedingly rich and plumply titled, so that for many years she had been one of the more prominent London hostesses, and still was. She entertained frequently in one manner or another, and invitations to her gatherings were quite "the thing" to have.

Rachel Besborough was also a widow, though not so repeatedly as Victoria, having been married to the same marquis for some fifty years before he passed on. She had quite a large family in her children and their offspring, though none still lived with her, so she was more often than not a guest of one of her friends.

Elizabeth Jennings, now, having never married, was quite likely the oldest "old maid" in existence, or so she said with a chuckle about herself. Not that she seemed to mind. She was Rachel's older sister, and so had never lacked having a large family to dote on.

This morning they were all gathered in Lady Victoria's large sitting room in her house on Bennet Street, where William and Anastasia had been staying since they'd arrived in London last week. Anastasia was standing up on a chair, undergoing her second and hopefully last fitting by Victoria's personal seamstress, the wardrobe of fancy gowns that William had promised her almost complete.

Those clothes were all that the ladies were waiting for to "launch" Anastasia on London society. Lady Rachel was keeping a written record, added to daily, of all the fashionable places Anastasia needed to be "seen at." Lady Elizabeth had formed a list of her own, of well-known gossips whom she had already begun visiting.

"Nothing like setting the stage in advance," she had said after returning from her first gossipy visit. "Lady Bascomb is just *dying* to meet you now, gel, and by tomorrow, so will be most of her friends. I swear, she can manage to call upon at least forty different members of the ton in a single day. Do *not* ask me how, but she can."

They had decided a little confusion would be just the thing to spark curiosity, and so each gossip Elizabeth paid a visit to was told something entirely different about Anastasia's history. With her mother supposedly being William's younger sister, who really had run off in her youth and had never returned to England, any and every background they created for Anastasia would be completely plausible.

The three ladies had in fact stayed up very late one night having a great good time designing some pretty outlandish scenarios, from her being the daughter of an illegitimate heir to a throne in Eastern Europe, to the daughter of a rich Turkey slave trader, to the truth, that her father was a Russian Prince. All of which got confided, in absolute secrecy, of course, to the many known gossips on Elizabeth's list.

It became William's task to find out when the marquis arrived in London, and to discover his habits, or at least his normal haunts. After all, this whole scheme was for his benefit, and wouldn't do much good if he didn't hear the gossip, or have a chance to see Anastasia in her new finery.

Once they'd set the scene, the invitations began pouring in. Anastasia, who had yet to make her first "public" appearance, was already in great demand by every hostess in town, thanks to Elizabeth's gossip-spreading talents. Her first appearance, though, would be at the costume party that Lady Victoria planned for the coming weekend.

Christopher would not be receiving an invite to this. It remained to be seen if he'd show up anyway, to denounce her, just to see what she was up to, or to claim her as his wife. Anything was possible—which was why the ladies were so excited. They could merely set things in motion. They couldn't predict the outcome.

The activity, the in-depth planning, it all helped Anastasia to get beyond the worst of her grief. And she didn't just have the loss of her grandmother and "husband for a night" to deal with, but also of the Gypsies, the people she'd grown up with, people she cared about and who cared about her. She'd said good-bye to them all, though she didn't expect it to be forever. Gypsies never parted for good except in death. They always expected to see old friends and acquaintances again in their travels.

The day of the costume party finally arrived.

Anastasia began to feel a certain anticipation, even though she didn't expect to see Christopher tonight, when he had been excluded from the guest list deliberately. After all, it wouldn't do to appear obvious in what they were doing. The whole purpose was to intrigue him, to make him regret her loss, to make him want her back, and to make it easy for him to ignore that "it just isn't done" by showing him just how it *was* done—by keeping the truth to themselves.

Ironically, the first impression she gave to *his* rules-rigid society was that of herself, the truth, because the costume she wore was no costume but her own clothes, her gold dancing outfit. To those gathered, avidly waiting to meet her, she appeared costumed as a Gypsy, and they loved it! She was a smashing success.

Although she did insist on beginning this "farce" with the truth, or a semblance of the truth, she still evaded most questions. The "mystery" is all-important, her new friends had reminded her repeatedly as they prepared for this debut. "Keep them guessing, keep them wondering, never reveal the *real* truth, except in jest."

Which was easy enough to do. Gypsies *were* masters of mystery and evasion, after all, an art she had been raised to know, despite the fact that she had rarely ever made use of such talents before now.

The night went splendidly well, surpassing her friends' expectations. Three quite legitimate, if impulsive, proposals of marriage, eight proposals of a less savory sort, one young man making a complete fool of himself by getting down on his knees in the middle of the dancers to propose to her at the top of his lungs, two other gentlemen coming to blows while vying for her attention.

Christopher didn't show up. Though it had been confirmed that he was in London, they couldn't be sure whether he had heard about her yet. But new gossip would be making the rounds tomorrow. He would hear about her eventually. It was only a matter of time . . .

Chapter 22

CHRISTOPHER COULDN'T MANAGE TO GET BACK INTO
the swing of things, now that he had returned to
London. He had finished his business at Haverston in haste, then shocked his factor by firing
him. Yet he made no effort to find a new factor.
He made no effort to do much of anything other
than staring into a lot of fires while analyzing the
things he should or shouldn't have done concerning Anastasia Stephanoff.

He could *not* get her out of his mind. It had
been nearly two weeks since he'd last seen her,
yet he could still picture her as if she stood before
him. Naked, enraged, under him in bed, the im-
ages haunted him like vengeful ghosts that
wouldn't go away.

He had gone back to her camp. He had sworn
that he wouldn't, knew that seeing her again
would serve no purpose under the circumstances,
yet two days after their final parting, he had rid-

den there again. He wasn't at all sure what he would have said to her at that point, yet he didn't get the chance to find out.

He was incredulous to find the Gypsies gone. He hadn't expected that. Rage quickly followed his amazement, enough that he'd had every intention of sending the law after them. They had claimed his property would be left as they'd found it, after all, yet they had left a grave behind, as well as a large pile of charred wood and metal that indicated one of their wagons had been burned.

Yet he'd no sooner ridden into Havers Town to find the sheriff than his rage was gone. Realizing who that grave might have belonged to was responsible for that. Anastasia's grandmother. And if that was true, then she must be grieving. Oddly, he wanted only to comfort her now. He had to find her first, though.

This he tried to do, sending runners to the closest towns. It was hard to believe they could find no trace whatsoever of the Gypsies. Vanished. Completely. And that was when he began to suspect that he might never see her again.

He was staring into the fire in the parlor at Haverston when he first realized that, and promptly punched a hole in the wall next to the mantel. Walter and David, both there to witness this, wisely said not a word, though they exchanged raised brows.

The next day they returned to London, where his friends quickly abandoned him to his foul mood. He barely noticed their absence, so little had he paid attention to their attempts to cheer him up.

It was their usual habit, though, to prowl one or more of London's many pleasure gardens or spas on a weekend, when they had no specific engagements to attend, and so that first weekend back in London, David and Walter both showed up at Christopher's town house again, to have another go at getting their "old" Kit back.

Some of the gardens could be reached only by river barge, having no land access. The gardens were so popular that many a Londoner kept a barge for the express purpose of visiting them with friends, rather than endure a delay in having to rent one. In their group, David had done the honors, simply because he owned property on the river where a barge could be easily docked.

They were fine places of entertainment, and not just for the aristocracy, but for all of London. Some, like the New Wells, near the London Spa, even housed strange animals, rattlesnakes, imported flying squirrels, becoming something of a Zoological Garden. Some had theaters. Most all had restaurants, coffee shops, or teahouses, arbors, shaded lanes, vendors, music and dancing, booths and raffing shops for cardplayers and gamblers.

The older of the gardens, Cuper's, Marybone Gardens, Ranelagh, and Vauxhall Gardens, were famed for their evening concerts, masquerades, and innumerable illuminations that made them so lovely at night, and most new gardens were mere imitations of these four.

For tonight, Walter suggested The House of Entertainment at Pacras Wells in northern London. Christopher agreed, though he couldn't say why, since he simply didn't care one way or the other. However, upon arriving, they went not to see the entertainment, but straight to the Pump Room, where his friends insisted he try the "waters" advertised as being a powerful antidote against rising of the vapors, also against the stone and gravel, and likewise, cleansed the body and sweetened the blood.

He almost laughed. They were obviously going to try any means to bring him out of the brooding he'd fallen into. Not that he believed in natural spring waters, but to humor his friends, who weren't being even the least bit subtle about it, he did drink a bottle, and pocketed a few more to take home with him.

Leaving the Pump Room, they ran into a group of acquaintances, five in number, who, unlike them, *were* actually there for the entertainment.

And two of the young men were well-known jokesters, which was probably why David suggested they join the group, hoping they could get a smile out of Christopher, where he and Walter had failed.

He couldn't have known he'd be making matters worse, but that was exactly what happened. And all because one of the young men, Adam Sheffield by name, was in a bad mood himself, but unlike Christopher, he had no qualms about complaining quite loudly about it to his friends. The reason was almost immediately revealed.

"How'm I supposed to meet her if I can't get near her? That old bird is too particular by half, I tell you, in who she invites to her events."

"No need to narrow it down to just her parties, old boy. If you didn't know, she's particular about who she lets into her house at *any* time. Party or no party, you can't just call on Lady Siddons. You have to be an acquaintance, or be with an acquaintance."

"As if she ain't acquainted with just about everyone, old as she is."

"We should have just crashed that silly party," another of them said. "I hear it was in costume. Who would have known the difference, with a few more Pans and Cupids running about the place?"

"Think I didn't try?" Adam told his friend.

"Why d'you think I was late joining you? But they were taking bloody head counts *and* names at the door."

"I heard her father was a famous matador," another of the group said now, which got the rest of them contributing to the discussion.

"A what?"

"You know, those Spaniards who actually—"

"Not even close," was said with a hearty laugh. "He's the king of Bulgaria."

"Never heard of it."

"As if that matters—"

"You're both wrong. He's not a king, but a prince, and one from some country where just about everyone's surname has an 'off' in it. Means 'son of,' or daughter in the case of the Stephanoff chit."

"Doesn't matter who her father is," someone else pointed out. "Long as her mother's from good English stock, which I've heard on good authority she is, being that her mother was Sir William Thompson's sister."

"So the chit is Thompson's niece?"

"Yes."

"Well, then, that explains why Lady Siddons has taken his niece under her wing. Sir William has been a neighbor of hers for several centuries."

"They're not *that* old, you dolt. 'Sides, how would you know? You don't run in those circles."

"No, but m'mother certainly does. Who do you think told me that Anastasia Stephanoff was going to be *the* catch of the season? M'mother almost ordered me to put in my bid for the gel."

"When no one's even met her yet? And why is that? Why keep her under such tight wraps?"

"She might be a guest of Lady Siddons, but that doesn't mean she's been hidden away until her launch tonight. Just means we don't know anyone who *has* met her yet."

"Well, half the bloody ton's meeting her tonight," another complained. "Why d'you think Adam's so put out, since *he* didn't get invited."

"Hardly half the ton." This was said dryly, if a touch resentfully. "Pro'bly just those with deep pockets, which don't include us."

"Speak for yourself, old boy," the oldest in the group said smugly. "My pockets are deep enough to suit any would-be husband hunter, but I didn't get invited either. But I'll tell you, Adam, if she's as pretty as I've heard she is, I might just ask for her m'self. Been thinking it's about time to settle down. Actually, m'father's been doing that thinking for me, if you get my drift."

"How do you know she's pretty?"

"Would she be the topic on everyone's mind if she wasn't?" one of them chuckled.

"That hardly signifies. Doesn't take a beauty to become *the* topic."

"Actually, m'oldest sister heard it from Lady Jennings, who's a dear friend of Lady Siddons, that the Stephanoff chit is uniquely beautiful, sort of a cross between a Spanish Madonna and a wanton Gypsy. Just the thing to intrigue a man, if you ask me."

The conversation continued in the same vein as the young bloods approached the theater, but Christopher slowly came to a halt. It took David and Walter a few moments to realize they'd left him behind. Returning to him, it wasn't hard to see that joining that group hadn't been such a good idea after all. His expression bordered on the furious.

"It was that mention that the chit they were talking about looks like a Gypsy," David guessed with a grimace. "What rotten luck."

But Walter said in a reasonable tone, "You know, Kit, you've refused to talk to us about that Gypsy of yours, why she left you when you'd offered to keep her in fine style, why you've been so angry about it. What are friends for, if not to hash things out with?"

"I never even told you her full name, did I?" Christopher said.

David, coming up with pretty good guesses tonight, exclaimed, "Good God, you're not going to say her name's Anastasia Stephanoff, are you?"

"The same."

"But you can't think . . . ?"

"Not bloody likely." Christopher snorted.

"Then don't let it bother you, Kit, if it's no more than a coincidence, that the two women share the same name," Walter suggested.

"A damned strange coincidence," Christopher replied, his original scowl a bit more pronounced. "Especially considering it's not a name that is even remotely common to England. Besides, I just don't like coincidences that happen to be *that* co-incidental."

"Don't blame you a'tall. Definitely strange. But let's get back to your Anna," Walter tried again. "Why did she leave you?"

Walter was pushing it. If Christopher had wanted to discuss his Gypsy with them, he would have done so before now. Yet considering the flaming jealousy he'd just experienced, when he *knew* those young men weren't even talking about his Anna, well, he obviously did need to talk about it, if only to get his mind off of that other girl, who was running around with his Anna's name.

So he said curtly, "Because she objected to my thinking *and* saying she was my mistress."

"Thinking?" David latched on to that word. "I know you got quite foxed the day before. Did you forget to square away the formalities and ask her?"

"No, I did some asking, but apparently not what I'd intended to ask," Christopher mumbled. "Seems instead of making her my mistress, I made her my wife."

Their identical shocked expressions merely confirmed why he should have kept this to himself. A man in his position just didn't make such appalling blunders.

David was the first to recover from his surprise. But he didn't point out the obvious, which Christopher wouldn't have appreciated, having said it enough times himself. *Everyone* knew what he'd done just wasn't done.

And his tone was deliberately calm as he said, "Well, that proves Thompson's niece really isn't the same girl, just in case we were doubting it a'tall. Your wife wouldn't be launching herself in the tried-and-true husband-hunting fashion, now would she?"

Walter rolled his eyes at that reasoning, but what he wanted to know was, "How does one get so drunk that they don't recall getting married?"

"By drinking *too* much, obviously," Christopher replied in self-disgust.

"I suppose," Walter allowed. "But of course, you've rectified the situation?"

"Not yet," Christopher mumbled so softly, he barely heard himself.

Walter certainly missed it, and rather than take

the hint that Christopher obviously didn't want to answer, he asked for clarification. "What was that?"

"I said not yet!"

The explosive answer still didn't stop his next question, "Whyever not?"

"Damned if I know." Christopher scowled.

David and Walter exchanged knowing looks at that point, but it was David who expressed their thoughts with, "Then perhaps we should hope that, for whatever strange reason she might have been in that Gypsy camp, your 'wife' and Sir William's niece are one and the same, after all. I'd make a call at the Siddons household tomorrow, indeed I would, were I you, Kit. Be nice if you were pleasantly surprised."

Would it? Christopher wasn't so sure, but he'd already decided to do just that.

Chapter 23

CHRISTOPHER WASN'T EXPECTING TO BE SURPRISED as he was shown into Lady Siddons's parlor, where her "guest" was holding court. Sir William's niece could be a raving beauty as the rumors indicated, but she wouldn't be the Anastasia he was looking for.

After giving it some thought, though, he didn't think the identical names were so coincidental. That would be too far-fetched. It was much more likely that his Anastasia hadn't given him her true name, that she'd met William's niece at some time in the past, liked her name, and decided to take it for her own as well.

Yet he had to find out for sure, thus his early morning visit to old Lady Siddons's house. And not expecting to be surprised just made his surprise all the worse when he saw Anastasia.

She was standing in the center of seven slavering men, all vying for her attention, wearing a morning dress that would have done a queen proud, wide-skirted, tightly corseted, her wild hair caged in a fashionable manner, frilled and laced. Black lace and powder blue satin, making her cobalt blue eyes so incredibly vivid.

For the first startled moment, Christopher actually thought there was merely a resemblance between the two women, so much did she look like an English lady, rather than the Gypsy he had first met. But only for a moment . . .

Their eyes met across the room. She immediately went very still. Then she blushed and lowered her gaze, as if she had something to be guilty about. But then she did, didn't she? Masquerading as a lady. Presenting herself on the marriage mart, when she was already married.

He was letting his jealousy supersede his delight in finding her again. He realized it, and yet those nasty emotions were too powerful to easily ignore, and were coloring his every thought. Even Adam Sheffield was here, obviously having had no trouble getting past the front door this morning, and looking utterly bedazzled by Anastasia. His friend, too, the one who'd mentioned putting a bid in for her himself, was gazing at her worshipfully.

Christopher had the distinctly violent urge to walk over there and knock their heads together, the whole lot of them. How dare they fawn over his wife and entertain lurid thoughts about her? And he had no doubt whatsoever that their thoughts were lurid.

A cross between a Madonna and a wanton, as had been noted last night, was apt by far. Anastasia exuded sexual promise, and yet seemed untouchable, a combination ripe for stirring a man's desire, yet making him hesitant to proceed, thus leaving him wishful and fantasizing.

Those who were doing no more than fantasizing, he would merely hurt. The others, though, and he could see there were several others who were actually entertaining thoughts of a more permanent nature, unaware that the lady was unavailable for anything permanent, Christopher was going to slowly take apart piece by piece . . .

"I am surprised to see you here, Lord Malory," was said by his side.

He hadn't noticed the dowager countess approaching him. He knew her by sight but couldn't recall ever actually speaking to her before. She, apparently, knew him by sight as well, to know who he was.

As for her wondering at his presence, he replied skeptically, "I doubt that, Lady Siddons, considering who your houseguest is."

"No, truly," she insisted, though she said it with a smile that merely confirmed his impression.

"After all, you were privileged enough to obtain the gem, yet foolishly tossed it away."

"I've tossed away nothing, madame," he said stiffly, well aware what she meant, and continuing in the same vein, "The gem is still legally mine."

Her brow shot up, indicating he might have actually surprised her this time, yet her tone was merely curious. "I find that passing strange, considering the connections available to a marquis that would expedite the disposal of matters of that nature. Perhaps you have merely been delayed in seeing it accomplished?"

"Perhaps I have no intention of doing anything of the sort," he shot back.

"Well now, that presents a dilemma. It might behoove you to make the gel aware of it, since she is quite under a different impression. Or do you think she's been launched just to gain your attention?"

"Actually, that she's been launched a'tall is beyond comprehension," he told her. "Or aren't you aware of who she really is?"

"Who she is? You mean aside from being your wife?" she rubbed it in, then, "I can't imagine what you're thinking. She's my dear friend's niece, of course. I don't believe you've made his acquaintance. Well, come along, my lord, and we shall rectify that."

She walked off, fully expecting him to follow her. He did, since he did in fact have a few pertinent questions to put to Sir William Thompson.

The old man was alone, standing sentinel next to a rather large fireplace, where he'd been keeping a "paternal" eye on his young "relative." Making quick work of the introductions, Lady Siddons left them alone there.

Christopher didn't mince words, asking right off, "Why have you claimed Anastasia as your niece?"

William didn't answer immediately. He glanced away from Christopher to stare again at the large group in the center of the room, his expression thoughtful. He took a sip from the cup of tea he held.

Christopher didn't get the impression that he was grappling to find an answer. He suspected he was being kept waiting deliberately. To prod his impatience? To punish him? No, that was too ulterior. Perhaps the old man simply hadn't heard him, a distinct possibility considering his age, which was likely in the seventies.

But then Sir William said in a mild tone that could have been discussing any mundane thing, rather than what was likely painful memories, "My sister disappeared some forty-two years ago, Lord Malory. I never forgave myself, at least not until very recently, for my part in it, for not taking her side when she fought with my parents over whom she was to marry. She chose to run away, rather than accept their choice for her, and we never saw her again, nor ever heard from her again. She had lovely black hair, you know. It's not inconceivable that Anastasia could be her daughter, not hard to believe a'tall, actually."

"But she's not, is she?"

William glanced at him again now. He seemed somewhat amused when he said, "Does it matter? When the society that you allow to dictate your actions thinks she is? You want to hear facts, my lord?"

"That would be wonderfully helpful," Christopher said dryly.

Sir William smiled at his tone. "Very well, it's a fact that I was traveling with those Gypsies myself. The reason isn't important, but I was in that camp when you arrived to tell them to leave. You wouldn't have noticed me, though. The truth is, you noticed nothing and no one else, once you set eyes on the lass."

The heated flush came swiftly, the truth of those words embarrassing, though undeniable. "She's uncommonly attractive," Christopher said in his defense.

"Oh, she is that, indeed, but what has that to do with anything, my lord? No, you have only to consider. There is love that takes a long while to grow, then there is love that is immediate. I never wondered at your interest in the lass. It was blatantly apparent."

Love her? Christopher started to snort, then nearly choked on his own derision. Good God, why hadn't he considered that? He had thought he was obsessed with her. He'd thought he was losing control of his own emotions. He'd thought he was letting lust get the better of him. Yet thinking back on it, he recalled how incredibly happy he'd been, waking up to find Anastasia in his bed that morning. He hadn't thought that he might be in love.

"The question, Lord Malory," William continued, "is what are you going to do about it?"

Chapter 24

HE'D COME TO HER. ANASTASIA HADN'T HAD TO GO out and be "seen" in places that Christopher might frequent, hoping to run into him. It wasn't going to take weeks, as she'd suspected it would. He'd come to her, and the very next day after her official "launching."

She shouldn't read anything into it, other than that Elizabeth's prior rumor-spreading had paid off, yet Anastasia couldn't help doing so. He was here, and so soon. And she discounted that he was staring green daggers at her. She had expected him to seriously disapprove of what she'd done, considering how he felt about commoners and nobles mixing socially, let alone more permanently.

She was doing a bit more than that, she was pretending to be something she wasn't, not her idea, but she certainly hadn't balked at it. It would be in line with Christopher's rigid beliefs to denounce her for it. But he didn't, at least not immediately. He spoke with Victoria. Now he was speaking with William. And all the while she was kept in suspense, waiting to see what he would do.

It was impossible to continue to carry on conversations with her admirers when her heart was slamming in anticipation, when her every thought was centered on the large, handsome man across the room, rather than on what was being said to her. If she'd said one word since he walked into the room, she'd certainly never recall it.

She was about to excuse herself and approach Christopher, unable to wait a moment longer when her future happiness was at stake here. But she didn't have to. He began walking directly to her, and his expression had only changed slightly. It was decidedly determined, implacable, and somewhat menacing, a combination that didn't bode too well for Anastasia's hopes.

She held her breath. It wasn't hard to tell that her attention was utterly transfixed, which had the men around her all glancing toward Christopher as well.

She anticipated an embarrassing scene at that point. What she didn't expect was a very calm, "You'll have to excuse Anastasia, gentlemen. I have a matter to discuss with her that requires privacy."

That, of course, was not met with agreeably, considering the men around her had been almost fighting to retain her attention. It was Adam Sheffield who pretty much summed up, or tried to sum up, their general reaction with, "Now see here, Malory, you can't just—"

Christopher cut that off curtly. "Can't I? Beg to differ, dear boy. A husband has rather pertinent rights, some of which even come in quite handy."

"Husband?"

That was twice more repeated in the shocked silence Christopher left behind him. He didn't stay to elaborate, had no intention of explaining himself. He simply took Anastasia's hand and led her out of the parlor.

She was too shocked herself to have protested, not that she wanted to protest. He stopped out in the hall to merely say, "Your room will do, lead on."

She did, up the stairs, down another hall, another, then one more. It was a large house. He said nothing else on the way. She was too nervous to speak herself.

Her room was cluttered. The maids didn't get that far in their cleaning until the afternoon. The bed was unmade. The dancing costume she had worn last night was draped over a chair. Several of her new gowns covered another chair—she'd had trouble deciding what to wear this morning, not used to all her choices being so fancy.

He took a moment to survey the room, after

closing the door. His eyes *would* linger on that bright gold skirt with the bangled hem. When his glance came back to her, it was distinctly questioning.

"I wore it last night at Victoria's masquerade," she explained.

"Did you? How—apropos."

His tone was just too dry for her frazzled nerves, making her reply stiffly, "Wasn't it? Nothing like presenting the truth and having no one believe it. But then most fools are made, they aren't grown."

He actually chuckled. "How true, and something I've become rather adept at myself lately."

"Making fools?"

"No."

With that simple answer, the stiffness went out of her, leaving only the nervousness. And she wasn't going to ask how he thought he'd made a fool of himself. She could name several times that *she* felt he had, but wouldn't.

Instead, she suggested reasonably, "Shall we discuss why you're here?"

"You mean you weren't expecting me, after launching yourself among the very people I socialize with?" He accepted her blush in answer, but still explained, "I'd heard the niece of a nobleman was calling herself by your name. I came here to find out why. Imagine my surprise . . ."

She had expected his surprise, and his anger. She'd seen the anger, but it wasn't present at the moment. Why it wasn't was what concerned her.

So she asked pointedly, "Why aren't you angry?"

"What makes you think I'm not?"

"You conceal it well, *Gajo*. Very well, what exactly have I done that you object to? Present myself as a lady when you feel I don't have that right?"

"Actually, what I'd like to know is why you've taken on this identity that isn't yours."

"It was not my idea to do, Christoph. I was hurt and angry enough to go about my way, never to see you again. But my grandmother—"

"Your grandmother," he cut in. "I saw the grave, Anna. Was it hers?"

"Yes."

"I'm sorry."

"There is no need to be. It was her time to go, and she was pleased to rest there in that lovely clearing of yours within sight of a road—symbolic of a Gypsy's existence. The worst of my grief is gone. She had long suffered with pain, you see, which made her welcome an end to it, so I can't begrudge her that."

"I'll put a marker—"

"No," she cut in now. "No, it was her wish to keep her name to herself, to have no evidence of it left behind. But as I was saying, Christoph, she still insisted you and I were fated to be. And William, who was traveling with us and heard her, thought you might benefit by being shown that appearances and origins don't mean that much, that—other things—are more important."

"Other things?"

She was not going to spell it out for him, so she shrugged. "To each his own. Some think power is the most important thing in life, some think wealth, some might say happiness, some might say—well, as I said, to each his own."

"You were going to mention love, weren't you?" he asked casually. "Isn't that what you feel is most important in one's life?"

She stared at him hard. He could be mocking her, but she didn't think so.

"No, love by itself is not enough. You can love and be miserable." Something she had been sure she was going to find out firsthand, but she refrained from saying so, merely added, "Love and happiness is what is most important. If they go hand in hand, there is no need to ask for more. But to get both, love must be given and returned."

"I agree."

Those two simple words started her heart slamming again. Yet she was reading too much into it. He might have claimed her in front of those men downstairs, might have given the impression that he was her husband, but of course, it was merely an impression. He hadn't told them that he was her husband, merely mentioned a "husband's rights." Cleverly done, and easy enough to back out of—unless he really *had* intended to make the claim in such a public manner . . .

She knew she was leaving herself wide open for devastation, yet couldn't seem to help it, wanting, needing, clarification. "What—do you agree with?"

"That love must be returned if given, for happiness to occur."

"But this is not what you, personally, consider most important, is it?"

"When my life was empty, or 'something was seriously lacking' in it, as you so aptly put it, I had no idea what that something could be any more than you did."

"I knew," she said softly.

"Did you? Yes, I suppose you did, and simply telling me what it was would have been met with skepticism at that point, as you probably realized."

"At that point?"

He smiled. "If a foolish man is lucky, he remains the fool for only so long, Anna, before he sees how to redeem himself and does so—if it isn't too late. I thought it might be too late, which is why I'm so grateful to Sir William."

"Grateful? For making me acceptable in your social circles?"

"No, for making it possible for me to find you again. I *have* tried, you know. I still have men out searching for your caravan."

"Why?" she asked breathlessly.

He came closer, stopped in front of her, lifted her chin. "For the same reason I have no intention of divorcing you. I want you in my life, Anna, any way I can have you. I know that now. It just took me a few days to realize that marriage, with its permanence, is indeed preferable. The scandal is so very insignificant in comparison."

She wrapped her arms around his neck. What she felt was in her eyes, which drew his lips to hers. There was no passion in his kiss, just a wealth of love and tenderness that sealed their fate more thoroughly than any words could.

Chapter 25

CHRISTOPHER TOOK ANASTASIA STRAIGHTAWAY TO his London town house, but they didn't stay there long. Within the week he ordered his servants to pack up all of his personal belongings to be moved to Haverston. Much as he might prefer city life, he quickly realized that his wife didn't, and he was much more concerned with making up for what a complete ass he'd been, about the matter of their marriage, than he was with his preferences at the moment.

He would have taken her to Ryding instead. At least it was a much more cheerful house. But she had expressed a desire to be near her grand-mother, and so to Haverston they went. He had, of course, remarked on the dourness of the place, to which she'd laughed and told him that could be easily corrected.

"I will hire an army of laborers," he promised

her. "It won't take much time a'tall to make that mausoleum habitable, I suppose."

"You'll do no such thing," she told him. "We will effect the improvements ourselves, so that when it's finished, it will be *our* home."

Wield a paintbrush himself? Hold a hammer? Christopher was beginning to realize already just how much his Gypsy was going to change his life. And he was looking forward to every bit of it.

Chapter 26

IT WAS THEIR FIRST CHRISTMAS AT HAVERSTON.
Christopher had always spent the holidays in
London—after all, it was a prime social season.
He had no desire to this year. Actually, he had no
desire to return to London for any reason. Every-
thing he wanted, everything he loved, was at
Haverston.

The house was coming along splendidly,
though it was far from finished, since they'd had
to slow down their remodeling when Anastasia
became pregnant. The main rooms were done,
however, and now held a cheerful warmth that
had nothing to do with the season, though it was
nicely decorated for the season as well.

For Anastasia, it was her first English Christmas
as well, and so a new, wonderful experience for
her. For her people, Christmas had always been a
time to visit as many towns as possible, as
quickly as possible because it was a time people

spent money on gifts, rather than just themselves, and the Gypsies had many gifts to offer. But that meant they were never in a place long enough to give it a festive look, to decorate a tree, or hang a wreath. That was a *Gajo* thing to do. But not for Anastasia—not anymore.

With her servants to help her, she had unpacked the many trunks that Christopher had had sent from Ryding, filled with Christmas heirlooms that had been in his family for generations, and they had spread them throughout the house together. He hung mistletoe in *every* room, and made the silliest excuses, to lure her under it every chance he got.

She made or bought gifts for all the servants. They delivered them on Christmas Eve, where she got to experience her first sleigh ride, since it had begun snowing earlier in the week, and a thick coat of snow now covered the fields and roads. It was quite fun, despite the cold, and they weren't gone long, since many of the servants lived in the mansion, but the warm parlor was a welcome respite when they returned home.

They spent the rest of the evening there, sitting on the sofa near the fire where a large Yule log burned, watching the small candles flickering on the tree Christopher had gone out and cut down himself.

Anastasia was feeling such peace, such contentment, despite the feeling that had come to her a few days ago that she must try and explain to her husband. It was different from her normal "gift," her insight, and yet it wasn't.

She was four months into her pregnancy. She wasn't actually showing it yet, nor feeling it, other than the brief bouts of sickness she'd had in the mornings for a while. Yet she felt a closeness to her unborn child that was akin to holding him in her arms already. And the feeling that had come to her had to do with him, yet not exactly with him.

It would be best if she could get it into words that made sense, and she tried to do that now, telling Christopher, "There will be one more gift for us to make, though it won't be for us to deliver."

He had one arm around her. His other hand had been idly caressing her arm. He turned to her now to say, not unexpected, "I don't understand."

"Neither do I, really," she was forced to admit. "It is just a feeling that has come to me about our son—"

"Son?" he interrupted in surprise. "We're having a son? You actually know this?"

"Well, yes, I had a dream about him. My dreams are usually quite accurate. But that has nothing to do with the gift we must make."

"*What* gift?"

He was starting to sound frustrated. She couldn't blame him. She often questioned herself, the feelings she got.

"We must put down on paper, how we met, how we came to love each other, how we defied our respective people to choose love rather than what was expected of us. We must write our story, Christoph."

"Write it?" He sounded uncomfortable. "I'm not very good with the written word, Anna."

She smiled at him. "You will do fine. I already know this."

He rolled his eyes at her. "I've a better suggestion. Why don't *you* do this writing that must be done—and by the by, *why* must it be done?"

"We must do this, not for our son, but for his children, and their children. What I have 'felt' is that our story will benefit one or more of these children. I don't know when it will be of benefit, or why, I just know that it will. Perhaps I will know more about it at some future time, have other feelings about it, but just now, this is all I know."

"Very well, I can accept that—I suppose. Yet I still don't see why we both must do this. It only takes one person to tell a story."

"True, except I can't write about *your* feelings, Christoph. I can't write about *your* thoughts. Only you can add these, to make our story complete. But if your style of writing bothers you this much, or if you've had thoughts you think I might question or tease you about, I will promise not to read what you write. This story is not for us, nor for our son, it's for those who will come after, that we will likely never meet. We can lock it away, so no one that we know will ever see it."

He sighed, then kissed her gently on the cheek to make his reluctant acquiescence a tad more graceful. "When do you want to begin?"

She hesitated for only a moment. "Tonight, on Christmas Eve. I have a feeling—"

"No more 'feelings' tonight," he cut in with a moan.

She chuckled. "I didn't say we have to write a *lot* tonight, just a beginning. Besides, I have another gift to deliver tonight that will take quite some time—in the delivering of it."

It was the sensual look she was giving him that had him raising his brow with interest. "You do? Quite some time, eh? You, ah, wouldn't consider delivering that present first, would you?"

"I could be persuaded to."

His lips came to her cheek again, and then moved down her neck, sending shivers over her shoulders. "I'm very good at persuading," he said in a husky whisper.

"I had a feeling you would say that."

Chapter 27

AMY CLOSED THE JOURNAL FOR THE LAST TIME WITH a satisfied sigh. It had been more than she could have hoped for. She was now fully at peace with her "gift." It *could* just be incredible coincidence, how lucky she was with her wagering, but she preferred to think she had inherited her luck from her great-grandmother.

Not everyone had stayed for the full reading, which had taken three days. Roslynn and Kelsey took turns seeing to the children, so they only heard every other chapter or so, though they would catch up, now that they could have the journal to themselves.

Amy's older sisters had decided to wait and read it at their leisure. Though they did pop in every so often to find out how the story was progressing, they mostly kept Georgina company, who was entertaining her visiting brothers elsewhere in the house. The rest of the Andersons didn't come to England frequently enough to suit her, so when they did, she liked to spend as much time as possible with them.

James and Tony, those rogues, had interrupted repeatedly with droll comments about Christopher Malory, whom they had immediately likened to Jason. Jason had sat through the entire reading in pensive silence, not even bothering to scold his younger brothers for their drollery.

Amy's mother, Charlotte, had been unable to sit for such long periods, and so like her other daughters, she decided to read the journal some other time. But her father, Edward, had stayed for all of the readings, and now came to kiss her brow before he took himself off to bed.

"I don't look like her, as you do," he told Amy. "But like you, I used to wonder why I was always such a good judge of people. That 'insight,' if you want to call it that, is what has aided my investments and made this family incredibly rich. But never being *wrong* makes one feel deuced unusual, indeed it does. Glad to know I'm not the only *strange* one. Indeed, much nicer to know there's a good reason why we've been so fortunate in our many endeavors."

Amy was amazed. Her father might have been the most jovial and gregarious in the family, but he was also the most pragmatic and realistic. She

would have thought he'd be the last one to believe in a Gypsy's gift.

Reggie, the only one close enough to have
heard Edward's quiet remarks to his daughter,
said with a grin, "Don't count yourself short,
Uncle Edward. It still takes a certain genius to
build the financial empire that you have. Being
able to accurately judge the people you invest
with helps, certainly, but you still did the picking
and choosing. Now, look at me. Like Amy, I took
after her in looks, yet I didn't inherit any of these
other gifts."

Edward chuckled at her. "I don't mind sharing
the credit, puss. And don't be too sure you didn't
inherit any gifts. Gypsy charm works its own
magic. And have you yet to be wrong in any of
your matchmaking endeavors?"

Reggie blinked. "Well, no, come to think of it, I
haven't." And then she beamed. "Oh, just wait till
I tell Nicholas that he never stood a chance, once
I decided to matchmake myself to him."

Reggie's husband had gone to bed several
hours ago, simply too tired to stay up to hear the
"ending." But the others in the room heard her
delighted remark and started commenting, some
with humor, some quite appalled . . .

Like Travis, who quickly said, "Just keep those
matchmaking tendencies of yours away from me,
cousin. I'm not ready to wear the shackles just yet."

"I am," Marshall said, smiling at her. "So do feel quite free to make me your next project."

"Never really thought of it before, but the dear puss really has had quite a hand in matchmaking a lot of us, myself included," Anthony put in. "She did fill my Roslynn's pretty head with nothing but good things about me, expounding on all my good qualities."

"That must have been bloody hard to do," James remarked dryly. "Considering how few good qualities you possess, old man."

"Look who's talking." Anthony snorted. "Can't imagine what George ever saw in you. But then she *has* come to her senses, hasn't she?"

That was hitting rather low, considering it was quite a raw spot for James at the moment, that Georgina still wouldn't talk to him about what was really bothering her, and their bedroom door was still being locked tight against him—especially since Anthony was having no such extended difficulties with his own wife.

So it wasn't the least bit surprising that James replied, albeit with his usual lack of expression, "That black eye of yours is starting to fade, brother. Remind me to rectify that in the morning."

"Not bloody likely. I'll be catching up on quite a bit of lost sleep tomorrow, if it's all the same to you," Anthony retorted.

James merely smiled. "It's not. And do be assured that I can wait until you've caught up. Wouldn't want you in less than top form."

Chagrined, Anthony mumbled, "You're all heart, you bloody ass."

"I'd prefer you two did *not* go at it again," Jason said as he stood up to take himself off to bed. "Sets a bad example for the children."

"Quite right," Anthony agreed with a grin, then to James, "At least *some* of the elders around here are possessed of wisdom."

Considering James was Anthony's elder by a year, there was little doubt that Anthony was getting in yet another subtle dig against him. James might have let it pass if his mood hadn't gone sour with the reminder that his wife was still annoyed with him.

"Which is fortunate," James said, giving his brother a sage nod. "Since some of the *infants* around here are possessed of none a'tall."

Derek, standing next to his father and seeing one of his stern frowns forming, whispered aside to him, "You know once they get started like that, there's no stopping them. Might as well ignore them. I get the feeling it's going to continue like this until Aunt George is smiling again."

Jason sighed and replied in an equally soft whisper, "I suppose I should have a talk with her. From what I've heard, her anger seems quite overdone."

"It does, don't it? Seems to indicate there might

be something else that's put the bee in her bonnet, that she ain't fessing up to."

"You've hit the nail squarely. But James has already come to that conclusion himself—not that it's helped any."

"Obviously, since he still ain't himself. Course, he never is, when he and George are having a tiff."

"Are any of us?"

Derek chuckled, likely remembering some of his own tiffs with Kelsey. "Good point. Deuced hard to analyze the situation when you're knee-deep in the doldrums."

Jason was ready to conclude that that might have been his own problem where Molly was concerned. The logic she had always used on him, while valid, always made him rage inwardly that it *was* valid. The situation, as it had stood, was frustrating beyond endurance, and who could think clearly mired in such emotional muck? Yet he now had hope, thanks to his grandmother's amazing gift.

Jeremy drew his attention back to the current barb slinging by remarking cheerfully, "Well, this 'baby' is taking himself to bed. At least *I* didn't inherit any sorcery-type silliness with these blue eyes and black hair that I got from the *grand-mère*."

Derek rolled his eyes at that and said in mild disgust, "No, you just cast the most potent spell of all, cousin, in having every woman who looks at you fall hopelessly in love with you."

Jeremy beamed. "I do? Well, hell's bells, I'll settle for that."

Anthony chuckled, putting an arm around Jeremy's shoulders to confide, "They're just jealous, puppy, that all the charm in this family fell on us black-haired Gypsies."

"What rubbish." James snorted. "You've about as much charm as the backside of my—"

Jason cleared his throat very loudly. "I think we've all been up far too long today," he said, and then sternly, "Go to bed, the lot of you."

"Would if I *had* a bloody bed to go to," James mumbled on his way out the door.

Anthony frowned and did some mumbling of his own. "Can't believe I'm feeling sorry for him. Gads, I must be exhausted. G'night, all."

Jason looked at Edward and shook his head with a "what can you do?" sigh, then turned to Amy to ask, "Do you need help, m'dear?" He indicated Warren, who was fast asleep with his head on her shoulder.

She smiled lovingly at her husband. "No, he wakes very easily."

She shrugged her shoulder to demonstrate, and Warren sat right up, blinked once, then said, "All done for the night, sweetheart?"

"All done for good," she replied, and handed

the journal to Jason for safekeeping. "I'll tell you in the morning what you missed."

He yawned, stood up, and pulled her to his side. "I'll let you know, by the time we get upstairs, whether I can wait until morning or not to hear how they handled those snooping townsfolk."

She moaned a bit, but then chuckled as she put an arm around his waist. "Same way you probably would have. They told them to mind their own bloody business."

"Excellent, the American way," he replied as he walked them out the door.

They left more'n one English groan behind them.

Chapter 28

JAMES PAUSED BY HIS WIFE'S BEDROOM AS HE DID each night, to see if the door would open. Tonight he was annoyed enough not to bother even trying. She'd been utterly unreasonable in her anger, utterly uncommunicative as well, refusing to discuss it. He really was at his wits' end on how to set things right with her, particularly when he hadn't done anything wrong to be setting right.

He needed a miracle to get out of this mess. That thought reminded him of the conversation he'd had with Jason the night the younguns had snuck into the parlor to open The Present. Before Anthony had found him in Jason's study and they'd started their commiserative drinking, James had found Jason there doing some drinking himself.

"I hope you've got more of that on hand, because I could use a full bottle myself," he told his brother when he entered the room.

Jason nodded. "Fetch a glass on the sideboard and start with this one."

James did, then took the seat across from Jason's desk, waiting for him to pour from the near-empty decanter next to him. When he did, he said pointedly, "I know why *I'm* drinking, but why are you?"

Jason didn't answer that, said instead, "James, you confound me. You, out of all of us, have a certain unique finesse in handling women—at least, you always did in the past. Where's it gone to?"

James leaned back in his chair and took a long swill of his brandy before answering, "Easy to handle women when you aren't emotionally involved with them, quite another thing when you love one to distraction. I've used every means I can think of to get George to at least discuss what's bothering her, but George is, well, George, and she won't budge until she's bloody well ready to. It's got nothing to do with Tony or Jack. I've at least narrowed that down. She merely used them as a convenient excuse to explode—at me. I'm the problem, but since I haven't done a single thing out of the ordinary that might have set her temper off, I'm bloody well in the complete dark."

"It sounds like she just hasn't figured out yet how to approach the matter with you, whatever it is. That could be part of the problem, her own frustration in being unable to express it," Jason suggested.

"George? Having trouble expressing herself?" James all but rolled his eyes.

"Not ordinarily," Jason agreed. "But this doesn't sound like an ordinary problem, or it *would* be out in the open already, wouldn't it?"

"Possibly," James allowed thoughtfully, then, "Bloody hell. I'm done with trying to figure out what's wrong. Everything I make a guess at just points out more clearly that this makes no sense a'tall."

Jason, staring at the glass in his hand, snorted. "Women make sense when they're upset? When did they ever?"

James chuckled at that, since it reminded him of the realization he'd come to a few years ago, yet he'd never broached the subject with his brother. It also gave him his answer to why his brother might be in need of a fortifying brandy or two. In a word, women problems.

So he asked baldly, "How long have you been in love with Molly?"

Jason glanced up, but his expression didn't show the surprise that question should have brought. "Since before Derek was born."

James couldn't quite conceal his own surprise at that answer and the obvious conclusion it brought. "Good God . . . well, damn it all, Jason, why the deuce have you never told any of us?"

"You think I didn't want to? I'd shout it from the rooftops if it were my choice, but it's not. Molly had valid reasons for wanting the truth about us kept secret, even from Derek—at least she managed to convince me those reasons were valid. I'm not so sure anymore, but that's a moot point after all these years of secrecy."

"Why don't you just marry the woman and have done with it?" James said reasonably.

Jason laughed without humor. "I'm *trying* to. I have been trying to since the divorce from Frances, but Molly won't budge in her refusal. She's got this gigantic scandal imagined in her mind and she refuses to inflict it on the family."

James raised a golden brow. "On the family? When has this family *not* had a scandal brewing of one sort or another?"

Jason raised a brow himself. "True, to which you, for one, made sure of."

James chuckled at his brother's censorious tone. "Let's not get into that. I'm reformed, don't you know."

Jason shook his head bemusedly. "I still can't credit how *that* came about."

"Love, of course. It does produce amazing miracles. Speaking of which, it's looking like I'll need one of those to get out of this confounding situation with George. If I find one, Jason, I'll be sure to pass it along, since you seem to be in need of a miracle as well."

Remembering that conversation with his brother, James had a feeling that Jason might have found his miracle, thanks to their grandmother, yet one hadn't dropped into his own lap yet. But enough was enough and tomorrow he'd tell his wife so. Tonight he was simply too tired. Tonight he'd probably say something he'd end up regretting, and then he *would* have something to apologize for.

He walked away, but no more than three steps were taken before he spun about and pounded on her door. To hell with waiting. He was tired, yes, but he was even more tired of sleeping alone.

From inside the room he heard, "It's open."

James frowned down at the doorknob, tried it. Damned if it wasn't open. Bloody hell. It would have to be open the one time he made a racket pounding on it rather than just checking it first.

He entered the room, closed the door, then leaned back against it, crossing his thick arms over his chest. Georgina was sitting on the bed, wearing the white silk negligee and robe that he'd given her last Christmas. She was brushing her long brown hair. He always enjoyed watching her do that—another thing he'd been denied lately.

He raised a brow at her and asked dryly, "Forget to lock the door?"

"No," she said simply.

The golden brow lifted just a bit higher. "Don't tell me you've gotten all maudlin over the elders' love story and decided to forgive me because of it?"

Her sigh was loud enough to hear across the room. "Maudlin, no. Finally realizing that putting this off isn't going to make it go away, yes, their story did help me to see that the unavoidable can't be avoided. So you may as well know, there's nothing to forgive you for, James."

"Well, I always knew that, but what the devil d'*you* mean by nothing?"

She lowered her gaze and mumbled something that he couldn't make out. This had him crossing the room to stand in front of her. He lifted her chin. Her large brown eyes were inscrutable. She'd learned how to do that from him.

"Let's try this again, shall we?" he said. "Now, what d'you mean, there's nothing to forgive me for?"

"I was never angry with you. The way I've been behaving had nothing to do with you—well, it did, but not for the reason I let you think. I was already upset about something else when Jack said what she did. I used that as an excuse, because I wasn't ready to fess up to the other. I didn't want to upset you."

"I hope you know, George, that you haven't made one bloody bit of sense. Didn't want to upset me? Do I look like I haven't been upset?"

His frown answered that question quite satisfactorily. She actually smiled.

"Let me rephrase that," she suggested. "I didn't want to upset you with what was really bothering me, which was not wanting to upset you at all."

He made a sound of frustration at that point. "I know it's American reasoning that makes what you say sound like gibberish to the English mind, but do try—"

"Rubbish," she cut in with a snort. "I'm just still hedging, is all."

"Good of you to own up to that, m'dear. Now own up to why."

"I was getting to that," she continued to hedge.

"Notice I'm patiently waiting."

"You're never patient."

"I'm *always* patient, and you're *still* hedging," he all but growled. "George, I'm warning you, I'm bloody well at the end of my patience."

"See?"

He gave her a scowl worthy of decimating an ordinary opponent. She was unaffected, well aware she had nothing to worry about from his scowls. But she was pushing it. Finally she sighed again.

"I know you love the twins," she said. "You can't help but love them, they're such darlings.

But I also know you were horrified at the thought of having them, when Amy and Warren produced twins, and him being my brother, you realized we might have some, too."

"Not horrified," he corrected. "Just bloody well surprised that they run in your family, when your family didn't have any to show for it."

"Horrified," she reiterated stubbornly.

He sighed this time, though only for effect. "If you insist. And your point?"

"I didn't want to horrify you again."

"Again?" And then he blinked. "Good God, George, are we having another baby?"

At which point she burst into tears. James, on the other hand, burst into laughter. He simply couldn't help it. But that just had her crying louder.

So he lifted her up, sat down on the bed and placed her on his lap, wrapped his arms around her carefully, and said, "You know, George, we're really going to have to work on your way of announcing these things. Recall how you told me about Jack's impending arrival?"

She did indeed. They'd been in the middle of a heated exchange on his ship, where she'd just got done calling James an English *lord*, a Caribbean *pirate!*

He'd replied, "I hate to point this out, you little witch, but those aren't epithets."

She'd shouted back, "They are as far as I'm concerned. My God, and to think I'm going to have your baby."

To which he had countered heatedly, "The devil you are! I'm not touching you again!"

She had stomped away with the parting shot, "You won't have to, you stupid man!" which had finally got the point across to him that she was already pregnant.

"And the second time, d'you recall that you actually denied you were pregnant? Told me you were just putting on a little weight, as if I couldn't bloody well tell the difference." He snorted.

She stiffened at that point. "You blame me for not mentioning it, after what you said when Amy had her twins? 'We are not having any, d'you hear!' Those were your exact words, you odious man. Well, we did have some, didn't we, and we may have some more, and some more, and—"

"How you do go on," he cut in with a chuckle. "My dearest girl, you shouldn't hold a man accountable for one unguarded moment of surprise."

"Shock," she corrected.

"Surprise," he repeated adamantly. "That's all it was, you know. And I did adjust to it remarkably well, if I do say so myself. In fact, you can give me twins every year if you're up to it, and I'll adore them all equally. You know why, don't you?"

She frowned. "Why?"

"Because I love you, and at the risk of sounding exceedingly conceited," he added with a smug grin, "I know you love me, too. Stands to reason, then, don't it, that anything that we produce from that love will be cherished, whether it comes in a single package or in pairs. I'll love them all, silly girl. Don't ever doubt that again."

She put her head against his chest with a sigh. "I have been rather silly, haven't I?"

"Considering where I've been sleeping lately," he replied dryly, "I'll refrain from answering that, if it's all the same to you."

She kissed his neck in apology. "I'm really sorry about that."

"As you should be."

It was his condescending tone that prompted her to reply, "Did I ever mention that four generations back, there was a rare instance of triplets in my family?"

"I know you're expecting to hear yet another 'Good God, George, we're not having any of *those* either,' but I'm going to have to disappoint you. Now, if I *didn't* think you were pulling my leg . . ."

She giggled, which more or less admitted she was doing just that. But then she asked curiously, since she had come upstairs early, "Did Amy finish the journal tonight?"

"Yes. Amazing gift my grandmother had. I prefer to think it was just incredible good guessing on her part, but who's to say for sure?"

"My, I did miss a lot, didn't I?"

James nodded. "You'll want to read it for yourself, if you can manage to get it away from Jason. I've a feeling he has someone else he'd like to have read it first, though."

"Molly?"

James chuckled. "So you noticed, too?"

"The softening of his edges whenever she's around? Who could miss that?"

"Just *most* of us," he replied dryly.

Chapter 29

"DID IT GET FINISHED TONIGHT?" MOLLY ASKED
when Jason joined her in her bed that night.

"Sorry, did I wake you?"

She yawned and snuggled up close to him. "No.
I've just missed you these last nights, so I tried to
stay awake tonight. Didn't think I was going to
manage it, though. I was just nodding off."

He smiled and pulled her close. He'd had no
chance to talk to her since that journal had been
unwrapped. She'd been asleep these last few
nights by the time he came to her, and gone in the
mornings, she rose so early. Nor, with the house
so full, was there much chance to find her alone
during the day to have a few private words.

And the subject of the journal wouldn't be discussed by the rest of the family, at least not in
front of the servants, which they all considered
Molly to be—with the exception of Derek and his
wife, and now James, who knew the truth about

her, that she was Derek's mother, that she'd been Jason's only love for more'n thirty years.

So Molly wouldn't know yet what was in the journal. However, she couldn't help but know that the family had all been camped in the parlor for three days, hearing it read. She had appeared in the doorway several times to shake her head over the fact that they were all still there.

"I want you to take the day off tomorrow and read it for yourself," he told her.

"Take the day off? Don't be silly."

"The house will get along fine without you for a day, m'dear."

"It won't."

"Molly," he said warningly.

She mumbled, "Oh, all right. It *could* wait until after the holidays, when the house isn't so full, but I'll admit to a certain curiosity about that journal, after having it in my possession for most of my life, yet not knowing what it was."

He sat up abruptly. "Most of your life? When did you find it? And where?"

"Well, I did—and I didn't. What I mean is, it was given to me when I was but a child of four or five—I can't remember which. I was told what to do with it, and when to deliver it, but not what it was. And I must confess that it was so long ago, Jason, that I put it away with some old things of mine and completely forgot about it ever since.

It's been up in your attic all these years, with my old childhood things that I have stored there."

"But you finally remembered it?"

"Well, no, and it was the strangest thing, how I found it again," she admitted.

"What do you mean?"

She frowned to herself, remembering. "It was when I first started fetching the Christmas decorations down from the attic. The sun had been out most of the day, which had caused the attic to be quite stuffy and warm, so I opened one of the windows up there, yet it didn't do much good other than let in a little cold air, since no breeze was stirring, and wouldn't have come into the room anyway, with only the one window open— or so I thought. Yet just when I was heading toward the door with my last load for the day, this great gust of wind tore through the room, knocking things all over the place."

"You'd left the door open, to account for such a strong cross breeze?"

"It was no breeze, Jason, it was a very strong wind, which didn't make much sense to begin with, when it hadn't been a bit windy that day. But no, the door was closed, which is why I found that wind so strange, least I did afterwards, when I had time to think about it. At the time, though, I was too busy picking the things up that it knocked over. It was when I came to this large folding Oriental room divider, that had fallen over on a stack of paintings, jarring several out of their frames, that I noticed my old things. I *still* didn't recall the journal, though, and wouldn't have bothered to look inside that old trunk of mine, except, well . . .".

Her frown got deeper. He almost shook her, to get her to finish.

"Well?" he demanded.

"Well, if the wind didn't gust once more in that corner, rattling the lid on the trunk something fierce. I swear, it seemed almost as if the wind was trying to open it. It really was the strangest damned thing. Gave me the chills, I don't mind telling you. And *that's* when I remembered that old leather-wrapped thing I'd put in that trunk long before I ever came to Haverston to work— and that I was supposed to give it to your family as a gift. Stranger yet, soon as I did open the trunk, the wind stopped completely."

He laughed suddenly. "I can just hear what Amy would say about that if she'd been there. She'd insist it was my grandmother's ghost, or perhaps even *her* grandmother's ghost, making sure the journal got delivered. Good God, don't ever tell her about that wind, Molly. She really will think this old place is haunted."

"Nonsense. It was just a wind, likely stirred up by the heat in the room."

"Yes, obviously, yet my niece is a bit fanciful, so let's keep that part of your discovery to ourselves, shall we?" he suggested with a smile.

"If you insist."

"Now tell me who gave it to you all those years ago. You aren't old enough to have known my grandmother."

"No, but my grandmum was. And it all came back to me when I found it again, what she'd told me when she gave the present into my keeping. She'd been Anna Malory's personal maid, you know."

He grinned at her. "Now, how would I have known that, when you never bothered to mention it before?"

She blushed. "Well, I'd forgotten about that, too. I don't remember much about my grand-mum, since I was so young when I knew her, and she died soon after she gave me that journal. And my mother never worked here at Haverston, so she'd had no dealings with the Malorys herself, nor ever had reason to mention them, which made it all the easier for me to forget about it. And it was more than ten years later before I came to work here myself, but even that didn't stir my memory."

"So Anna Malory gave it to your grandmother to deliver?"

"No, she gave it to her to give to me. Let me tell

you what my grandmum told me, and maybe you'll understand. I certainly didn't at the time, and still don't, but here it is, best as I can remember. My grandmum was already Lady Malory's maid, but the lady summoned her one day, told her to sit and have tea with her, that they were going to be the best of friends. Grandma said the lady often said strange things, and one of them she said that day. She said, 'We're going to be related, you know. It won't be for a very long time, and we won't see it happen, but it will happen, and you'll help it to happen when you give this to your granddaughter.' "

"The journal?"

Molly nodded. "Lady Malory had more to say about it, specific instructions actually. My grandmum admitted she'd thought the lady was daft at the time. After all, she didn't have a granddaughter yet. But the instructions she was given was to have her granddaughter—me; I'm the only one she ever got, after all—deliver the present to the Malory family for Christmas in the first quarter of the new century. Not to any specific member of the family, just to the family. And being a gift, she wanted it to look like a gift. And that's all she had to say about it. No, wait, there was one other thing. About the time of delivery. She said, 'I have the feeling that's when it will be of the most benefit.' "

Jason smiled slowly and gave his grandmother a silent thank-you. To Molly he said, "Amazing."

"You understand it, then?"

"Yes, and so will you, I think, as soon as you read it. But why didn't you leave a note with it, so we would have at least known who it was for, and who it was from? Not knowing turned it into quite a mystery, which is why the younguns didn't wait for Christmas to open it."

"Because it was for all of you, of course." And then she chuckled. "Besides, if it turned out to be nothing important, I wasn't going to own up to putting it there."

"Oh, it was important, sweetheart, and more than that, a valuable heirloom for this family. And I'm most definitely looking forward to hearing what you have to say after you read it."

She gave him a suspicious look. "Why do I get the feeling I'm not going to like whatever's in that journal?"

"Possibly because you're so pigheaded stubborn about certain things."

"Now you're really starting to worry me, Jason Malory," she said in a grumbling tone.

He grinned. "No need to fret, love. Only good things will come of it, I promise."

"Yes, but good for *whom*?"

Chapter 30

CHRISTMAS MORNING DAWNED BRIGHT IF CHILLY at Haverston, though the parlor where most of the family was gathered was quite comfy, with a nice fire crackling. Jeremy had lit the small candles on the decorated tree. Though the extra light wasn't needed, the flickering flames fascinated the children, and the sweet scent from the candles was a nice touch.

The last to arrive were James, Georgina, and their three younguns. Jack ran immediately to her oldest brother, Jeremy, whom she adored, and got her usual tickle and hug from him. Then, typically, she headed straight for Judy, ignoring everyone else, though she would make the rounds to greet the rest of her large family after the two young girls finished their morning whisperings.

Anthony, never one to let a prime moment pass, said to his tardy brother, "Now that you've managed to find that bed of yours again, having trouble getting out of it, eh?"

Anthony had got most of his teasing done yesterday, though. When he'd seen James in such obvious good spirits, he'd been unable to resist taunting, "What? No longer in a mood to pass out black eyes?"

"Put a lid on it, puppy," his brother had replied with a snort.

That never worked, at least not with Anthony anyway. "George has forgiven you, I take it?"

"George is having another baby, or babies, as the case may be," James said drolly.

"Now, that's what I call a nice Christmas present, news like that. Congratulations, old boy."

Just now, though, it wasn't James who replied to Anthony's renewed teasing, it was his own wife who, in her charming Scots burr, said, "Put a lid on it, mon, or you'll be wondering where your own bed has gone."

To which James burst out laughing, and Georgina said, "It wasn't *that* funny. Notice your brother isn't one little bit amused."

"Course I did, love, and *that's* what's funny," James replied.

Anthony did some mumbling and shot James a disgusted look before he leaned close to whisper something to his wife that had her smiling. Obviously, notorious charmer that he was, he'd just patched things up nicely.

The present-opening began soon after, with the children all gathered on the rug before the tree. Judy noticed the missing Present on its pedestal, and went to Amy for questioning. She and Jack hadn't come near the parlor during those days the journal was being read, having much more adventurous things to do at their age.

"It was just a book?" Judy asked after Amy answered her first question, obviously disappointed that what had caused her and Jack such interest was actually not at all interesting in her mind.

"Not just a book, love. It tells the story about your great-grandparents, how they met, how it took them a while to realize that they were meant for each other. You'll want to read it someday."

Judy did not look impressed, and in fact was already distracted, watching Jack open her next present. But several of the adults were close enough to have heard her questions, and reminded of the grandparents they all shared, had a few more comments to make.

Travis said, "I wonder if he ever liked this place, considering how much he hated it at first."

"Course he did, since *she* was in it," his brother replied. "Makes a world of difference if you've someone to share things with."

Anthony commented, "Find it remarkable that he

agreed to brighten the place up himself. Wouldn't catch me wielding a bloody hammer."

"No?" his wife said pointedly.

"Well . . . perhaps." Anthony grinned. "Wonderful thing, the proper incentive, specially when it yields wonderful results."

Roslynn rolled her eyes, but it was Derek who said with a chuckle, "You'll have to admit, they did a good job on fixing the place up. For all its huge size, Haverston still has a homey feel to it."

"Only because it's been *your* home," his wife replied pointedly. "To those not raised here, it has more the feel of a royal palace."

"My thoughts exactly," Georgina agreed.

"American thoughts don't count, George," James told his wife dryly. "After all, we know quite well you won't find such grandeur in those primitive States of yours, barbaric as they still are."

Anthony chuckled at that, nodding across the room to where Warren was sitting on the floor before the Christmas tree with one of his twins on each knee, quite involved with helping them to open their presents. "Wasted that one, old man. The Yank didn't hear you."

"But this Yank did," Georgina replied, giving James a jab in the ribs to show how much she appreciated his disparaging remarks about her country.

He grunted, but it was to Anthony that he replied, "Do be a good chap and remind me to repeat it later, when he is within hearing."

"You may depend upon it," Anthony replied.

They were, after all, united when it came to their nephews-by-marriage, against them, that is, despite their merciless barbs reserved for each other when the "enemy" was not around.

Reggie came by, passing out a few presents, one of which she dropped in James's lap. It was from Warren.

"See if that doesn't change your mind about keeping today, of all days, friendly," she said.

He raised a brow at her, but opening the package, he chuckled. "Hardly, puss," he said, examining a small bronze caricature of an obvious English monarch looking decidedly silly. "Couldn't ask for a nicer gift, though."

Since it was a gift meant to provoke, James *would* be delighted with it. Warren *was* his preferred and most challenging barb-slinging choice, after all, with Reggie's husband coming in a close second.

"Famous," Reggie said, rolling her eyes. "Though I should be relieved. At least my Nicholas will be spared, now that you have your target for the day."

"Don't count on it, m'dear." James grinned wickedly. "Wouldn't want him to feel neglected just because it's Christmas."

Molly appeared in the doorway just then. Jason hadn't spoken to her since she had started reading the journal. She had finished it late last night, long after he'd gone to bed. He came to her now with a hopeful look, and she knew exactly why he wore it.

But reaching her, he glanced up at the doorframe they stood under. She followed his gaze to see the mistletoe hung there as it was every year. Before it even occurred to her that he might do something outlandish like kiss her with his *entire* family in the room and possibly watching, he kissed her, and quite thoroughly, too.

A few breathless moments later, he said, "Do I need to ask my question—again?"

She smiled, knowing exactly which question he meant. "No, you don't," she whispered, so they wouldn't be overheard. "And my answer is yes, though with one condition."

"Which is?"

"I'll marry you, Jason, if you'll agree that we won't tell anyone about it, aside from your family, of course."

"Molly—" he began with a sigh.

"No, hear me out. I know that's not what you were hoping I'd say, after reading about your grandparents. But things were different for them. She was a stranger to the area. The people here and in Havers didn't know her most of their lives.

It was easy for them to ignore inquiries, or put them off, so that no one ever did really know the truth. But you can't deny that they didn't own up to the truth, that only a select few ever knew— and besides, her father *was* a Russian noble, even if her mother wasn't."

He rolled his eyes. "And your point?"

"You know I can't say the same, Jason. And I still won't bring more scandal on your family, when it's already borne so many scandals in the past. If you can't agree to keep a marriage between us secret, then we'll just have to go on as we have been."

"Then I suppose I'll have to agree to those terms, of course."

She gave him a suspicious look, considering she had been anticipating much more of an argument from him. "You wouldn't agree now, only to change your mind after we're married, would you?"

He feigned a hurt look before asking her, "You don't trust me?"

She scowled. "I *know* you, Jason Malory. You'll do or say just about anything to get your way."

He grinned. "Then you should know that I'd never do anything to get you seriously annoyed with me."

"No, not unless you thought you could talk me around it. Need I remind you that I'd consider this a serious breach of promise?"

"Need I remind you just how happy you've made me, agreeing to be my wife—finally?"

"You're changing the subject, Jason."

"You noticed?"

She sighed. "As long as we understand each other."

"Oh, we do, sweetheart." His smile was so very tender. "We always have."

Behind them, they heard a cough, which reminded them both that they weren't alone. They turned as one to face the room, and found every member of his family staring at them. Molly started blushing. Jason was grinning from ear to ear, and he didn't waste time explaining why.

"Allow me to announce," he said, taking Molly's hand in his, "Molly has given me the greatest Christmas gift I could have asked for in agreeing to be my wife." Which, of course, started everyone talking at once.

"About bloody time," James commented first.

"You can say that again," Derek said, and with a whoop of delight, came forward to hug his parents.

"It's too bad this wasn't settled sooner," Reggie remarked, smiling. "We could have had a Christmas wedding today."

"Who says we can't?" James replied. "I happen to know the elder has had a special license ready and waiting for quite a few years now. And if I know my brother, he isn't going to give Molly a chance to change her mind."

"Goodness! So this didn't just develop?"

Nicholas chuckled at his wife. "Take a good look at Derek and Molly, standing there together, sweetheart. That ought to give you your answer."

Reggie did, then said, "Oh, my. I think Uncle James said it aptly."

And Amy giggled. "He did, didn't he? Of course, I've known for the longest time, having caught them kissing once. I just didn't know it would one day lead to this."

"And to think I had no hand in matchmaking them," Reggie sighed.

James chuckled at his niece. "How could you, when they were in love before you were even born?"

"I realize *that*, but you said it yourself, Uncle James. They've been a bit tardy in getting around to marrying, and I consider it my department to push these sorts of things along."

Anthony laughed at that. "Don't think you could've helped this time, puss. Actually, come to think of it, I'd say it took The Present to do it."

And James said dryly, "You only just figure that out, dear boy?"

Anthony's brow rose, but before he came back with a rejoinder, Charlotte was heard from. "A

Christmas wedding, how utterly wonderful. I think I'm going to cry."

"You always cry at weddings, m'dear," Edward said, patting her hand.

That being the first remark from Edward, and hardly what Jason was expecting from his closest brother, particularly since he'd been the one most vocal against his divorce, Jason asked, "No comment about an impending scandal, Edward?"

Edward looked a bit embarrassed as he admitted, "We've muddled through all the other scandals this family has created. I imagine we'll muddle through this one just fine." And then he grinned. "Besides, now that you're finally marrying for the *right* reasons, I couldn't be happier for you."

"There doesn't have to be a scandal," Reggie said. "Or have you all forgotten The Present so soon? I don't see why we can't take a leaf from those old friends of Sir William Thompson's. Gossip is an amazing thing, after all. If so many conflicting things are heard about the latest major on-dit, then no one can really point to the truth and hold it up as fact. No one knows for sure what is the truth, thus what will be believed is what one chooses to believe."

But Molly was shaking her head. "My case isn't the same as your great-grandmother's. People around here knew my father."

"Yes, but did they know his father, or his father before him? For all you know, Molly, you could have a lord or two up your ancestral tree. It's a rare family that doesn't have a few ancestors conceived on the wrong side of the blanket in one century or another."

Derek chuckled at that point and told his mother, "You know once Reggie latches on to an idea, she rarely lets go of it. Might as well let her have her fun with the gossips. After her success in Kelsey's case, she will anyway."

Molly sighed, having had her one stipulation to the wedding, that no one else should know about it, taken out of her hands. Jason, understanding, pulled her closer to his side to say for her ears only, "Remember what my grandfather Christopher had to say on the subject?"

She glanced up at him in surprise, but then she smiled. "Yes, point taken."

"Good. And I hope you've noticed, not one objection from my family."

That reminder got him a poke in the ribs. "Rubbing it in is not allowed. And besides, they aren't objecting because they all love you and want you to be happy."

"No, it's because you've always been part of this family, Molly. We're just going to make it official now—and about bloody time."

Home for the Holidays

They don't need ribbons nor pretty wrappings,
they need only be delivered,
a smile, a hug,
to share with someone you love.

Chapter 1

VINCENT EVERETT SAT IN HIS COACH ACROSS THE
street from the fashionable town house in London. It was one of the colder nights of the winter
season, but he had slid the window open so he
could see clearly across the street. He wouldn't be
surprised if snow was imminent.

He wasn't sure why he was there, subjecting
himself to inclement weather. He didn't doubt
that his secretary, Horace Dudley, would serve
the notice that gave the occupants two days to vacate the house. It wasn't that this was another
stepping-stone in his decision to ruin the Ascot
family, who lived there. It was more likely that he
was simply bored and had had no other plans for
the evening.

Even the decision to ruin this particular family
wasn't an emotional one. Vincent hadn't experienced any real emotion since his childhood, nor
did he ever again want to know such pain. It was

much, much easier to exist with a stone for a heart, made simple matters such as evicting a family during the Christmas season just a matter of course.

No, the methodical destruction of the Ascots wasn't emotional, but it was personal. Vincent's younger brother, Albert, had made it personal, when he had put the full blame for his failed business and finances on George Ascot.

Albert had lost most of his inheritance, solely on his own. However, he had learned from his mistakes. He had taken what little was left of it and tried to start a business that would support him, so he wouldn't be a continuous drain on Vincent. And to give himself some pride. He had bought several merchant ships, opened a small office in Portsmouth. But apparently Ascot, an established shipping merchant himself, had been afraid of the competition and had set out to undermine Albert's efforts at every turn, to break him before he even began.

These were the details in Albert's letter, which was all he'd left behind before he disappeared, that and an astounding number of debts that continued to land on Vincent's door. Vincent feared that Albert had taken himself off to quietly kill himself somewhere where he wouldn't be found, as he had threatened so many times. What else was he to think, when Albert's letter had ended with "This is the only way I can think of, to no longer be an embarrassment or burden to you"?

Albert's demise had left Vincent without family, though to be honest, he'd never really felt a part of his own family, so his lack of one now hardly made a difference to him. His parents had died just after Vincent reached his majority, within a year of each other, leaving only the two brothers. With no other relatives, even distant ones, the brothers should have been close. Not so. Albert might have felt a closeness, or more to the point, a dependency, but then Albert expected the world and everything in it to revolve around him, a silly notion that their parents had fostered by making him their joy, their amusement, their favorite. Vincent had merely been the reserved, boring heir they never took notice of.

It was amazing that Vincent had never hated his brother, but then you had to experience emotion to hate. By the same token, there had been no love, either, for his weakling of a brother, merely a tolerance because he was "family." That he had picked up the gauntlet, as it were, on Albert's behalf was more a long-standing habit, as well as a matter of pride. It was a blight on his own name, that George Ascot had successfully crushed an Everett without consequences. He would soon know differently. It was the last thing that Vincent could do for Albert, to at least pay back Ascot in kind.

The snow he had been expecting arrived, just as

the door opened across the street to Dudley's knock. Vincent's view was hampered by the white flakes, but he could still make out a flowing skirt, so a female had answered the knock. Ascot himself wouldn't be there. Reports were that he had set sail on one of his ships in the first week of September, and more than three months later, had yet to return to England. His absence was making this retaliation simple. When Ascot did return, he would find his credit canceled with many of his merchant suppliers, and his home lost to him due to lack of payment on demand.

Vincent hadn't decided yet whether to continue his campaign after tonight or to wait for Ascot's return. Tonight's eviction would be a decisive blow, the culmination of several weeks' work, but hardly satisfactory when Ascot wouldn't be there to know of it yet.

Actually, this whole matter of revenge was rather distasteful. It wasn't something he wanted to do, had ever done before, or likely ever would again, but was something he felt he *had* to do this one time. So he would as soon get it over and done with. But Ascot wasn't obliging in that, being out of the country for longer than expected.

He should have returned by now. Vincent had counted on his being back by now. Waiting was not something he did well. And waiting in his coach, in the cold, when he didn't need to be there and still wasn't even sure why he was there, was starting to annoy him, especially since Dudley was taking his sweet time delivering the notice. How bloody long did it take to hand over a piece of paper?

Across the street, the door finally closed. But Vincent's secretary still stood there facing it, unmoving. Had he accomplished his task, or had the door been closed on him before he could? What the devil was he doing, standing there in the snow doing nothing?

Vincent was about to leave the coach himself to find out what was going on, when Dudley finally turned about and headed back toward him. Vincent opened the coach door, more in his impatience than to get Dudley out of the biting cold sooner. But Dudley didn't rush inside when he got there, he didn't enter the coach at all, was once again just standing there in the snow, as if he'd gone totally daft.

However, before Vincent could ask about this strange behavior, Dudley announced, "I have never in my life done anything so despicable, my lord, nor will I ever do so again. I quit."

Vincent raised a questioning brow at him. "Quit as in—?"

"You will have my formal resignation on your desk in the morning."

Vincent savored a moment of amazement. It

wasn't often that he could be so thoroughly surprised. But then his impatience returned.

"Get in the bloody coach, Mr. Dudley. You can explain yourself when we are out of this damnable weather."

"No, sir," Dudley replied stiffly. "I will find my own way home, thank you very much."

"Don't be absurd. You won't find a hack this time of night."

"I will manage."

With that, the secretary closed the coach door and started marching down the street. Ordinarily Vincent would have shrugged and dismissed the man from his mind, but he was in an impatient frame of mind, which was as close as he came to being emotional.

He found himself leaving the coach himself and marching after Dudley to demand, "What the devil happened at that house to give you leave of your senses?"

Horace Dudley swung around, his face suffused with emotional color rather than paled from the cold. "If I must have further discourse with you, my lord, I fear I will disgrace myself beyond regret. Please, simply accept my resignation and leave it go at—"

"The devil I will. You've been with me for eight years. You do not just resign over a small matter—"

"Small!?" the little man burst out. "If you could have seen the stricken look on that poor girl's face, it would have broken your heart as it did mine. And such a pretty girl. Her face is going to haunt me the rest of my days."

Having said so and apparently believing it, Dudley scurried off down the street once more, refusing to speak more of it. Vincent let him go this time and turned a scowl on the house in question.

The property belonged to him now. He'd called in a considerable number of favors to coerce the previous owner to ignore his verbal commitment with George Ascot and sell him the deed instead. Ascot had had a gentlemen's agreement with that previous owner, had paid him a very large portion down on the town house and agreed to pay off the balance within a few years. There still being a mortgage, he was not yet in possession of the deed.

Vincent had bought the deed and sent a demand for the balance from Ascot to be paid immediately. He was well aware that Ascot wasn't in the country to receive the demand or arrange to borrow elsewhere to pay it, thus he would lose the house and everything he had put into it—and only find out about it upon his return, when it was too late to salvage his investment.

It had been a well-aimed blow at Ascot's finances, as well as his reputation, since it wouldn't go over well with his creditors that he had been evicted from his residence. Vincent certainly hadn't expected to lose his valuable secretary over the matter, though.

A pretty girl, eh? She must be the daughter. No other female in that house would be so affected by the eviction, to wear a "stricken" look, since Ascot only had one female in his family, a daughter who had just reached marriageable age. His wife had passed on years ago. There was also a young son.

Vincent found himself approaching the door to the house, just out of curiosity, he assured himself. But after knocking and waiting several long minutes, with snow continuing to collect on the shoulders of his greatcoat, he concluded that curiosity was a silly thing by all accounts, and his own didn't need to be satisfied.

He turned to leave. The door opened. Pretty? The girl standing there haloed in the soft light behind her took his breath away. This was who he had evicted into the snow-covered streets? This exquisitely beautiful, forlorn creature? Bloody hell.

Chapter 2

Larissa Ascot stood in the open doorway staring at the large form before her, but she wasn't really seeing anything. Snow was blowing in her face, but she didn't really notice that either, or even feel the cold.

It was too much, all at once, much too much to deal with on top of everything else that had been visited upon her in the last few weeks. The butcher, as well as the baker, both denying her further credit until the current accounts were settled. Her brother, Thomas, sickening and needing constant attendance. Her father's banker apologizing, but patiently explaining why she couldn't have access to her father's funds without his permission. Watching the household funds, which had been ample and should have lasted nearly a year for incidentals, dwindle down to nothing because she had been forced not only to settle with those nasty merchants who had shown up at her door demanding immediate payment on out-standing debts, but also to pay cash just to put a bit of food on the table.

Most of her servants had already been let go, an event that had made her literally sick to her stomach in the doing. Many of those servants had been with her family for years, had made the move with them from Portsmouth to London three years ago when her father had expanded his business and relocated there. It had been horrible for them to lose their jobs during the holiday season, but just as traumatic for her to have to be the one to tell them. But she had been unable to pay them this month, and with her father already a month late in returning, she could no longer assure them that he would be home soon to settle with them.

And now this . . . this eviction. Unexpected, completely without warning. The little man had said a demand had been sent by the new owner through the posts, that there had been ample warning, but she didn't read her father's mail, so she hadn't seen it. New owner? How could Mr. Adams, whom they had bought the house from, sell it out from under them? Was that legal? When there was only a few thousand pounds remaining before the house was completely theirs?

She couldn't comprehend why all this was happening, why merchants they had dealt with for several years now no longer trusted her family to settle with them at the end of the year as was their custom, why they had lost their home. One day to leave. They were to vacate by tomorrow, pack up everything and be gone. How? She didn't have any money left to hire wagons to move them. And to where? Their old home in Portsmouth had been sold. They had no other relatives. The old family estate near Kent was merely a property, uninhabitable, and besides, the doctor had warned that if Thomas didn't remain in bed and out of drafts, he wouldn't recover, could even take a turn for the worse.

"Are you all right, miss?"

The body standing before her slowly took shape, a tall man in a greatcoat that was deceiving of form; skinny, fat, it was hard to tell in one of those coats, not that it mattered. Larissa was merely trying to focus on *something* that might draw her out of the mire her mind was still in. Somewhat handsome, though that was hard to really discern when his cheeks and long nose were covered with snow. Not too young, perhaps nearing thirty . . .

"Miss?"

The question? Ah, was she all right? If she began to laugh hysterically, would he still wonder?

"No, I don't believe so," she said honestly, though she realized she'd just opened the door on further conversation that she didn't want, so she added quickly, "If you're here to see my father, he isn't home."

"I know." At her frown, he continued, "I'm Vincent Everett, Baron Everett of Windsmoor."

"Baron of— You're the new owner?"

Incredible. Such gall, for him to show up after his devastating blow had already been delivered. Was he there to gloat, then? Or merely to make sure that they would comply with the eviction so he wouldn't have to send round the magistrate to physically oust them? Which was going to be the case anyway. There was simply no way that she could get everything they owned out of the house by tomorrow, even if she had someplace to move to.

She supposed the furnishings could be stored at her father's office on the docks. She and Thomas might even have been able to sleep there temporarily—if her brother weren't so sick. But that office was drafty even in the summer. To subject Thomas to the cold that floated up from the Thames was unthinkable. Yet what other choice did she have? There was no money left for lodgings, no money left for food. She had put off selling their possessions, hoping with each day's passing that that would be the day her father would return and make everything right again. But she'd put it off too long. Now there was no time left . . .

Her instinct was to close the door on the baron. He might own the house now, but she was still in possession of it—for one more day. But he hadn't said why he was there yet. And just because her world was falling apart didn't mean she had to abandon common courtesies. She could give him at least five more seconds to state his busines, *then* she would close the door on him.

"Why are you here, Lord Everett?"

"My secretary was rather upset."

"The man here before you?"

"Yes. And from what he said 'm beginning to think a—misunderstanding ay have occurred."

"Misunderstanding? I h ve a letter of eviction. It's quite clear, actually nd if it weren't, your secretary read it alo so I couldn't possibly—misunderstand."

She heard e bitterness in her tone, found it appalling at she could so reveal herself to a comple stranger, but couldn't manage to contain uch overwhelming emotion. Better a bit of ger, though, than tears. The tears would come, would have arrived already if she hadn't been so dazed by this last and worst shock, but hopefully she could hold them back until she was alone.

"I did not say 'mistake,' miss," he corrected her. "I was referring to something else, which cannot be cleared up until your father's return. So I will need an address where you can be reached after tomorrow."

The fight went out of her, leaving her shoulders drooping. Had she really thought, just for the barest moment, that his "misunderstanding" might mean they wouldn't lose the house after all?

"I don't have an address to give you," she replied in a near whisper. "I truly have no idea where we will be after tomorrow."

"A quite unacceptable answer," he said with some impatience in his tone. He then reached into a coat pocket and handed her a card. "You may stay at this address until your father makes other arrangements for you. I will send my coach in the morning to assist you."

"Can we not just . . . stay here . . . until this matter you've mentioned is settled?"

There was the barest hesitation before he replied succinctly and emphatically, "No."

She'd had to force that last question out of her. It went completely against the grain for her to have to ask, beg as it were, for anything, and in particular, from a stranger. But if he was going to supply lodging as his card indicated, why could he not supply this lodging? had been her desperate thought. But a foolish thought, obviously.

And his "no" was the catalyst that sent him on his way, a dark shadow quickly fading to nothing in the swirling snow.

It was another moment or so before Larissa thought to close the door and did so. She even managed to take herself upstairs to check on Thomas. He was sleeping fitfully, the fever that visited him each night still lingering.

Mara sat beside his bed, sleeping in the comfortable chair drawn there. Mara Sims had been Thomas's nanny, and Larissa's as well. In fact, she had been with them as long as Larissa could remember. She had refused to abandon them just because her wage was a bit tardy, as she put it. Her sister, Mary, had likewise refused to leave.

Mary used to be their housekeeper, but when they'd lost their cook back in Portsmouth, she'd admitted that she much preferred the kitchen domain and had taken a downgrade in position to do what she loved best. The haughty housekeeper who had replaced her had been the first to quit right after the creditors began showing up at the door. Amazing how the news of their financial difficulty had spread through the neighborhood so fast.

They would have a roof over their heads . . .

Larissa should have been experiencing some relief about the new lodgings, the biggest worry out of the way, temporarily at least. But as she went to her room and began the miserable chore of packing her personal belongings, she couldn't quite grasp the relief she should be feeling.

Nor had any gratitude shown up yet where the baron was concerned. His offer of alternate lodging had been for his convenience, not theirs. It wasn't help in the traditional sense, was simply that *he* wanted to keep track of them for his own purpose, whatever that was. The "misunderstanding" apparently wasn't anything drastic that might alter their changed circumstances.

She was probably still too dazed by it all to feel much of anything just yet. Which was just as well. At least she wouldn't be crying all night long while she packed. And the tears actually held off until the wee hours, when she went to sleep with them on her cheeks.

Chapter 3

VINCENT STOOD BEFORE THE FIREPLACE IN HIS
bedroom, a snifter of warmed brandy in hand. He
was staring at the dancing flames as if mesmerized, yet he wasn't actually seeing the fire. It was
a piquant face that he saw, framed with bur-
nished gold locks and eyes that were neither
green nor blue, but a light blending of both colors
in a unique shade of turquoise he'd never seen
before.

He never should have gone to have a look at
Larissa Ascot. He never should have got anywhere near her. She should have remained face-
less, merely "Ascot's daughter," an indirect
casualty in his small war. But having seen her, the
decision to seduce her had been the easiest decision yet in his campaign against the Ascots. Ruin
her for marriage, another blow against the family's good name. That had been his thought when
he had handed her his card. On reflection,

though, he knew it was just an excuse, and a paltry one at that.

It had been a long time since he had wanted something, really wanted something, for himself. He wanted her. Revenge gave him all the excuse he needed to have her, would ease his conscience—if he had one. He wasn't sure if he had one or not. The lack of emotion in his life included guilt, so it was hard to tell.

The next day he was in the entry hall to greet her when she arrived at his home. Her surprise was evident.

"I thought the address you gave me would be for another property of yours that you let out, one that was presently vacant. If I had known you were offering the hospitality of your own home, I would have . . ."

"Declined?" he supplied with interest when she failed to finish. "Would you really?"

She blushed profusely. "I would have liked to."

"Ah." He smiled at her. "But we can't always do as we like."

No indeed, or he would carry her straight away to his bed. She was even more beautiful than he recalled, or perhaps it was merely the bright daylight in the hall that revealed more of her perfection. Petite, narrow of waist, finely garbed in a fur-trimmed coat over mauve velvet skirts. A small, narrow nose. Dark gold brows, more a slash than an arch. Unblemished skin except for a small mole on the corner of her chin. Tiny ear-lobes with teardrop pearls hanging from them. She was every inch a lady, merely lacking a title that said so.

The Ascots had not been poor, likely were still well off. They were gentry. There was even an earl somewhere in their ancestry. They were quite socially acceptable to the *ton*, even though George had gone into business, which was not so frowned upon these days as it used to be. Albert had tried to do the same . . .

The only reason that Vincent had found it so easy to ruin Ascot's financial reputation was that he was not in the country at the moment to put an end to the rumors that had spread about his dire straits. His prolonged absence had set his creditors to panic.

She came with an entourage, two women in their late fifties who looked nearly identical, and a pile of blankets that his coachman had carried in for them.

"We have bedding," Vincent thought to point out.

Larissa was still blushing over being there. Her blush brightened more as she explained, "That's my brother, Thomas. He has a dreadful cold. He wanted to walk, but the illness has sapped his strength."

The blankets wiggled. The son was sick? Why had none of the reports he had on the family mentioned that? Vincent was pricked by his elusive conscience, but only for a moment. He nodded at his housekeeper, who had been apprised of the impending guests. She in turn nodded at the coachman to follow her. The two elderly servants did as well.

They were alone for the moment, there in the wide entry hall. Vincent wasn't sure how to proceed. He was used to dealing with women in a straightforward manner. His title and wealth had always opened more doors for him than not, and the "nots" simply weren't worth the effort. So he had never actually resorted to a planned seduction before. And the few that had been planned against him all seemed to include food in the agenda for some reason beyond his comprehension, as if women naturally assumed that a man without a wife must be starving, when any man of his position would have a perfectly good cook on staff, which he did.

However, the thought of food reminded him, "You are in time for luncheon."

"No, thank you, Lord Everett, I couldn't possible intrude," she replied.

"Intrude on what?"

"Your family."

"I have no family. I live alone here."

It was a simple statement of fact, not meant to elicit sympathy from her. Yet he didn't mistake the brief show of it that crossed her face before she recollected that she was in the enemy's camp, so to speak.

Her attitude was understandable. She was not bubbling over with gratitude for his assistance, just the opposite. Her stiffness, her reticence, both spoke volumes. She no doubt saw him as the enemy, whether she was really aware that he was one or not. He'd put her out of her home. That alone would bring dislike, possibly even hate. Which was why the show of sympathy was so interesting. She had to have quite a compassionate nature to feel sympathy, however brief, for someone she likely despised at the moment.

She had given a paltry excuse to decline eating with him, and having disposed of it, he wasn't going to give her another opportunity to refuse a simple meal, especially when it was such a perfect opportunity for them to become better acquainted. He took her arm and led her to the dining room, sat her down and moved away from her to put her at ease. He'd noticed her nervousness as well as her shyness, or rather, her disinclination to look at him directly, and in his experience, there was only one reason for that . . .

It was fairly obvious that despite any resentment toward him that she might be harboring, she was still attracted to him.

It was not unexpected. Women of all ages were drawn not only to his looks, but to the challenge he represented. They wanted to crack his shell. They couldn't grasp the fact that cracking it would gain them nothing, since he had nothing inside it to offer.

As for Larissa, he would have to take full advantage of her attraction to him, to get around her present dislike. And perhaps use her sympathy to his advantage as well. Actually, he decided that anything would be permissible in this seduction. He would be absolutely ruthless about it if he had to be. For once, having a lack of emotion and conscience was going to be quite beneficial.

He took the seat across from her and gave a nod to the waiting servants to begin the meal. It wasn't until the first course was over that she noticed that he was staring at her in a sensual manner. Her blush was immediate when she did notice. He did not stop.

Vincent had been told on numerous occasions, in numerous ways, that his eyes revealed his emotions. Which was quite amusing to him since these occasions were usually during sexual interludes and his passions were tepid at best. It was the color of his eyes that gave the impression, he supposed, of more desire than was actually present. Amber jewels, molten gold, devilishly wicked, sexy, he'd heard it all and discounted it all. His eyes were merely a very light shade of brown with a few gold flecks, nothing extraordinary, in his opinion. Of course, living with them for twenty-nine years made them quite ordinary to him.

But if Larissa imagined heated desire in them when he was only admiring her beauty over the entrée, well, that was to his good. He would much prefer to not have to spell it out, this seduction, if she was too dense to realize he was seducing her. And it wasn't as if she could run off and hide from it, when she had nowhere to run to. He needed only assure her that the choice would be hers to make, and he would do that at an appropriate time. Less than an hour after her arrival was definitely too soon.

Still—he didn't stop staring. He knew he should. He simply couldn't.

He found it incredible that Ascot had managed to hide this exquisite daughter of his from the *ton*, to keep her under wraps, as it were. This was their third year in London. Surely someone of note would have discovered her by now, particularly since the family had lived in one of the more desirable neighborhoods, well populated with titles. Yet she wasn't engaged or being courted, and her name had never reached the gossip mills.

This would have been her come-out Season—if her father had been home to "bring her out."

He decided to ask, "Why is it you're unknown to society here?"

"Perhaps because I've made no effort to be known," she replied with a light shrug.

"Why not?"

"I didn't want to move to London. I grew up in Portsmouth, was perfectly happy there. I hated my father for bringing us to London. And for the first year we were here, I behaved like the foolish child I was and tried every way I could to make my father regret the move. I was an utter brat. I spent the next year trying to make it up to him, to make our home here a real home. Meeting my neighbors wasn't part of either agenda . . . My God, why did I just tell you all of that?"

Vincent burst out laughing, wondering the same thing. And she looked so surprised—at herself. That was what he found most amusing, that he disturbed her enough to cause her to forget standard protocol.

"Nervous chatter, I would imagine," he supplied helpfully, still smiling.

"I'm not nervous," she denied, but she looked down as she said it, still shying away from his direct stares, which he had no intention of stopping.

"It's normal to be nervous. We are not well acquainted—yet."

"Well acquainted" implied many things, and she apparently objected to all of them. "Nor will we ever be," she retorted stiffly, then thought to add, "I know why I am here."

"You do?" he asked with interest.

"Certainly. It was the only way that you could be assured another meeting with my father when he returns, to straighten out this mysterious misunderstanding of yours—which you refuse to explain."

A pointed reminder that he was not being completely truthful with her, which he in turn pointedly ignored, since he had no intention of revealing his real motives. Revenge worked best when it struck in surprise, after all. But he did want to know just how much of an upper hand he held at the moment, where she was concerned, since she was now a prime piece in the equation.

He had made assumptions, when she had confessed she didn't know where her family would be moving to. He had pictured her destitute and living on the streets. But those earbobs she was wearing said otherwise. Yet he wanted her to have no other recourse than to remain right where she was. The last thing he wanted was for her to be able to up and leave his house once she realized he was going to make every effort to get her into his bed.

It made the difference between a speedy,

straightforward campaign for him, and a long, tedious one during which he would have to be careful of every word he said to her. And time *was* of the essence, since her father could return at any moment to rescue her from ruination.

It wouldn't be too difficult, however, to assure that she was destitute, or at least to have her think so, and to that end he said, "If you have any valuable jewelry, you can lock it in my safe while you are here. My servants are trustworthy, or most of them are, but we have a couple new maids that haven't proven themselves yet."

"I do have a few nice pieces, from my mother. They would have been sold only as a last resort. There are paintings, however, that I should have sold already. I prevaricated too long, thinking my father would return sooner. I should see to their disposal tomorrow."

"Nonsense. You've no need to sell off your belongings now. You can wait here for your father. He will rectify everything when he returns, I'm sure."

"I'm sure as well, but I don't like being without any money whatsoever, and I really did go through the last of our funds for Thomas's medicine. He will also need more . . ."

"Your furniture is being stored as we speak. I repeat, there is no reason for you to dispose of it. My personal physician is also due this week, to examine my staff—something I arrange for each year at this time—so feel free to use his services for your brother while he is here. But how is it possible that you are completely without funds? Is George Ascot that inconsiderate that—"

"Certainly not!" she cut in indignantly. "But our creditors heard some ridiculous rumor that he wouldn't be returning and demanded I clear their accounts. And not just one, but all of them showed up at our door. They wouldn't believe me that he would soon be home. I was forced to deplete my household funds to satisfy them. And then Thomas caught that horrid cold that got worse and worse until I feared . . ."

She broke off, overcome with emotion. Strangely, Vincent found himself wanting to put his arms around her to comfort her. Good God, what an absurd thought—for him. He shoved the inclination aside. He was making progress, in getting her to talk. He wasn't going to muck that up with some silly urge to fix everything for her, when her plight was all his doing in the first place.

"And then I added to your woes." He managed to feign a convincing sigh.

She nodded, in complete agreement. She was also back to not looking at him. No matter. He *had* made progress. She had opened up, and easily. But then she seemed to have a wide range of easily pricked emotions, and it was not difficult at all to manipulate emotions if you knew which cords to yank on. He was learning hers.

"I still don't understand why you bought our house, or how you bought it for that matter, when it was already sold to us," she remarked.

"Simple business, Miss Ascot. I acquired the deed from the possessor of the deed. It's what I do, buy and sell, invest, supply what is in demand at opportune times to reap huge profits. Be it a certain style of architecture, a piece of art, or whatever, when I hear that someone is looking for something in particular, I make an effort to supply it, if it's within my means and inclination to do so."

"You're saying you have a buyer for our house already, that that's why you purchased it out from under us?"

"My dear girl, your father was given the opportunity to pay the remainder of his debt to complete his own purchase. Had he done so, the deed would have been his."

"But then you would have purchased the house for nothing, would have seen no profit on it."

"True, but that is a chance I take in what I do. I either reap excessive rewards, or I break even. Occasionally I even take a loss, but not enough for it to have kept me from becoming quite rich in my endeavors."

"That implies you have made your own fortune," she concluded.

"Indeed."

"No grand inheritance, then, when you gained your title?" she asked next.

It was easy to see that she was trying to discomfit him, and perhaps catch him in a lie. She wasn't very adept at table-turning, though.

He was amused by the effort. He didn't even mind sharing a few particulars of his life with her. Actually, he supposed he was a prime candidate for extreme sympathy, if all the facts of his life were taken into account. Not that he would ever reveal all those facts, but a few to work on her sympathies certainly wouldn't hurt.

"My title came with the entailed family estate in Lincolnshire, which I refuse to ever step foot on again, since it holds nothing but bad memories for me. The rest of the family wealth, mediocre as it was, was left to my favored younger brother, now deceased."

He said it without inflection, yet the frown lines came immediately to her brow. She really was too compassionate for her own good. It was going to be her downfall—where he was concerned.

Uncomfortably she announced, "I'm sorry, I didn't mean to pry."

"Of course you did. It's human nature to pry."

"But polite to refrain," she insisted, determined to be at fault for the moment.

"Stop chastising yourself, Larissa. Politeness is not required of you here."

"On the contrary, politeness is mandatory at all times," she countered.

He smiled. "Is this a reminder for yourself, or do you really believe that? And before you answer, take note that I have just dismissed formalities between us in the use of your first name. You are invited to do the same. Keep in mind also that people are allowed their moments of impoliteness, when warranted, especially between close acquaintances."

Her blush was back in full bloom. So was her stiff tone as she stood up to say, "We are barely acquainted, nor will I be here long enough for that to change. I will in fact make an effort to be as unobtrusive as possible while in your house. Now if you will excuse me, *Lord Everett*, I must check on my brother."

He sat back with his wineglass in hand, which he swirled once before finishing off. She wanted formality between them, had just stressed it. He wondered how her formality, and her politeness for that matter, would hold up once he had her naked body snuggled next to him in bed. Not very well, he hoped.

Chapter 4

THOMAS WAS SETTLED IN AND LETTING MARA spoon-feed him. He didn't like being treated like a baby. He truly hated it. But during the worst of his fever when he had insisted on feeding himself, he had never finished his meals because he was simply too weak.

Having caught him in the stubborn lie that he wasn't hungry, merely because he was too tired to finish on his own, Larissa no longer gave him the choice. He'd be fed or he'd be fed, and those were the only options he had until he was completely well again.

The room that he had been put in was much larger than his room at home. So was the bed. He seemed so small in it. But then he was small for his age, both skinnier and shorter than other boys of ten. Their father, a tall man himself, had assured him that he would catch up soon enough, that he hadn't sprouted himself until he was twelve.

Thomas might be behind other boys his age in height, but he was far superior in intelligence. If he weren't so stubborn at times, and prone to a temper tantrum on occasion, Larissa would swear there was a full-grown man inside that little body. His keen observations were often just too adult-like. But his boundless energy, when he wasn't sick, was a firm reminder that he was still a child.

His energy, or current lack of it, contributed to his being a really rotten patient, full of complaints. He didn't like staying in bed, and hated the weakness that had come upon him since the onset of the fevers.

As she approached the bed, Thomas wouldn't look up at her, still pouting over the move, as if there had been some way she could have prevented it. She wished she'd had the luxury to do a little pouting of her own, but all she'd been able to do was cry.

She tried to sound cheerful, however, when she asked, "No chills from that cold ride here?"

"Cold? You had me so buried in those blankets, Lari, I roasted."

"Good, roasting is fine as long as you didn't catch a chill."

Mara tried to hide a smile, unsuccessfully. Thomas glared at them both. Larissa "tsked."

Thomas called her Lari only when he was annoyed with her, because he hoped it would annoy her as well, it sounding like a man's name. When all was right with his world, he called her Rissa, as their father did.

"Why did we have to come here?" Thomas brought his real complaint out in the open—once again. "This room is like a hotel room."

"And how would you know what a hotel room looks like?" Larissa countered.

"I went with Papa once, to meet that French wine merchant at his hotel."

"Oh, well, yes, this house is much bigger than ours, and it does seem very—impersonal, from what I've seen of it so far, like a hotel. Baron Windsmoor has no family, though, which I suppose accounts for that."

"We won't have to stay here long, will we?"

"Not long a'tall," she assured him. "Just as soon as father returns—"

"You've been saying that for weeks now. When is he going to return?"

It was hard to remain cheerful when Thomas was asking the very things that she had been asking herself—and had run out of answers for. Two months was all he was to be gone, which would have allowed a week, two at the most, to conduct his business. He had promised to be home by the beginning of November. It was now a full month beyond that. Bad weather might be responsible for some delay, but four weeks worth?

No, she could no longer hide from the fact that something must have gone terribly wrong on his journey. Ships were lost at sea all the time, with no one ever really knowing what had happened. There were even pirates rumored to still roam the very waters that their father would have sailed through, ready to pounce on a heavily laden merchantman. She'd had time and plenty to imagine the worst, shipwrecked, stranded on a deserted island, starving . . .

Her worry had become so intense it now seemed a part of her. She wanted desperately to share it with someone, needed a shoulder to cry on, but she had to do without either. She had to be strong for Thomas's sake, to continue to assure him that everything would be all right, when she no longer believed that it would.

To that end she said, "The best-laid plans don't always lie down right, Tommy. Father hoped to secure a new market in New Providence, but what if there was none there? He would have had to sail to the next island then, wouldn't he? And if there was nothing there, either?"

"But why did he have to sail so far when he could have found a new market closer to home?"

She gave her brother a stern look. "Haven't we discussed this before, and several times? Weren't you listening to me the last time?"

"I always listen to you," he grumbled. "You just don't always make sense."

She didn't take him to task for that, knew very well that he was merely being defensive because his illness was making him forgetful. He'd either been half-asleep during most of their recent conversations, or his fever had been raging, so it was no wonder he couldn't remember them all.

"Well, let's see if we can both make sense out of what happened, because I still don't understand it all either," she told him, hoping that would make him feel better. "Most companies in the same line of business enjoy some friendly or even not so friendly competition. That's the nature of business, you'll agree?" She waited a moment. He nodded. She continued, "But when one bad apple gets into the pot, it can ruin the whole pot."

"Can you stick to specifics please?"

She "tsked," but did. "That new shipping line that opened late last summer, The Winds line, I believe it was called, was a welcome addition to a thriving market—until they proved to be completely underhanded. Instead of seeking their own markets, they set about stealing those already in good hands."

"Father's?"

"Not just Father's, though they did seem to single him out the most. He never told me about it himself. He wouldn't, not wanting to worry me. What I know, I overheard when his captains or clerk came to the house. Apparently The Winds was trying to put him completely out of business, *and* nearly succeeded. I'd never seen him so furious as he was those last few weeks before he left, after all but one of his ships returned to port without their scheduled cargoes, because The Winds captains had followed his and overpaid in each port."

"Even that nice French wine—?"

"Yes," she cut in, trying to keep him from talking so much, since that seemed to wear him out, too. "Even he ignored the contract Father had with him to sell to the higher-bidding captain."

"But what good is a contract if it can be so easily broken?"

"From what I heard, they weren't exactly broken, just some flimsy excuses given as to why the merchandise wouldn't be forthcoming. The nature of business, I suppose," Larissa said with a shrug she wasn't really feeling, adding, "It's hard to fault the merchants when they had the chance to reap huge, unexpected profits."

"I don't find it hard to fault them a'tall," he disagreed. "Contracts are made for good reason, so the market can be dependable."

She should have known better than to fluff it off, when Thomas was being groomed, even at his young age, to take over their father's company someday. "Be that as it may, this happened all across Europe. The Winds ships showed up in every port that ours did. Rather easy to conclude that it was deliberate, that they were specifically following our line to obtain *our* cargoes. And *that's* why Father sailed so far from home. He couldn't compete with The Winds, which was paying unheard-of prices, or he would have made no profit on the cargoes."

Thomas frowned. "I think this is where I don't understand. How was that other shipping company going to make any profit if it was paying so high for its cargoes?"

"They weren't. They apparently had money to throw away on this particular tactic. Secure the market first, then worry about getting the prices back to reasonable later. It was merely a ploy, and one that worked. Father couldn't risk sending his ships back to the same merchants, only to have the same thing happen again, so in that, The Winds line won; they now have those old markets."

"Do you think Papa was able to find new markets, then?" Thomas asked.

"Certainly," she said, trying to sound confident. "And he had planned to expand to the West Indies eventually. So this may turn out to be a very good move in the end."

"Though forced on him before he was ready."

Often she wished Thomas weren't so smart and would just accept an explanation when given as most children did at his age, rather than question and point out all the flaws in her logic. "Would you like me to tell you what I think?"

"Do I have a choice?"

She smiled. "No, you don't. I think this is going to turn out very well in the end. I doubt The Winds line will survive very long, and when they go under, Father will be able to get back his old contacts, and with the new ones he gains from this trip, why, he'll probably have to buy new ships to keep up with it all."

"And *I* think you're just hoping The Winds will go under, when they aren't likely to, if they had such deep pockets to begin with, to get away with what they did."

"Oh, I'm not talking about their finances. I'm talking about the bad will they've spread, starting out in such an unethical manner. Consider, the merchants who sold to them for the huge profits know exactly what they were up to, and anyone that underhanded can't be trusted. But many of the goods involved are perishable, in need of timely delivery—and trustworthy captains to arrive on time. If The Winds line is late in the future, the cargoes could spoil before they are even picked up, and of course, they won't be bought spoiled. Do you see what I mean?"

"So you're thinking that Father's old contacts will want to deal with him again, because he's well established and, of course, trustworthy?"

"I think they will prefer to, yes . . . and will you look what we've done. We've put Mara to sleep with all this talk of business that she doesn't find the least bit interesting. But no wonder, it's time for your nap as well."

"I'm not tired," he complained.

"I saw those eyes drooping."

"Didn't," he grumbled.

"Did, too. And besides, you need the rest whether you sleep or not. When your fever is completely gone, then we can negotiate an end to these naps."

He conceded. He loved to negotiate, which was why she'd mentioned it.

She headed to the door. But he stopped her there with one last question that she really wasn't prepared for.

"Where are we going to put the Christmas tree this year, Rissa?"

It wasn't the question, but the quaver she heard in his little voice as he asked it. It was her undoing. She hadn't even thought about spending Christmas without her father. She hadn't thought that far ahead, couldn't, because there was too much grief awaiting her down that road.

"It's too soon to think of the tree, this early in

the month. But we'll have one, Tommy, even if we have to share the Baron's—"

"I don't want to share, I want to put on the decorations we've made. You did bring them with us, didn't you?"

No, she hadn't. They'd been stored in the attic and had gone with the other furnishings to wherever Lord Everett had had them taken.

"They'll be here when it's time," was the best she could offer him at the moment. "So please don't worry about it. Just get better, so you'll be able to do some of the decorating yourself."

She had to get out of there. Tears were already streaming down her cheeks, which she didn't want him to see. It wasn't going to be a normal Christmas for them this year. She was afraid, so very afraid that they would be spending it without their father.

Chapter 5

LARISSA WASN'T SURE HOW SHE FOUND THE BED-
room that she had been given, when she could
barely see through her tears, and no one had answered any of the knocking she had done on all
the doors between hers and Thomas's, so she'd
had to peek into each room. But she finally did
spot her trunks piled at the foot of the bed in one
of the last two rooms at the very end of the hall, a
much longer distance from her brother than she
cared for.

Had she thought Thomas's room was immense
compared to his old one? The one she had been
given was even grander. There was even a separate dressing room attached to it, with a large
bathroom off of that, and another connecting
door led to still another bedroom, which, to her
shock, she realized was the baron's bedroom.
She'd been put in the lady's half of the master
bedroom suites. Good heavens, why? Surely a

house this size had other rooms for guests, and hadn't she just passed at least a half dozen in the hall?

This wouldn't do, must be a mistake, and she would have to tell the housekeeper—just as soon as she could manage to stop crying. To accomplish that, she sat down on the edge of the bed and gave in to all the emotions that were crowding in on her. Oddly enough, a few of those emotions were new to her and took over, drying up the well.

She had let Thomas distract her, purposely, since she knew he could. It was why she had raced to his room. But she was alone now, her thoughts once again disturbed by that strange luncheon she had shared with the baron.

She didn't know what to make of him, but he had flustered her beyond anything she had ever experienced. It wasn't that he was so very handsome that he had taken her breath away for a moment, when she'd had her first good look at him there in the bright hall. At least it wasn't *just* that.

Tall and broad of shoulder, Vincent Everett had one of those athletic-type bodies that could, if the man didn't have a meticulous tailor, make him look stuffed into the current fashions. The baron's tailor was obviously the meticulous sort, though, since he cut a fine, dashing figure instead, despite his excess in muscular limbs.

So much, the snow and his greatcoat had concealed from her last night. Black hair, not just black, but darkest pitch, angular cheeks, a strong, decisive chin, a narrow nose, features that fit together so perfectly, it was amazing just how handsome he was.

Still, that was only a small part of what had so rattled her. What had been most disturbing was those golden eyes of his that seemed to talk to her. Unfortunately, everything they said was naughty— Good God, how fanciful. He really had disturbed her beyond rational sense—yet his eyes did seem to be expressing things that weren't proper. A mere trick of the light, no doubt. Certainly not intentional. He probably didn't even know the impression his stare gave others. And it was probably her own heightened emotions that caused her to imagine more than what was really there.

What had been merely a simple business deal for him, just another boring financial transaction, had been a calamity for her in the loss of her home. She couldn't help the antipathy she felt toward him for that. But that strong emotion was probably why everything else he made her feel was much more exaggerated.

As she'd eaten, she had had trouble swallowing each bite. There had been so much churning going on in the region of her belly that she had feared she was going to heave right back up what little food she got down. And yet he had continued to stare. Most rude. Most nerve-racking. Yet because he had done so nearly the entire time she was with him, she had to conclude it wasn't deliberate, wasn't meant to discompose her, was probably just a normal, if rude, habit. Perhaps even a business tactic he had perfected and now unconsciously used in every aspect of his life.

She had seen one merchant try such a tactic on her father once, staring pointedly at him in an effort to cause enough doubt that the price they were negotiating might be raised before verbal commitment was made. It hadn't worked on her father, but it had been amusing to watch.

It took several knocks before the sound broke through Larissa's troubled thoughts and she rose to open the door. Vincent Everett stood there. She had just been hoping that she might be able to avoid any more encounters with him while she was here, yet there he was. And standing so close that she could smell the musky scent of him, feel the heat that he radiated—or was that the heat of her own embarrassment?

She thought to step back, would have run to the far side of the room if it wouldn't point out clearly to him how much he disturbed her. The little space she did gain made no difference, though, because he was doing it again, staring.

And such heat in those amber eyes! She had the impression of being completely stripped for his perusal. And the embarrassment was the same as if she really were standing there naked before him.

"Your jewels."

She wondered briefly if he'd just said it, or was repeating himself. She wouldn't be the least surprised.

"Excuse me?"

"I was afraid you might forget." And the look he gave her now said he'd been right, she was a complete scatterbrain. "But I don't want to be indirectly responsible for causing you any more distress, which would be the case if your jewels turn up missing."

That jogged her memory. "Oh, yes, the new servants that haven't proven themselves yet. Just a moment."

She moved quickly to her three large trunks, which had been stacked neatly like a pyramid at the foot of the bed. Rummaging through the one on top didn't reveal her jewel box, but unfortunately, it was the heaviest trunk, since it contained her personal books. This would have been no problem if she had time to unpack it first. But with the baron waiting at the door, it was necessary to move it out of the way to get into the two trunks below it.

She knew very well she couldn't lift the thing herself, but she could drag it off the top with a little effort, and started to do so. But the baron's arms were suddenly on both sides of her, reaching for the handles on the ends of the trunk to move it for her.

He should have said he would do it. He should have let her move out of the way first. Her heart slammed in her chest. She was trapped between him and the trunks, could feel his chest against her back, his breath on her neck. She was going to faint, she knew it, knew it, was going to expire right there on the spot.

"Sorry," he said after an unbearably long moment, and he moved one arm to let her out of his trap.

Again her instinct was to bolt to the other side of the room, far, far away from him. She desperately wanted to, but she refused to let him think she was afraid of him, which was what he would surely think. He was the enemy, after all. And she wasn't afraid, not really. What she felt was far more disturbing than fear.

He set the heavy upper trunk aside, probably could have done so with one hand, it seemed so effortless to him. And he didn't move back to the doorway as would have been proper. They were alone, after all, completely alone, *in a bloody bedroom no less*, which went beyond improper, was in the realm of compromising. So she dove into the next trunk as soon as it was cleared, the sooner to get him out of there, and thankfully came up with the narrow, wooden jewel box this time.

"There are only these few pieces that were my mother's, and her mother's before her," she said as she thrust the box at him. "They are valuable, but the value is more sentimental to me than anything—"

She gasped instead of finishing. He had placed his hand over hers on the box to take it from her, probably because he hadn't taken his eyes off of her long enough to glance down at what he was reaching for. It was a shock to her, staring into his eyes as his warm palm slid over the top of hers, slowly, too slowly, before he finally took the box from her. She was totally undone again, blood racing so fast she really did think she would faint this time.

That touch they had just shared, which had completely shattered her composure, meant absolutely nothing to him. He glanced down as he flipped open the box to look inside at the long strand of pearls and the pearl and ruby butterfly pin therein.

"I understand," he said tonelessly before looking up at her again with gold eyes that seemed even hotter, though it was probably just the light again that made them seem so. "And these?"

Before she realized what he was referring to, or going to do, he flicked one of the earrings she was wearing with his finger. His other fingers brushed against her neck as he did so, an accident surely, yet she felt the shiver clear down to her toes. She swayed as her knees started to buckle. She forgot how to breathe. In a desperate effort to regain control of her senses, she closed her eyes—and heard a groan. His? Surely not.

She focused on the subject, or what she thought was the subject. It took several long moments to dredge it up. The slamming of the lid on the jewel box helped, startled her enough to open her eyes again too.

"The earrings are always with me, either worn or resting beside my bed when I sleep."

"I'm not taking any chances where you are concerned. Give them to me."

It was a harsh order or seemed to be, since his voice had gone quite raspy. Did he mean the earrings? She wasn't sure. She couldn't think clearly again. But just in case, she yanked them off and thrust them at him, then nervously let them drop before his hand actually got close enough, too afraid that she might end up touching him again. It was too soon, though, and he wasn't quite quick enough to catch them before they fell to the floor.

Embarrassed that her nervousness was so very

obvious, she thoughtlessly dropped to one knee to pick the earrings up, overlooking the fact that he might do the same. They butted heads on the way down. She lost her balance, ended up sitting on the floor. And before she could recover on her own, he was helping her up.

This was truly her undoing. She was rendered speechless by the shock of it. Instead of offering his hand, which she most certainly wouldn't have taken—he must have known that—he lifted her up, grasping her beneath her armpits, as one would a very small child. It should have been impossible, at least from the floor. But he used his own chest for leverage. And in those brief seconds she felt his palms near the sides of her breasts, felt those breasts pressed firmly to his chest before he let her go. Mere seconds. Yet the impressions would last her an eternity.

The pearls hadn't been picked up yet. He did that now, as well as retrieving the jewel box he'd set down while assisting her. The earrings he closed tightly in his fist rather than put them in the box. For once, he seemed as agitated as she, but it was only a brief display, gone so swiftly, she figured she must have imagined it. He did turn toward the door, however, his errand complete, eager to be gone.

She wouldn't have stopped him. It was crucial that he leave before she fell completely apart. But her mind simply wasn't in its proper working order, and with the trunks still in her view, she recalled . . .

"Oh! I was going to find your housekeeper . . . I seem to have been put in the wrong room. I should be closer to my brother—"

She would have said more, but he interrupted her. "You were situated correctly. I usually have guests over the holidays, and these particular guests can't be made to think they are being given special treatment, you understand, when they are business associates. And rather than move you— if you are still here at that time—it was much easier to just place you here now. Is there a problem with the room?"

"Well, no, but—"

"Good, then think nothing of it."

He continued out the door before she could argue further. The second the door closed, she collapsed on the bed. She was visibly trembling. Her nerves were so frayed she felt like screaming. Her heart was still beating erratically. Good God, what had that man just done to her?

Chapter 6

VINCENT CLOSED HIMSELF IN HIS STUDY, WHERE HE
could be assured of no interruptions. His staff
was well trained, knew not to bother him with incidentals when his door was closed, his secretary
being the sole exception. His bedroom would
have guaranteed no interruptions at all, but his
bedroom was too close to her.

Never in his life had he gotten drunk in the afternoon. Today just might prove an exception.
Not that the brandy he had poured for himself
seemed to be helping. He had hoped that it
would calm him, or at least get his mind off of
Larissa Ascot long enough for his body to settle
down. It was doing neither.

Just as he shouldn't have gone to her door last
night, he most certainly shouldn't have sought her
out in her room today. And the jewelry had merely
been an excuse for him to do so. He had simply
wanted to be in her presence again, had been so

stimulated by her during lunch that he was loath to stay away from her when she was nearby.

But that had been a mistake. Seeing her with a bed near to hand had brought The Seduction to mind. It was a perfect setting, after all, to begin it. And he'd thought he could handle it, was even progressing nicely—until he got caught in it himself.

He had never felt desire like this, so completely out of his control. It still amazed him, the strength of it, and the overwhelming urge he'd had to toss her on that nearby bed and ravish her in absolute, unrestrained abandon. Not that he knew much about ravishing, or doing things without restraint, for that matter. But he knew it was too soon to do anything of the sort with her.

She'd been aroused, yes—good God, how easy that had been—and likely would have offered only a token protest before giving in to that arousal. But that was not what he wanted. He wanted her complete surrender, wanted her begging for everything he planned to give her. Her ruination was going to be her own doing, merely helped along by him. His blasted conscience, which seemed to be rearing its silly head at this late stage in his life, wasn't going to be pricked when he was done with her.

He had now removed any other options for her

as well, leaving her no choice but to accept his hospitality. He had already arranged for her furniture to be "stolen," which was the story he would give her if she mentioned again needing to sell it. Having had anything of value moved to a separate location, he could even take her to the warehouse where it was stored if necessary, to show her that what remained hadn't been worth stealing, so wasn't worth selling either.

And her jewels would be inaccessible for her, the key to his safe unfortunately "misplaced"—for the time being. He hadn't locked them away yet, though, held one of the earrings in his hand now, unconsciously rubbing it along the side of his cheek. He had watched them sway in her nervousness and thump gently against her neck. They'd still been warm when he'd picked them up, her heat in them, and he'd grasped that warmth tightly in his fist on the way out the door, unwilling to let it go, when he had just forced himself to let *her* go.

It was such a simple plan, this seduction. How in the bloody hell did it suddenly seem so complicated? But he knew why. He hadn't counted on the effect she had on him, hadn't planned on being charmed by her blushes, entranced by her beauty, fascinated by her myriad emotions, nor aroused by an innocent touch and set on fire by her own desire. *He* was the one who had been seduced, and most thoroughly. And he wasn't sure if he could manage to subject himself to that again, without bringing it to a natural conclusion.

He should distance himself, timewise, at least until he could get these unexpected reactions of his under control. Avoid her completely for a day or two. But there was no time for that. No more touching, then. The touching had been his own undoing. Surely he could conduct this seduction without physical contact. Work on her sympathies instead. Even resort to a bit of natural courtship of the less obvious sort. Seduce her mind first, then her body.

Satisfied with the new plan, Vincent finished off the brandy and didn't refill his glass. And he was glad of the distraction when the knock sounded at the door now. Since it was only his secretary who ever intruded here, it wasn't surprising to see Horace Dudley enter.

Vincent had forgotten, however, that he might need to be looking for a new secretary. A distinctly annoying thought. But just as stiff of form as he'd been last night when he marched off down that snowy street, Horace carried the promised letter of resignation in hand. Vincent didn't give the little man a chance to present it.

"Put that away, Mr. Dudley. I have already rectified what you found so objectionable, leaving you no reason to desert your position here."

"Rectified? You've allowed the Ascots to keep their house?"

Vincent frowned over that absurd conclusion. "After all the effort and favors I called in to acquire it? No. But the lady is staying here until her father returns, so she won't be sitting on some street corner, huddled in a blanket, half-buried in snow."

Horace cleared his throat. "I hadn't quite imagined such a dire circumstance, m'lord, but apparently you did."

Vincent's frown took on deeper lines. "Not a'tall, and beside the point," he said briskly. "You will agree, however, that you no longer have reason to look for a new position?"

After the tongue-lashing he had received from his wife last night over his high morals, which wouldn't put bread on the table, Horace was happy to say, "Indeed, and thank you, m'lord."

"Back to work, then. You may concentrate now on those two investments we discussed last week. Oh, and summon my physician to the house."

"You are feeling poorly?"

"No, but let the staff know that he'll be here to take care of any illness or physical complaints they might have."

"You should know they won't come forward, m'lord. Physicians are much too expensive for minor—"

"I'll take care of the charges."

Horace blinked. "That's quite—generous of you. Are you sure you aren't feeling poorly?"

The frown became a definite scowl. "I haven't gone daft, man, and I always have ulterior motives. Just make sure, if he's asked by Miss Ascot, that he tells her he sees to the staff here each year at this time. And have him look in on her brother while he's here. The boy has apparently been sick for some time now."

"Ah, now I understand. You don't want her to feel indebted to you."

Vincent almost laughed at the misconception. Indebted would be nice, but would have to wait for something else to inspire it. His only concern now was to keep the lady from trying to pay for a physician herself. Horace didn't need to know that, however, so Vincent merely nodded, allowing him to think what he would.

Chapter 7

VINCENT MANAGED TO DISTRACT HIMSELF FOR THE remainder of the afternoon. But by the time the dinner hour was approaching, he was so filled with anticipation of seeing his beautiful house-guest again that he knew damn well he didn't dare. Not yet. Not when just the thought of her entering the room set his blood to racing.

Bloody hell. This just wouldn't do. There was the chance she might not come down to share the meal with him. But just in case she felt common courtesy would demand it, he left the house. There was only one cure for his current dilemma, and there were several residences where he could find it.

He decided upon Lady Catherine. A widow of several years, she never failed to welcome him into her home. And since she was somewhat of a recluse, he rarely found her already entertaining when he called on her, as tended to be the case with the other women he shared company with. He didn't keep a mistress, had never found the need to when he had so many invitations from the women of his acquaintance that he couldn't keep track of them all. The few he regularly visited were the least complicated of the lot, enjoyed the independence that widowhood gave them, and wanted from him no more than he was willing to give, or at least strived to give that impression.

Catherine was a handsome woman a few years older than Vincent. She was indebted to him. He had arranged for her to acquire the house of her dreams, the one she had fallen in love with as a child and had wanted ever since. She had been unable to convince the owner to sell to her when she'd become a rich widow. It was how Vincent had met her, when he'd heard what she was after.

He hadn't lied to Larissa when he'd told her how he made his fortune. Catherine had paid him an exorbitant fee for finding out what it would take to get the owner of the house to sell—in that particular case, a racing stable in Kent which the man had never thought to acquire himself, even though he was an avid horseman, and an invitation to meet the queen, both easily obtainable.

Catherine was still indebted, or felt she was. She really did love her house. Vincent often wondered if that was why there was always plenty of extra food available when he showed up unexpectedly, even though Catherine would otherwise have eaten alone.

The lavish meal, he enjoyed as usual, for she had a splendid cook. He even enjoyed her company, her fine wit able to amuse him occasionally, when he was a man who didn't find much amusing. She expected him to stay the night with her. He had planned to. It was why he was there. But as much as he had been overcome with desire that day, he felt absolutely none that evening.

It wasn't Catherine's fault. She was as lovely and accommodating as usual. It was Larissa's fault. She still wouldn't leave his thoughts, even for the few hours he spent with another woman.

He left directly after the meal. Catherine was disappointed and had trouble hiding it, though she tried. He'd never done that before. But had he stayed, he probably would have embarrassed them both.

He returned home with dread, though, knowing full well that he was going to have a problem with Larissa's close proximity that night. How utterly insane, to have put her in that particular room, with no locks on the doors between them. There were no guests expected over the holidays. He had wanted her where he could reach her. He had been thinking, foolishly, of *after* The Seduction, when he expected to continue to share her bed, at least until her father's return, and so had arranged the easiest access to it. He had *not* counted on being tempted beyond reason before he had her.

He'd been right. He was unable to sleep. He'd been right, too, that he'd be unable to resist entering her room that night. He had an excuse ready, in case she awoke. She didn't. She slept very soundly. He didn't even try to be quiet, wanted her to wake. She didn't. She was driving him crazy.

Somehow, and he'd never know where he dredged up the will, he managed to get out of there without disturbing her. He even managed to get to sleep, probably because it was now near dawn. He'd actually spent most of the night in her room in a state of heightened anticipation that had finally drained him to exhaustion.

And he dreamed that she stood at the foot of his bed, watching him sleep, as he had done to her . . .

It wasn't a dream. Larissa had been unable to sleep as well, though in her case, she didn't know what was bothering her so much that all she could do was toss and turn and pound on her pillow every few minutes in vexation that sleep was avoiding her. She'd heard Vincent come down the hall, had known it was he, because their doors were the only ones at the end of the hall. She'd heard vague sounds after that, nothing distinguishable—until the inner door to her room opened and she went so still, she briefly forgot to breathe.

It was he, and all those feelings he had acquainted her with that afternoon came back, just knowing he was there. She couldn't imagine what he wanted, wasn't going to ask. When she realized he wasn't going to wake her to tell her, no amount of curiosity got her to open her eyes. She pretended sleep. She didn't want to know, really didn't.

Her heart pounded so loudly she was sure he must hear it, and still he didn't wake her. He made enough noise that she probably would have woken easily—if she weren't pretending to sleep. Then he was quiet, so quiet, she could no longer be sure he was still there. Yet she couldn't relax, wouldn't open her eyes to find out for certain, either. A wise choice, because when he did finally leave several hours later, she heard him clearly, heard his sigh, too.

She unwound with the closing of the door. She hadn't known she'd been so tense the whole while, and was sure to be stiff for it in the morning. But instead of turning over and finally getting to sleep herself, she found herself following behind the baron. Not immediately. She did *not*

want to come face-to-face with him after that
nerve-racking ordeal. Yet slowly she passed
through the dressing room and into the bathroom, then stood at the door there that connected
to his room, with her ear pressed to it.

Ten minutes passed, twenty. Her ear was starting to ache. The room was cold, too far away from
the fireplace in the other room to have caught any
of its warmth, the portable brazier in the corner
unlit. Shivers were already passing down her
spine in continuous trips. And then she did what
would very likely be the most stupid thing she
had ever done or ever would do. She opened his
door.

She told herself she just wanted to be assured
that he had gone to bed, that he wasn't coming
back. Yet when she saw him lying there in his big
bed, she was drawn forward despite better sense
that warned her not to.

She was mesmerized. There was enough light
from the fire he had restoked to see him clearly.
His room was warm as well, which was why she
didn't leave immediately. At least that was the excuse she gave herself for standing there at the foot
of his bed, staring at him. That his chest was bare,
even of a blanket, had nothing to do with it.

It was *such* a wide chest. Lightly sprinkled with
hair, though because the hair was as pitch black
as that on his head, it seemed a much thicker mat.

He really did have the body of a man who enjoyed athletic endeavors quite often. His upper arms were as thick as small tree trunks; even his neck was thickly corded.

His jaw was dusted with dark stubble. He must have to shave more than once a day. Her father's facial hair was like that, grew back so quickly that, like most men, he simply sported a beard and merely kept it trim. She wondered why the baron didn't, wondered so many things about him. Was he lonely without family? Whom did he talk to when he needed a friend? Did he have a lady in mind to start a family? Someone he was already courting? Did he even want a family of his own someday? He must. He had a title to pass on. Didn't titled gentlemen take that sort of thing quite seriously?

Not that she would ever ask him any of that. Not that she really cared, was only mildly curious. It was perfectly natural to wonder about the man who had evicted her from her home, then offered temporary lodgings in his own—and caused her so many unusual feelings.

He stirred. She thought his eyes might even have opened, though it was hard to tell. But her heart was suddenly slamming in her chest again. She ducked down behind the bed and crouched there for what seemed an eternity. Even so, she pretty much crawled out of there on all fours, to keep from his immediate view. Her cheeks were flaming. Common sense had returned. She knew she had done a stupid, stupid thing and wasn't taking any more chances.

Chapter 8

It was a muffled thud, coming from beyond two closed doors, but it was enough to wake Larissa. She didn't find out what the noise had been, though, until she wandered, blurry eyed, into the bathroom, and found one of the household footmen kneeling on the floor there in front of the door that connected to the baron's room.

The man's presence startled her to full wakefulness. Wide-eyed now, she just managed to cut off a shriek of surprise, in fact.

But a thorough glance revealed his tools and that he had been installing locks on the doors. It was the doorknob on the one he was working on, accidentally falling to the marble floor, that had made the noise that woke her.

This he apologized for profusely while he explained in embarrassment that he was supposed to have been finished with his task before she arose, so he wouldn't disturb her. Walking in and finding a man in her bathroom was indeed disturbing, though not nearly so much as it would have been if the man had been the baron instead.

The housekeeper was there as well, supervising, though on the other side of the door in the baron's room. She made her own presence known by dragging the footman out of there for the time being.

Her parting remark cleared up any remaining confusion, or it should have. "He'll finish up, miss, when you go down for lunch. The baron wasn't aware that these doors were without locks. Didn't think of it myself, either. Nothing wrong with that, of course, if a wife were installed, but with a guest, well, you understand . . ."

Larissa understood perfectly, the *need* for a lock on each of the two bathroom doors. What she didn't understand was why they were being installed now, after the fact, as it were. And at the baron's request, obviously.

The lack of locks was most likely why she had been unable to get to sleep last night to begin with. She realized that now. She'd tried to lock the doors as soon as she had retired to her room last night. That she couldn't must have added to her unease at being in a strange house—with very good reason as it turned out.

But with the baron installing locks, she had to

wonder what really happened last night. She had assumed it was he who had entered her room, but she hadn't opened her eyes, not once, to make sure. And then it occurred to her, who else it could have been.

One of those new servants that hadn't proven themselves yet. The baron had been worried enough about them to have her lock up her jewelry. One of them could well have been trying to rob her last night, but didn't leave in time when she showed up for bed. The thieving maid could have hid in the dressing room until she was asleep, then tried to sneak out.

Fear could have frozen the thief in her room— or she realized Larissa wasn't asleep. She hadn't moved, after all, not once, in her pretense. The maid could have been waiting in an agony of fear for Larissa to make some kind of sleep sound to assure her she wasn't awake, yet she never did. And opening the outer door to the hall would have brought in some light. Had she been awake, she most certainly would have started screaming, or so the thief could have thought.

It was a perfectly viable explanation, much more realistic, really, than that the baron had stood there for hours by her bed, watching her sleep as she had thought. And the thief had finally given up with that sigh she had heard and gone back into the dressing room to hide the rest of the night, because Larissa never did stir enough to let her think she could escape without her notice.

Yet she had given the thief her escape when she had, soon after that, entered the bathroom to listen at the baron's door. The maid could have slipped out of her room with ease then. Larissa wouldn't have heard her. She was listening for sounds on the other side of the door, not behind her.

Good God, the baron must have seen her in his room last night, and *that* was why locks were going on the doors this morning. And he'd been there all along in his room. She was the one who had intruded, without reason, or without reason from his perspective.

Larissa groaned and buried her face in her hands. She was never leaving that room. No, she couldn't stay there, it wasn't really her room. But she was never going to face the baron again. Couldn't. Such embarrassment went beyond anything of her experience.

She'd leave his house. She had to. He was kind enough not to insist on it himself, had ordered locks instead. But she simply couldn't stay there now and risk seeing him again. What he must be thinking—how utterly mortifying.

And then she groaned again. To leave, she *had* to see him. He had her jewels in his safe. He also had the address where the rest of their possessions had been taken. She couldn't get either without speaking to him. And if she had to speak to him, she was going to have to explain to him what had happened last night.

Had she ever dreaded anything so much? She didn't think so. But prevaricating had put her in this mess to begin with. If she had sold the jewels sooner, or started selling off the furnishings, she would have had a bit of money on hand to take them to a hotel until she could figure out what to do, instead of coming here.

Having inquired of the first servant she passed the baron's whereabouts, she was taken to his study downstairs. She was told he could be found there most mornings after he returned from his daily ride, though not often in the afternoons, when he made social and business calls elsewhere. Today was an exception.

She wasn't really listening to the servant's chatter as she was led there. Her cheeks were already flaming in anticipation of seeing Lord Everett. She had to force one foot in front of the other to walk into his presence.

It was a nice-looking office, accommodating, the chairs about the room designed for comfort rather than just utility, so anyone who joined him there would feel at ease—at least anyone but her. Several lamps had been lit, since the day had turned out quite dark and dreary, with snow still falling in short bursts. The rose-colored lamp domes went quite well with the ruby drapes. She was trying to look at anything but him, but that didn't last long.

He sat behind a large desk. He was reading a newspaper. He didn't glance up. It was probably no more than a reflection from the lamp on the desk beside him, with its rose shade, that made his cheeks look as pink as hers must be. Wishful thinking, to hope he was embarrassed, too.

"Someone was in my room last night. I thought it was you, but you were sleeping."

She blurted it out—and realized, too late, that she was *admitting* to having entered his room in the middle of the night. How else could she have known he was sleeping? Had he not known of her intrusion, he certainly did now.

"It could have been me."

It took several long moments before that statement broke through her embarrassment, and then she blinked in confusion. "Excuse me? 'Could have' implies you don't know. How is that possible?"

"I've never awakened to find myself walking about, yet I've been assured that I do just that on occasion, take strolls while I'm asleep. Not often. And I don't go far, apparently. If I did, I would have to consider having myself locked in at night, which I would rather not do. But it did occur to me that I might wander into your room during one of these strange occurrences, which is why I ordered the locks, to prevent any chance of that happening."

He was taking the blame on himself, even if he wasn't at fault. She was relieved by his explanation. Her embarrassment even subsided. He hadn't seen her. And she had the means to secure the room on all sides now, whether she was in it or not, so she wouldn't have to worry about thieves either. He had removed her reason to leave.

She should still leave. There was something just not right about her feelings for the baron. She should despise him and nothing more, yet there was more.

She almost said as much, that she would begin immediately looking for other accommodations. But then she remembered her brother, and the new physician who had examined him yesterday, assuring her that he should be up and about in no more than a week—if he continued his present convalescence. And he had stressed, repeatedly, just as their own doctor had, that Thomas was to avoid drafts at all costs, which might cause him a relapse.

She had forgotten all that in the misery of her embarrassment, which was still another reason why they should leave the baron's house. He simply filled her mind too much, to the exclusion of all else.

She could wait at least another week, though, for her brother's full recovery. But in the meantime, she could find an auction house that would assist her in disposing of the more valuable furnishings, and a jeweler who would offer her a fair price for her mother's pearls. She could no longer depend on her father coming home to make everything right again for them, when she had finally admitted to herself that he might never be coming home.

She was also going to have to obtain employment to support herself and Thomas. Their father's numerous assets were going to be denied them until he was officially declared . . . She couldn't say it, even in thought. But she had no idea how long that would take.

A quick glance out the window reminded her that it was rather late to get started on all of that today, nor was it a pleasant day to be walking about London, when the snow that had begun to fall last night continued to appear periodically. The last thing she needed was to catch a cold and end up confined to a bed herself. In the morning, then—if she could manage a normal night's sleep.

She made haste now to leave the baron's presence. "I'm sorry to have bothered you. I'll leave you to your reading now. And thank you for thinking of the locks."

"Don't go."

Chapter 9

IT WAS JOLTING, HEARING THAT "DON'T GO" FROM Lord Everett, particularly since Larissa had just been thinking about leaving his house. It took a moment to realize he meant for her not to leave his study, rather than his house. It still had sounded plaintive, his tone, almost desperate, which was why it had been so jarring to her.

He *was* lonely. She was sure of that now. It shouldn't bother her, though. He was nothing to her, after all; no, worse, he was a despicable, evicting landlord. Unfortunately, her heart, soft as it was, ignored that. It did bother her that he was lonely; it went right to the core of her compassionate nature.

She glanced back at him, raised a questioning brow to force him to elaborate. That seemed to confound him. He needed a reason to keep her there, but apparently didn't have one handy. His request had been impulsive, and had revealed too much of himself. She took pity and moved toward the window, giving him more time to find his "reason."

She expected to hear something trite, but in the end he surprised her, even made her rethink her conclusion that he was lonely, for which she was quite glad. She didn't *want* to feel any sympathy for him, after all.

It was a subject that he no doubt intended to cover with her, and it could merely have slipped his mind for a moment, which had given her the wrong impression. But he knew he had something to bring up, had asked her to stay so he could, then couldn't recall what it was.

Perfectly logical; it happened to everyone on occasion. For her to have surmised that he was lonely, merely because a subject eluded him for a moment, was rather far-fetched on her part. Wishful thinking again? Absurd. She merely needed to stop making assumptions about him.

"Did my physician attend to your brother yesterday?" was his forgotten question.

"Yes."

"Good. I wanted to make sure that my servants didn't keep him so busy that he might have run out of time to see everyone who needed his attention, but he left before I could speak to him."

She smiled. "No, I believe he mentioned that Thomas was his first patient of the day."

"And the boy's progress?"

"Still recovering nicely, though he must continue bed rest for another week or so."

"He must have deplored that news."

"Ah, you remember what it was like to be that age?" she replied.

It was a natural question following his remark, yet it brought an immediate frown to his brow that she couldn't help wondering about. She refused to ask what caused it, though. The less she knew about him, the better off she would be, she was sure.

So she continued as if he hadn't just caused her a great deal of curiosity. "Yes, Tommy hates having to remain in bed. He's never been this ill before, at least not with anything that required such a lengthy convalescence, which is why I try to spend as much time with him as I can. We also had to let go his tutor, so I've been filling in there as well. Though with nothing better to do, Tommy is so far ahead in his studies, I don't know why I bother."

"Intelligent boy?"

The frown had left as quickly as it came, making her think she might have imagined it. "Very. It was why he was being taught at home. The headmaster of his last school refused to advance him to a higher age group, yet what he was being taught was nothing that he didn't already know."

"Such decisions can be made for other than academic reasons," he pointed out.

"We're aware that Tommy will have a difficult time with his peers, if he enters college too young. The teasing began long ago from those his age, because his thinking is more adult in nature than childlike. He will probably work with our father for a few years, then enter college at the appropriate age—at least that was . . ."

She couldn't finish, having touched on the probability again that her father wouldn't be there in the future. Nor had she even thought yet what his continued absence was going to do to his business.

The shipping company wouldn't be turned over to her for disposal until he was officially declared dead, yet in the meantime it would fail, so there would be nothing left to turn over. She couldn't run it herself, didn't have the necessary knowledge to do so. Thomas was too young yet to take over. And the clerk who had been left in charge couldn't continue indefinitely either, making decisions that were beyond his capabilities.

"That was the plan?" the baron guessed, unwilling to leave the subject alone. "Before what?"

"Before these rumors started, that my father isn't going to return."

There was a moment of silence as her eyes glistened with unshed tears which he couldn't help but notice. "You think he's dead, don't you?"

"No!"

Too much emphasis. Too much despair. An obvious lie which he ignored.

"There are countless reasons that could have detained him, none of which include any dire circumstances," he told her. "You have been inconvenienced by the delay, but there is no reason to think it is anything other than a delay."

The word he'd chosen, "inconvenienced," almost brought forward a bitter laugh from her. Was that how he viewed an eviction, as no more than an inconvenience to the tenant? Yet she did realize that he was trying to bolster her hope, which she had finally abandoned. She just wished she could borrow some of his optimism, but it didn't work. Her own had sustained her this long, but was now gone.

She couldn't talk to him anymore. The lump in her throat was all but choking her. But there was nothing more to say. She'd already answered his reason for detaining her, that and more.

And then she looked at him. A mistake. She should have walked out while she still had some of her wits about her. She might have been able to manage a few words in parting at the door. But looking at him, she saw the concern in his golden eyes that he probably didn't realize was there, and burst into tears. Impossible to stop. Impossible to control.

It was too far from the window to the door. She didn't make it before his hand was on her shoulder, stopping her, then his arms were gathering her close.

It was what she had needed for several weeks now, a shoulder to cry on. That it was the shoulder of the very person responsible for some of those tears pouring out of her didn't seem to matter much.

He held her close, and tightly, as if he were overcome with emotion himself. He wasn't, surely. He was just trying to comfort her and probably wasn't sure how to go about it, was probably quite unaccustomed to women falling apart in front of him.

It *was* comforting, having his arms around her, his solid chest to lean on, and so nice that she was loath to end it. But when the tears started to dry up, she started to become aware of him in a different way, in the way that so disturbed her and rattled her common sense.

She stepped back quickly, breaking his warm embrace. "Thank you, I'm fine now."

She wasn't, but it was the correct thing to say to him. Unfortunately, he was too perceptive, and blunt enough to remark on it.

"You aren't."

She really was, at least for the moment, in the matter that had needed comfort. It was something else altogether making her tremble now. And she was afraid to look at him directly, to see what was in his eyes this time. She suspected that it would be a terrible risk, to subject herself to that molten fire if it was there again. Her emotions were just too fragile at the moment to withstand it.

So she turned away toward the open doorway and even passed through it before she said, "I *will* be."

Whether he heard her, or would have argued the point, was moot. She didn't give him a chance to, practically ran all the way to her room.

Chapter 10

LARISSA HAD BEEN TOLD LAST EVENING, WHEN SHE
had gone down to dinner and had eaten it alone,
that the baron usually wasn't at home in the
evenings. Quite understandable for a member of
the *ton*, particularly during one of the more
prominent social Seasons, which was in full
swing, to be attending one social gathering or another. So he rarely ate at home, which for her had
been good news.

It was why she went downstairs tonight. She
wasn't expecting to see him again that day. Besides, she had no reason to offer to take her meals
in her room, so it would be quite rude to do so.

He joined her.

Having assumed he wouldn't, it was quite disconcerting, watching him walk into the room,
offer her a curt nod, and take his seat across from
her. Her embarrassment returned over the outburst of tears he'd been witness to that afternoon.

Horrid emotion, to be so uncontainable and embarrass her like that. But at the time, she hadn't thought of that, hadn't thought of anything except the grief pouring out of her.

He wasn't going to remark on it, though, for which she was most grateful. He said a few words to the servant who poured his wine. She had declined wine herself, didn't usually drink it with dinner, but she caught the servant's eye now and indicated she'd changed her mind. She needed something, anything, to help her get through this meal, now that she wouldn't be having it alone.

The silence between them was embarrassing in itself. They ought to be talking to each other. It was the civilized thing to do. Surely she could manage some normal conversation that wouldn't lead to a burst of emotion. And she had Thomas's request still in mind.

He'd asked her again today about adding their Christmas decorations to the baron's tree. She didn't plan to be here for Christmas, hoped to find other accommodations by then, though she didn't tell Thomas that. And just in case she had trouble finding a suitable place in time, she really ought to cover the subject with the baron.

It was a simple request, after all. Nor could she imagine why he might deny it. And it was conversation! Desperately needed, because the continued silence was beginning to heat her cheeks.

She began, "I've noticed you haven't brought in a tree yet for Christmas. When do you usually decorate one?"

"I don't," he replied simply as he sat back with his wineglass in hand and gave her his full attention.

She should have realized that. She simply couldn't imagine him doing anything so festive. He no doubt left the task to his servants, then merely enjoyed their efforts.

So she rephrased her question. "But when do you usually have one decorated?"

"I don't," he replied yet again.

She was so surprised she couldn't hide it. "Are you saying you don't have a tree put up—ever?"

He raised a brow at her. "Why are you having trouble with that fact?"

"Because—I've never not had a Christmas tree myself. I thought everyone . . . But how did you celebrate Christmas as a child?"

"I didn't."

She thought of her own many Christmas experiences as a child, the fun in decorating a tree, the excitement as presents gathered under it . . . That he had never experienced any of that, she simply couldn't comprehend.

"You *are* English, aren't you?"

He laughed. She saw nothing funny in the subject. Thomas was looking forward to decorating a tree with his own lovingly crafted ornaments. He *would* have a tree to do so if she had to go out and cut one down herself.

"Quite English," he answered after his laughter wound down to a smile. "I merely never had anyone to share the holiday with."

She blushed. "I'm sorry, I didn't know you were orphaned that young."

"I wasn't," he said with a shrug. "My parents died after I had reached twenty."

Larissa stared at him. She also gave up. His family must have simply been—strange.

If he had a wife, the lady would insist on a tree. With that thought occurring, she asked him, "Why have you not married yet?"

It was the wine. She never would have asked such a personal question if she hadn't gulped down her first glass of wine and was already working on the second, nor asked it so bluntly. She wished the footman with the wine bottle would go away. No, actually, she wished he were standing closer rather than so far across the room, he wasn't even within hearing distance.

The baron didn't take offense, though; he even answered her. "I have yet to find a compelling reason to marry."

She should have apologized for the personal question, instead pointed out, "But you have a title to pass on."

"My father's title. I despised him, so why would I want to preserve his title?"

"That's rather harsh," she replied. "Surely you didn't really."

"You're quite right. The hate didn't last more than a few years. Indifference prevailed thereafter."

"You're serious, aren't you? I've never known anyone to not love their parents."

It was probably her surprise that made him chuckle. "You've led a sheltered life, Larissa. You've never known anyone to not have a Christmas tree either. Shall I tell you how easy it is for both to occur?"

She should have said no. Knowing more about him was not going to be good for her peace of mind, she was sure . . .

"Yes."

He finished off his own wine before he began. "I grew up on the family estate in Lincolnshire, which I haven't been back to since my parents died."

"Why?"

"Because I have nothing but feelings of inadequacy there, and the memories that caused them."

She changed her mind abruptly. "You don't have to delve into those memories—"

"It's quite all right," he interrupted. "Believe

me, those feelings are gone. In fact, I have no feelings remaining at all, where my parents are concerned. They were social butterflies. They did their duty in producing the required heir, myself, then proceeded to ignore me. I was turned over to servants to raise. Quite a normal occurrence, in the *ton*."

That was true, she supposed, though not as frequent as his "normal" implied. Nor did it explain why he had hated his parents, but she didn't need to point that out, because he continued.

"My brother, Albert, came along a few years after me, unplanned, unwanted really, and turned over to the servants as well. Consistent of them, so I didn't realize yet that my parents simply didn't like children, at least had no time to share with them. They were never at home, after all, so neither of us was actually ignored, it was more like we were—forgotten. I even became close to Albert briefly, before they took him away."

"Away?"

"With them. You see, by his fourth year, he became the 'court jester.' It's how I've always thought of him. He went out of his way to amuse people—and succeeded. He was quite good at it. While I, on the other hand, had no such qualities. I was too serious, too reserved. If I ever laughed as a child, I don't remember it.

"On one of my parents' rare visits, they discovered this. They had brought home guests. Albert managed to make most of these guests laugh. He was entertaining. My parents suddenly found him of value in their socializing, and worth spending time with, so of course, he must travel with them."

"But not you," she said in a quiet tone, not a question, an obvious summation.

"No, certainly, I was the heir and already being tutored. And I wasn't amusing. But they did finally bring Albert home, when he had to begin his own schooling. And they came to visit much more often, stayed for months at a time now. They missed Albert, after all. And when he wasn't in school, they took him off again with them."

"On holidays," she guessed, holidays like Christmas.

"Yes."

Larissa felt like crying—for him. He had said it all matter-of-factly. It meant nothing to him now. But dear Lord, it must have bothered him as a child, when his brother was lavished with attention, and he was given none. Inadequate, he had mentioned. Yes, he would have felt that, would have felt left out, unloved, unwanted . . .

She cried anyway, couldn't stop it despite trying to, silent tears, at least, that she was able to quickly swipe away before he noticed—or he was pretending not to notice. He probably hadn't liked having to offer comfort to her that afternoon, and didn't want to have to do so again. He wouldn't attribute her tears to anything to do with him, thankfully. Why would he, when they barely knew each other? He'd think she was thinking of her father again—if he even noticed the new tears.

Stupid, stupid emotions, to have her crying like a ninny so frequently these days. But she felt so sorry for Lord Everett, to have had such a horrid childhood, such a cold and unloving family.

He must hate his brother, too, if he was still living. He'd said their closeness had only been brief. And that left him no one. He was so alone—so in need of someone to care about him.

"So you see now why I have never celebrated Christmas," he ended.

She did indeed, and nearly cried again. She really was going to have to work on this emotional weakness of hers, as soon as she figured out how one became hard and indifferent—like the baron was. And her immediate problem hadn't been solved either, so she mentioned it.

"My brother has been raised in a more . . . traditional—manner."

He raised a brow at her. "You're saying you intend to celebrate Christmas—here?"

"Certainly, *if* we are still here."

"And that will require a tree?"

She sighed. "Yes."

"By all means, then. I wouldn't want the boy to not have what he's accustomed to."

"Thank you. We'll put it up in his room, if you'd rather not have it downstairs in the parlor."

"Nonsense, might as well do it right, if you're going to do it."

"We'll need our decorations. They were stored in the attic—"

"I'll have them fetched."

"You're very kind."

He burst out laughing. "No, my dear Larissa, I can be called many things, but kind would certainly never be one of them."

Chapter 11

VINCENT FOUND OUT ONLY AFTER LARISSA HAD LEFT his house that she was gone. Her brother was still there, as were her clothes, so he didn't panic. She obviously meant to come back. He was still annoyed, since he had planned to advance his seduction that morning.

Too much progress had been made yesterday for him not to take advantage of it, and before it became redundant. She had revealed how vulnerable she was in his study, that her father's continued absence had become more than just a worry to her. Such grief made her ripe for comforting, and comforting could come in many forms.

He had offered the most basic form yesterday, no easy task for him, to hold her like that, feel her body trembling, and then let her go. She had felt so right in his arms. He'd never experienced that rightness before.

Her tears and grief were real; he hadn't doubted that for a moment. He just didn't think they were necessary yet, so they hadn't affected him much. She might doubt her father's return, but he didn't, which was why he was still under a time constraint, to get her seduced soonest, before Ascot came to collect her.

If he thought otherwise . . . well, there would no longer be the need for any further revenge on his part. Seducing her was going to ultimately hurt the father. If the father was dead, it would only hurt her—a thought he shied away from. Not that she wouldn't still find a husband eventually. She was too beautiful to remain unmarried for long—another thought he shied away from.

It was really too bad that her father had to be such an underhanded bastard. And amazing that he had raised such a caring, compassionate daughter. Was the son the same, or was it only from the mother's influence, which had been denied the boy? Vincent's reports revealed that she had died with the second child's birth. But Larissa would have had eight years in the mother's care, long enough for her to have developed the softer qualities of her gender.

Compassion had poured out of her last night. He had never thought how deplorable his childhood would seem to someone else. He had lived it, but had put it behind him. Even speaking of it wouldn't bring up those old feelings of pain and loneliness that he had buried so deep in order to survive them. But she had envisioned it all and had cried—for him.

What he had told her was the truth, but just a brief version of it. To no one would he ever admit how many nights he had cried himself to sleep as a child, or the anguish in thinking it was *his* fault that his parents didn't love him, or the misery each time he stood alone at the window and watched them ride away with Albert, leaving him behind. To experience, every time they had had to deal with him, their impatience to have it done so they could continue with more interesting endeavors. To never have had a single hug or tender touch, even from his mother.

It was nothing to Vincent now because he wouldn't let it be. He had made of his heart a rock void of emotion—in self-defense. But that Larissa would cry for him, when she had so many bitter feelings against him that should take precedent, still amazed him.

He had done his best to ignore those tears, because he didn't want her getting defensive about it, which would have ruined the effect it had had on her. But he did mean to take advantage before she had time to remember why she should spare him no sympathy at all.

So he became annoyed that she wasn't available

that morning. Yet when several hours passed and she hadn't returned, he began to worry.

It could not have been a simple walk she was doing. That wouldn't have taken this long. She must have some purpose. Yet she had gone out alone, without escort. London was no place for a young woman, and especially one as beautiful as she was, to walk about alone.

He finally sent people out to look for her. When that produced no results, he went out himself to try to find her. He questioned the neighbors at her old address. He went to the docks to her father's company office, which was nearly deserted now, with only a single clerk remaining. He even went by the warehouse where he had stored her possessions, even though he knew that was pointless, since he hadn't given her the address of it yet, but he'd run out of options.

By the time he returned home, only to be informed she *still* hadn't shown up yet, he acknowledged that his worry was getting out of hand. He went straightaway to her brother's room, which he should have done sooner. If anyone would know where she had gone or why, the boy would.

He found the child abed, propped up with pillows and reading a hefty volume of Greek mythology, of all things, surely not by choice, though no one was with him at the moment to insist. Took his studies seriously, did he? Or perhaps he was simply so intelligent that he craved knowledge constantly, of any sort.

These were vague thoughts that didn't last more than a second due to Vincent's own craving for knowledge—about Larissa. "Where is your sister?"

He should have at least introduced himself first, realized that with the blank stare he was getting and started to correct the oversight. "I'm—"

"I'm sure I know who you would be, Lord Everett," Thomas interrupted without the least change of expression. "My question is what is it that you require of my sister that has you so impatient to see her?"

"I am not the least bit impatient."

The book was set aside. The boy even crossed his arms in a manner that indicated he would wait until he heard the correct answer. And his direct gaze was actually disconcerting. For a moment Vincent felt as if he were in the presence of the girl's grandfather, rather than her ten-year-old brother. A brief moment.

In a tone gone stiff, Vincent explained, "While you both reside in my house, you are afforded my protection, which makes you more or less my responsibility for the time being. Yet I can't assure her safety if she intends to traipse about London by herself."

"Does she know you are accepting responsibility for her?" Thomas asked.

"I assume—"

The boy interrupted again with the offering, "You can't assume where Rissa is concerned."

"Regardless, she has been missing since early this morning. Is that a normal habit of hers, to go about town without an escort?"

"No indeed, she rarely goes about town at all. She's been quite the recluse, my sister, since we moved to London. Wasn't always the case, least not in Portsmouth. Think this city intimidates her."

"Then why the devil would she go out in it alone?" That question merely gained a shrug from the boy, prompting Vincent to clarify, "You have no idea, then, where she might have gone today?"

"Possibly to collect our Christmas decorations? I'm afraid I have been nagging her—"

Vincent interrupted impatiently this time. "No, I told her I would have them fetched."

"Then to my father's office?"

"No, the clerk there said she hadn't been by," Vincent replied.

"You've already been searching for her?"

This was asked with a raised brow that looked quite odd on a ten-year-old face. Yet the implication was still there that the boy had just drawn conclusions from that information that were no doubt wrong, yet drawn nonetheless.

"Did I mention responsibility?" Vincent almost growled. "I thought so. Of *course* I would find it necessary to look for her, when she's bloody well been gone for half the day."

"Do you realize how upset you sound, Lord Everett? Do you take all of your responsibilities this seriously? Or just my sister?"

Vincent sighed and got out of there. He wasn't used to dealing with children, and he certainly wasn't used to dealing with little adults in child form. Silly boy, to try and credit Vincent with emotions, of any sort.

Chapter 12

LARISSA WAS WALKING IN THE HOUSE JUST AS VINcent came downstairs again. She looked cold. She looked tired. She was windblown and damp from snow drizzles that she'd probably been caught in more than once. She was infinitely beautiful even with wind-chapped cheeks.

The anger came immediately to replace the worry he'd undergone, now that he could see she was unharmed, and he blasted her with it the second he reached her. "Don't *ever* leave this house again without taking one of the footmen with you! Do you have no sense at all, to not realize what could happen to you out on those bloody streets?"

She stared at him, and stared. She was probably too tired to muster any expression. Finally she said simply, "They aren't my footmen to command."

"Then consider them henceforth at your beck and call—!" he growled, only to be cut off.

"Nor did I have a choice in the matter. I had to go out . . . so I went."

He gritted his teeth. "There is no 'had to' involved. The only rational choice would have been to stay indoors on a day like this."

"That wouldn't have found me a jeweler willing to pay a fair price for my pearls, nor an auction house interested in the paintings and other objects of art I mean to dispose of," she told him.

Vincent almost panicked. He'd already assured her that she didn't need to sell anything. There had to be a reason that she'd subjected herself to horrid weather and risked her own personal safety. He was either frightening her away, or she was running from things she didn't understand.

She was an innocent. She might not realize yet that the strong feelings she had been experiencing were sexual in nature and perfectly normal. Yet he couldn't explain—and end up frightening her even more.

There was no need to panic, though, since he'd already planned to let her think that her valuables had been stolen or were otherwise unavailable to barter for currency. He would have preferred not to have to lie to her about them, but wouldn't feel too much remorse in doing so. Any means to keep her under his roof was permissible, as far as he was concerned, short of locking her in.

"I thought I assured you that you are most welcome to stay here until your father returns."

"And if he doesn't return?" she asked in a quavering voice. "No, Lord Everett, we can't continue to accept your charity, which is what it is. You required an address of us. That is why we are here. But I assure you I will have an address for you before we leave—I just need to go out and find one, which I intend to do."

"Nonsense," he countered. "You can at least wait until the beginning of the New Year. Surely you can give your father a few more weeks to make an appearance. Or do you mean to disrupt your brother's Christmas as well as his recovery, when you don't have to? And after we just agreed that you shall have your Christmas tree?"

She worried at her lower lip in indecision, seriously chewed on it. He wished she hadn't, because he now had an overwhelming urge to help her chew on it. Such lovely lips she had. Did she realize what her simple action was doing to him?

"I suppose a few weeks more—"

Vincent gave in to the urge. He had meant to further his seduction today, to draw it closer to the inevitable conclusion. And he could see no reason, really, to wait any longer for that conclusion. Once she shared his bed, there would be no more talk of leaving, which was the deciding factor for him. And the sooner she did, the longer he would have to enjoy her, before her father arrived to take her away.

He didn't expect to lose himself so deeply in the magic of his own creation, but he did. He wouldn't have carried her straight upstairs either, where any number of passing servants would notice, it being only late afternoon, but he did that, too. He had planned to ask her to leave her door open for him tonight, so it would be entirely her decision. He had simply meant to so heat her with desire today that there would be no other decision for her to make. And he certainly hadn't expected to so dazzle her with one kiss that she was completely his in that moment, to do with as he would.

It was too stirring a kiss, too craved to not be. They were both ignited by it instantly, bodies crushed together, taste and senses exploding in sensual delight. It was her dazed look when he finally let her go that had him picking her up and carrying her upstairs. She had no time to come to her senses. She was still clinging to him when he got her inside her room. Unfortunately, he'd had a little time himself, and a scowling stare from his housekeeper on the way, to jolt him out of his own rashness.

This *wasn't* how he meant to have her. It *wasn't* going to salvage his conscience later, that he had given her no opportunity to think, let alone decide to embrace ruination for a few moments of immense pleasure.

He forced himself to set her down in the middle of her room. He kissed her again, gently now. He waited for her eyes to become focused.

Then cupping her face in his hands, he told her, "You've exhausted yourself today. Take a nap before dinner. I may not join you. I doubt I'd be able to keep my hands off of you long enough to eat. I will join you later, though, if you will leave your door unlocked for me tonight. Follow your heart, Larissa. I promise you pleasure unimagined."

Incredible, to have left her there. If he didn't think himself an utter fool for doing so, he might have been proud of himself . . .

And he made sure that his housekeeper saw him returning downstairs.

Chapter 13

LARISSA DID INDEED TAKE A NAP THAT AFTERNOON. It refreshed her, though it didn't help to clear her confusion over her latest encounter with the baron.

She wasn't sure exactly what had happened between them, or what he had implied would happen. He had sounded like a parent—or a husband—when she had entered the house and he had railed at her for what he considered reckless behavior. And since he had never been either, what was she to think? He cared. It was patently obvious. In the brief time she had known him, he had come to care about her.

And that incredible kiss. She had still been cold, standing there in the entryway. He had warmed her completely. She had still been slightly trembling from it. She had trembled even more from his kiss.

She had never experienced anything even re-

motely like it. She had left Portsmouth without
ever having had any real interest in any young
man; thus she'd never let one kiss her. And she
had spent her first year in London pouting, which
didn't include any socializing, nor was much
done in the last two years, other than with her father's business associates.

She had never realized how lacking she was in
social congress with young men she might like,
let alone be seriously attracted to, as she was to
the baron. She had been promised a Season that
would most likely find her a husband, and had
been perfectly content to wait for it.

She was in no hurry, after all, to leave her family, who were still in need of her. But her father
had expected her to marry soon, now that she
was of age to do so. Her brother did, too. She had
been resigned to it herself, even slightly looking
forward to it finally, when the trouble started
with her father's business. And now—she was resigned to not having a Season after all.

He cared about her.

She was still having trouble grasping the impli-
cations of that, other than that the thought
thrilled her. She wasn't quite naive, though, about
what he'd meant by not being able to keep his
hands off of her, nor about what would likely
happen if she did unlock her door tonight.

Her father had found her alone with a young

man the year before they'd moved to London. It wasn't what he'd imagined; the fellow was the brother of one of her good friends, and she'd been talking to him about his current romantic interest, who happened to be another of her friends.

But her father had felt compelled to explain to her about men's unruly desires, a most embarrassing conversation for them both, but most enlightening, too, about things she could only have guessed at before.

The baron cared about her *and* he desired her. His remarks had cleared that up for her, where before she never would have believed either of him—which was one reason for her prior confusion. She simply hadn't believed he was interested in her that way—nothing he had said supported it—so the heat she'd seen in his eyes couldn't have been from passion. But it was. She didn't doubt it now. And it had been there almost from the beginning.

Could she marry him, though, after what he had done to her family? He was directly responsible for their losing their home. But it hadn't been personal, had been just another business transaction for him, and of course, he was in a position to make complete amends for it, had already made some by bringing them into his own house.

She could marry him; indeed, that thought thrilled her, too. And it was what he must have in mind. She was of good family, after all. He wouldn't consider making love to her without offering marriage. He had probably just been too overcome with impatience to mention it yet.

She could understand that. She was skirting around his "pleasure unimagined" remark, didn't dare think of that, or she would have been overcome with impatience herself, nearly was already. She was even counting the minutes until she would retire tonight.

She almost didn't go down to dinner. Vincent had said he wouldn't be there, but if he was, she didn't think she'd get much eating done. But she went, and it was a solitary meal, or at least it was until an unknown gentleman walked in, clearly expecting to find the baron at his meal. His surprise was evident, to find her there in the dining room instead.

"Oh ho, are you for me?" was the first thing he said to her.

He seemed absolutely delighted by that prospect, whatever he meant by it. She wasn't quite sure.

"Excuse me?"

"A sop to keep me happy until Vincent finds what I commissioned him to?"

That didn't clear up the confusion. "I'm afraid I don't know what you're talking about."

He blushed now, apparently realizing he'd made

a mistake. "Beg pardon, miss, truly. Lord Hale here. 'Fraid I wasn't expecting to find a lady in this bachelor residence, and one alone—or are you not alone? Here with your father? Never say with a husband?"

She was on firmer ground now. "I'm awaiting my father here."

"Is Vincent a business associate of your father's, then?" he asked.

"No, he recently became our landlord—and evicted us from our house."

She shouldn't have added that. It was certainly none of his business why she was there or how she'd got there, and now she was the one blushing for letting her bitterness over that show.

It also surprised him enough to say, "The devil he did. Kicked you out? So you'd end up here?"

"Well, no, that had nothing to do with it. He's offered us temporary lodging so that he can be assured of speaking with our father when he returns. Some misunderstanding that needs to be straightened out."

"Then your father isn't actually—here? You're here alone?"

"No, my brother is with me, and several of our servants," she replied.

He seemed disappointed by that. "Ah, everything on the up and up, then. Oh well, I'll get over it, I'm sure."

He wasn't making much sense again, but no matter, he seemed harmless enough. He was about the baron's age, not nearly as tall and rather chunky of build, with light blue eyes and a rag-mop of unruly black curls that seemed designed to look so unkempt. He would even be considered handsome if one didn't compare him to the baron, who was too handsome.

Since he didn't seem inclined to leave, simply stood there in the doorway sighing as he gazed at her, she thought to ask, "Did you have an appointment with the baron?"

"Not really, just my weekly check on his progress, though he was probably expecting me, since I show up about this time each week. I'm a bit impatient to receive what he's finding for me."

"Which is?" she asked rather stiffly, thinking he might be the gentleman who had wanted their house so badly that Vincent had bought it out from under them. But then she blushed. "I'm sorry, that was presumptuous of me."

"Not a'tall. It's a painting. A special painting that I simply *must* own for myself. Price is no object. I know, I know, silly of me to put so much stock in possessing something, but there you have it. I'm the first to admit I'm eccentric. And I've run out of things to spend my money on. A deplorable state of affairs. Rather boring, too."

She smiled. She couldn't imagine anyone so

rich that it became boring. And as long as he wasn't the fellow who had coveted her home, she had nothing against him, was even grateful to him for taking her mind off of what she expected to happen later tonight.

"I'm sure you'd be welcome to stay for dinner," she offered. "I don't think the baron will be joining us, though. I'm not even sure he's at home just now."

"Oh, he is. The butler wouldn't have let me in the door otherwise. I suppose I should seek him out." Another sigh. "But I'll see you again soon. Depend upon it. Think I might be stopping by daily now for reports. Yes, I just might."

Chapter 14

"HOW MUCH IS SHE GOING TO COST ME?"

It took a moment for Vincent to realize that Jonathan Hale wasn't talking about the painting he'd hired Vincent to find for him, which he had been known to refer to as "she," because of its title, *La Nymph*. But only a moment, since he did happen to have been thinking about the same "she" when Jonathan entered his study.

He still asked, "Who?"

"That dazzling wench you've left to dine alone across the hall."

Vincent stiffened. "She isn't for sale."

"Nonsense, everyone has a price."

Trust Jonathan to think so. Vincent had known the viscount long before Jon came to him to find *La Nymph* for him. It was common knowledge among the *ton* that Hale was obscenely rich, which had heretofore made it a simple matter for him to be able to obtain anything his heart desired.

He was used to naming a price and getting what he wanted. That he'd finally found something that he couldn't have was not a matter of the item being unavailable; it had merely not been found as yet. Which was why he had approached Vincent and offered him a ridiculous sum of money merely to locate the painting for him. Jonathan would then negotiate with the current owner himself to buy it.

It was one of the harder commissions that Vincent had accepted. He was more in the habit of barter, of give and get, of finding out what was needed to obtain something, and supplying it. But what he was doing for Jonathan Hale was more or less searching for a rumor.

The actual existence of a painting called *La Nymph* was confirmed, but not the notoriety about it. It was reputed to be of a beautiful young woman so erotically depicted that it had an aphrodisiac effect on anyone gazing upon it, male or female. It was reputed to have kept one of its previous owners, an earl in his seventies, in a constant state of sexual readiness. It had caused marriages to be ruined. It had caused one man to go insane. It had sent another to the poorhouse.

Hearing of all this, Jonathan had decided he *had* to have it in his collection. Whether the painting did what it was reputed to do erotically didn't matter to him, he wanted it because it was so notorious.

Some said *La Nymph* had been commissioned by one of the kings by the name of Henry, that it was of his favorite mistress, but with so many kings of that name, no one had ever figured out which one. Some said it had been created in revenge by the artist, that the young woman in the painting had been his love and had spurned him. Most people who heard about the painting simply didn't believe in its existence. It was a joke. A hoax. Titillating dinner conversation.

Vincent would have been inclined to believe the latter if his search hadn't produced some valid information about the last known owner of the painting. He had been a gambler by the name of Peter Markson who had won a painting called *La Nymph* in a card game several years ago. A lucky stroke for him, since he was apparently not very good at gambling, and in fact had had to leave the country to escape debtor's prison. He'd used the painting to pay for his passage, then was taken ill at sea and died aboard ship.

The captain of that vessel held possession of it next, his name unconfirmed. He didn't keep it long, though, turned it over to the owner of his ship, because after he took it home with him, his wife then threatened to leave him if he didn't get it out of her house.

This was information picked up on the docks, so not really dependable. It made a good tale for seamen to pass about once they heard of the erotic nature of the painting, but was suspect because the names of the ship, its captain, and its owner were never the same twice. Apparently each old salt who wanted to tell the tale made sure it was about a captain or ship he knew or had sailed on.

Yet it was the closest Vincent had come to finding out anything about *La Nymph*. And Peter Markson really did leave the country in disgrace, having lost everything he owned on the turn of a card. That was the only fact that Vincent was inclined to depend on.

As for Jonathan's sudden keen interest in Larissa, that was understandable. She'd had the same effect on Vincent when he'd first seen her, of wanting her at any cost. But with Jonathan, he couldn't take it seriously, because he knew the man's preferences where women were concerned.

So he gave him a thoughtful look and said, "I suppose her price would be marriage."

He had thought that would put Jonathan off, since he was a confirmed bachelor who preferred not to dabble with innocents, when there were so many well-experienced ladies more than willing to entertain him for a pretty bauble or two. And Jon didn't look too happy with the "price."

"Hmmm, hadn't planned to marry," Jonathan complained. "What need when I've all the women I could ask for, and a few carts full of bastards as well to pick an heir from? Marriage never struck me as being a fun thing to do. But I suppose it wouldn't hurt to try it."

That gave Vincent pause. "You aren't serious."

"Why not?"

"For the very reasons you've stated. You've become accustomed to variety in your women. A wife doesn't provide that."

"Mistresses do."

"Then why marry?"

"To have her."

"Then why have mistresses?"

Jonathan frowned. "For the variety—and why are you trying to talk me out of it?"

"Because you merely want to possess her. You have no intention of devoting yourself fully to her. Having come to know her since she has been staying here, I think she deserves better than that in a marriage."

"Or you planned to marry her yourself," Jonathan all but accused.

"No."

Jonathan raised a skeptical brow. "Then you can't object to my courting her. I'll even make my intentions clear, if you insist, that I have no desire to give up my present way of life, merely want to add her to it. All up and up. The truth. Sounds challenging, don't it?"

"You think to sway her with your wealth?"

Jonathan grinned. "Of course."

It was amazing, how strong the urge was to wipe that smile from the viscount's lips with his fist. Emotion again. It was sneaking up on Vincent too much lately, and in fact his emotional outburst today in the hall when Larissa had returned from her errands had quite shocked him later when he had time to reflect on it.

He should have made love to her this afternoon. She'd been willing—at least, she hadn't been objecting. Then this conversation with Hale wouldn't have bothered him very much. He would have been done with her himself, would have accomplished his goal. What matter, then, if Hale courted her or even married her?

The thought still didn't sit well with him. Before, after, it made no difference, he did *not* like the thought of her marrying Jonathan and being merely another acquisition in his vast collection. And she was vulnerable right now. Thinking her father wasn't coming back, that she and her brother were soon going to be without an income, the few valuables she meant to sell unable to support them indefinitely, she just might jump at the chance to marry one of the most wealthy men in the realm, no matter the reasons offered. Vincent had intended to use that same vulnerability to get her into his own bed.

This bloody revenge thing was turning him into someone he didn't much like. A cad, no doubt about it. At least Hale's intentions toward the girl were honorable, if unsavory, while Vincent's were just the opposite.

In a moment of conscience, he said, "Court her by all means, and good luck."

He actually meant it, was thinking only of Larissa's best interests in that moment. He even hoped that she'd had enough time to realize how foolhardy it would be to leave her door unlocked to him tonight, because conscience or not, that was one temptation he knew damn well he wouldn't be able to resist, wouldn't even try.

Chapter 15

LORD HALE KEPT HIM LONGER THAN EXPECTED, chatting about inconsequential things that nearly brought Vincent to rudely show him the door. He restrained himself, just barely, and only because Jonathan was a client. But when Vincent finally got to his room, he was in a state of frustrated impatience that he couldn't seem to control.

He dismissed his valet, tore off his clothes, and donned a robe. Then did nothing. He stood in the middle of his room and stared at the bathroom door, and didn't take a single step toward it.

It was going to be locked, he knew it was, and he didn't want to find that out for certain. And if it was, he knew he'd be up all night, trying it again and again, in hope that she just hadn't got around to opening it yet, when if it wasn't open by now, it probably wasn't going to get opened at all. Either way, it was going to be a long night.

Everything in him insisted he open that door immediately, yet he was so loath to face the disappointment of it being locked that it was an actual fear. Another emotion she was making him feel . . .

How in the bloody hell had this become so important to him? She was just a lovely conquest, wasn't she? She would be an hour or two of pleasure, no more. She would also be another notch in his campaign of revenge, though that was a point that didn't seem to matter much now, was no more than a sop for his conscience.

He didn't like this hold she had on him, when he didn't understand what it was. The seducer had become the seduced. He wanted her now at any cost and that frightened him. He should leave her be. He should get her out of his house even, put her back in her own if necessary, anything to get her beyond his manipulation. With her here and so accessible, she actually had more control over him than he did her. That had been proven today when she had held his emotions, his every thought, his body, all at her whim. Thank God she was too innocent to know how to use that against him.

Larissa stood there in the bathroom for nearly an hour, staring at the lock on the connecting door. She wasn't going to turn it. Rational thought had

prevailed, even though it was making her miserable. She'd marry Vincent, yes, but she must have
his proposal first. That was the proper order to go
about these things.

But the promised "pleasure unimagined"
wouldn't leave her thoughts either, which was
why she was still standing there, abject over her
decision, and unaware that she was trying to find
a way to get around it. Her pulse was racing as
she imaginined him on the other side of that door,
waiting.

Surely he had realized himself by now that a
proposal was required before they indulge in any
more pleasure of any sort, let alone the kind she
was sure he had in mind. He could have intended
to ask her tonight, though. She could be denying
them both for no good reason.

She unlocked the door. Vincent proved that
he'd been waiting for the sound of it when it
opened only seconds later. They stared at each
other. Like liquid gold, his eyes were so hot they
seared, melting away any last trace of indecision
she'd been feeling.

He shrugged out of his robe, left it on the floor
there. She was still fully dressed, now uncomfortably so. Yet she was so mesmerized by his golden
eyes that she didn't even think to look at him, at
all of him, nor was the option there for long,

when his hand slipped behind her neck and drew her close to his body.

Their lips met and melded. It was a ravenous kiss, echoing hunger long denied in them both. Her knees buckled, they became so weak, but there was no danger of falling, she was held so tightly to him.

She was so new to this sort of sensual kissing— this was only her second experience of it—yet he was so skillful at it himself, guiding her, prompting when needed, that her inexperience wasn't given any opportunity to interfere. Not that any hesitancy or inadequacies stood a chance of being noticed amidst the pleasure of tasting each other so fully, they became lost in that kiss.

A groan finally broke it—his. She barely noticed, she was so enthralled by what she was feeling. And swiftly she was carried to his bed. Not hers. She didn't notice that yet either. But it wasn't long before she was noticing something quite extraordinary . . .

Had she really thought all pleasure would derive merely from being held and kissed by him, just because it was so nice by itself? But then how could she have known otherwise? His "pleasure unimagined" had been unassociated with anything specific in her mind, because she had no specifics to draw from other than loose generalities. But it became very associated with his hand on her breast.

Spontaneous reactions went off in numerous parts of her body from that simple placement of his palm. Gooseflesh, butterflies, wet heat, and that was only the beginning. He continued to kiss her and catch each little gasp of pleasure that escaped her, and many did as he began the next lesson in sensual touching.

Even the removal of her clothes was an erotic experience, he did it so slowly, with such thorough caressing of each limb and curve exposed. Amazing that if she touched the underside of her knee, she'd feel nothing, yet his fingers there made her shiver. That it was Vincent touching her made all the difference, and such a difference, such a wealth of new sensations to marvel at.

He had her mind and body so consumed with him and the pleasure he was introducing her to that she wasn't sure what made her realize she'd reached the point of no return without hearing what she needed to hear from him. Not that she had the will, or, certainly, the desire, to stop what was happening either way. It would make her pleasure complete, though, to have confirmed what she already took for granted.

The words came out between the gasps, and not very coherently at that. "I thought . . . Shouldn't you . . . There is the question of . . ."

He must have understood what she was trying to say, because he replied, "This isn't the time for important questions that could tie up the tongue."

So misleading, that remark, and yet so reassuring. She assumed that he was talking of asking her to marry him. And she had to agree, after her own garbled speech, that it was rather impossible to put two thoughts together at the moment. Besides, there was no opportunity to say more, when he was distracting her with his kisses again.

His large body covered her gradually, carefully, so as not to alarm her. She was beyond that, comforted instead by his weight, even as the pressure heightened her arousal. He grasped her hands, held on either side of her head. He kissed her deeply as he took possession of her. The pain was so swift, it was there and gone before she really felt it or had time to stiffen against it, and was as soon forgotten in the onslaught of pure sensual delight that followed, of feeling him buried deep within her.

Briefly she thought that was the end of it, that nothing could be better. How naive. Even his "pleasure unimagined" didn't do justice to the incredible bliss that steadily grew as he began moving in her, then burst and spread through her body in unrelenting waves.

In those few moments of utter ecstasy, nothing

else mattered. They would work out the marriage arrangements later, she was sure. For now, she savored the knowledge that Vincent Everett belonged to her.

Chapter 16

THE PROPOSAL OF MARRIAGE DIDN'T COME AFTER the lovemaking as expected. Not surprising, though, when Vincent removed his weight from Larissa, pulled her close to his side, and promptly fell asleep. And she lay there also, too much savoring the whole experience, the happiness she was feeling, and the unexpected comfort of being held by him even in sleep to consider waking him now when she finally realized that part of the evening's agenda hadn't been finished.

She wasn't worried about it, though. Taking things for granted had a way of removing doubts and leaving room only for positive thoughts. She knew she couldn't stay there in his room to sleep the night with him, much as she would have liked to, but had that to look forward to when they married. And before the comfort of his closeness put her to sleep as well, she carefully got out of bed, gathered up her clothes so she'd leave no trace of herself there for any servants to find, and tiptoed back to her room.

She didn't lock the doors between their rooms, didn't even think to. Nor was there a need to now. Making love with Vincent changed so many things, not just her outlook or her future, which was now secure. *She* was changed, and she felt confident in the intimate knowledge she had gained. And she eventually fell asleep with a smile on her lips.

It annoyed Vincent that Larissa wasn't in his bed when he awoke the next morning. He knew it shouldn't, knew she'd been right to leave, would have taken her back to her room himself if he hadn't fallen asleep. Thus his annoyance made no bloody sense in his mind.

And his mood only got worse. Every little thing annoyed him that morning as he dealt with his secretary and his staff. He found himself snapping at the lot of them, and for no good reason.

Unfortunately, that mood didn't leave him before luncheon, and when he joined Larissa in the dining room, he ended up snapping at her as well, before he could stop himself. "My cook is threatening to quit if *your* cook does not stay out of his kitchen!"

He'd all but shouted it, and managed to shock them both. That was certainly not how he'd meant to greet her, and definitely not how he *should* have greeted her, when this was the first time he was seeing her after stealing her virginity last night. It didn't matter that one thing after another this morning had conspired to cause him boundless frustration—and that was just another excuse.

He knew why he was a fuse already lit, he just hadn't owned up to it yet. And he was furious with himself for cowardly refusing to examine the root of his annoyance, and instead taking it out on others—even her.

He was feeling an incredible amount of guilt over what he'd done last night. He'd never in his life enjoyed anything so much, yet now was overcome with regret for it. Because he had no intention of marrying her, when he knew that was what she was expecting from him now.

The original motive of revenge wasn't helping to ease his conscience at all in the matter of his becoming her lover, when he had counted on it doing so. The only thing that might help now was to not let it ruin her reputation as he'd planned to. As long as it didn't become public knowledge, she could still find a good marriage.

He didn't doubt that Hale would marry her either way. He was smitten by her beauty, could care less whether she was a virgin. But could he stomach watching another man pursue her, when

just speaking of it last night, he'd wanted to
punch the man in the face?

Larissa recovered first from his outburst, explained calmly, "I'm sorry. When I told Mary this
morning that we would be living here permanently now, she no doubt decided she could make
herself more at home here, and she feels most at
home in a kitchen."

Vincent flushed. And he couldn't correct her
about living there permanently—not yet. His silence on the matter would confirm it in her mind,
but that couldn't be helped. He still expected her
father to show up, even if she didn't. And when
Ascot did, then Vincent could be done with this
bloody business of revenge, deliver the final blow
to the man, and then get on with his own life.

He mumbled something about their both keeping their servants in line, and hoped she'd leave it
go at that. She did. She even smiled at him, which
had the effect of making it worse. He couldn't
leave it go himself now. She was such a sweet,
gullible chit, and he'd been an absolute bastard in
his dealings with her from the start—and was still
going to be. The least he could do was make her
happy in the meantime, and keep his foul moods
to himself.

He moved around the table to her side. He
would have kissed her if they were alone, but
there were servants entering and leaving, so he

merely bent down and whispered to her, "Forgive me for that boorish greeting. And thank you for the most wonderful gift I've ever received."

"What gift?"

"You."

He could feel the heat of her blush, though he was standing behind her and couldn't see it. Her cheeks were still pink when he took his seat across from her and gazed at her. But he detected the barest trace of a smile, proving it wasn't embarrassment making her cheeks glow.

The meal progressed. She chatted aimlessly merely to fill the silence, nothing of import, merely relaxed conversation that he found himself enjoying. She could be amusing when she wasn't nervous, and she wasn't the least bit nervous with him at the moment.

But then she mentioned the Christmas decorations again. He'd already had them fetched. He could just tell her that and nothing more. But this was too ideal an opportunity to mention that the rest of her stored valuables were gone, not when she was requesting them, but while she assumed she wouldn't have to sell them now, so the loss wouldn't hit her so hard. They'd be "found," of course, after her father returned. Vincent had no intention of stealing anything from the Ascots, other than their good reputation.

He didn't consider dispensing with the theft

story. He'd already seduced her, yes, but now he had to worry that she would ask him directly about marriage, and if she did, he wasn't going to lie about it. Which would put her back to thinking she had to leave, which he still wasn't willing to let her do. When her father returned would be soon enough to give her up. So having her think she had no means to leave would still be beneficial—for him.

To that end, he managed a suitably grave expression before saying, "Speaking of those Christmas decorations, they arrived here this morning, but I'm afraid some bad news was delivered with them."

"They've been damaged?" she asked in alarm.

"Not that I'm aware of," he quickly assured her. "But apparently there was a robbery late last night at the warehouse where your belongings were stored. The report from the attendant who keeps a watch on the place was that it was a selective robbery, which isn't uncommon, since it can be accomplished in the least amount of time."

"I've been robbed?" she said incredulously.

"*We* have been robbed," he clarified. "I had a few valuables stored there myself. But most of your possessions are still there. As I said, the thieves were selective. They took only what they considered valuable and easily movable, paintings, vases, and other small pieces of art. They were in and gone in under ten minutes, which was the amount of time the attendant was indisposed."

"I had plans for those paintings," she said in a forlorn whisper.

He hadn't counted on her stricken look. He now knew exactly how his secretary had felt that night when she'd turned this look on him. Vincent didn't have the luxury of resigning from what he'd started, however, without admitting he was a despicable liar.

He could, however, lessen the blow, and assured her, "I'm not writing this off, Larissa. The robbery has been reported to the authorities, but I've already assigned my own people to track down these culprits. What was taken *will* be recovered. If your portion isn't found by the beginning of the New Year, I will replace the value myself."

"You . . . don't have to do that," she replied. "It's not your fault—"

He didn't let her finish. "I disagree. It was my warehouse, after all, and I should have had it protected better. I'm afraid I'm not used to owning it yet, and frankly, I wasn't planning to keep it, just haven't got around to disposing of it yet."

"Then why did you buy it?"

He relaxed. Her expression was merely curious now, the horror gone from it. He'd managed to ease her mind and accomplish his goal, and all because she didn't have a suspicious bone in her pretty little body.

"I didn't buy it. It came into my possession a few months ago, was the last asset from my brother's business that didn't succumb to his creditors when he died."

"Oh, I'm so sorry."

Bloody hell, there it was again, sympathy for him pouring out of her. She'd just been delivered a devastating blow, yet had room to feel compassion for him as she realized what he'd said meant his brother had only recently died.

He quickly made light of it in offering her a shrug and a slight change of subject. "Have you no other assets at all, aside from your jewels?"

"There is a piece of land in Kent that's been in my family's possession longer than anyone can remember. There is a ruined castle on it, believed to have belonged to one of our ancestors, an ancient one. But that rumor has never been confirmed. Unfortunately, it only takes one generation to go by, uninterested in preserving family history, for that history to be lost."

"The land is valuable, though?"

"I suppose it is, but I can't sell it. My father hasn't been declared dead yet, for me to be able to. The same goes for his company, his ships, any stored cargoes or valuables he has locked in the small storeroom at the company, none of which I can dispose of yet. And his personal belongings, jewelry and the like, sailed with him."

Vincent stiffened. Talk of ships in relation to her father brought a very unacceptable—to him— thought.

It hadn't occurred to him, until that moment, that Larissa's father fit the description of the current possessor of *La Nymph*, and that she had paintings she meant to sell . . . No, that would be too easy, too convenient—and make her family incredibly rich. But just in case it wasn't a coincidence, he would visit the warehouse after luncheon to examine those paintings himself that had been moved to the secured storeroom in the back of the building. And he hoped, he really did, that he wouldn't find *La Nymph* there.

Chapter 17

VINCENT RETURNED TO HIS HOUSE IN A MUCH better mood than he'd been in upon leaving it. The trip to the warehouse showed that the Ascots were in possession of seven old paintings, two by well-known artists, but none of them the notorious *La Nymph* that he was searching for. So he didn't have to face the dilemma of making the Ascots very rich, something that just did *not* fit into his plans for their ruination.

And then he had his mood utterly ruined again by finding Jonathan Hale in his parlor with Larissa and her brother, Thomas, who'd been allowed out of the sickroom for the express purpose of decorating the Christmas tree. Such a homey scene, and so foreign to him.

It was the laughter and smiles, the sheer enjoyment they were having, that hit Vincent the worst. He wasn't part of it, nor ever would be. And it wasn't even strictly related to Christmas, though that was the present reason for it. They simply knew how to have fun doing simple things, while the concept of fun had never been part of his own life, even as a child.

More than once his brother had tried to show him how to have fun, would drag him from his studies, explain some imaginary game, then be disappointed when Vincent couldn't get the hang of it. There were simply too many real concerns always plaguing Vincent as a child for him to let go of them long enough to have fun. But that Albert had tried to include him in that aspect of life was one reason he had tolerated his brother's many weaknesses throughout the years. Albert had tried to teach him. Vincent hadn't really tried to learn.

Larissa noticed him standing there in the doorway and gave him a brilliant smile. She took his breath away, she was so incredibly beautiful. Jonathan saw it as well and stood there mesmerized. Thomas, noticing both men, rolled his eyes toward the ceiling. Obviously he was used to men behaving like idiots around his sister.

"I didn't think you would return in time to help," she told Vincent, motioning him forward.

He didn't move. "Help?"

"It's your tree, really. Our decorations are only being added to the contributions your servants have already made. Look at this one from your grouchy cook." She pointed out a small shiny spoon that had a hole punched in the end of it so it could be tied to a branch with a bright ribbon. "He even blushed as he put it on."

"I have no decorations to add."

"There are plenty here to choose from. Come, put this angel on the top."

There was a sturdy chair placed next to the tree, to use to reach the upper branches. Vincent simply couldn't picture himself standing on it, yet he found himself walking forward. *She* was the draw, not the silly tree, which had no business being inside a house.

He took the ornament from her, glanced at the top of the tree, which was a good three feet above his head. He stood on the chair. She stood behind it, holding the back to keep it steady for him. He looked down at her, caught his breath yet again. She looked so delighted. It was too easy to make her happy. She took joy in such little things.

He placed the angel on the top of the tree. Not correctly, apparently, since she began to direct him to try again, and again. Hale started making jokes about angels becoming fallen in his hands, which fortunately, Larissa saw no double meaning in, but Vincent certainly did.

Finally she clapped and said, "Perfect!"

Thomas, standing across the room to view it from a different angle, said, "It's crooked."

"Bah, don't listen to him, Vince, he's being ornery."

Hale chimed in, "Crooked."

"See? Majority rules." Thomas chuckled.

"You don't have a majority yet without my vote," Vincent heard himself saying.

"Well, then, what's the verdict?"

Vincent stepped off the chair, moved about the room looking at the tree from different directions, keeping them waiting while he seemed to give it serious thought. Finally he stopped next to Thomas and said, "Crooked. You fix it. I obviously don't have a knack for it," and he lifted Thomas up to straighten the ornament, which he did.

Across the room, Larissa pealed with laughter. "Now it's crooked."

It was infectious this time, her laughter. Vincent heard himself joining in with the others and was amazed at how good it felt. He sat back after that and watched them finish, making a comment here or there, pointing out a few barren spots on the tree that could use some help.

He still couldn't quite believe that he had joined their festive group and actually felt a part of it. But then that was Larissa's doing. It wasn't that she had a knack for taking command, was more that people simply wanted to please her by doing whatever she requested of them.

Vincent couldn't *not* invite Hale to dinner after all his help, much as he would have preferred it otherwise. While the child had been present in the parlor, Hale had been the perfect gentleman, merely part of the group. But now with the boy sent back to his bed, Hale turned every bit of charm he could muster in Larissa's direction.

Vincent was disgusted. He would have said something to warn Jonathan to back off, but Larissa was doing too good a job of evading, and for the most part, ignoring or simply not understanding some of the more subtle overtures coming her way. And he realized, after a while, that he had nothing to worry about.

For the time being, and until she learned the truth, she considered herself soon to be married, which meant she would ignore any offerings from other men. Yet because Vincent hadn't asked her to marry him yet, she couldn't use that as an excuse to refuse invitations from others; she had to be creative in her turndowns instead.

She was doing an admirable job of that, much to Jonathan's chagrin. Yet she did it in such a way that Hale didn't lose hope, much to Vincent's chagrin. He would have preferred the man go away and not come back. No such luck, he was sure. And he did notice, when she declined going to the theater, that she seemed rather disappointed to have to refuse.

He wondered then if she had ever been to the theater before, and rather doubted it. Reclusive, she had been, from all accounts, and unknown to the *ton*. Her father could have taken her, but she had only just come of age, and taking her prior to that would have been inappropriate.

He decided to invite her himself, when he joined her later tonight. A small thing that might give her a lot of enjoyment. The least he could do, and besides, it might distract her from asking pertinent questions that he needed to continue to avoid himself.

Chapter 18

As a distraction, inviting Larissa to the theater worked wonders. She had intended to address the issue of marriage that night when Vincent joined her in her room. That had been fairly obvious by her nervousness. And she even began the question he didn't want to hear.

But having expected it—since he was quite aware that while they were alone was really the only chance she would have to bring up anything that personal—he was swift in cutting her off with the invitation. And before they were done discussing the particulars of him taking her on such an excursion, he was kissing her. And of course, once that began, there were no further thoughts about anything other than the pleasure to come.

The guilt was still there and bothering him, but it didn't stop Vincent from making love to Larissa again that night. *That* was a compulsion that far outweighed any remorse he might be feeling. And his conscience did seem to absent itself nicely once he gathered her in his arms. It was only later, when she wasn't near him, that the guilt would set in to bedevil him again.

He avoided her the next day up until it was time to leave. She had claimed that she had appropriate clothes for such an outing, since her Season wardrobe had been made long before the new Season began. He had cautioned her against anything too fancy, and she had complied. The clothes did determine which theater they would go to, after all, and there were many to choose from, the more esteemed establishments frequented by the *ton* to the common variety that one might find a chimney sweep standing in line for.

She had done exactly as he'd asked. Her rose velvet gown could have been worn for day wear with the short, fur-trimmed cape covering the deep scoop of the neckline. But once the cape was removed, the gown was definitely evening wear, and definitely too elegant for a theater frequented by the lower masses.

One of her servants accompanied them. Chaperonage was good, in his opinion. It kept him from touching Larissa, kept him from seeming the least bit proprietary—kept him from ravaging her in the coach on the way to the theater district, which might have been a definite possibility, as lovely as she looked that night.

It turned out to be a complete blunder on his part, however, to take her anywhere where she would be *seen*. She enjoyed it immensely, yes, but he could have found some other way to amuse her.

The results began the next morning. No fewer than seven young dandies showed up at his door to call on the young beauty they had glimpsed with him last evening. And worse, he wasn't there to fend them off, had gone on his morning ride in the park. By the time he returned home, Larissa was holding court in his parlor, next to her Christmas tree. And the parade of young bucks continued that afternoon with another five gentlemen calling.

The only thing that Vincent was able to console himself with was that Larissa was still declining all invitations. How much longer that would last, though, when she didn't have an actual verbal commitment from him yet, was the burning question he had to deal with.

She was his on borrowed time. When her father showed up, she wouldn't be his any longer. And unlike her, *he* didn't expect that time to continue more than a few more days. Which was the only reason his current evasive tactics were going to work. Her question couldn't be put off indefinitely, when it was too important to her to get an answer. And he was sure she would like to be able to say officially, "I'm engaged, leave me alone," to all her new admirers.

When Lord Hale showed up that evening, he had already heard about the excursion. Not surprisingly, he was quite put out with Vincent for introducing Larissa to the *ton*.

Jonathan even went so far as to accuse him, "You've already asked her to marry you and been accepted, haven't you? You're just waiting for her father to return to England to make it official. 'Fess up, Vincent. I'm wasting my bloody time here, aren't I?"

"What, pray tell, does the one have to do with the other?" Vincent asked him.

"You wouldn't feel confident in showing her off unless you already had her committed to you. Or are you going to try to tell me that you didn't know you'd have half the *ton* knocking at your door after they got a look at her? Now, I know you well enough to know that you don't like to entertain here. So what does that leave in assumptions, eh? That you couldn't resist showing her off, just as I'd planned to do *after* I got her committed to me. I'm not fool enough to do it beforehand, and neither are you."

Vincent only just managed to resist laughing.

Should he 'fess up to being the fool Hale had just described? He really hadn't thought of the repercussions that would result from taking Larissa out for an evening's entertainment. He had wanted to distract her. He had wanted to offer her some amusement, nothing more.

And he *had* tried to avoid the *ton* by going to a less prestigious theater, but only so he wouldn't have to fend off questions about her from acquaintances they might run into. That had backfired, of course, due to the play in question having received excellent reviews, which he hadn't been aware of, which was a sure draw for the theater-frequenting crowd, including those from his social circle. But then, unlike Hale, he wasn't hoping to marry Larissa, so wasn't thinking about keeping other men from noticing her.

They had gathered in the parlor after dinner. Larissa had just excused herself to retire. It had been a strenuous day for her, apparently, being admired by so many.

Hale was obviously disappointed to see her go—he had arrived late himself and so hadn't had a chance to spend much time with her today. That might account for half of his annoyance.

"I believe I've already mentioned to you that I have no plans to marry Larissa or anyone else for that matter," Vincent said.

"You have eyes. The girl is nigh impossible to resist."

"Nonsense," Vincent maintained, and even managed to keep a straight face doing so. "She's beautiful, yes, but I have no desire to complicate my life with a wife."

"You'll need to marry sometime."

"Why? You hadn't planned to, prior to meeting Larissa. Nor do I require an heir."

"You've a title to bestow," Jonathan pointed out.

"My title can rot. I have nothing I care to leave to anyone."

"That ain't normal, Vincent."

Vincent shrugged to show how little he cared for normality, though he did add, "Besides, this is redundant. I have not asked the girl to marry me, nor will I. As to your concern over my taking her to the theater, did it not occur to you that I might have simply wanted to distract the girl from her worries? Or weren't you aware that her father's tardiness has her assuming the worst? And besides, I *thought* I was taking her to a play that wouldn't be frequented by our crowd. Bloody ill luck that it was such a good performance that word of it has spread."

"Her father could be dead?"

Trust Jonathan to surmise that and be already

thinking how to put that information to good use in his campaign to win her. "Highly unlikely."

"But possible?"

"Anything is possible, of course. But it's more likely that he will show up within the week, that whatever has detained him, he will make an effort to finish up. He will want to be home for Christmas, after all, to spend it with his family. Larissa, unfortunately, has it set in her mind that something has gone terribly wrong, and once a fear sets in, it's hard to shake. I've tried to convince her otherwise, with little luck. So I tried a distraction instead."

Jonathan frowned. "She hides it very well, that she's worried. How did you find out?"

"Having her burst into tears in front of me when we had been speaking of her father was a very good clue," Vincent said dryly.

"I would be quite happy to take over the matter of distracting her. No reason for you to be bothered, when she means nothing to you. And you've already done quite enough in allowing the girl and her brother to stay here until their father returns. Which reminds me, why *did* you evict them from their home?"

Jonathan was overstepping the bounds of their relationship in asking questions that were none of his business. He knew that, of course. His slight blush said as much. Yet he wasn't going to retract the question, because his interest in Larissa naturally included all information he could gather about her, and he no doubt hoped Vincent would realize that and supply some of it.

Vincent sighed. It wasn't his habit to lie, yet he seemed to be doing a great deal of it since he'd met Larissa. And having assured Jonathan that he had no interest in the girl himself, he couldn't very well tell the viscount that she'd been brought into his home so he could seduce her, or that his goal was to ruin her family's good name. That would be information Hale would relish sharing with Larissa, if for no other reason than he'd expect her to be grateful.

So he found himself continuing the lie he'd already begun with her. "It was a business decision carried out before I was aware that George Ascot wasn't in the country and so unavailable to move his family elsewhere. When it did come to my attention that his children would be left homeless and without guidance, I brought them here to await his return."

"Ah, well, glad to hear you aren't completely heartless," Jonathan replied.

Vincent frowned, remarking, "Not to say I admit to having a heart in that context, but just what was heartless about my actions?"

"Evicting them during the holidays," Jonathan clarified. "Rather harsh, that."

"Bah, just what do the holidays have to do with conducting business as usual?"

Jonathan blinked. "Well, actually, nothing, now you mention it. It's just that this particular holiday is synonymous with generosity and goodwill."

"Sorry, but unlike you, I have no sentimentality toward this holiday, nor any preconceived notions about it. For me it's just another day."

"Now, that's sad, Vincent."

"Why?"

"Because you've obviously never experienced the joy and cheer that go along with the generosity and goodwill. Quite uplifting, if I do say so myself. Enemies call truce. Neighbors remember they have neighbors. You find good cheer and well-wishes everywhere you look. You can't say you've never experienced any of that."

Vincent shrugged. "Not that I recall."

"Bloody hell, I thought you were English," Jonathan grumbled, which caused Vincent to burst out laughing and the viscount to demand, "What's so funny?"

"Just that Larissa assumed the same thing, when I mentioned I'd never had a Christmas tree before."

"So this one here that *you* helped to decorate is just for her?" Jonathan snorted before he got an answer. "For someone who's never experienced the generosity of the season, you're being damned generous where that chit is concerned. A word of advice, then. You might want to tone that down a bit, or *she* might get the idea that you're interested in her, when, as you say, you aren't."

Chapter 19

ASSUMPTIONS HAD A WAY OF EASING DOUBTS, BUT they also crumbled when subjected to too much time and scrutiny. Such was the case for Larissa. And after a bit more than a week had gone by since the night she had succumbed to temptation, she finally had to conclude that if Vincent was going to ask her to marry him, he would have done so by now. Which meant he wasn't going to.

Oddly enough, she wasn't devastated by that conclusion. But then he hadn't broken any promise to her. He hadn't deceived her in any way. She had done that to herself with her silly assumptions.

He had been as much a victim as she of the powerful attraction between them. The end results just didn't equal the same thing for them both. She had naturally thought marriage, being a romantic at heart, while he apparently simply took his pleasure where he found it. She couldn't blame him for that. She figured it was as natural for him to do as it was for her to have expected more.

She supposed it might have hit her much worse, that he didn't want to make their relationship permanent, if she weren't already grieving over her father and what his absence meant. Ironically, she knew she had Vincent to thank for keeping her mind off of that grief.

Night after night he had come to her room. It had been addicting, his lovemaking. She had waited in breathless anticipation for his touch each night. All of which had added benefits for her that he certainly wasn't aware of, because when she was with him, she thought only of him, but when she wasn't, her grief would set in again.

She had no longer been able to hide that grief from her astute brother either. Which was why Thomas no longer asked her when their father was coming home. And she had caught Thomas crying the day he finally realized that their father wasn't coming home. But by silent agreement, they weren't going to speak of it—not yet.

So she had much to be grateful to Vincent for, not just for giving them a home for the holiday, but for his many and varied distractions when she might otherwise have wallowed in complete despair.

She still locked her door again that night, the

night before Christmas. She might be grateful to Vincent, but she couldn't continue to have an intimate relationship with him, now that she knew that was all he wanted from her.

It wasn't easy, though. It should have been. She was rather numb, after all, over the new conclusions she'd drawn. But he came as usual, softly called her name from the other side of the locked door. She didn't answer. And she knew she had tried to deceive herself again, because it was hurting more than she'd thought, that he didn't care about her as much as she'd hoped.

The tears that soaked her pillow that night were for what might have been . . .

For Thomas's sake, Larissa wore a bright, cheerful expression as she woke him and dragged him down to the parlor to open his presents, which she had bought and had hidden away many months ago. He had tucked a few under the tree for her as well, when she wasn't looking, carvings he had made himself, and some for Mara and Mary, who joined them for the fun of present opening.

Of course, it wasn't a normal Christmas for them. It wasn't their house, wasn't even their tree that they'd put presents under. But that had nothing to do with giving. Christmas wasn't about a place, after all; for them it was about family, and

sharing, and love. And that was where it wasn't
normal, since they weren't a complete family this
Christmas and were sore missing that complete-
ness on such a traditional day of gathering together.

Mara and Mary helped them to forget, ohing
and ahing over Thomas's whittling skill, which
was improving each year, and over the little trinkets Larissa gave them, which, fortunately, she
had bought before the money ran out. Mary
didn't stay long, though, anxious to get to the
kitchen, which was Larissa's real gift to her, having talked Vincent's cook into letting Mary cook
the Christmas goose for dinner, which she did so
well.

She didn't worry about Thomas getting over-
excited either, as he tended to do on Christmas,
though she would have a week ago. But he was
recovered from his sickness finally, thank God,
not quite as full of energy yet, but much more his
usual buoyant self.

"May I have a word alone with your sister?"

Vincent stood in the open doorway. He looked
a bit hesitant to enter the room.

Thomas, to whom the question had been ad-
dressed, didn't glance his way, nor was there any
inflection in his voice when he replied, "Not if
you're going to make her cry again."

"Excuse me?" Stiffness now.

"Her eyes are all red—"

"Thomas, hush!" Larissa cut in, thoroughly embarrassed by now. "That has nothing to do with him," she added, and blushed a bit more for the lie. "Please, take your new soldiers and go upstairs. I'll join you shortly."

Thomas gave her a disgusted look that indicated he knew very well she was lying. But Mara, much more tactful, helped him gather his new wooden soldiers and books, and half prodded, half dragged him out of the room.

Vincent wasn't nearly as astute, or deliberately chose not to be, because as soon as they were alone, he said, "You were crying over your father again?"

"No."

He blushed now. Well, if he hadn't wanted the truth, he shouldn't have asked a question that would lead to it. And she didn't take pity on him. It was time for plain speaking between them. He had repeatedly avoided or evaded her questions when they were alone at night, and in the day there was never the opportunity to speak of anything personal with so many servants always near to hand. But for once they were alone, and he wasn't kissing her to distraction or cutting her off with silly remarks until he *could* kiss her to distraction. In fact, for once, he was the one with burning questions.

"Why wouldn't you answer me last night?"

"Probably for the same reason you never answer me," she replied.

"What are you talking about?"

She gave him a sad smile. "Come now, Vincent, obtuseness doesn't become you. Anytime I ever begin to mention marriage in your presence, you pounce on another subject so swiftly, I don't even have time to blink. Very well, so marriage is a subject we will never discuss. And now that I've come to realize that, it is rather obvious, isn't it, why my door will henceforth remain locked?"

He frowned. He also started to approach her. She quickly held up a hand, even took several steps back.

Letting him touch her was out of the question, not because it was out in the open now, that he had no intention of marrying her, but because she was too malleable in his arms. But oh God, why didn't the knowledge she now possessed stop her from wanting him? She should despise him—again. She shouldn't be wishing fervently that he would deny it and assure her that yes, of course they would marry.

"You don't really want to do this to us, Larissa, do you?"

His tactics were on the rise, and he had many that he knew would work, including that husky tone he'd just used. How was she going to survive this?

"I don't, but you do. Whether we continue as we were, or we say good-bye today, is entirely up to you. I can only follow my heart."

"Your heart isn't telling you to shut me out."

No, it wasn't. She hadn't realized she had fallen so deeply in love with him. She had begun this only thinking it would be nice to marry him. She hadn't thought why it would be so nice. But all the little things she knew about him had gotten to her, first to her compassion, then into her heart. The overwhelming attraction she felt for him was merely a side benefit—or a curse.

She tried to point out what he seemed to be missing. "Temptation is a lure of the forbidden. By all that's right, you are forbidden to me. Preference has no bearing. If it were just me, if I had no others that I am responsible for, then it might not matter so much. But I have a young brother to raise now—on my own. And he will be taught by example, just as my father would have taught him, the correct path."

"Your father wouldn't have been a good— Never mind." He cut himself off.

He raked a hand through his black mane. His frustration was evident and mounting. Or was it anger? It was hard to tell with him, when he so rarely showed any emotion—other than passion.

She didn't doubt for a minute that he liked their current relationship and wanted it to continue.

The emotion he was displaying was because he didn't want her to end it. But she had no choice. He might care for her, but not enough to want to make her a permanent part of his life. And what did that leave her? What exactly had he envisioned for her? Being his mistress, when her upbringing simply wouldn't allow it? Or had he envisioned no more than a brief love affair that was ending sooner than he'd expected?

She was starting to feel some frustration herself, which was welcome, really. Anything to distract her from the pain squeezing at her heart.

"Vincent, I don't know what you want from me. Do you even know?"

"I know I don't want you to leave me."

"Only marriage would assure that."

"Blast it," he exploded. "I *can't* marry you."

She frowned. "Why not?"

"Because of your father."

Confusion filled her, and with it, alarm. "What about him?"

"There are things you don't know."

"Then tell me!"

"You revere him, Larissa," he replied. "It's better if you don't know."

She paled, drawing her own conclusions yet again. "He *is* dead, isn't he? And you've known all along. You've received proof—"

"*No!*" He pounced this time, before she could

step back again, but only to grab her shoulders. He shook her once. "No, it's nothing like that. Ah, bloody hell, it's not worth it anymore. *You're* more important. But your father is only detained. There's no reason to assume the worst. In fact, I wouldn't be surprised if he showed up today at my door—"

The knock at the front door was too loud to miss hearing, and too prophetic not to strongly affect Larissa. She went utterly still. She held her breath in hopeful anticipation. But it was too much anticipation to wait. She broke out of Vincent's hold, heard him sigh, but ignored it. She ran to the open doorway of the parlor, stared as his butler rushed to deal with the loud visitor.

"I didn't mean he would literally show up this minute, Larissa," Vincent said behind her in a voice that was already starting to reveal sympathy.

She ignored him again, wouldn't listen to denials anymore. This was her *last* hope. Dear God, let it be her father. She'd never ask for another thing, never . . .

It wasn't her father. It was a big, burly man standing there, asking if this was where the Baron of Windsmoor lived. She didn't hear any more after that. A ringing began in her ears. Her vision blurred. She grasped the fact that she was fainting and almost laughed, because she was made of sterner stuff than that. Wasn't she? She had probably just held her breath too long . . .

Vincent caught her before her legs completely buckled. She heard him calling her name, trying to keep her there when her mind was insisting on the oblivion of nothingness. He sounded like her father. Stupid mind playing tricks on her now. He demanded she open her eyes. No, she didn't want to. No more disappointments. She'd had too many.

"Rissa, please, just look at me."

Vincent had never called her Rissa. She opened her eyes, then forgot to breathe again.

"Papa?" she whispered. "Is that really you?"

For an answer, she was pulled into an old, familiar embrace, one of warmth, comfort and love, and everything-will-be-fine-now, an embrace she had grown up depending on. It was he. Oh, God, it was he, alive, and home, and alive, alive . . .

Great, racking sobs of emotion overcame her. She couldn't help it. Her prayers had been answered. The season of miracles had given her one.

Chapter 20

"WHY ARE MY CHILDREN HERE?"

It was the first thing George Ascot said to Vincent once they were alone. He was a big, heavyset man in his middle years. His light brown hair had a bit of gray at the temples; the trimmed beard had much more. His eyes were disconcertingly the exact shade of blue-green as Larissa's, with that same warmth indicative of a compassionate nature, falsely so in his case, of course.

Vincent had stood there silently and watched the tearful reunion, witnessed the love and tenderness pouring out of the father for the daughter, which had somewhat surprised him. But what had he expected? Just because the man dealt viciously with his competitors didn't mean he couldn't love his family. Even a devil could love his children if he had any and be no less evil, he supposed.

Larissa shouldn't have left them alone. She had

finished her crying, and finally her laughing, and had run upstairs to fetch her brother to give him the good news. She hadn't even asked yet what had detained her father. That wasn't very important to her apparently, now that he was safe and sound—and home.

Vincent could have offered the man excuses. He could have made amends as well. If she hadn't left them alone, he might have, for he'd already decided that his revenge wasn't worth losing her. An amazing discovery which she had only just forced him to realize. But as he stood there alone in the hall with the man responsible for his brother's death, the feelings returned that started it all. And unfortunately, those feelings governed his response.

"You left them without guidance or wherewithal; they had nowhere else to go," Vincent said.

George would have had to be deaf to miss the disgust in Vincent's tone, and although he didn't understand it yet, he still took offense, replying stiffly, "Rissa had ample household funds."

"When there were panicked creditors hounding her to settle accounts?"

"Panicked? What could possibly—?"

"Rumors that your underhanded business practices led you to financial ruin perhaps?"

"Preposterous!"

Vincent shrugged, unimpressed with the man's

florid-faced indignation. "You weren't here to prove otherwise, were you? In fact, your prolonged absence only confirmed and strengthened the suspicions that you weren't planning on returning to England at all."

"My family was still here! No one in their right mind would conclude that I would abandon them!"

"Someone without ethics wouldn't worry about throwing his family to the wolves. It happens all the time. Besides, how were your creditors to know that your family wasn't already making plans to abandon England as well?"

George became infused with even more indignant color. "You sound as if you believe those ridiculous rumors."

"Perhaps because I do."

"Why? You don't even know me."

"Don't I? Did you not learn my name before you sent your driver pounding on my door?"

George frowned at that point, explaining, "I come home to find my house empty of my family and all furnishings. My nearest neighbors inform me that I can find my family, at least, at Baron Windsmoor's residence and give me the address Rissa left with them. No, actually, I got no more than your title before I hied it here in all haste. Is your name relevant? Just who are you, sir?"

"Vincent Everett."

"Good God, you aren't related to that black-guard Albert Everett, are you?"

Vincent stiffened now. "My brother, now referred to as deceased."

"He's dead?" George asked in surprise. "I'm sorry, I didn't know."

"Don't be a hypocrite, Ascot," Vincent said in disgust. "Sorrow from the man who drove him to his death just doesn't smack of sincerity."

"Drove him—!" George gasped. "What madness are you spouting now?"

"So now you would claim ignorance? Very well, let me refresh your memory, then. Albert used what little was left of his inheritance to start a business that would support him. Unfortunately, he picked your line of business, and you went out of your way to make sure that he knew the added competition wasn't welcome."

"That isn't—"

"Let me finish," Vincent interrupted. "You undermined his efforts at every turn, had your captains escalate the bids on the cargoes he was after, so he couldn't hope to make a profit on them. You made sure his business would fail, and so it did. You crushed my brother thoroughly, so much so that he killed himself rather than admit to me that he had lost everything. You didn't really think his family would let you get away with that, did you, Ascot?"

The indignation was gone. The older man was red-faced with fury now, though his voice managed to remain calm as he replied, "You have that a bit backwards, sir. If your brother's business failed, it was because he was buying cargoes—*my* cargoes, already contracted to me—at ridiculously high prices, so he was unable to sell them at even close to a return on the investment. I had assumed he had an unlimited supply of funds to do this, which is why I gave up trying to regain the markets he was stealing from me, and sailed west to find new markets. I hadn't heard that he failed, or I wouldn't have left."

"So you're saying that Albert tried to drive you to ruin, and ruined himself in the process?"

"Exactly."

"That's rather convenient, you'll agree, an easy claim to make against a man who can't step forward to deny it, because he's dead."

"The truth is not always easy to swallow, sir, though it can usually be verified. You have only to question my captains, or perhaps the merchants involved, who ignored valid contracts with me to reap quick profits from your brother. These cargoes weren't on the open market to be bid upon as you mentioned, they had set prices already agreed upon. Or perhaps question your brother's own captains, who can tell you that their orders were to obtain cargoes at any costs.

Now, whether his captains acted on their own or under his direction, the results were the same. They followed my ships specifically, showing up in all the same ports."

"So now you would put the blame on his captains?" Vincent said.

George sighed. "Actually, I put the blame where it belongs, on your brother. I spoke to him before I left England, to try to find out why he was throwing away good money on underhanded tactics, rather than put a little effort into finding new markets for himself where he could have made easy profits. In all fairness, he struck me as a man who simply didn't know what he was doing, but was too proud to admit it. Ironically, his tactics would have worked if he had enough money to see it through. Obviously he didn't have enough, and instead, he ruined himself and nearly ruined me in the process."

Vincent shook his head. "Do you really think I would believe you over my brother? I know his faults, and he has never denied them, nor his mistakes. So why would he lie in this instance? He claimed that you, and you specifically, caused him to fail."

"I can't imagine why he singled me out for blame, and I suppose I will never know, since he's deceased. But I'm obviously wasting my breath professing my innocence to you, when you refuse to see beyond the few facts you have been told. So be it. But if you believe all that, why would you help my family?"

"What makes you think I've helped them?"

George stiffened. It was the tone that alarmed him. "What have you done?"

Vincent didn't answer. The moment was at hand, the moment he had worked for, when all he had to say was, "Paid you back in kind," and he couldn't say it. He couldn't go on with this. Not because he believed Ascot; he didn't. But he was himself as much to blame for Albert's death as Ascot was. He hadn't pulled the cords that led to Albert's decision, as Ascot had, but he had done nothing to influence that decision either.

He hadn't recognized it before, had merely seen this revenge thing as doing his duty, more or less. But there was guilt involved, his own, for failing to pay more attention to his brother, for failing to develop a relationship with him in which Albert wouldn't have hesitated to bring even this worst failure of his to Vincent's attention, rather than give up all hope and kill himself instead.

Their parents had spoiled and coddled Albert so much that he was unable to stand on his own after their deaths. He had needed constant bolstering. Having that cut off abruptly by their deaths had hurt him. Vincent could have helped, could have weaned him slowly from his dependence, or at least tried to instill some confidence. Instead he had viewed Albert's weaknesses with disgust, while doing nothing to help his brother overcome them.

"I repeat, what have you done?"

"Nothing that can't be rec—"

"Having somehow managed to buy our home, he then kicked us out of it so we would have no place else to go," Larissa said at the top of the stairs in a dull voice. "Then brought us here so he could seduce me—with no intention of marrying me—which he did quite easily. He took full advantage of my vulnerability in thinking you were dead, Father. He used my grief to aid him, because I needed a distraction from it, and he was that; indeed, he was quite the distraction."

She was staring down at Vincent without expression, as if all emotion had been sucked out of her—or she had no room left for any more. Her brother was standing next to her, staring daggers at Vincent as he slipped his hand into hers to offer comfort. The boy sensed she was in pain even if she wasn't showing it.

Had they heard everything? Yes, they must have for her to have drawn such an accurate conclusion. But unlike him, they, of course, believed their father without question, that he had done no wrong. And Albert wasn't there to prove otherwise, never would be. Not that it mattered; they would still believe their father, despite the fact that it was Albert who had been ruined, not Ascot.

And if Ascot was telling the truth? No, it wasn't possible, and besides, if Albert had been in the wrong, then Vincent had also been in the wrong to seek revenge on his behalf. That thought didn't sit well with him at all—indeed, positively sickened him—yet it was no worse than what he was feeling now, looking up at Larissa. Such utter dread. He felt as if he had just lost the most valuable thing in his life, and so he had, her respect, her sympathy—her love.

He *should* continue with his revenge for his brother's sake, but he couldn't, because of her. Yet he was going to suffer the consequences either way. Even if he set everything to rights, it would not make a difference with her. He'd sought retribution against a man she saw as innocent, and used her to do it. She'd never forgive him for that. Not even if he managed to convince her that her father was the real culprit. Not that he could, when he only had Albert's letter as proof, and she could claim that was fake.

Yet he had to try. The fear washing over him that he had lost her was more than he could bear.

He said, "There is a letter that will at least explain my actions—"

"I don't doubt you had good reasons for doing

what you did," she cut in. "Does that excuse harming the innocent to gain your goal?"

"No," he was forced to reply. "No, the goal became merely an excuse, once I met you."

She blushed. He knew she understood he was saying her seduction had been personal, had nothing really to do with the revenge. But as he'd known, it made no difference. Nor was he allowed to explain further. Her father had recovered by then from his shock in hearing that his daughter had been compromised. He was quite straightforward in his reaction. No demand for marriage, just a very furious fist that caught Vincent by surprise. The Ascots were gone by the time he regained his senses.

Chapter 21

"She didn't take her Christmas ornaments with her when she left? I wonder why, when they hold such great sentimental value for her."

Vincent didn't answer Jonathan Hale or acknowledge his presence. He didn't want the company, but hadn't thought to tell his butler that he wasn't receiving visitors today. He'd been sitting there in his parlor, alone, staring at Larissa's Christmas tree and recalling that day it was decorated, the enjoyment he'd had, the laughter . . .

He'd felt a part of something that day, rather than the outsider always looking in, as was usually the case for him. That was Larissa's doing. She shared with everyone, excluded no one. She'd made even his servants feel that her tree was their tree, got Jonathan involved in its decoration just because he happened to be there. For her it was an event that began the sharing of the season.

He didn't answer Jonathan, because he was afraid he wouldn't be able to get any words out without their sounding as choked as he felt. But the viscount either didn't notice his preoccupation or chose to overlook it.

Jonathan knew Larissa was gone, that her father had taken her away, and that their whereabouts were presently unknown. He wasn't happy about that, and Vincent was surprised he hadn't asked, "Have you found her yet?" which was his usual first inquiry when he stopped by each day now, and had been for the last week. The painting, his reason for coming there, was rarely mentioned anymore. It had become quite secondary in importance to his pursuit of Larissa.

"Some of them had been made by her mother, you know," Jonathan continued. "A few were even made by her grandparents, and one, that she prized the most, a great-grandfather had whittled. Seems to be somewhat of a tradition in her family, the making of Christmas ornaments. Found that rather quaint myself. Even contemplated making an ornament and giving it to her as a Christmas present, but gave up that idea quick enough. Just ain't talented in that way."

Vincent sighed and finally glanced at his visitor. "There is no news to report," he said, hoping that would send Jonathan on his way.

"Didn't think there would be. I'm just in the habit of coming by daily now. Didn't think you'd mind, and I've decided to take it upon myself to cheer you up."

"I don't need cheering."

"Course you don't," Jonathan said dryly. "You aren't the least bit sick to your guts with missing her. It's too bad you didn't realize sooner that you'd been lying to yourself all along about her."

"Wouldn't have taken you for a man to jump to false conclusions, Jon."

Jonathan chuckled. "Still lying to yourself, or just to me?"

"Go home," Vincent mumbled.

"And let you wallow in all this misery by yourself?" Jonathan said as he dropped down on the sofa beside Vincent. "Now, here I thought the old adage was that misery loves company. I know I ain't enjoying wallowing in mine alone."

"You know bloody well that Larissa would only have been another acquisition for you. You didn't form any deep attachment to her."

"True, which is why my misery is quite mild compared to yours."

"I'm *not* miserable."

Jonathan snorted over that denial. "You're so deep in the doldrums you can no longer see daylight. 'Fess up, man, you were an utter fool not to get the gel engaged to you while you had the chance."

"You don't understand what was going on here," Vincent gritted out.

Jonathan raised a brow. "Apparently not," he allowed, but added, "Did you?"

"Excuse me?"

"Did you realize that she was in love with you? I saw it, though I tried my damnedest to ignore it, of course. Didn't fit with my plans, after all, for her to get so attached elsewhere that my millions wouldn't tempt her. True love just don't come with a price tag, unfortunately."

"I really don't want to talk about this."

"Why not? Or don't you plan to do things right, if given a second chance?"

A second chance? Vincent hadn't thought that far ahead. He *was* making an effort to find Larissa. He *did* plan to lay the truth at her feet, all of it. But he wasn't very hopeful that it would do any good, other than to clear his conscience. And after nearly a week had gone by, he wasn't very hopeful that he'd ever see her again.

He didn't expect her to personally come back to collect what she'd left behind, but he had counted on at least someone, even if only a servant, show-ing up to do so. But she hadn't sent anyone by to claim her jewels from him. She still didn't even know where those furnishings of hers had been stored. Demanding one or the other would have given him someone to have followed to lead to her, but no one had come.

Hotels and inns had been searched. He had people scouring the whole town and watching Ascot's office around the clock. The ship George had returned in was still in the harbor waiting for permission to dock, so at least he was still in the country. But there was simply no clue as to where he had taken his family off to.

Jonathan apparently got tired of waiting for an answer to his last question. With a sigh he said, "I have a confession to make."

Vincent winced mentally. "Don't. I'm not in the mood for confessions."

"Too bad," Jonathan grumbled. "Because this one is coming whether you listen or not. I came to you to find *La Nymph* for me, not just because I desire to own that painting. There are countless others I could have hired to find the painting, and for much less cost to me. I came to you in particular because I like you, Vincent, I like your style, like the fact that you've never tried to ingratiate yourself with me to get something out of me, as is the case with most people I know. I have no friends, you know, no real friends, that is."

"Nonsense, you don't go anywhere that people don't flock to your side—"

"Leeches, the lot of them," Jonathan cut in, disgust in his tone. "They don't care about me or what I'm feeling, they only care about how they can manage to get some of my money into their pockets. And that's always been the case, even when I was a child. I was born rich, after all."

"Why are you telling me this?" Vincent asked uncomfortably.

Jonathan's cheeks bloomed with a bit of color, but he still admitted, "Because I had great hopes that you would become the close friend I've never had. And since nothing else has worked to accomplish that thus far, I'm falling back on the old premise that confidences are a sound basis for developing lasting friendships. And besides, you don't seem to have any close friends yourself. Do you?"

Vincent saw no reason to deny it. "No."

"Well then—"

"You haven't gathered yet that I am rather reclusive?" Vincent pointed out.

"Course I have, which is one of the things I like about you. And just because I flit about here and there doesn't mean I enjoy doing so, just that I'm so bloody lonely, I crave companionship of any sort, even from sycophants, if that's all that's available."

Vincent was beginning to get embarrassed over these "confidences," not so much because Jonathan felt a sudden need to pour out his guts, but because his confession was sounding much too familiar. He hadn't realized they had quite so much in common, neither of them willing to trust anyone enough to get close to them, neither of them willing to risk being hurt if anyone did.

"Are you feeling sorry for me yet?" Jonathan asked hopefully.

"No."

"Bloody hell . . ."

"But you're welcome to stay for dinner."

The viscount laughed.

Chapter 22

IRONICALLY, LARISSA WAS SITTING IN FRONT OF A
Christmas tree at the same time that Vincent was.
She was also alone, also recalling the decoration
of that other tree. This one wasn't hers and hadn't
been preserved well, was mostly brown now,
with pitifully broken branches and a pile of fallen
needles beneath it that the servants couldn't manage to keep up with. It belonged to the Applebees, good friends of her father's who still lived
in Portsmouth. He had taken her and Thomas
straightaway there after they'd left Vincent's
town house.

Despite Larissa's state of shock when they arrived there, it wasn't lost on her that she hadn't
once considered the Applebees as an option when
she had agonized over where to take her brother
when they lost their home. She would have
thought of them eventually, because they really
were very old friends of her father's, and she *had*

thought of them after she was already moved into Vincent's house, as well as her many childhood friends in Portsmouth, any one of whom would have opened his or her door to her. But by then she had conveniently ignored their existence for the simple fact that she had *wanted* to stay in the baron's home.

Of course, Thomas's illness had been the deciding factor; at least she had convinced herself of that at the time. It was better for him not to make that long trip to Portsmouth while he still had that lingering fever. But they could have managed it, could have sealed up a coach against drafts and got him there as quickly as possible if it had been necessary. Vincent's offered hospitality had made it unnecessary. And Larissa's desire to get to know Vincent better had kept her from considering those other options, even if she hadn't owned up to that at the time.

They had been staying with the Applebees now for nearly a week. It had taken that long for the shock to wear off completely for Larissa. The knowledge that she had been used in a plot for revenge had utterly crushed her. Everything she had supposed about Vincent Everett had been wrong. She had fallen in love with someone who wasn't real, who was a complete fake.

Her father had wanted to comfort her, but after her first outburst of tears when he tried, he had decided the best way to help her get over her heartache was to not discuss it at all, which meant not discussing Vincent. She was grateful for that. She really couldn't bear to talk about him yet, when just thinking about him could start the tears flooding again. But she had been in such a state of despair that she hadn't done much communicating with her father at all yet.

She still didn't even know what had kept him from returning to London for so long. If he had mentioned it, and she supposed he probably had, she hadn't been listening. When she was around, a lot of whispering tended to go on. The Applebees were kind, but if they had been told why she was mired in such misery, they no doubt pitied her.

They were a large family. William and Ethel's four children had married and had young families of their own, and all came to visit their parents at this special time of the year. The house was full. It was a large house, though, so there had been plenty of room for the Ascots, and Thomas had many youngsters to keep him quite occupied. A blessing that, because if her father might be kindly avoiding the subject of her unhappiness, her brother certainly wouldn't have if he could have found her alone. Fortunately, with so many people in the house, it was rare to find anyone alone—until today. The Applebees' four married children had all left to go back to their respective homes that morning.

Because of that mass exodus, Larissa had had the parlor to herself for several hours now. No more pitying whispers. No more attempts to cheer her when she couldn't be cheered. But no more relief either, with the numbness of her shock finally fading. And much too much introspection now and mental browbeating—and anger.

The anger had sneaked up on her, not really unexpected, just all at once it was there and a lot of it, and now bitterly contained just below the surface. Having been used and deceived so easily marked her clearly as a naive fool. And Vincent had done it so easily. That was the quelling blow. She'd almost begged him to dupe her. Every tactic he'd used on her had worked, not because he was so adept at fooling people, but because she had wanted to believe that he cared about her.

Good God, he must have hated touching her, hated making love to her, despising her family as he did. And how he must have laughed at how easily she had succumbed to his seduction and his lies. Everything between them had been a lie, everything she had believed about him, a lie . . .

"Do you want to stay here with Thomas while I return to London?"

The question came from her father, who had just entered the room. At least she heard him right off this time. She recalled a number of times in the last week when he'd had to wave his hand in front of her face and repeat himself to try and get her attention.

"When are you leaving?" she asked.

"In the morning."

He was going to find them a new home. She vaguely remembered that being discussed last evening during dinner. If he went alone, he'd stay at the London office. If she went with him, he'd need to get them rooms at a hotel. She saw no reason to incur the extra expense. She hadn't asked him about his finances. It wasn't her place to ask. In the few conversations that she'd managed to hear when she wasn't so deep in self-pity, she gathered that he'd found new markets in the Caribbean and was no longer worried on that front.

"I'll stay here," she replied.

"You're feeling better?"

There was a great deal of concern in his expression. There was also some hesitancy in his tone that wasn't like him. Her state of nearly deaf distraction since his return must have begun to seriously worry him. But she saw no reason to hedge about the subject now.

"Better, no. Fully cognizant again, yes."

He smiled gently. "A little absentmindedness never—"

She cut in, "I might as well not have been here,

Father, for all the awareness I've had lately. Do you know, I don't even know what detained you from returning home when you were supposed to. Each time it has occurred to me to ask you, we haven't been in the same room, and then I as quickly forgot about it again. But I'm sure Thomas and everyone else knows by now. I'm sure you've mentioned it to me as well . . ."

"Three times, actually." He chuckled, then surprised her by saying, "Damn me, never thought I'd reach the point where I could laugh about any part of that ill-fated trip."

"Ill-fated?"

"From the moment we entered the warmer waters of the West Indies. The island we came to first wasn't a major one, though we were so happy to see land of any sort, we stopped there anyway. But as soon as we docked, we were met by the local magistrate and a full troop of guards, and charged with attacking one of the local plantation owners. The man was there to support the charge, and quite a gruesome account he gave of it, that his plantation house burned to the ground, including his barns, that our ship just sat offshore and continued to rain fire down upon his property for no apparent reason."

"Someone actually did that to him?"

"As it turns out, no. But at the time, Peter Heston was an old and well-respected member of the community whom not a single person on that island would even think of doubting, while I and my crew had never been there before and could have been pirates for all they knew. We were found guilty before there was a trial. The actual trial was a mockery where Heston repeated his ghastly tale. No other witnesses were necessary for us to be sentenced to prison."

"Prison!" she gasped, incredulous. "You were actually put in prison?"

"Yes," he replied. "And with absolutely no hope of getting out of it, when we knew that the entire island thought us guilty."

He shuddered unconsciously. She couldn't even begin to imagine how horrible that experience must have been for him and his crew. He'd never been in jail before, never suffered any real physical hardship that she was aware of. Nor should he ever have experienced anything like that, when he was a good, honest man who would never do anything that might get him arrested, much less sent to prison.

Which was what she couldn't help but point out. "But you didn't do anything!"

"No, and our ship's guns were quite cold to prove it," he agreed.

She frowned, getting a bit confused now. "Then why were you even arrested, much less put to trial?"

"Because our proof of innocence required immediate clarification, which didn't occur."

"For someone to examine the guns?"

"Yes."

"Why didn't they?"

He chuckled again. She was surprised herself now that he could, especially after he replied, "Probably because we were about to be lynched on the spot. This was midmorning, you see. And quite a few people had noticed the town guard heading for the docks and followed them. There was a huge crowd by the time we docked, and everyone there was able to hear Heston's accusations. Understandably, the magistrate wanted to break that up quickly, and could only do so by getting us off the dock and into his jail."

"When it would only have taken a moment or two for verification?"

"It was a very tense situation, Rissa. There were other plantation owners in that crowd who were no doubt thinking it could have been *their* houses that we might have destroyed. And when an issue becomes personal like that, emotions can be quite heated. We really were in danger of that mob of angry islanders taking the law into their own hands. Frankly, we were rather glad to be put behind bars until the matter could be straightened out. Knowing ourselves innocent, we didn't really doubt at the time that it would be straightened out, so we were more concerned with the angry crowd than with the charges being filed against us."

"Yes, I suppose the immediate threat would have been of more concern," she agreed. "But you said the man's house hadn't really burned down. Why weren't you released after that was discovered."

"No, I said no one else had done it to him," he corrected her.

She blinked. "He burned down his own house?"

George nodded. "But that didn't come to light soon enough to keep us out of prison. And at the time, the magistrate had two completely conflicting accounts on the matter, so whom do you think he would be inclined to believe?"

"Heston, of course."

"Exactly. The man's plantation really had burned to the ground. Our ship's guns hadn't been fired. These were facts that we were assured were both going to be investigated right after we were all secured in the jail. But too much time had passed, on getting us secured and getting the crowd to finally disperse. And since it wasn't immediately proven that the guns weren't heated the least bit from use, it couldn't be proven at all. Yet there was a burned-down plantation, proof for the other side, and the word of one of their own well-known and respected citizens."

Larissa shook her head. "How did the truth finally get discovered?"

"When Peter Heston's wife finally returned to the island. She had been there that day when Heston went completely mad. She had known his mind wasn't quite right for a long time, but she had never warned anyone, since his increasingly strange behavior had seemed harmless. But early that morning she came upon him starting the fires. He was raving that there were pirates hiding on the property and the only way to flush them out was to give them no place to hide by burning everything to the ground."

"There weren't any, though?"

"No, it was all in his mind. She tried to stop him, of course. But he didn't recognize her. He thought her one of the pirates and tried to kill her as well."

"How horrible for her."

"Yes, though she did manage to escape, and by the quickest means possible. Unfortunately, that was by boat. They lived on the coast, had their own small dock where Heston kept a fishing vessel. She used that, leaving the island completely rather than going to town to get help."

"I think I would have rather been out in the water where he couldn't reach me than still on the island where he might catch up to me, if I were her."

"Yes, I suppose you're right. Never looked at it from her perspective, merely from my own, which included her long delay in returning. I would have preferred she come straight to town to report what had happened, thus leaving my crew and me out of the incident completely, but she was so frightened by having her own husband not recognize her, call her a pirate and try to kill her, that she wanted only to get as far from him as possible."

"Where did she go?"

"She had a daughter by her first marriage, who lived on a nearby island. Unfortunately the daughter wasn't home, was on a shopping trip to the mainland."

"Unfortunately?"

"It was the daughter who convinced her that she had to return to get help for Heston, who was obviously quite crazy now, before someone did get hurt by him. Heston's wife had been thinking only of her own safety, which included never returning to her own home. Which was why so much time passed before she did return and the truth was learned."

"Why was there no one else around to witness the fire and how it started? Had they no servants at all?"

"That was one of my own questions, answered by one of the jailers. It was common knowledge that Heston had had bad crops for three out of the last four years. Other plantation owners in the area had suffered from the same bad weather, but it wasn't all a weather problem, not for all three of the bad years. Most of it was likely part of his decline; he simply wasn't attending to his crops properly. But the Hestons were barely making a living by then, because of so many failed crops. The plantation workers were seasonal, so none were around this time of the year. But the house servants had been let go a few years ago. And they lived on the far east end of the island, with no other neighbors close by."

"It is amazing indeed that you can laugh about any of that misadventure."

He grinned at her. "It really wasn't that much of a hardship, their prison. What I find amusing myself is there was no one else in it. The place had been closed up for years. They had to open it and clean it up just for our benefit. There was even a debate to just keep us in the jail instead, though it was finally decided the accommodations there just weren't big enough to contain an entire ship's crew."

"The island was that small?"

"Compare it to one of our country villages and you can imagine the size, and how everyone would know everyone else, which tends to keep down crime. The only reason they even had a prison on the island was it had many years ago been converted from an old fort, which was no longer in use. But we were well fed for our brief sojourn, and not mistreated. The worst part of it all was our boredom—they had yet to decide how to put us to work—and our outrage and sense of hopelessness. In fact, we spent all our time there plotting escape, which we probably would have succeeded at eventually had we been forced to stay there much longer."

"What happened to Peter Heston?"

"Considering he went berserk in town when he saw his wife there, and tried once again to kill her, proving to everyone just how crazy he is now, he's been moved to another island that has a religious order which runs a house to care for the aged and mentally imbalanced. He'll live out his days under the supervision of the nuns there."

"And the townspeople who convicted you out of hand, based on one man's word?"

"Oh, they were duly repentant, so much so that we have been given exclusive shipping rights to all their crops for the next five years."

Larissa raised a brow at her father's new grin. "You find that adequate recompense?"

"Hardly." He chuckled. "Particularly after it came to light that the island was dying due to being so far off the normal shipping lines that they couldn't get ships to come their way."

She huffed indignantly. "So you will be a benefit to them if you agree to contract their crops."

"Certainly, but it satisfied my own goals," he replied. "I will in fact probably have to buy another ship or two to accommodate an entire island—now that I know my old markets are available again."

She could have wished that the conversation had not turned indirectly to the Everetts. But the fact was inescapable that had Albert Everett not forced her father to seek new markets in the West Indies because he stole his old ones, he wouldn't have spent time in prison, would never have had to leave England, so they wouldn't have lost their house—and she wouldn't have met Vincent.

"I am glad you can find something amusing about all this," she said bitterly. "I can't. I thought you were dead. I thought nothing else could have kept you away from home for so long. I imagined shipwrecks, horrible storms, yes, even pirates. Never would I have imagined you detained in a prison, because I know you would never do anything that might break any laws."

He put his arms around her, advising, "Let it go, Rissa. It's all over now. I'm home, safe, in good health, and have even benefited from the mishaps of the journey. Don't be angry on my account."

"I'm not, I'm furious that the Everetts have

done us such an injustice and yet won't pay for it."

"We know how pointless revenge is."

"I know." She sighed.

"And you don't mean *the* Everetts, you mean Vincent Everett in particular. His brother apparently met justice at his own hand."

Chapter 23

ALBERT WASN'T DEAD.

It took a while for Vincent to assimilate that fact. He thought hoax. He thought cruel joke. He even thought of George Ascot. After all, how better for Ascot to completely absolve himself of any wrongdoing than by imparting the information contained in the letter that was delivered to Vincent, which painted Ascot as innocent? And it was hand-delivered by a sailor. There was no proof that Albert had written the letter; even his signature could have been a copy.

That thought didn't last long. The letter was from Albert. The tone in it was his, impossible to duplicate without knowing him well. And references were made that Ascot couldn't have been aware of, without seeing the first letter.

Albert wasn't dead.

It should have been elating news and just that, instead of the incredible shock it was. But then it came with a confession that just about everything in Albert's first letter had been lies and excuses. He placed all blame now where it belonged, on himself. No apologies, not even for giving the wrong impression about his death. Albert hadn't realized he had done so, so he had no idea that Vincent might have picked up the gauntlet for him.

I know you were probably expecting to never hear from me again. I was rather foxed when I wrote you that farewell letter, but I do vaguely recall saying I would never be back. That hasn't changed. I have no desire to ever return to England, where I feel so inadequate to my peers. Where I live now, everything is on an equal footing. Even a beggar can pick himself up by his bootstraps and start over. Which is what I've done.

I did think you might like to hear of my progress, in getting my life in order. And perhaps a better explanation is due, at least a sober one this time, of what brought me to complete failure.

It was so hard to compete with you, brother. You were such a bloody success. Everything you touched turned to gold. I know I shouldn't have felt a need to compete with that, but I did, and that was where I went wrong. Success didn't come to me quick enough, so I tried to rush it. And when that didn't work, I turned more and more to drink, which was truly my downfall.

It got to where I didn't know what I was doing half the time. I hired captains who were less than honest. One was rumored to have been a pirate in his younger years, but since he promised to make me rich, I ignored the rumors. I let them advise me. Everything they told me sounded reasonable; at least when I was foxed it did. But they were under the mistaken impression, which I gave them, of course, that I had an endless supply of blunt backing me. Well you might imagine how some business strategies might work in that case, where they wouldn't otherwise.

I'm not making excuses. I've done that all my life, but no more. My failure was the culmination of a lot of bad decisions, all of them mine. I never should have started something that I had no experience in, and when it began to turn sour, I wallowed in self-pity and drink instead of seeking proper help. I was blaming everyone else at the time, including other shippers, because I simply couldn't own up to the fact that I didn't know what I was doing. So someone else had to be the culprit, not I. Childish, I know, but at least I can recognize that now.

I left England in a panic, of course. My letter to you then might have indicated that, though I confess I don't recall everything I said to you in it. Ironic that neither of my two ships was in port at this moment of desertion, so I stowed away on another ship—and was discovered the first day out to sea and put to work scrubbing decks. At least they didn't boot me off the ship in the middle of the ocean.

I haven't had a drink since I left England, nor do I want one. Being completely broke on my arrival in America, I had the choice of begging or getting a job. Pride notwithstanding—that had been completely crushed when I was on my knees swabbing decks—I found a job as a baker's helper. Really nice chap, the baker. He's taken me under his wing, teaching me his craft, and is even talking about expanding, now that I've become so adept with the ovens. I don't mind saying my muffins are good enough to drool over.

I don't expect to become rich here. I no longer have a burning desire to do so. I find satisfaction now in a simple day's work and wage. Even my pride has returned, due to the praise of our customers.

I hope this letter reaches you before Christmas, and leaves you with a smile and the assurance that you no longer need to worry on my account. My gift to you is that baby brother has finally grown up. Do keep in touch, Vince. The only thing that I miss about England is you.

The letter was a nice gift, would have been even nicer if it had arrived before Christmas as intended, before Vincent confronted George Ascot with what he had thought to be the truth. He wasn't going to make excuses for himself either. He'd been wrong in his beliefs, and wrong to seek revenge of any sort, particularly when, as Ascot had said, a little investigation would have pointed out some of the discrepancies in his brother's false accusations.

Once more he was mired in guilt, and not just for failing his brother. Albert had managed to land on his feet and was getting on admirably with his life, while Vincent now had to deal with his own shortcomings. He had wronged an innocent family, severely wronged them, and he wasn't sure how to make amends for that, if he even could. Returning what he had taken from them wouldn't be enough, not to satisfy him. Nothing was going to help there, when in his rash undertaking he had ended up hurting the woman he had come to love.

Chapter 24

GEORGE ASCOT WAS FINALLY FOUND. TWO DAYS before the New Year arrived, he showed up at his company office in London. He even spent the night there, giving Vincent ample time to arrange around-the-clock surveillance so that he could be followed when he left. It also gave him the opportunity to speak privately with Ascot himself.

Apologies were owed, whether they would be accepted or not. He at least wanted to assure the man that the vendetta was over. He didn't expect the visit to assuage his guilt. Not even complete forgiveness or understanding would do that, when he couldn't manage to forgive himself.

The office was locked when he arrived. He chose the earliest hour possible just after dawn, well before Ascot's clerk was due. He was aware he might catch Ascot still sleeping, but they would at least be assured of privacy at that hour.

George hadn't been sleeping. But he certainly

wasn't receptive to his visitor either. Having opened the door, he took one look at Vincent and began to close it again.

"A moment is all I ask," Vincent said.

"When it's all I can do to keep from bloodying your face, a moment is too long."

George's expression said he wasn't exaggerating. He looked absolutely furious. And he was a big man. He might well be able to do considerable "bloodying" even if Vincent defended himself. Of course, Vincent's guilt wouldn't let him defend himself, but neither would a beating help him to get rid of it, so he would prefer discourse to violence.

"I am here to offer apologies and an explanation, though the latter is more for my benefit than yours."

"An apology when you think me guilty? Or have you found out that I'm not the villain you took me for?"

"I set out to ruin you. An eye for a eye. I make no excuses for that, other than I really did think you indirectly responsible in contributing to my brother's death. But you were correct that I was lax in not verifying the facts. I have since learned the truth."

"Not from me, you didn't," George said bitterly. "You refused to believe me."

"Would you have taken the word of a stranger over that of your brother?"

"If I had such a weak-kneed brother, I just might," George said.

It was the contempt in the tone, rather than the actual words, that caused Vincent to flush with embarrassment. "He was weak, yes, but he wasn't known to lie. However, he was also foxed when he wrote his parting letter, doesn't even recall much of what he said in it, and to give him his due, he didn't suspect that I might mistake his intentions and seek revenge on his behalf."

"Doesn't recall? Are you saying he didn't kill himself after all?"

"I have only just received another letter from him, a sober one this time. He has settled in America. He now takes all blame onto himself for his failure here."

"Which leaves you having pursued vengeance against an innocent party."

"Given the information I had, in my mind, it wasn't fair that you would escape without any consequences at all, when you had set out to ruin a competitor and had succeeded, perhaps more than you had planned, but succeeded nonetheless. But my original information was wrong, so yes, I have myself become the villain in this whole debacle, due to my mistaken beliefs. For this I do humbly apologize and will make amends as you see fit. I begin with these."

"What is this?" George asked skeptically, accepting the packet of documents.

"The deed to your home, in your name, all debt satisfied. The address is also there, where your furnishings are stored. I have also set about correcting the rumors about your financial straits. Your presence again in England confirms the falseness of the original rumors. If you have any further difficulty over this matter—"

"I will see to it myself."

"As you wish," Vincent replied, realizing he was insulting the man in implying that he couldn't handle the situation on his own. "I merely didn't want you to have to be bothered correcting what I set in motion, if I have overlooked any other effects it might have had."

"If you wish to make amends, do so by staying away from me and my family, so we can forget that you exist. What you did to me is moot, even somewhat understandable. What you did to my daughter—"

"Had nothing to do with this."

"Do you really expect me to believe that?"

"It's true only that had I not begun this, I wouldn't have met Larissa. But from the moment I saw her, I was smitten beyond anything in my experience. I'll admit I lied to myself. She was off-limits to me by normal means. I couldn't marry her because she was your daughter, the daughter of an enemy. Yet I couldn't not try to make her mine. So revenge became merely an excuse for me to ignore my own conscience in the matter."

"You're talking about an innocent child that you took advantage of!"

"I'm talking about the *woman* I love. She's a child only in your mind, sir. And had you not returned when you did, I would have tossed all my efforts to the wind to obtain the only goal that has any meaning for me now—I would have begged her to marry me."

George snorted his skepticism. "Convenient to say when you know she won't have you, that she despises you for what you did to her."

Vincent sighed. "Not convenient, merely late in the discovery. Even on Christmas eve, I hadn't yet realized just how much I love her. I had done everything possible to keep her in my house. I lied to her, misled her, just to keep her from leaving me."

"You *admit* that?"

"Yes. I was still convinced that marriage was out of the question, a betrayal, as it were, to my brother. But on Christmas morning she finally demanded to know if my intentions were honorable as she'd assumed or not, and if not, she was leaving me. I knew then that revenge was meaningless in comparison to losing her. But before I could let her know that, you arrived."

"You hardly sounded as if you had just come to that realization during our discourse."

"My anger with you got in the way."

"I will consider that fortunate for my family," George replied stiffly. "Now if you are finished, Lord Everett, I don't believe we have anything further to say."

"Will you allow me to see your daughter? She is owed an apology as well—"

"She is owed some peace over this matter, or don't you realize how devastated she was by your revelations. She is only just beginning to recover. Stay away from her."

Chapter 25

STAY AWAY FROM HER? VINCENT COULDN'T. HE
would have liked to have permission to approach
Larissa, but with it or without it, he had to see her.
But she didn't return to London so that he could.

George moved back into the London house,
had their furnishings fetched and reinstalled, and
filled the place with servants again. He'd been
quite busy, taking care of normal business that required his attention after such a long absence, as
well as visiting all those merchants who had panicked at the first hint that he had deserted England.

The reports that Vincent was receiving were
that a lot of groveling was done by the merchants.
Not unexpected of a merchant class that depended on the goodwill of their customers.
Whether George was forgiving or not was moot
and of little interest to Vincent. The people he had
following George were reporting basic actions,

they weren't getting close enough to overhear conversations.

The empty town house was a home again by the end of the year, but a home without children; at least Larissa and Thomas hadn't returned to it yet. Vincent was beginning to worry that Larissa wasn't going to return at all, and because of him. Not an unfounded worry. George could have sent her word about their meeting and his desire to see her. Her absence in London could well be her response to that. Which was why, when Ascot left London, Vincent was not far behind him.

Portsmouth turned out to be the final destination. Vincent wasn't surprised. He'd actually had the inns and hotels searched there, being aware that was where the Ascots had lived prior to relocating in London. With no luck, of course. But a little information had been gathered about the Applebees before he knocked on their door the next day, so he knew these were old friends of the Ascots.

He wasn't denied entry. He might have been. But the Applebees' butler apparently hadn't been warned to turn him away. But then the Ascots probably hadn't expected him to show up in Portsmouth either. He still didn't hold much hope of actually seeing Larissa, though. She'd be told he was there. It would be her decision and likely a denial. But he got lucky . . .

* * *

Larissa stopped halfway down the stairs when she saw Vincent being led to the parlor. The urge was to turn about abruptly. She didn't want to talk to him again—ever. But it would be cowardly to rush back to her room, and besides, her anger wouldn't let her do it. She wasn't numbed by shock this time. Her anger brought her down to the bottom of the stairs, where he had moved to the moment he saw her.

She was going to slap him, as hard as she could. An action worth a thousand words so there would be no mistaking what she felt for him now. But she didn't do it. Standing that close, she was caught by the golden glow in his eyes, then entrapped for several long moments as her body reacted in myriad ways to being near to him again.

Good God, how could she still be attracted to him? How could she desire him still, when she despised him beyond reason? When his hand reached toward her cheek, her knees nearly buckled. His caress was imminent. It was going to destroy her resolve and make her forget, briefly, why she never wanted to see him again.

"Larissa—"

"Don't touch me!"

She jumped back, nearly tripped on the stairs. Her pulse was racing. That had been too close, her senses returning nearly too late to stop him.

"Don't touch me again," she repeated in a

calmer, though scathing tone. "You use that as a tactic to bend my will to yours, but I'm aware of that now and won't be—"

"Larissa, marry me."

Moisture sprang immediately to her eyes. "You ask too late."

"I know, but to not ask would be one more regret to add to the rest."

She should have turned to leave then. She should have ignored the pain in his eyes that was ripping at her heart. That she couldn't bear to walk away from him yet infuriated her, and that came out in her tone.

"Nothing you can say will rectify what you've done, so why do you put us both through this?"

"Because I need to wipe the slate clean, and there are still things you don't know that must be confessed before I can do that."

"Your *needs* are no longer a concern of mine."

"Hear me out at least. It won't take much of your time. And I actually have more fuel for you to add to the fire, lies I told you, and why I did."

"I've already realized that just about everything you've ever said to me was a lie," she replied. "There's no need to confirm that."

"Hardly everything," he said with a sigh.

She had the feeling he wanted to caress her again. Was he experiencing the same pull that she was, which was almost irresistible? Very well, so perhaps he hadn't hated touching her, hadn't laughed at how easy it had been to seduce her. Perhaps this powerful attraction really was mutual. But that changed nothing. He had still used her to get at her father. He hadn't hesitated to trample the innocent on the path to his goals.

It was probably guilt that had brought him there. She understood why he might be feeling it now. But she didn't care. She was done feeling sympathy for a man who didn't deserve it. And assuaging his guilt would only be a benefit to him. It would be nothing but pain to her, to hear it all spelled out, how he'd used her.

Yet the words came out before she could stop them. "Make your confession, but please keep it brief."

He nodded. He smiled softly. He had to stuff his hands in his pockets to keep from touching her.

"The lie began from the start. I brought you to my house because from the moment I first saw you, I wanted you. That had nothing at all to do with your father. He would have been easy enough to find at his office, once he returned. Fortunately, you didn't point that out when I mentioned needing an address so I could find him."

"I was too upset that night to think of anything," she said in her defense.

"That was rather obvious and to my benefit, because I was so taken with you, I wasn't thinking very clearly myself, so probably wouldn't have been able to come up with a better excuse to move you into my house. But it worked. You moved in. And then I faced the dilemma of how to keep you under my roof as long as possible, because I couldn't bear the thought of being denied even one extra day with you, when I'd already accepted the fact that our time together would be limited, and end, once your father returned. Keeping you without funds or the need for them was my solution to that."

"Need for them?"

"You had mentioned your brother would need a physician, so I had mine summoned for you. His visit wasn't an annual occurrence as you were told, he was there specifically to see to your brother."

"One kindness on your part doesn't excuse—"

"Rissa, that was no kindness, that was to keep you from selling any of your possessions to pay for a physician, which would leave you with coins in hand to find lodging elsewhere. To further insure that you wouldn't be selling anything, I invented that excuse to lock up your jewels. My servants are actually all quite trustworthy."

"Had I requested them back?"

"The key to my safe would have conveniently—for me—gone missing."

After that confession, it occurred to her to ask,

"There was never a theft at the warehouse where our things were stored, was there?"

"No. I merely had anything of value there moved to a different location, in case you wanted to go there to see what was left. It would have all been returned to you, which was why I mentioned my own involvement in searching for the 'thieves,' so you wouldn't wonder at how easily the items could be recovered. Stealing from your family wasn't on my agenda."

"No, just thoroughly ruining us."

The bitterness in her tone was thick enough to cut, bringing a frown to his brow. "Are you deliberately failing to see that these are two unrelated issues?"

"Hardly unrelated when you managed to accomplish two goals with one—"

"From the moment you entered my house," he cut in, "your father was all but forgotten in my mind. I lived and breathed *you*. You consumed my every thought. Everything I did was done to obtain you. But I convinced myself that the only way I could have you was with the excuse of revenge. I couldn't have you by normal means, couldn't marry you because your father was my enemy—"

"He was never your enemy."

"At the time he was. In my mind he was. At least allow that what one believes is a truth for *him* for however long he believes it. I saw your father as being directly responsible for my brother's ruination, which also made him indirectly responsible for his death. Yet I was merely going to ruin him financially. I wasn't going to exact any harsher revenge. An eye for an eye, as it were. He could rebuild, reestablish. Albert was dead, or so I thought. Your father wasn't."

"Why are you telling me this when it doesn't pertain to me? You seduced me with no intention of marrying me. *That* pertains to me! Admit it."

"I have admitted it. I merely wanted you to know why I felt that I couldn't marry you, and why it finally didn't matter."

"I know why it doesn't matter. My father told me your brother isn't dead as you'd thought. He was your motive; now you have none. That doesn't excuse what passed before."

"He told you that, but he didn't tell you I'd already realized it was over before then, before your father arrived Christmas morning. Or don't you remember what we were discussing just prior to his showing up?"

"I recall you saying you couldn't marry me because of my father."

"After that, Rissa. I realized during that conversation that you were all that mattered to me. I told you so, if you'll try to remember. The vendetta was over as far as I was concerned. I even tried to tell your father that nothing had been done that couldn't be rectified, but you interrupted with your interpretation of what I'd done."

When he was admitting to all these lies, was what he was telling her now to be believed? She'd be a fool to let him dupe her again, but then she was a fool for standing there listening to him at all.

"Are you done confessing?"

It was probably her stiffness that made him realize he was getting nowhere with her, that nothing would breach the shell of her bitterness. His expression turned so sad it nearly made her cry. But she wasn't going to relent, she wasn't . . .

"No, actually, you might as well know that I was in your room that night, the night you thought I was, awake, and driving myself crazy with wanting you. That silly story about sleepwalking was a lie. The locks were put on your doors because I couldn't trust myself not to enter your room again without permission."

"And what you told me of your past, to gain my sympathy?" she recalled. "All lies as well."

"Your sympathy is a wonderful thing, Rissa, and yes, I used it. But it wasn't necessary to invent a pitiful past to stir your compassion. Everything I told you of my childhood was true. I had merely never told anyone else about it before, because I despise pity." He smiled wryly. "Your pity

I wanted, though. Your pity is such an amazing thing."

"Your lies were pointless."

"Excuse me?"

"I could have left at any time if I had really wanted to. Your lies wouldn't have stopped me."

"You had your brother to think of, not just yourself. You wouldn't have left without funds."

"No, certainly, but there were a few more valuables stored at my father's office that I never mentioned to you, a titled painting and several antique maps my father had intended to sell, but didn't get around to doing before he left. The maps would have fetched a nice price."

"And the painting is *La Nymph*."

She blinked. "How did you know that?"

His laugh was quite hollow. "A logical guess, since I happen to have been searching for that painting for a client for several months now, and it was known to be in the possession of a ship owner, just not which one."

"Why that painting in particular?"

"Have you seen it?"

She frowned. "Actually, I recall my father rushing me out of the storeroom the last time I visited the office when he was there, because he didn't want me to see it. He mentioned something about it being inappropriate for innocent eyes, so I assumed it was a nude."

"Indeed, but a rather risqué one by all accounts," he replied. "And my client will likely pay you a half million pounds for it."

She blinked again. "Is he out of his mind?"

"No, just very eccentric, with more money than he will ever be able to spend."

"You're teasing me. I don't find that very nice under the circumstances, but then why should that surprise me?"

He sighed. "I swear I'm not. You know him well enough. It's Jonathan Hale who wants to get his hands on that painting so much that he's hired me to find it. Now I've found it. It's in your possession. I'm sure he'll be contacting your father about it just as soon as I tell him."

"Why would you tell him, when it will be a benefit to my father? You did realize that, didn't you?"

"If you would stop being suspicious of my motives long enough to think about what I've told you today, you'd have an answer to that. Have you never done anything that you bitterly regret now?"

"Aside from meeting you?"

He blushed, but continued relentlessly, "Didn't you tell me how you despised your father for moving you to London and regretted how you treated him for it?"

"You compare childish pouting to what you did to me?" she demanded incredulously.

"No, I am merely reminding you that none of us are perfect. We cannot always do as we aspire to; we too often act on emotions that shouldn't be released. I wasn't used to being controlled by emotions, Rissa. Good God, I was even under the foolish belief that I didn't have any, since so many years had passed without anything provoking mine. Then I met you and I suddenly had *too* many emotions stirring all at once."

The golden heat was entering his eyes again. She began to panic. She'd managed to remain un-affected by his closeness this long, or at least to give that impression, but she didn't think she could withstand again being devoured by those seductive eyes of his.

"You've finished. Please go."

"Rissa, I love you. If you're never going to be-lieve anything I say to you again, at least believe that."

She left instead, ran up the stairs to hide behind a locked door where she could cry in peace. She wished he hadn't come. She wished those last words of his weren't going to haunt her, but she knew they would.

Chapter 26

LARISSA DIDN'T GO DOWN TO DINNER THAT NIGHT.
Her family was returning to London in the morning, which allowed her to use the excuse of packing to avoid a last night of socializing. A kindness
on her part, that she not inflict her rotten mood on
the Applebees.

How could she have been so unlucky, to have
come downstairs today at the precise moment
that Vincent was being led across the hall? And so
foolish not to have taken the cowardly route as
had been her first impulse, instead of giving him
a chance to speak to her.

She could have recovered, eventually, without
hearing his grand confession. Now she knew the
worst, but also the best—if she could believe it.
And there was the rub and the source of her sorrow. She couldn't believe it.

How does one trust again after being so thoroughly lied to? She'd never been lied to before,

thus had never figured that out for herself. And Vincent was asking too much of her, to forgive, to forget, to accept him as he was without suspicions. How could she do that when he could lie so convincingly, so expertly, that she'd never be able to know when he was being truthful with her?

Of course, everyone made mistakes and had faults, but not everyone had such ruthless faults as Vincent did. Someone else might be able to overlook them, to say that only love mattered, but she had too many doubts for that someone to be her. Yes, she still loved him. The wrenching in her heart today made that bitterly obvious. But she despised everything he'd done and she'd never get beyond that simple fact long enough to forgive him.

She was dreading going to bed, knowing she wouldn't get much sleep that night. So her father's knock at the door was very welcome, even if the subject that he brought in with him wasn't.

"I was informed that Lord Everett paid you a visit today," he said as he joined her in front of the fireplace where she had been sitting, staring blankly at the dancing flames. "I hadn't realized that he might follow me here to find you, or I would have seen to it that he never get past the door. I hope you know that I had expressly forbidden him to see you, to no avail, obviously."

"It's all right," she replied. "I doubt he'll try to see me again."

"You turned him down, then?"

"You knew he was going to ask?"

"I'd gathered that was his goal, yes. He claims to love you. Do you have reason to doubt that after your experiences with him?"

"Yes—no," she corrected, then with a frustrated sigh, added, "I don't know anymore."

"I'm sorry, Rissa. I know you haven't wanted to talk about what happened. But I have assumed, from your state of melancholy, that you love the man."

"I did. I don't now."

He smiled gently. "Would that it were so easy to turn love off and on with a few simple words. Here, take these and read them," he said, handing her two letters. "I've had them in my possession for several days now. I wasn't going to show them to you, since they might upset you again, but perhaps that decision was a mistake on my part."

"What are you talking about?"

"Those letters. They were given to me when Everett handed over the deed to our home. I didn't know it until he was gone. How much do you know about the brother?"

"Not much. He rarely spoke of him. When he was mentioned, it was in connection with Vin-

cent's childhood, which was pathetically lonely—
he *says* that wasn't one of the many lies he told."

"You don't believe it?"

"I honestly don't know what to believe anymore. As for Albert, they weren't close except for
a very brief time when they were young. Albert
was their parents' favorite, you see. He went
everywhere with them, while Vincent was never
included. I gather that Vincent was in the habit of
cleaning up his brother's calamities, though, a
brotherly duty, as he saw it. Mind you, everything I just told you came directly from Vincent, a
known liar."

He ignored the bitter tone, said, "You'll find
those letters enlightening, then."

She stared at her father, waited for further explanation. He gave none, merely nodded at the
letters now in her hand. She read them, both.
They were Albert Everett's letters to Vincent. She
had to read the first one again to make sense of it,
then once more.

Finally she said, "This first one does paint a
rather dastardly picture of you, doesn't it?"

"Yes, from a child crying foul. And Albert even
admits it in the second letter, that he hadn't
grown up yet, at least not to a point where he
would take responsibility for his own actions."

"You would think that Vincent would have suspected as much."

"When, as you say, he didn't really have much association with his brother?"

"You're defending him?" she asked incredulously.

"No, just trying to see this mess from his perspective—and well aware that given the same set of circumstances in my own family, I probably would have acted exactly as he did. Actually, I may well have acted much worse and have called the man out who had so ruined a member of my family that he chose to kill himself."

"But revenge is pointless. You've always said so. You've raised us to believe the same."

"Revenge is, yes, and particularly when you don't have the means to inflict it. But when you have a victim driven to the point of death, and the one responsible escapes without any consequence whatsoever, then it's a matter of trying to visit justice on the guilty one."

"You really *are* defending him."

George chuckled. "No, because we don't really have all the facts and never will have them. Even Albert admits he was drinking heavily most of the time that the events occurred, so wouldn't remember exactly what brought him low. Lord Everett is guilty of drawing his own conclusions. But given the known facts, his conclusions were hard to dispute."

"Not if he had bothered to find out what sort of

man you were," she insisted. "And that you would *never* do anything so reprehensible—"

Another chuckle. "You needn't get indignant on my account at this late stage, Rissa. It's over. Our lot has actually improved because of it. The only casualty involved is you, but even that can be rectified."

"By marrying him?" she snorted.

"Only you can decide your destiny at this point," he replied, and headed toward the door. But he paused there long enough to add, "I read that first letter again and again, and then I played a little 'what if.' I suggest you do the same. Read the first letter and imagine it's from Thomas, grown up to manhood, of course. But imagine that he wrote that to you. Then ask yourself what you would do about it."

Chapter 27

VINCENT WASN'T QUITE CERTAIN HOW IT HAP-
pened, but Jonathan Hale now considered him
his best friend. Ironically, Jon wasn't far wrong.
Vincent did in fact welcome his company now.
He supposed it could just be that he needed the
distraction. But Jon was much more relaxed, in
thinking them friends, which in turn made him
more amusing, so his company really was enjoyed. However, it didn't take much for Vincent
to realize that without Jon's visits and amusing
chatter, he'd have no break at all from the painful
moroseness that otherwise filled his mind from
morning till night.

Failure was so alien to him. He succeeded at
most all of his endeavors, except the one most important to him, the only one that mattered. And
how arrogant, to think he could convince Larissa
to give him another chance if he could just talk to
her. She did still care for him. He had seen that in

her eyes. But it wasn't enough. Would anything be? Laying everything, every lie and little deceit, on the floor before her for a fresh start hadn't helped.

He hoped he had merely tried too soon, that more time was needed for the biting edge of his deception to dull. But if she couldn't find it in her heart to forgive him, or at least to understand why he had done what he had, then no amount of time was going to help.

Jonathan had at least benefited from Vincent's brief visit to Portsmouth. The Ascots hadn't taken advantage of him, knowing how much he would have paid for *La Nymph*. George had charged him only what he felt the value of the painting was, which was much less than what Jon had paid Vincent in commission. Ascot really was as good and honorable as Larissa had made him out to be. Which just made Vincent feel even more rotten.

And how did one get on with one's life, when one refused to cut the cords to do so?

One of the cords Vincent wasn't letting go of was the Christmas tree in his parlor. He wasn't going to remove it. It could rot there, until nothing was left but dead bare branches, but it was staying there in his parlor until Larissa showed up for the ornaments on it.

Jonathan was right, they *were* valuable to her, and Vincent was counting on that, that she wouldn't send just anyone by to fetch them for her, that she would come herself to collect them. And when she did, she wasn't going to be handed a filled trunk that she could immediately leave with, she was going to have to spend a bit of time there removing the ornaments from the tree herself.

It was his last hope. A little time with her alone. And perhaps she might remember, as well, the fun they'd had decorating her tree. He was counting on that, counting on other memories associated with his house to remind her how wonderful their lives could be, if she would give him another chance.

He took precautions as well, going out only when he absolutely had to. She might think she could come there without seeing him, but he had left strict orders that he was to be summoned if she showed up, and not let in at all if he wasn't there, which would force her to return when he was. And so he waited.

She did come, and in the late morning when he was usually home, so she was making no effort to avoid him. He found her still in the hall where she'd been asked to wait. She appeared nervous. It was actually hard to discern, when her beauty overwhelmed him, but he did notice it, the chewing at her lower lip that she stopped when he appeared, her hands clenched tightly in front of her.

It was perhaps that nervousness, rather than her desire to leave soonest, that had her blurting out immediately, "I've come for our Christmas ornaments. I couldn't bring myself to fetch them sooner."

"I understand you'd rather not see me."

"It wasn't that. I just wanted you to have a normal Christmas tree for once. We made do, sharing the Applebees' tree for the remainder of the season. But I knew you wouldn't, that if we stripped your tree, you'd leave it that way."

"Why?"

"Excuse me?"

"Why did it matter to you?" he asked.

"Because it was your first tree."

"So? I've gone this long without having one. I could have gone the rest of my life without having one."

"That's why, because you don't care. Because it saddens me that you don't care."

He smiled gently. "Rissa, a Christmas tree is nothing if you have no one to share it with. You said as much yourself. It symbolizes a season that is celebrated in sharing. Come. Let's share this one for the last time."

He moved to the parlor, didn't wait for her, knew she would follow. He was rather proud of the condition of her tree, watched eagerly as she entered the room and saw it. She was amazed, clearly. He had hoped for a smile, though, instead of just surprise.

"You changed it, brought in a new tree. Why?"

"It's the same tree," he insisted. "I've been pampering it myself, watering it twice a day. It decided to survive a little longer."

He was joking that the tree might have had any say-so in the matter, but she was too sentimental not to agree with him, and with the smile he'd hoped for, she said, "So it did, and quite beautifully, too. I don't believe I've ever stripped a tree looking this healthy before. Are you *sure* you didn't bring in a new one?"

"Did I forget to assure you that I'd never lie to you again?"

She blushed. There it was, standing between them again, everything he'd done, everything he regretted. And how utterly foolish, to let that subject come up so soon. He'd wanted her to relax first, to recall the fun they'd had in this room.

"Do you realize that saying it isn't an assurance, when the assurance could be a lie as well?"

"Your doubt is tangible, Rissa, and understandable. But have you realized that most of the lies were to keep you here? I wanted you so much, I was committed to doing anything in my power to have you come willingly to me. I'm sorry for the deceptions having to do with your father. I made mistakes. I'm far from perfect. But I won't apologize for wanting you, or for making love to you, or for anything I did to make you mine, if only for a little while, because saying I'm sorry for *that* would be a lie."

Though her cheeks were a bit brighter from his bluntness, she didn't reply. She even moved away from him so she could stare at the tree without looking at him. Her expression had given him no clue, either, to how his statements had affected her, other than to embarrass her.

He tried again. "I was never going to marry. But then I was never going to fall in love either. It was an emotion I thought I was immune to. You've proven me wrong. I just wish I had realized it before Christmas day. Had I recognized it sooner, we would have been engaged before your father returned; hell, I might even have dragged you off to Gretna Green to make sure we were married before his return."

He paused, waited hopefully, but she still just stared pensively at the tree. His last chance, and she was shooting it down with her silence. Of course, that was answer in itself. She'd had enough time to harden her resolve. But he hadn't anticipated indifference.

He moved behind her, started to put his hands on her shoulders, but stopped himself, afraid she'd bolt if he touched her. "Rissa, say something."

"I read your brother's letters."

"And?"

"And I might have done the same thing you did."

He went still, held his breath. "You're saying you forgive me?"

"I'm saying I love you and can't find any way around that."

He didn't give her a chance to take it back or try to correct what she'd just said. He swung her around, gathered her close, kissed her deeply. That she yielded immediately was his answer and filled him with such relief, there was barely any room left to contain his joy. She was his again! And he wasn't going to lose her this time.

"You came here with the intention of forgiving me?" he said.

"I thought it might be possible."

Her grin was infectious. He returned it, hugged her tightly. "Elope with me."

"No, we do this the proper way this time. You'll have to speak to my father."

He groaned. "He's made his feelings clear. He doesn't like me."

"You'll find he's probably changed his mind about that," she told him. "He knows I love you. He's the one who made me see that I was being too hard on you. But if I'm wrong, *then* we can elope."

"You really mean that, don't you?" he asked her in amazement.

She cupped his cheeks in her hands so tenderly. "I was letting my hurt overrule my heart, when I knew deep down that you were still the man I fell in love with. I'm sorry it took so long for my heart to take over again—"

"Shh, it doesn't matter now. Nothing else matters, except that we're together again. I'll speak to your father immediately."

"You'll help me take down the Christmas tree first," she said.

He chuckled. "I knew that tree was going to bring us together again."

"It's almost a shame to take it down, when it's still so green."

"Then don't," he suggested. "Or is that part of the ritual?"

"Well, it does sort of put Christmas to rest until the next year."

"Who says it has to be put to rest? I rather liked your concept of 'sharing.' "

She smiled, reached for his hand to hold it. "We won't need a tree for that."

He brought her hand to his lips. "No, I don't suppose we will."

Chapter 28

"OH . . . OH, MY."

That didn't quite express Larissa's degree of surprise, it was more indicative of her speechlessness when she finally noticed the large painting hanging on the wall at the head of Vincent's bed.

They had been married that morning, just a small gathering of family and friends. Viscount Hale had wanted to throw them the biggest party London had ever seen, but Vincent had adamantly refused, mentioning something about theaters and what had happened the last time the *ton* got a look at Larissa, and that he'd like to keep her to himself for a while more as they settled into marriage.

Jonathan understood perfectly, if Larissa didn't. She had enjoyed the theater, but she wasn't sure she would enjoy a huge London bash, so she was rather glad her husband had declined the offer.

Her father had welcomed Vincent to the family

with open arms, as she had predicted. Her brother hadn't. Having witnessed the turmoil of her emotions while she was falling in love, and blaming many of those tears on Vincent, Thomas had taken a "wait and see" attitude. For him, Vincent was going to have to prove that he could make Larissa happy. She was sure it wouldn't take long, though, when she was already happier than she could ever have thought possible.

"Oh, my," she said yet again, causing Vincent to chuckle this time as he came to stand behind her next to the bed.

She was staring at an exquisitely beautiful, naked young maiden cavorting with four satyrs in a woodland glade. That was the modest description of *La Nymph*. The depicted scene was actually much more lurid, and anyone with any degree of imagination could make whatever he or she wanted to out of it.

"Our wedding gift from Jonathan," Vincent explained, his hands resting on her shoulders.

"We don't have to keep it, do we?"

He laughed. "No indeed, and in fact, it's only on loan to us. He expects it back, though I don't doubt he's glad to be rid of it for a while. He was somewhat amazed to find the notorious effect of the painting quite true, at least for him." He explained to her, briefly, the history of *La Nymph*, ending with, "The day he brought it home, after purchasing it from your father, he ended up visiting four of his mistresses, quite an exhausting experience, I would imagine."

She turned around, stared at him wide-eyed. "He had that many—lady friends?"

His hands began to caress her neck. "More than that, but he only managed to get around to that many that day."

She huffed a bit indignantly. "And there I thought he was interested in me for marriage; at least that is the impression he gave."

"Oh, he was." He grinned. "He did indeed want to marry you."

"When he kept company with so many other women?" she all but snorted.

"What he would have offered you in a marriage was more money than you could ever imagine. He wasn't offering faithfulness. He would have been up front about it, though, explaining to you that variety is the spice of his life. It would have been entirely up to you if you wanted that sort of marriage."

"He actually thought I could be . . . ? Well, *bought* is the word that comes to mind."

Vincent smiled, his thumbs beginning to circle her cheeks, then her earlobes. "He had hoped so. You became his newest goal for a while. But he began to see where your true interest was—and mine as well—and bowed out of the running with no hard feelings. Actually, now that he considers me his best friend, he's quite delighted that you've married me instead."

"A friend, yet he can give you something like that?" she said, nodding at the painting again.

"A joke, sweetheart, in poor taste in that it has nothing to do with love, everything to do with sex, but he meant no harm by it. But then it doesn't have quite the same effect on me as it does on him."

"No?"

"Some people are stimulated by what they see, as in the case of the painting. For others, visual makes no difference; touch is their only stimulation; it must be what they can feel. And for still others, there is emotional stimulation; the heart must be involved."

"You fall into the third category?"

"I'm not sure which might have been the case before I met you, but I'm quite sure which is the case now. Love makes the difference for me. You are my only stimulation."

She hadn't been immune to the caresses she had been receiving, but his words thrilled her beyond measure. "I believe we just might have all three categories covered tonight," she said breathlessly. "Though the latter two are preferred."

"I'll get rid of the first," he offered.

He went to the head of the bed to flip the painting around to the wall. Neither of them was expecting there to be another painting on the back of it, of the exact same scene, just rendered from behind.

They both laughed. "Now, that is too funny," Larissa allowed. "Even the artist realized that not everyone would appreciate his work. Quite determined, wasn't he, that it not be hidden from view?"

Vincent grinned, grabbed a sheet from the bed, and draped it over the painting. "And I'm quite determined that your wedding night be perfect in every way."

He came back to stand before her, cupped her cheeks in his hands. The golden glow was in his eyes, though his expression was intensely serious for a moment.

"I love you so much, I'm not sure how to express it, Rissa. You've brought light into what was darkness. I existed, but I wasn't living. Can you understand what I mean? You filled a void in my life I didn't know I had."

"Don't make me cry," she said, moisture gathering in her turquoise eyes.

He smiled gently just before he hugged her close. "I don't mind your sympathy tears. They show me how much you love me."

"I'd rather show you in other ways."

"You do. You show me in so many ways, but I'll

never get enough. I'm so *glad* that you're my wife, Rissa. And I promise to make you glad of it also, every day, for the rest of your life."

She wiped the tears from her eyes, gave him a brilliant smile. "You've already begun."